A Hand to Hold in Deep Water

A Hand to Hold in Deep Water

SHAWN NOCHER

BLACK STONE
PUBLISHING

Copyright © 2021 by Shawn Nocher
Published in 2021 by Blackstone Publishing
Cover and book design by Alenka Vdovič Linaschke

Printed in the United States of America

First edition: 2021
ISBN 978-1-0940-9521-9
Fiction / Women

1 3 5 7 9 10 8 6 4 2

CIP data for this book is available
from the Library of Congress

Blackstone Publishing
31 Mistletoe Rd.
Ashland, OR 97520

www.BlackstonePublishing.com

For my family, my everything

PROLOGUE

Lacey and Tasha

JUNE 2004

She and I are lying on the dock, peering through the planks at an especially large jellyfish, the breadth of a dinner plate, thick and milky, drifting beneath us in the brackish water. They're common in the river this time of year, something to do with the salinity, but these larger ones with their ruffled pink insides are more unusual, and we watch in rare silence.

This river, this lovely, lazy, undulating St. Mary's River, is full of surprises—some scaldingly beautiful, like the feeding frenzy of blues we saw last week. The dorsal fins of the massive blues, black blades swirling in the roiling water, stirred the river into an ethereal brew, boiling and flashing, glinting with desperate leaping minnows.

Other surprises, like the jellyfish, are mesmerizing and disconcerting if only in that they remind me to be careful should I risk a swim. You never know what lies beneath the surface.

"Can I touch it just a little bit?" she asks. "If I'm very, very nice to it?"

She asks as though she doesn't quite believe me that its tentacles would sting her if she were to wade too close.

"Tasha, honey, it will sting you and it will hurt. It can't help it. That's just what jellyfish do."

"Is it a boy jellyfish or a girl jellyfish?" she wants to know. She is four. This is the question du jour. She asks the same thing about the dog she sees trotting up Route 235, the crow that caws from the telephone wires, the squirrel that chits at us from the back porch, demanding the surrender of her popcorn. Even the honeybee—the one that stung her tiny foot yesterday and squirmed on the ball of it until it pulled free of its own stinger and died a wretched little death while she howled into my neck—even the bee prompted the same question.

"Was it a boy bee or a girl bee what stung me?" she had asked in between sobs.

"I think it was a boy," I told her, cradling a small pink foot with one hand and holding her against me with the other. I thought to tell her they were all boys, that the queen, the only female among them, was sitting fat and pretty on her throne while the males, *the boy bees*, spent their life's energy finding ways to keep the queen happy and amused so she wouldn't abandon them. I thought to tell her this, but instead I made a paste of baking soda and salt and slathered it on the sting until her breath was less ragged and her tears had dried to reveal clean pink streaks down her dirty cheeks.

But now we are watching the jellyfish puff and billow and ripple below us and I can't tell her if it's a boy or a girl.

"I don't know," is all I can say, because I try to always tell the truth.

"It's a girl," she says, with such certainty. "It has pink in it."

"Yes," I say, "probably a girl."

She is on her belly and, like an otter, she pushes up with her tiny forearms and rolls to her bottom to look at me. She wears a pint-size yellow bikini that is, frankly, quite ludicrous in its effort to conceal. The top is made of two yellow triangles, no bigger than the triangles of peanut butter and jelly sandwich I make for her every afternoon, and because the top ties at the back of her neck, and because she is a squirmy child, the triangles have fallen to reveal nothing more than two copper-pink nipples, flat as pennies on her chest. Between the top and the bottom is a small round ball of a belly bearing a tiny twist of a belly button. Her belly button is something that, even at four, continues to fascinate her. She curls over her own body in order to peer into it. "Why do I got a belly button?" she asks me again.

I turn over to my back and pull my T-shirt up to feel the sun on my ribs. "Your belly button once had a long tube coming out of it that connected you to me when you were in my tummy. Remember? I told you this?"

"And we were like one person—right?"

"Right."

"And all the stuff I needed to be born came from you in my belly button—right?"

"That's right." I roll down the top of my running shorts and feel the sun's warmth spread to my hip bones, pat my stomach and remember the mound of her that once rose in it. A small motorboat goes by, and the wake sets the water to slapping against the piling. There is a whiff of diesel in the air and I open one eye to a small dissipating billow of dark smoke.

"And all little kids get a belly button from their mommy, right?"

"Uh-huh."

"But not from their daddy, right?"

"Right," I say, but we are treading dangerous territory here, so I remind her that her daddy took care of me so I could take care of her.

"Then Daddy left, right?"

"No, honey." And this is where it gets tricky. "Daddy just lives somewhere else. He just doesn't live with us."

"Right," she says, with a kind of conviction that makes me certain she is filing this under *Things to Remember*.

Suddenly, she gasps and I feel her finger poke into my stomach. My eyes fly open and I sit up. "Quit it, Tasha—you're tickling me!"

"You have a belly button, too!" she says.

"Well, of course, silly, everyone has a belly button. You've seen my belly button. It's just like yours."

Her little brows furrow and then rise in surprise. "Then you have a mommy, too!" she says. "Did you get your belly button from when your mommy took care of you and got you ready to be borned?" But she's too excited to wait for an answer. She is on her knees peering deep into my stomach and trying to push my upper body back so that she can find it again in the fold of my waist. Her hands are sticky on my skin and I grab one and kiss it to distract her as I am pulling my shirt down. "That tickles, stop!"

"Let me see, Mommy."

"Tasha, everyone has a belly button. Everyone has to have a belly button to be born."

"But I didn't think you had a belly button, Mommy. I didn't remember you did!"

"Why on earth not?"

"'Cause I didn't know you had a mommy. Where's your mommy?"

I look at her now, her eyes searching mine.

"Where's your mommy?" She is still. The boat has moved farther down the river and its motor is just a soft hum, expectant, waiting. There is a shift in the air and a faint breeze shimmies off the river, lifting strands of her hair so that they twist and fall along her face. I push her hair back from her eyes and she tilts her head, juts out her chin, takes in a tiny patient breath that she will hold until I answer her.

I take a breath of my own and, as much as I try not to, I cannot help but imagine. I imagine her standing stock-still and blinking into the sunlight where only a moment before I had been standing. Where one moment she was a mother's daughter, and in the next she is alone with only terror rising in her throat and a button of a scar to remind her of me.

"I don't know," I manage to say. "I just don't know."

PART 1

Spring 2005

CHAPTER 1

Chicken Farming

MARCH

Willy hates chickens, has hated them as far back as he can remember, so the fact that here he is, nearly seventy years old, getting up to feed the chickens, well—it just doesn't sit so good with him.

He pulls on his coveralls and shuffles down the hall to wash. There is no dignity in it—chicken farming. He's selling eggs, for God's sake. Turning on the spigot, he hangs his head over the bowl and waits. In his younger days he would have cupped his hands to puddle the first icy chokes of water, splashing his face until his eyes were wide and a forelock of hair hung dripping over his nose. Then he would have peeked in on Lacey, cracking her door just a bit so that it would make a small creak like old bones, always just a little taken aback to see her still sleeping through the clanking of pipes, before he headed up to the barn to start the chores.

But these days he is kinder to himself. He lets the water run warm before soaking a washrag and pressing it to his face, letting its warmth put a thaw to his knuckles beneath the rag. And he is alone now, no one to check on. No pressing chores other than those chickens.

"Damn chickens," he mutters to himself just as he does every morning, but as much as he tries to muddle himself in gloom, he can't deny that today is different. Today marks the beginning of Lacey and the girl's visit.

He tries not to expect too much, not to want anything out of the visit, but it's been nearly a year since he's seen them both and he can't deny that there's some anticipation in the air. He hardly slept the night before, which is unusual for him. He's never had any trouble with sleep, rising easily and rested at the first crack of dawn. But last night he had woken a number of times, not tossing and turning, but waking to the dark and lying still for lengths of time, noticing the way the shadows changed in the room each time he woke, leaving them slightly rearranged as if the dark itself was a shifting thing.

Fact is, he has to admit, he's been missing the both of them. He's seen Lacey and Tasha only a handful of times since Tasha was born. She is five now, but he can remember the first time Lacey came back to the farm with her. She had been just a baby, a bitty little thing, a newborn.

It had been a January day, one of the coldest on record, and while he had hoped to visit with her and the baby sooner, the weather along the Pennsylvania–Maryland line had been miserable, wet, and icy for weeks. He'd just lost his smallest banty—pretty little red hen, but lousy layer—a few days earlier. Found her frozen, like an oddly feathered rock, on the floor of the coop. Hens weren't laying in the cold anyway, hunkered down and fluffed, blinking at him as if to say, *What did you expect?* He had tacked up more foil-sheathed insulation along the roofline, and they had clucked and grumbled at the disruption. That evening he had phoned Lacey, checking on her and the baby, and told Lacey to sit tight and he would come down to see her and the baby at the college where she taught, soon as the weather turned. She had told him not to come. The weather was just as bad down in southern Maryland. In fact, she had said, even the brackish river had frozen. She was looking out her window to it right now, she said, and the river was iced over deep and thick, cracking in places, and making ungodly creaks and shrieks as it did so. No, she had agreed, it was not a good time to travel. She was just going to hunker down with the baby and stay warm.

Willy doesn't travel much. Never had much use for it, doesn't like traffic or icy roads or motels or staying in someone else's place. Doesn't like the smell of someone else's sheets or the sound of unfamiliar night noises. But a few days later, just as the weather had started to warm a precious few degrees and the ice had slid down off the roof of the barn in heaving sheets, just when he thought it might be time to pack the truck and head on down to southern Maryland where Lacey lived and get a look at this new baby girl she had brung into the world, just around then she had done what she always did and beat him to it—in this case showing up loaded with not only the baby but diaper bags and portable baby contraptions. They were cumbersome things that folded in complicated ways and then unfolded to become something else altogether. Portable cribs and strollers and special places for changing diapers and such. What looked like one thing turned out to be another, and he watched in amazement as she unsnapped and unzipped and unbuckled to reveal a little muffin of a baby, pink-faced and squalling from the back of her car.

The baby wailed in a terrible way and then, once Lacey had settled herself into a kitchen chair, Lacey had startled him again by lifting her breast up out of her shirt to nurse the infant. That surprised him, the round fullness of it, the wide blue vein that ran through it, and the way the baby's mouth bobbed first and then suctioned to the dark nipple. He had turned his head from her, started to rise from the chair he sat on across from her, maybe thinking he'd make some coffee, pop some bread in the toaster, or offer to scramble some eggs.

"Willy," she said to him as he rummaged through the breadbox on the counter. "She's got to eat, for crying out loud."

Well, he knew that. That wasn't the point. He'd raised dairy cattle for most of his life and certainly understood what was going on here. But the way she was, not caring for any privacy. And besides, he hadn't even said anything about it.

But Lacey knew him. Over the next few days he could feel himself flush every time she opened her shirt, and then he'd get to squirming so, trying not to look, that he'd have to get up and pretend to need something from another room, or if she was set at the kitchen table he'd pace the floor behind her or fuss with a rag at the counter. But then—and he could have sworn she did it just to ruffle him—she'd get up, the baby still latched to her breast, and swing the chair around with her foot and then sit again so she'd be facing him still.

On her last morning before heading back with the baby, she had been sitting in the parlor, still in her flannel bathrobe with her bare feet resting on a small needle-pointed stool.

"You cold?" he asked. The baby was at her breast again, and he knelt down at the woodstove, his back to her, and opened the front of it, digging at the coals with the poker, and with some small satisfaction, stirring up a shimmer of sparks. He heard the tiniest *smack-pop* of the baby coming off the breast. "What kind of name is that—Anastasia?" he had asked Lacey. "Is that a Russian name?"

"You know it's a Russian name, Willy," she said, distracted. "Cold War is over, you know." He turned around to see her wiping at her breast with the lapel of her bathrobe. "Her father teaches Russian history. I told you that."

"He picked her name?"

"He picked her name," she crooned, lifting the baby to her face and kissing her nose. "*We* picked her name," she corrected herself. "And we think Anastasia is a *beautiful* name, don't we, Anastasia?" The baby gurgled and pursed her tiny lips.

What he wanted to say, though he didn't dare, was how could she let a man who hadn't even married her name the baby. And where was he anyway? But Willy wouldn't ask. There were always questions he couldn't— or wouldn't—ask. Questions he was afraid would come out of his mouth half-formed and end up meaning something altogether different from what he was thinking and so, better to stay away from them.

"It's complicated, Willy," she said. Lacey knew him, always seemed to know just what he was thinking.

"Huh?"

"It's complicated. I told you this. We'll get married. There are just things to work out." She ran her finger along the baby's cheek. "Besides, I'm thirty-one years old. I wanted this baby."

"Thirty-one," he mumbled. "Just ancient. Surprised you're not dead yet."

Lacey just smiled at him. "You know what I mean."

But he didn't, not really. "That baby needs a daddy."

She lifted the baby over her shoulder as it spit up a dribble of milk that ran down the back of her robe.

"Uh-oh, sit tight," he said. And he went to the kitchen and returned with a dishtowel. "Just a little spit-up." He wiped at her back and then across her shoulder with it. "Got it." He looked at the baby resting milk-drunk on Lacey's shoulder. "I'm sure it will work out," he said.

"Can you watch her for a bit, Willy? I need to get in the shower."

She lifted the baby from her shoulder up to Willy's arms. "Here you go, Grandpa." It was the first time she'd said that. *Grandpa.*

The baby hiccupped and settled into a long coo that trilled like a dove and then, even with her eyes closed, he could have sworn she smiled. The moment was all too brief, but in an instant that smile had changed everything about her little face, and Willy had felt his heart melt into a puddle.

Now Lacey is coming home for a visit. It's spring break at the college where she teaches, and she and the girl will be arriving sometime today. Mac, the child's father, has long since moved on—just as Willy suspected he would—and it's just the two of them now, just Lacey and Tasha.

Willy had never gotten used to Mac anyway. There had been a few awkward visits from the three of them the first year or so after Tasha was born, and truth be told, Mac unnerved him, though he couldn't exactly say why. Maybe it was the way he fussed in the kitchen, talking aloud like he was on some fancy cooking show. *I'm thinking of julienning the carrots,* he would say. *Lace—how do you feel about me pureeing this gazpacho a bit more?* Or maybe it was the way he was always draping an arm over Lacey's shoulders whenever she held Tasha on her hip, clustering the three of them together and smiling up at Willy as if Willy was expected to take a damn picture. It seemed to Willy that he did it for Willy's benefit, as if to say, *Look at us, look at the three of us.* And then there were his constant questions about the farm. *What was the source of the TB outbreak?* That was a question that rankled Willy to the bone. In all his years of farming he had maybe five calves come down with scours. It was a record to be proud of. He ran the cleanest barn for miles around the county and that was a fact. Mac then went on to explain to Willy, as if Willy didn't already know this himself, that he understood bovine TB to be a *zoonotic disease* and were any farmhands—or Lacey—exposed?

Willy figured Mac had been doing a little research. They were sitting in the Adirondack chairs, out beside the pond, and Lacey had just gone into the house to put Tasha down for a nap. He explained with a measured tone that while his farm was found not to be the source, he was in fact the first to recognize the symptoms in one of his own cows. The heifer had a nasty swollen udder, oozing pus and crusting over, and he had separated her out from the herd. Doc Asher had administered a full spectrum of antibiotics and still she was no better, the udder turning hard, the heifer dropping weight, hanging her head listlessly, baying mournfully, refusing to eat. He, *Willy*, had been the one to ask for the TB test that would confirm his worst fears. In the telling of it to Mac, he worked to keep his voice even, concluding with the fact that of course all the people had all been tested. And everyone was fine—just fine.

Eventually, Mac had faded away, moving out of Lacey's cottage and then taking a new teaching job in Virginia. But with Mac's disappearance, Willy also can't help noticing that the visits from Lacey and Tasha have become less frequent as well. It occurs to him that maybe Mac's leaving left questions hanging like a bad smell in the air around Lacey. He knows he'll never bring it up to her, never say, *I told you so*, but still, it's there between them—all this leaving and all the holes filled with a stinking silence.

It's been nearly a year since he last saw Lacey and Tasha. With so much time passing between visits, he isn't sure Tasha will remember him. She's always been shy with him at first.

Willy comes down the stairs now, slowly, easing to each step and knowing just which ones will creak with the weight of him. It will take a few minutes to work the kinks out of his knees. By the time he has jiggled the cord to the percolator to get the coffee brewing and slipped on his boots by the kitchen door he's beginning to feel his joints come together in a familiar way.

He heads out the door to the coop. It's late March, and the air feels thick in his lungs, full of rich, rotted odors. His boots crackle across paper-thin crusts of ice and then suck at the mud underneath.

He looks to the pastures, pastures that had once been tight and manicured by the herd. Now they are a tangle of overgrown brambles, black and wiry against the pale morning. A rough winter has tumbled many of the stones that fence the land.

Willy knows the stones, knows the sharp-edged heavy feel of particular ones that fall, year after year, and have to be lifted from the ground and placed again. There is less and less sense to it now, to the lifting and placing. Now he is a chicken farmer.

He lets himself into the chicken yard and the gate heaves on its hinges, setting the hens in the coop to murmuring, softly at first, almost politely, but as he reaches the coop, the sounds become more distinct, building to a fury of clucking and warbling with a jarring squawk rising out of the fray now and then.

He opens the door to the coop. Plywood, warped and insubstantial, not like the barn had been. The barn had been something to see. After the herd had to be destroyed, he'd still tended to it for a few years. But when he'd finally accepted the fact that there would not be another herd—well, it just hadn't seemed so important to fix things right away. When the weather vane toppled and hung swinging in the rain, he had tried to go up to the roof and fix it, but he got dizzy and couldn't get his breath. It hung that way for weeks, teasing him. Finally, a second storm moved in and it just gave up on him, disgusted, and flew off, ripping along the chicken yard and tangling in the chicken-wire fencing, which, of course, did have to be fixed. The weather vane rested now, defeated, in a pile of discarded tires and cinder blocks behind the chicken yard.

A young couple from Long Island had bought the remains of the barn and hauled it away piece by piece. They were going to build an addition to their home, authentic post-and-beam construction, they told him, with *reclaimed materials*, whatever the hell that meant. He wasn't sure, but it sounded illegal, like they were taking back something that was never really theirs in the first place.

They'd sent a crew of six men to dismantle it, and Willy had watched from a distance, grateful that Lacey wasn't around to witness the tearing down. He'd watched the destruction from his second, smaller barn, more of a large, freestanding garage, aluminum over concrete, where he now kept his tractor, chicken feed, his tools—the ones he imagined he couldn't do without—and the old '66 Ford F100, good for salvage parts and some memories.

All the farmers, the few that remained, have moved to aluminum barns. Course it's easier, less upkeep, goes up in a day and doesn't require the help of neighbors to raise. But Willy hates to call it a barn. It's a garage as far as he is concerned. Lacey always called it the *loud barn* because of the way her voice bounced off the cavernous inside of it, ricocheting off the metal walls.

The old barn, built by Willy's daddy, a few Amish boys, and a handful of neighbors, actually *was* post-and-beam construction and had been meant to stand the test of time. The beams locked together and petrified into place in a way that made Willy a little proud as he watched the men shout to one another as to the best way to go about bringing it down.

The husband and wife had come to supervise, and the husband couldn't help but reach out at each barn board that passed by him, having to touch it and marvel at the hand-hewn timbers and the richness of aged oak and hemlock.

When the crew finally slammed the doors on the bed of the semi and fell about to lighting their cigarettes and spitting over the splintered debris, the wife had stood over the stone foundation and clapped her hands like a child and Willy knew Lacey would have found her foolish.

Willy cursed the damn TB that had robbed him of his herd. Five local herds had had to be destroyed that year, but Willy was the only one too old to rebuild. The government had paid him a pittance on each head, but he'd never been much of a spender, so he could get by. He'd taken to tending the chickens instead. He turns a small profit on the eggs, which surprises him some, given his heart isn't in it, but his eggs are good, and people even asked for them by name at the local market. *Mr. Willy's eggs*, they call them.

Now he swats gently—because that is just his nature, and maybe because he is far too aware of just how much he doesn't like them—at the fattest hen to get at her egg. Their cackle and dander irritate him. And their eyes, bright little beady things that he's never gotten used to. He shuffles through a confetti of feathers and holds his breath. He always holds his breath as long as he can in the coop. He's never gotten used to the smell.

Lacey never minded it. The chickens had been her idea anyway. She was soon to turn six that year, six years old and alone with Willy. He'd married her mother only a year before, but May had run off and left him with Lacey.

He kept tending to her, in a daze, just as if she'd been part of the herd, until it occurred to him that she was his for keeps. May wasn't coming back. Lacey was staying. At least, that's what he thought then. In the end, it seemed that Lacey also left—not all at once, but over time. The chickens stayed.

He is wiping the eggs in the sink when he hears the car pull in the drive. It isn't even eight o'clock yet and he isn't near ready. Not that he has any solid idea of what he should have done to prepare for her visit, but he knows somehow, just knows, that there are things he should have done—laundered sheets, for instance, or picked up something special at the grocer. Towels, maybe, he should have laundered the towels. Lacey could manage to use two, three at a time. That had always confounded him, the way she went through the towels as a teenager. And the last time she and Tasha had visited, he must have recovered five or six hanging from bedposts and doorknobs after they left. He should have laundered towels.

He goes out the back door and down the stoop to the gravel drive where her car sits, the engine still humming.

"I left really early this morning," she says through the open window. She tips her head back against the headrest. "God, I'm beat." She turns off the engine, and the car gives a small rattle before completely surrendering, like stones in a can. She comes up out of the car in one long fluid step and then stands in front of him, with her hands at her waist, arches her back, and then reaches her arms up over her head. "Hey, Willy." She smiles and tosses her arms around him. "I look like hell, I know," she says.

He steps back from her, looks her up and down. "Nah," he says. "You look nice." And then he leans in and hugs her again, not knowing if she expects it or not, but he couldn't have stopped himself if he wanted to. It is always a little awkward between the two of them at first. Sometimes it's hard for Willy to know what is expected of him. She holds on to him a little longer than he would have thought, and he notices that she smells of coffee and maybe of cigarette smoke. He spies a mounded knot of blankets on the back seat and sidesteps Lacey to peer through the back window. Tasha is asleep in a booster seat, her head flopped to her shoulder in a way that makes Willy's own neck hurt. He looks expectantly to Lacey.

"She slept the whole way," Lacey says.

He peers through the window again but catches his own reflection in the glass and becomes suddenly aware of how he looks. He takes off his cap and stuffs it in his front pocket, raking back his hair with the fingers of his other hand.

"Want to get her up?" he says, nodding to the window. Lacey is looking around the place. He sees her eyes rest on the raw spot in the earth where the barn once stood and feels something ooze in his heart, his shoulders curling around his chest. It's been nearly three years since the barn came down, and still, watching her look at it again makes it hurt like an old sore scratched fresh.

"Want some coffee?" he offers.

"I've had enough coffee to wire Manhattan," she says.

He doesn't know what she's talking about. Sometimes it's like that. Sometimes there are gullies between the two of them that he just doesn't know how to get over.

He looks at her now. She doesn't look so different from the last time, skinnier maybe, but he knows she likes herself skinny. Her curly hair—that wild hair that used to make her cuss like a sailor on Friday nights and had been responsible for at least one hairbrush sent sailing through an open bathroom window many years ago—is as long and wild as it has ever been, but now she wears it with the front pulled back smoothly and the rest winding down her shoulders, as if she and her hair have come to a reconciliation of sorts.

"Uh-oh," Lacey says. "Here comes trouble." She nods behind Willy.

Tasha has climbed out of her booster seat and is pressing her face up against the window from inside the car, studying Willy. She unlatches the door, scrambles from the car, and moves quickly to Lacey's side, wraps her arms around Lacey's thigh. Lacey puts her hand gently to the back of the child's head. "Say hello, Tasha."

"Hello, Tasha," she mimics her mother and giggles, turning to bury her face in Lacey's side and then rolling back to look up at Willy.

She doesn't look like Lacey. She is fair, her skin nearly translucent, her hair so blonde and—unlike Lacey's—corn-silk straight, cheekbones that sit too high on her face for a child. But when she peers up at Willy and breaks into a bashful smile, there is something in the bow of her lips and the way her cheeks blossom that is sweet and familiar.

Lacey had been sending pictures of the girl in between visits. But of course, it wasn't the same as really seeing her. She's changed so much in the past year. He watches her eyes dart from Willy to Lacey and back again, sees the way her hand plays at Lacey's thigh, the fingers splayed and then curling into a ball. Nope, you couldn't see that sort of thing in a photograph.

Tasha untangles herself from Lacey and runs ahead to the house. Lacey nods to Willy. "Let the games begin," she says.

"How's the college work?" he asks.

"The college work sucks," Lacey says, pulling a pack of cigarettes from her sweater pocket and shooing Tasha up the back stoop and then following her through the door.

Lacey sits down at the kitchen table, kicks out a second chair, and spreads her legs across it. She runs her fingers down the length of a cigarette before sliding it back in the pack.

"Don't worry," she says to him. "I don't smoke in the car with her."

Willy just shrugs his shoulders. "I didn't say nothing," he says, turning his back to her to finish up with the eggs he left at the sink.

How does she do that? How does she always seem to know just what he is thinking?

He remembers the first time she surprised him like that. He'd been a young man then, just pushing up against the brink of forty, but still a young man, not feeling the gravel in his joints too much, not thinking so much about the way his skin fit over his bones.

He'd only married May six months earlier and he was still getting used to having a five-year-old around. She was bold for such a young thing, piping in with her opinions—*boys are stupid, green beans give me headaches, some of the farmhands smell funny.* And she was forever scampering between the cows in the stanchions, no matter how many times he told her it was a fine way to get herself crushed to death. It spooked him some, the way she would barge into the bathroom while he sat on the toilet and not even notice the compromising position he was finding himself in. Just popping in to tell him *hurry on up in here 'cause Momma says supper is ready and what's taking so long.*

On one particular evening, he had just finished up with the herd and was sitting on the back stoop preparing to light his pipe. She came meandering down from the barn and nudged him with her knees before sitting down beside him. He scratched the match across the cinder block, and she watched him draw the flame into the bowl. He felt her watching him and he sucked hard at the stem, drawing the flame down into the bowl and letting it rise again, amusing her, he was certain. He had thoughts weighing on his mind, but he tried to clear them away, focus on the girl. She'd been under his feet all day, following him through the barn, stooping down and peering with him at one of the heifer's damaged teats as if she had something to say about it, clambering up the paddock gate and riding it as he tried to lock up for the night. He'd even caught her sticking her little fingers into one of the heifer's cavernous nostrils. Couldn't explain *why* she'd do such a thing. Just said matter-of-factly that she *felt* like it.

"Willy," she had said, nudging her shoulder into his where they sat on the stoop together, her voice small and papery, like it might blow away. "I don't think my momma likes it here no more."

"Now, girl," he said, patting her knee, "what makes you say such things?" But his heart had already tightened in his chest because he'd been thinking the same thing, the very same thing. May wasn't happy, and it didn't seem right seeing as he had thought for sure she would be. He had been so proud to bring her home on their wedding day, and after that first night with her, feeling so good, he couldn't imagine she would feel any different from him.

That was just the thing that confounded him—that he could feel one way and she could feel another. Of late, when he touched her, she just lay still, not saying *no* to him, but like she'd taken out her heart and set it aside. And just last night, when he'd lifted his head from the sweet-salty crook of her neck, she lay wide-eyed and staring at the ceiling, and he couldn't go on.

It was a terrible thing, to feel connected to a woman and then find out you weren't really touching her at all. Something like that made a man start asking questions that he didn't want to know the answers to.

But even then, at that moment, with Lacey tucked against his shoulder and his hand patting her knee, he couldn't have possibly imagined that May would disappear the way she did, that she could just quit the life they had like it meant nothing, leaving him and little Lacey without even so much as a *so long and see ya later*. Gone. Like a breath that's been inhaled and exhaled and done with.

Tasha prances over to the sink now and stands on her toes to look in the basin. "Did all those eggs come from Mommy's chickens?"

Lacey's chickens. Now some memories are hazy and hard to bring back, like the way May felt to him on that first night, after her bath, the way her skin was still bathwater-warm and soft and giving in places. He hadn't known a woman's skin could yield to him like that. He was always trying to bring the feeling back, even years later, but it all felt so faded and cool, like the sheets, and he knew he couldn't be remembering it right because his imagination had to keep working at it harder every time.

But, Lacey's chickens. He can remember that.

She was turning six and her hair was a tangle of ringlets that made her look like something out of an old Tarzan movie from his own childhood. It had been a few months since May had disappeared, and he was just starting to see Lacey differently, thinking maybe he ought to figure out how to manage that mop of hair and not let her head off to school with a scab of jelly drying around her mouth and her socks unmatched. He was prideful of her, too, and his pride was unshakeable, but May had done all the tending to her and without May, there was that gully between the two of them now.

It was October, and the school had called him in to discuss her disruptive behavior. She was smart enough, they assured him, but he knew that already. He wanted to explain that she just had her own way of doing things and didn't much care for instruction of any sort. And he wanted to tell them that she was a whole lot better off if you just let her figure things out on her own—she was that kind of child. But the teacher, a pretty young thing with no children of her own and a disturbing way of looking at him without blinking, went on to explain that Lacey always seemed distracted, couldn't sit still in her seat, and just that morning had had to be reprimanded—*repeatedly*—for spitting in the school yard. Willy didn't see as this was a behavioral problem, but he didn't say anything, just made a mental note to explain to Lacey that it was fine for the farmhands to spit but it was not something a little lady should be doing in public. He didn't tell the pretty teacher that he wasn't her father, and he didn't tell her about

May—not exactly. "It's just the two of us now," he had said. She said she was sorry to hear that.

"I don't want to go to school anyhow," Lacey told him later that night.

"You got to go to school, Lacey."

"You know what I want for my birthday?" she said. "I want chickens, baby chickens."

"Now what are you gonna do with chickens? Chickens is the dumbest thing I ever heard of for a birthday present."

She began to fidget with her fingers, pulling at them the way she had for a long time after May vanished, wrapping one around the other and twisting.

"I don't want any dumb chickens anymore," she said. "I was just teasing you, Willy. I don't want dumb chickens."

He tugged at one of her curls and watched it spring back to her cheek. "Not so dumb," he said. He ran a finger over her brow. "Not so dumb."

For her birthday he brought home three chicks in a cardboard box, and she named them Huey, Dewey, and Louie. The next day he bought a Polaroid camera.

Now, so many years later, standing at the sink with Tasha bouncing on her toes beside him, he remembers that the chickens didn't bother him so much when he had the herd. They didn't matter then.

With Tasha peering into the sink beside him, he says to Lacey over his shoulder, "I'm thinking of getting rid of the chickens."

"What would you do around here?"

"Plenty to do," he mumbles, but he knows it isn't so. "I could hay the upper fields."

"Can I see the chickens, Willy?" asks Tasha. "I like chickens." She peers up at him expectantly. He looks down to her beside him and notices gray circles beneath her eyes, like soft pale bruises.

"They smell," says Willy.

"Chickens don't smell, do they, Mommy?"

Maybe it's their eyes he takes issue with, their cold little stupid eyes.

"Well, do they?" she asks again, putting her hands on her hips and flipping her head with a sharp nod.

Lacey reaches out and wraps her hands around Tasha's waist, pulling her to herself, smashing a mother's kiss on her forehead before Tasha can twirl out of her arms.

"You need a haircut," Lacey says to Willy. "You want me to cut your hair?"

"I get it done in town now," he says. "Been awful busy."

"Who cuts it? God, Willy, it looks like you've been doing it yourself."

"Young fella, don't remember his name."

"Let me do it. I always did a good job for you." She comes up behind him and tugs at the ends, forking her fingers and running them through the ends over his ear.

"Okay, Lacey." He should have cut it before she came. "That'd be fine. Meantime, me and the princess is gonna do some chicken farming."

Tasha runs ahead, scattering the few chickens that a moment earlier had clucked and drifted aimlessly in the chicken yard. Now they run from her, their wings lifted to their sides and flapping futilely, their tail feathers up and fanned, bobbing their heads and squawking at the indignity of it all.

"Here, chicky, chicky," she calls. "Willy, they won't come to me."

"Course not," he says.

"Why don't they like me?"

"Ain't you. Chickens don't like nobody." But he remembers the way the first three chicks had followed Lacey around the yard. He has pictures of it. They lined up right behind her and followed her all over the place, along the edges of the pond, even into the kitchen some days, and when she walked along the top of the stone fences they'd cheep and hop at the stones as if they'd rather dash themselves to death than lose sight of her. "Except when they're bitty chicks," he says.

He opens the door to the coop, and she walks in ahead of him. The hens snap their heads up and down as she walks the length of their laying boxes. She stops suddenly at the smallest red banty, her scabbed head sunken deep in a fluff of feathers. "Oh, look," she says, leaning into the hen. "Her head is all pecked to bits."

"It's called pecking order." He'd had to explain it once to Lacey, too.

He watches her small finger reach out to touch the hen who only snugs her head in deeper and blinks, but lets Tasha touch her fluffed breast feathers.

"Poor little thing," she croons, tilting her head and peering closer. He looks at the hen now and realizes it is worse than he thought, now that he's really seeing it. The scabbing concerns him. It's always best to let the hens work out the order on their own, but once blood is shed things can take a quick turn for the worse.

"I got some ointment," he says. "We can tend to that later." He is thinking he's going to have to remove the big apricot, the one whose shackles are fluffed even now as she skirts around Tasha's ankles and squawks. The bird's a good layer and generally keeps order in the house, but he can't have her bullying to the extent that blood is drawn. He shoos her away from Tasha, who hardly seems to notice, and she clumsily flaps to heft herself to a low perch a few feet away. The air is thicker and dustier from her attempted flight, and he pulls a handkerchief from his pocket, moves it once in front of his face to clear the air, puts it to his nose, and blows. Then he wads it up and sticks it in his back pocket.

"Mommy wouldn't like that," she says. "Shouldn't blow your nose in your banana. Now you can't wear it on your head, 'cause you went and blew your nose in it."

"In my what?" He pulls it out of his pocket and studies. "In my ban-*dan*-a," he says. He lets loose with a wild hard laugh that surprises him some. "It's called a ban-*dan*-a."

"That's what I *said*," she says, narrowing her eyes and walking out of the coop.

He follows her out, taking a moment to secure the yard with a length of chain. "But that's what it's for." He struggles with the task of having to make it right with her, getting angry with himself for wanting her to like him.

"You know what the Easter Bunny is bringing me?" she says.

"Nope," he says, feeling fairly certain he's been pardoned.

"A bunny."

"Is that so? Now what makes you think that?"

"I just know, that's all. 'Cause rabbits are my favorite thing and 'cause that's what I want."

"That don't make no difference—what you want." But she is skipping ahead now and he's glad she hasn't heard him. "A chocolate bunny, maybe," he calls to her.

"A real one!" She stops, turns, crosses her arms, and watches him, dragging one toe back and forth across the grass in front of her, and then considers him a moment before wandering back to him. "I can go slow if you want. Mommy says old people are slower than regular people."

"Is that so?"

Willy follows her through the kitchen door just in time to hear her tell Lacey, "Chickens *do* stink, Mommy."

"I love it here," says Lacey to Willy. "I really do." She is looking out the window over the sink to where the barn had stood. The tumbled stone foundation is jagged and crumbling. The concrete floor, visible through the places where the foundation has completely fallen away, sprouts spindly twisted saplings, mulberries most likely, that have straggled through cracks in the last few years. Under a damp gray sky, it all looks like an ancient ruin. The pair of rust-blotched paddock gates dipping down where the two come together, straining against their hinges, skeletal vines clambering up over the iron bars. The fields beyond lie fallow, damp and beiged by a long winter. The pond, a pool of cold obsidian framed in brambles, is perfectly still, not a ripple to be seen.

"It's changed a lot."

"Not so much. More the same than different," she says, letting the curtain fall and turning to him.

"Oh, not sure about that," he says.

She is quiet but looking right at him, and there is something hopeful in her face that he can't quite read, something that makes her cross her arms and breathe deeply. But then she drops her arms. "I'm sorry, Willy," she says. "I'm sorry I haven't been back much."

He waves her off. "Aw, well."

"It's just that—I don't know."

There isn't any explaining it. He knows that. Things change; wives run off, herds get sick, chickens lay eggs, barns come down.

She shifts on her feet and stands up straighter. With a fresh voice she asks, "Where do you keep the shears? I couldn't find them in the mending box."

Willy gets the shears and a thin black comb from the medicine cabinet and carries them down the stairs the same way he had taught Lacey to carry them, pointed down and with his hands wrapped well around the closed blades.

When he gets back to the kitchen Lacey is at the open kitchen door. "No farther than the fence, Tasha!" she yells. "Stay away from the pond—okay?"

She shuts the door and turns to Willy. "That child is way too comfortable around water," she says. "She can't really swim yet," she explains to Willy. "But she sure doesn't have any fear of the water." She motions to a chair and Willy dutifully hands her the comb and scissors and sets himself down. She flips a dishtowel around his neck, goes to the sink and runs the comb under the spigot, comes back to him and begins to drag the wet comb through his hair. "Tasha like my chickens?"

"They *do* stink," he whispers.

She laughs. "I know, Willy."

He sits up a little straighter for her and feels the gentle tug of his hair running through the teeth of the comb, a trickle of water trailing down his neck.

"There's something I wanted to ask you," she says. "And you can say no if you want. I'll understand."

He never could say no to her. She knows that about him. Oh, he could be mad at her, wonder about her, but he can never say no.

"I'm not teaching this summer. God, I need a break from the SOBs, Willy. Sometimes I think they don't give a rat's ass about what I'm teaching. That's the thing that gets me." She snips over his ear, leans down a bit, and snips again. "You wouldn't believe the papers they turn in. Crap, all crap." She puts her hand under his chin and lifts it. "I need some time off, so I told David—that's my department head—I said, 'David, you can get some other fool to teach your remedial English flunkies this summer.' That's exactly what I told him."

Willy knows he is expected to say something, but nothing comes to him. "Is that so?" he finally says.

"This is the thing." He can hear her take a deep breath at his back. "Willy, could Tasha and I stay here for the summer? There are some things we need to do—no big deal, really." She gently places her hand to the top of the back of his head and he bows it, tucking his chin. A pane of sunlight spreads to the kitchen floor only inches from his feet, a splash of summer. He imagines it would be warm if he slid his foot into it.

"It would be good for us," she is saying. "For both of us. And Tasha likes it here, likes you, and the chickens, of course."

He is thinking about what a colorless day it has been, how flat the sky had seemed, and now, well, now the sun is inching its way across the floor.

He knows he shouldn't answer right away, that he should offer to think about it. Maybe he should have some conditions, reasonable ones, of course. After all, she should know he'd gotten pretty used to living by himself, set in his ways and all.

"That'd be fine, Lacey," he hears himself say.

Suddenly, he can hardly sit still thinking about it all, imagining how things will be. He'll whitewash the coop for sure. And it isn't too late to plant the timothy. He can get at least one good cutting. It might be a little thin the first year, but by the following summer—

"Willy," she says, laying her hand over his shoulder, knowing him again the way she does. "It's only for the summer."

There is a rap at the door's window, and he looks up to see the girl's lips and tongue pressed against it. She waves quickly and runs from the window, leaving only a moist round impression and a steamy spill of breath.

"Probably just for the summer," she says. "Okay?"

"Sure," he says, but his voice is tangled in his heart so that it rattles some. "Sure," he says. "I know that."

CHAPTER 2

Coming Home

Lacey is gathering the sheets from the two bedrooms she and Tasha will be sleeping in. First, she strips the nubby white chenille bedspreads from a room with two twin beds where Tasha will be sleeping and tosses the sheets and spreads to the hallway. She is certain nothing has been washed since the last time she was home almost a year ago.

The room connects with another smaller room where there is an old three-quarter spool bed. The coverlet in this room is a crocheted piece, buttery yellow, whether by age or design, she can't be sure, can't remember.

She walks to the window and pulls back the thin, gauzy curtains. Dead flies are crisping in the windowsill and she can't help but wonder if she's just done something very stupid by asking Willy if she can come back for the summer. She leans down to the sill and blows. Fly carcasses flutter up to her face and swirl back down again.

She can hear Tasha downstairs talking Willy's ear off, rambling on and on in that way of hers, something about the *circle of life* and Simba's father falling off a cliff—and a wiggly tooth, which is just not possible, not for another year or more. After all, she's only five and Lacey is fairly certain that she couldn't possibly be losing a tooth yet. But, like all things having to do with being a mother, there is never anything that she is completely sure of. Other than that she adores her daughter, and even that, she's never quite sure she's doing that right, either.

Lacey would like nothing more than to crumple in a heap on top of her old bed, the one where the old mattress is so broken down and soft that the center of it is a deep nest, a feathered hole. But as tired as she is, sleep is both sassy and elusive these days. Lacey thinks of it as a tease—she wants it and it crawls so close, like a lover full of promises, but just as she feels its breath locked in hers a gear shifts in her brain and she is snapped wide awake. It's been like that now for days, and while she's tried all manner of seduction, from cajoling to ignoring it, she's pretty darn sure that the only chance she has of catching it is to be hit over the head with a lead pipe and subsequently slip into a coma.

Last night, the struggle had been especially miserable and by 4:00 a.m. she had given up, tossed off her covers, and decided that if she wasn't sleeping, she might as well be driving. Tasha, on the other hand, seemed to have no problem sleeping and barely mumbled when Lacey scooped her from her bed, set her in her booster seat, and padded her with pillows and quilts for the four-hour drive north to the farm.

The first couple of hours were fine, but near sunrise she was in serious need of some coffee. She pulled into a Starbucks drive-thru near Annapolis on Route 2 and ordered their largest dark roast with a shot of espresso.

The coffee had done its job, maybe too well, and by the time she had arrived at the farm she had that sick, surreal sort of feeling that comes from lack of sleep and too much caffeine, made all the worse by a feeling that something nasty was creeping up on her and she didn't have the wits or dexterity to get out of the way.

She looks around her old room now. Doilies are everywhere and when she lifts one from the chest of drawers, it leaves a filigreed dust pattern behind, a giant snowflake. Her mother made these, and Lacey knows she made most of them even before the two of them came to live with Willy. In her mind's eye she can see her still, the thick needles working at the threads, and she can feel herself rising up on her toes and leaning over her mother's thigh, peering deep into her lap, trying to see what her mother was seeing, trying to imagine what would soon trail from that frenetic dance between her mother's fingers and the needle.

Lacey had been living with Aunt Virgie and Uncle Price at the time, above the hardware store in town, less than two miles from the farm. But whether the memory comes from when May was living with them or it was only one of her visits, she cannot now recall. May eventually came to live with them as well, but Lacey knows that for some time she herself lived there with Aunt Virgie and Uncle Price. May lived far away and would come and stay with them for a time and then leave again, and these leaving times were fraught with confusion, so much so that even now, as Lacey stands fingering the doily, she can feel the tug of her mother's skirt between her fingers. And she can hear the grown-up noises, the murmurings and the deeper breaths and sighs between her momma and her aunt, and she is certain, even now, that Aunt Virgie was the voice pulling on May to stay, not to go back to wherever *back* was, and May was the smaller voice, the one that sounded a lot like Beauford, Auntie's black collie, whimpering on a squirrel chase in his sleep. And always Lacey was hopeful, even in her tiny little two- or three-year-old heart, that Auntie would win this time—and how could she not—because Auntie was the center of the world, a beautiful fat fleshy world of hugs and chocolates and warm baths, and who wouldn't want to be here in this world?

But always May left, until one day she didn't. One day she stayed and that day led to the next and the next and they became a family of sorts—the four of them, Uncle Price and Aunt Virgie, Lacey and May— and then to moving in with Willy and they became a *real* family of Willy and May and Lacey. Though, finally, May left again. And the last time there were no tears.

Lacey looks in the mirror now, licks a finger, and smooths it over one eyebrow and then the other. She pulls her sweater off over her head and stands in front of the old mirror with its blooming silver blemishes. She's wearing just a gray tank top, and she tucks it into her jeans but has to stand on her toes to see where the shirt meets the top of the jeans because the mirror is hung too high. It's always been this way. She used to pull a chair over to the bureau to try to get a full-length view of herself, but that always cut off her head and even still, she couldn't see her feet. It almost makes her laugh out loud now, to remember that there was never anywhere she could see her full self in this house. Putting herself together for school or an occasional date involved putting herself together in three parts, none of which she was ever able to reconcile with the others. Even today, she never knows for sure what shoes go with what dress or blouse or pants and so she is more or less resigned to loafers or flip-flops, boots in the winter, which she imagines work with everything. There had once been a pricey pair of muckety-muck designer heels reserved for parties and special evenings, but they made her calves ache and she was never quite sure they went with what she was wearing anyway and so she stored them away a long time ago. And as for her hair, she has also resigned herself to either up or down, depending on the weather mostly, and whether she wants it off her neck in a steamy St. Mary's summer or serving as a sort of wooly scarf on colder days.

Aunt Virgie liked to pull it back with clips and pins and she could fashion it into a mammoth twist on the top of Lacey's head, which always made Lacey feel like she had a pile of rags balanced up there but left her neck feeling cool and helped keep the knots from forming at the nape of her neck.

Even after May disappeared, Willy still brought Lacey by the store. He'd need something—steel hinges, spools of wire, bags of lime, ten-penny nails, and chicken wire—and just as soon as Willy brought the truck to a stop in the lot out front, Lacey would be out the door like a shot and running up the narrow stairway at the back of the store to find Auntie and get her hugs. She would find the woman swooshing her broom across the wooden floor or melting chocolate to make candies for the orphans at Villa Maria (*chocolate tells them they're loved*, she liked to say), or simmering something on the stove for supper, canning tomatoes, bleaching rags—the woman was industrious. She was never caught sitting down. In fact, Lacey has not a single memory of the woman sitting. Even when she set out a meal she bobbed up and down, hefting her large bust and wide backside between the backs of chairs and the walls of the small apartment to fetch this and that condiment, second helpings, sweet tea, *extra ice for your drink*, or *top off your coffee?*

Sometimes Lacey thinks she should remember more about her childhood, but not having siblings means there's no fact-checking, there's no one to bounce the smaller moments off and see if they might come back a little bigger, a little broader, add a dash of color or a point of view that makes everything stick in the memory banks a little longer.

What made it worse was that after May left, Lacey couldn't even bring herself to ask Willy about her. She'd get a feeling every time she'd think about her, like she was going to be sick, and also because she didn't want to know because she just kept on hoping May would come back, like she used to, when they lived over the hardware store. But deep down she knew that if she asked and Willy told her that she wasn't coming back, then it would have to be true that May was gone, and she was certain she would just die from the hurting inside. Sometimes Lacey thinks maybe she did die, slowly. She remembers it like a dying time, with the same feeling she has growing in her gut right now.

Lacey scoops up the sheets in her arms. They smell damp, a little sour, and she's thinking she should open the bedroom windows and let the mattresses air a bit as well, so she drops the pile on the floor and goes back into the suite of two rooms to begin opening windows.

There is a single small window in the first bedroom, between the two beds, and this one opens easily, but in her own bedroom the larger window is stuck hard. She balls her fist and bangs along the edges with the heel of her hand. Eventually, there is the distinct crackle of wood releasing from the frame and the window goes up in fits and starts, forcing her to jiggle and bang a time or two more before she gets it up all the way and then, once it's up, she realizes there's no screen in it. She leans out over the ledge and sees the screen directly below, out of reach on the sunporch roof. It's easy enough to step right out on the roof—onto what she always considered as a teenager to be her own balcony. It's slanted, of course, but angled perfectly for sunbathing and had once made for an excellent smoking porch.

Lacey folds herself through the window, stepping out maybe just a little more gingerly than she once did, but the muscle memory is there, and it feels so natural that she immediately wishes she had her cigarettes that are in her sweater pocket on the bed. She lifts the screen and realizes its aluminum frame is bent beyond repair. She angles it to slide it back through the window and leans it against the interior wall of the room. Amazingly, she can still smell wet stale ash on it.

Coming back through the window she pushes the thin curtains out of her way, but a breeze from behind her whips them around and they tangle and curl around her face as she steps back into the room. The air between the outside and the inside was so distinctly different a moment ago but a sudden spring wind has melded the two and now, with the curtain wrapped around her face and twisting at her ankle, she can smell dust and pine and ash, and maybe there is the bite of onion grass in the air, wafting in on the breeze at her back.

Lacey picks up the laundry from the hallway and heads downstairs to the cellar to start the wash, but just as she comes through the kitchen, she sees Tasha's rump poking out of the icebox.

"What are you up to?"

Tasha pulls her head out of the icebox and a fat pickle rests in her mouth like a big old cigar. She crunches down hard and juice dribbles down her chin. "Yum," she says, smacking away at the pickle.

The back door swings open and Willy is wiping his muddy boots at the stoop. He comes into the kitchen with Lacey's quilted overnight bag on one shoulder and Tasha's pink duffel on the other. "That everything?" he says.

Lacey nods, thanks him, and says to Tasha, "That's the dill." She shifts the wadded sheets to her left side and uses the thumb of her right hand to wipe juice from Lacey's chin. "Willy likes his pickles thoroughly dilled."

"Your momma used to like 'em that way too, as I recall," says Willy. He sets Lacey's bag at the bottom of the steps and hangs Tasha's smaller one from the banister. "She used to eat pickles for breakfast. Remember, Lacey?"

"Sure do." She has opened the cellar door and is reaching along the wall with one hand to find the light switch, balled-up sheets balanced on her hip.

"Could I eat these for breakfast, Mommy?" Tasha bites hard again and pretends to swoon with pleasure but before she can quite pull off the drama, her face pinches hard and her eyes fly open. She drops the pickle and her hands fly to her mouth. She squeals and then begins to cry in tiny little hoots, dribbling pickle mash from her mouth.

"Mommy, Mommy . . ."

Lacey is amazed at how quickly Willy gets to her, even before Lacey can drop the sheets and bolt across the kitchen. Willy has one big paw of a hand on the back of her head as she spits pickle mash to the floor. "There you go," he says. "There you go. Bite your tongue?"

She both nods her head and shakes it at the same time, and Lacey is more confused now. She kneels down beside her and Willy says, "Let's take a look in there."

Lacey is holding Tasha's hands while Willy uses his thumb to pull back her lip and deftly, with two thick fingers, goes in quickly, plucks his hand from her mouth, and presents her with a perfect little jewel of a tooth.

"Well, see, sugar? See? You just lost that wobbly ol' tooth," he says.

"Oh, my goodness, Tasha—you lost a tooth? You lost a tooth, sweetie. That's all." And she is so relieved she sits down on the floor and hugs her. "That's all it was—your first lost tooth!"

Tasha sniffles and begins to smile shyly, with her tongue searching her mouth, and then broader as Willy's hand *scritch-scritch*es up and down her back.

"It just scared you," says Lacey. And she gets up from the floor to get a clean dishrag, runs water over it, and calls Tasha to the sink. She wipes Tasha's mouth and the dishrag comes away blood streaked. Willy pulls a chair up to the sink and motions to Tasha to climb up, but she continues to stand there, choking a little, spitting into the rag Lacey holds.

Willy lifts her to the chair and turns the tap water on warm, pulls a box of salt from the cupboard and mixes her a glass of warm salt water. "Don't drink it, just swish it around your mouth and spit it out," he says.

She swishes and spits in the sink and Lacey watches swirls of pink roll through the porcelain basin. It bleeds much longer than Lacey would have thought.

"She'll be just fine," says Willy to Lacey.

"Of course, she will," says Lacey quietly, and she smooths her hand down Tasha's cheek. "It's just a tooth is all." But all she can really think of is that Tasha is scared, *was* scared, maybe not so much now with the two of them hovering around her but when it happened, well, the look on her face. That look.

The bleeding finally slows enough that Lacey tilts Tasha's head back to peer into her mouth. "Let's have a look," she says. Tasha opens her mouth like a baby bird and Lacey is horrified. Her gums are puffed white and swollen and tiny canker sores have erupted behind her lips. Tasha's eyes open wider and Lacey is certain Tasha has seen the flash of fear on her own face. She pulls her to her. "Oh, you're just growing up so fast!" she says as brightly as she can while she squeezes her daughter to her and feels the splash of her own flopping stomach.

December 18, 1972

   My heart feels like it's all stretched out, working out the kinks it got from being tied up in a knot for so long. My brain is plumb wore out from thinking. Lately I been thinking about sin. I ain't always so sure where the blame ough-ta land when it comes to sin. Seems too often the wrong person's got to make amends for sin that ain't of their own doing—like sin got a mind of its own and places it's just bound to get to—come hell or high water.

   Now even with the days passing on, things having changed so much, me being so far from the island and right comfortable up here, I can still feel sin hanging on me like an itchy old blanket thrown over, rotted in spots with mold, raising up a dank kind of smell that pinches at the insides of my nose and don't go away, not really, no matter how long I been trying to get used to it.

   For just one minute once, I didn't believe in sin. It was the very minute Lacey was born. She just come out with a pop—the last push being so easy given all the pushing and grunting and swearing and crying I been doing the whole night and all the live-long day. There she was, pop-swish, and she was in this world, squalling like a storm come in and her black hair slicked to her head like a cap of lace. For just that piece of time, as Miss Bunny wiped and wrapped her, and the sounds she was making settled down into little bursts of wind, I knew, there just couldn't be no such thing as sin. Not so long as she was lying there blinking into this bright new world.

December 20, 1972

   I have always liked the feel of one of them real good pens going across paper. I been told I have nice penmanship, but I won't be getting much of a chance to write no more on account of having left the island. Aunt Virgie says I should go to school up here, in Maryland. She took me for a drive to the high school here. It was bigger than any building we got on Ocracoke Island, bigger even than the packing plant. And all them kids, just looking so different from me, more like the tourists that come in the summer to Ocracoke. They got boys looking like girls and girls looking like boys. Aunt Virgie had pulled into the parking lot and there was a wide drive ahead of us that swung in a circle in front of the school and was filled with long yellow buses, one after the other.

She says we can just go in and have a look. She was hopeful with me. You look much better, she said. No one will ask anything, promise you, May. It's all healing real good. She was turning my face to hers when she said it, looking at me careful. But she was just being nice. I knew it was still looking bad, and I still weren't seeing too good out of the one eye, the worser one.

There were six wide doors across the front of the building and wings that stretched out to either side and rose three stories or more. As we sat there and I considered going in, a bell rang what made me jump right there in my seat and then all the doors, each and every one of them, burst open from the inside and there was laughter and curse words flying in the air and people moving around us but not really seeing us, just swarming like hornets, and climbing on buses and running through the parking lot. Cars were starting up and right next to us a girl stood aside a little hump of a car, a bug. I didn't see her at first with my right eye watering so bad and so she just come up out of nowhere. She held a cigarette in one hand and shoved a backpack to the back seat. She put the cigarette in her mouth and tilted her head back and took a big draw off it like it was the most important thing she'd done all day. She was no more than three feet from me and when she turned around and saw me and Aunt Virgie she just looked at me with that what-are-you-staring-at look, but I looked away so she would think maybe she was mistaken, though I was staring at her. At her hair, which was short in the front and long in the back and bleached a color of yellow that almost looked green in the sunlight, and at her clothes. She had patches on her jeans—American flags and a sunflower and on her bottom was a big red apple with a bite took out of it. A boy come running out of nowhere and grabbed her round the waist, swung her round and she kissed him for a long hard kiss and then she held the cigarette to his lips and he drew on it too, also looking like it was the best thing he had done all day. Then they kissed again like they was taking a sample of one another, tasting and stopping to consider and tasting again, and I looked away planning on not looking back again until they were done. Aunt Virgie smiled at me and said kindly that this might take a little getting used to, but I need to finish school.

But I knew I weren't going in there. Right then I was missing my old schoolhouse, but especially I knew I would miss writing. Miss Connolly was forever putting my poems and such up on the bulletin board in the front parlor of the schoolhouse. And I liked the look of it, all my pretty writing and my name swirled across the top of the paper, May DuBerry, claiming it as my own. I suspect she was liking my writing as much for the prettiness of it as she was for the words it was saying. Yes, I have always liked the look of my words on paper, though it can be embarrassing. It's kind of like looking at yourself naked in one of them long mirrors, liking what you see, but not being sure you're really supposed to—and certain it ain't for no one else to see. And words on paper can be a permanent sort of thing, lying round to be found like a dirty old pair of underpants shoved under the bed.

But I will keep this diary here. I can do my writing in it and maybe tell the story of how things were and how things are and someday how things will be.

As for school, I asked Aunt Virgie, what about Lacey? She told me she would take care of her, just as she done the last three years.

I know, though, that it's time for me to start taking care of her. Things are changing and I will write down the changing of them.

December 22, 1972

We have put to rest the issue of me going to school here. At least for now. I have promised to think on it again after Christmas, but I have learned that as I am soon to turn seventeen I don't actually <u>have</u> to go to school.

Lacey wants Silly Putty for Christmas. I saw some across the street at the pharmacy a few days ago and now I'm fixing to buy her some. Daddy sent me twenty dollars and said to buy myself something nice with it. They got some perfumes too, and some nice hand creams. I might get Aunt Virgie some of the hand creams. There's one that smells like roses and another like honeysuckle and I can't decide between the two. And maybe for Uncle Price I will buy him a new wallet as he holds all his dollars together with nothing more than a rubber band and he keeps his driver's license in the cash register drawer. It's so hard though, to leave here and go downstairs through the store, past the men who all hush up tight when I walk by. They don't really know nothing about me, though I know they speculate some.

It's getting real near Christmas and I'm afraid Daddy is likely pretty drunk by now. That's okay. Sometimes being drunk keeps him out of trouble. He says Little Jim keeps asking about me, wants to know how I'm doing, if I'm going with anyone. She got a fella? is what Little Jim wants to know. Now who would want to be with me with my face still all so puffed up and swollen and this yellow color rising up out of my eye socket (special thanks to him). Saddest thing of all is sometimes I think about him still and not in such a bad way as he deserves, neither.

Problem is with Little Jim he has a way of being that makes a body forget what he really is like deep down. He has a way of walking where he just bounces up on the balls of his feet and rolls right into his next step. If you're watching from behind (which is the safest place of all—watching him go), well it just sort of makes a girl's backbone slip and you can't help but think of going on after him. When he's standing still he likes to lean back into something, like a doorway or a piling or his truck (that boy loves his truck), and he tips the toe of his right boot over his left leg and scratches in the grass or the sandy gravel. All the while he'll be talking to you he'll lean back from his own hips, his arms all tight and this little smile dancing around on his face, and when he bends forward to say something to you, it don't matter what he's going to say, cause you just been flattered by the very fact he chose to say it to you. At least, that's how it was with me.

One thing you learn quick with Little Jim is don't get too comfortable. He'll go along like you're just teasing, one on the other, and then that smile falls off his face fast as you can blink.

Miss Bunny says she don't see why I felt feelings for such a boy in the first place. With so many decent boys round me, why would I choose to be taken up by the one boy who got the mean streak in him? Miss Bunny says it's sometimes in a girl's nature to be drawn to such kinds and I am just damn lucky there ain't too many men like Little Jim in the whole of Ocracoke. There are fine men and women living among us, she says, and she is right, too. For I remember how the women took care of Mama at the end and how the men let Daddy drink hisself mean and stupid but never left him alone for longer than it might take to relieve hisself till they got him sober enough to be working the boats again.

It was winter when she died. I was only twelve (not so long ago, but ages ago just the same), and the northwest wind been coming in hard for days over the sound. It's a wind so cold and raw that it gets inside your bones and turns the marrow to ice. The men say it cripples up the fingers in an instant when their hands get wet inside the gloves and they are clawing at the nets. The sea trout was running thick and deep in the shoals, but there was men who didn't go out, taking turns instead watching over Daddy who hung around the ice house acting like he was useful of a sort, but too drunk to be more than dangerous.

After we put Mama in the ground Daddy went on a bender for near a good five days, leaving me alone in the house to feel my feelings. Les Tate brung him home one morning, dragging Daddy to the door. He was shaking and pale and his eyes were skittery, like he weren't too sure about what was next or what already gone and happened. He smelled real bad, like something left out in the sun to rot and even though I was worried sick over him and feeling such sadness over Mama, such a kind of loneliness I didn't know was possible, I still didn't want him in Mama's house without a good bath. So I done what Mama would of done and drew a bath for him and told him to set on in it. Then he set there till I told him to get on out. I think he would of set there till a crust of ice run all around him.

He went directly to bed, naked as a jaybird, and it weren't even noon yet. I watched him sleep through the day, checking in on him, thinking on what Mama would do. But Mama was gone and I could not feel her anywhere. I remember heating up the chowder someone had brung by after the wake and burning my lips and tongue on it, thinking to myself how was it possible to burn my lips like that when the rest of me was so cold and maybe it wasn't a burn at all, but just the difference between the cold of the house with Mama gone and the hot of the soup on the tenderest part of myself.

He didn't get up again till the next morning when Les Tate banged at the door, yelling, trout was running thick and he was a fisherman—goddammit. I watched his naked backside rise up and stumble into his oilskins.

I could feel the sadness over Mama swelling in my gut right then, like a thing come to life and worming through my insides. There was such a heaviness to it, the way it had hold on me and weighed me down. I lay froze like that till nightfall, wishing I could turn myself inside out like a pocket, dump the load of it, wishing breath didn't come so easy and I could just will it to stop moving through me.

Lacey was waking from her nap and so I had to break from this to go to her. She called first for Aunt Virgie, who is down in the store and it hurts my feelings some. It's me here, Lacey, I said to her and she said Momma? like she was happy and surprised. She has a Fig Newton in her hand and she don't like the insides as much as the outside and is trying to nibble off the doughy part she likes best. I will write again later.

CHAPTER 3

The Morning Of

The next morning Willy came in from the henhouse to Tasha dancing around the kitchen clinking the three quarters Lacey had tucked under her pillow. She smiled at him and held out her small hand to show him.

"How did the tooth fairy get in the window, Willy? How do you think she got it open?"

"Magic," says Lacey, just now coming into the kitchen. She wears an oversized, old T-shirt that hangs nearly to her knees and thick socks scrunched at her ankles.

"Thought I heard something last night," says Willy. "Sounded like a fairy. You know how noisy they can be."

"What'd ya hear, Willy? Did you see her?"

"You hardly ever see 'em," he says. "Maybe just a little flicker of light, but they do make a lot of noise sometimes. Their voices are kind of squeaky and you can't really understand what they're saying. But when they hover over your pillow like a little helicopter, their wings hum and the little bells on their shoes make a jingling noise." He sets the basket of eggs down on the counter, leans down to her, and whispers, "I thought I heard a fairy last night." He looks over to Lacey where she is leaning against the counter. "Ain't been fairies around here in a long time," he says, standing up and catching her eye.

"Looks like they're back!" says Tasha, reaching under her nightgown and twisting her quarters into the fabric of the waistband on her underpants.

Lacey tells Willy she and Tasha need to go into Baltimore city, to Johns Hopkins. Tasha needs some blood work done. She has an appointment, Lacey explains. No big deal. Just some things that need looking into.

"Everything okay?" he asks. But Lacey doesn't answer him, just looks at him and away.

"I'll go with you," Willy offers.

"That's okay, Willy. It's no big deal—really."

It makes no sense to him, but something in the way she won't look at him makes him hold his tongue.

"Do I need a shot, Mommy? I don't want any shots. Do they need to suck my blood out again?"

Willy watches Tasha's eyes get larger and the way she is pulling her upper lip in and out of her mouth.

"Oh, honey . . ." Lacey pushes herself from the edge of the counter and kneels down in front of her. Just as her arms come up around Tasha, Tasha pushes her hands against Lacey's chest. "No, Mommy, no." She squirms out of Lacey's arms, flinging Lacey's hands from herself. "I don't want to go!" She spins away but Lacey stays with her knees planted to the floor and her arms open.

"It's okay, honey. Be a big girl, Tasha."

Tasha dives back into her mother's arms again, rolls her head side to side on Lacey's chest. "I don't want to be a big girl, Mommy. I don't want to. I want to stay here and feed the chickens." She starts to cry in earnest now, wrapping her arms over Lacey's shoulders, and looks up at Willy through her tears. "I want to stay here with you, Willy."

"Well, Willy can come with us. How about that?" Lacey says.

"Can the chickens come, too?"

"Just Willy."

The coffeepot perks, bubbles, and spits on the counter behind Willy and he takes two mugs out of the corner cupboard and sets them on the table.

Tasha sniffles and peels herself out of Lacey's arms, plops herself down on the floor, and reaches under her nightgown and into her underpants to find her quarters.

"What time's your appointment?" asks Willy, setting a box of Cheerios on the table. "She like these?"

Lacey nods. "Not till ten-thirty. I'm figuring an hour's drive with parking and all."

"'Bout right," says Willy. "Like I said, I'm happy to go along."

"Sure, Willy." She sips at her coffee and then twists her face into a knot. "One thing, though," she says, sliding her mug across the table. "We have *got* to stop for a decent cup of coffee. I can't believe you still drink coffee made in a *percolator!*"

"What's wrong with my coffee?"

"Basically, just the taste."

"They got them fancy coffees in town. We can stop on the way." He puts a bowl and a spoon on the table, checks the icebox quickly and a little anxiously for milk, and is pleased to remember he had just bought a quart three days ago.

"Want some cereal?" he asks Tasha. She scrambles into a seat at the table and Willy slides the chair up closer to the table itself. Her chin is nearly resting in the bowl as he pours the cereal into it.

"Town sure looks different. New supermarket?"

"Yep, looks like Carroll's Market's going to close down now. Franny don't want to run it anyhow. I heard she might sell to one of them fancy gourmet shops—sell a lot of French food, you know the stuff."

"I love French fries," Tasha pipes in.

"Silly goose," says Lacey. "Yeah," she says to Willy, "last time I talked to her she mentioned they were thinking of selling. But I think Duffy wants to hold on to it. Who knows? What about the hardware store? How are the nephews lately?" She is referring to Lyle and Clint, technically Lacey's second cousins, but known throughout the community as *the nephews*.

Price's Hardware. The first place he met May, who had been living upstairs over the hardware store with her aunt Virgie, uncle Price, and little Lacey at the time.

Price had been a round man who heaved his weight side to side when he walked. He liked company in the store but wasn't given much to conversation. Price's two young nephews who worked for him, Lyle and Clint, were the more social sort. But regardless of who was doing the talking, customers always felt welcome to hang behind the steps that ran up the back of the store where they could chat amongst themselves or with the nephews, smoke their cigarettes, help themselves to a mug of coffee, or just linger until the morning sun took a bit of the bite out of the air.

"Boys seem to be doing okay with the place," Willy says now to Lacey. "Lots of competition with them big stores these days." He turns to her from the sink. "They ask after you, you know."

Lacey nods as she offers a hand to Tasha who is scooting out of her seat. "No more, that's it? You can't eat any more?"

Tasha shakes her head, side to side.

"I'll stop by and see them," she assures him.

"That'd be nice."

The day Willy met May he had come into Price's Hardware for some tin snips and a new winch. A few men had gathered in the back. Willy never had much to say to the other men. No matter. He knew he was welcome to drop a nickel in the jar, pour himself a mug of coffee, and rest his back-side against a hissing radiator.

The men all heard the door at the top of the steps open and May was making her way carefully down the steps with a tray of clean mugs. There was no railing on the back steps, and she moved close to the wall as she descended, watching her own feet as best she could.

Setting the tray on top of two old filing cabinets that had been pushed together, her eyes went to the men and quickly away.

She was tiny, slender, little more than a wisp of something. But the first thing Willy noticed was the yellow-green remnant of a fist-size bruise on her left cheek and the smoldering purple on the underside of her chin. She used both hands to tuck her hair behind her ears, trailed her fingers down her neck, and looked around, careful not to look directly at any of the men as Frankie Ray thanked her for a fresh mug and Garret Crow shuffled his feet some before offering to fix her a cup.

"Oh, no, thank you," she said. "I just come down to find Lacey."

She headed toward the front room and called Lacey's name.

"Here, Momma!" came Lacey's reply. "With the boys!" And with that, little Lacey, just barely three years old and as much a fixture in the store as the WD-40 display and the rolls of chicken wire, came flying into the back room with her arms wide and landed face-first in May's skirt.

All the men grinned and shouted greetings, teasing little Lacey as they always did. They were clearly uneasy around May, but Lacey was altogether different. Following right behind her were Lyle and Clint.

They were twins, big, good-looking boys who would one day grow into big good-looking men. They had a fondness for each other's shenanigans and teased and fooled with each other mercilessly, Lyle calling Clint *PeeWee* on account of Lyle being a mere one inch taller than his twin, and Clint, the more mischievous of the two, once going so far as to put a dead mouse in one of Lyle's work gloves.

"You know," says Willy to Lacey now as she wipes a spill of milk from beside Tasha's bowl. "They done real good with it, Lyle and Clint. And the new garden center they opened next door is doing real good, too."

"That's great."

"Course, it's all them boys have ever known. Not sure what would happen if they had to close." He knew something of having to change one's ways, of knowing one thing and then not having it anymore. He remembers now how they had loved to play with Lacey in the store, even if it meant catching hell from their uncle Price.

When May had come down looking for Lacey that day, Lacey had run to her and buried herself in May's skirt, Lyle coming from the front room right behind her. "She's just causing trouble over here, as usual," Lyle had called out to May.

All the men, including Willy, knew that Lacey adored the boys and followed them around the store for as much of the day as she was allowed to. She poked her head into drawers, sifted her tiny hands through lug nuts and copper washers, and stood on her toes to blow small piles of sawdust into the air.

She loved the big spools of chain link in the back of the store and she'd enlist the help of one or the other of the nephews to help her spin the spools so that the chains smashed and clanked rhythmically on the floor. Uncle Price would yell, what the hell was them two ninnies up to anyway and say he was gonna kick their stupid butts if they didn't stop fooling around back there. Lyle would scoop her up quick and give her a jiggling while Clint rewrapped the chain link and teased her about getting them in hot water again.

Lacey had spun out of May's skirt and stormed stiff-legged and serious toward Lyle, poking a finger into his thigh.

"Lacey, stop it," May said.

"We ain't afraid of her, May," Clint said.

Lacey, distractable and curious, wandered to where the men gathered. She moved in and out among them, slapping her feet in the puddles made by the snow melting from their boots.

Willy wasn't used to children and she spooked him some, but the other men were perfectly comfortable with her, not minding at all when she tried to move them out of her way to get closer to the nickel jar, which, even on her toes, she was unable to reach.

"She ain't sick, is she?" asks Willy now, nodding to the sunporch where Tasha sits cross-legged on the floor showing her quarters to a small stuffed lion poking from her bathrobe pocket.

"We need some more tests." Lacey sips her coffee and grimaces. "God, this is awful coffee, Willy," and she tries to smile but Willy notices how she draws in her lower lip in a way that makes her sputter when she answers him. She gets up and shuts the door to the sunroom. "I don't know," she says softly to Willy. "It looks like—the truth is, Willy, there may be a problem. The *un*official diagnosis is acute lymphocytic leukemia."

"Leukemia?"

"That's just a possibility," she says. "We don't know for sure."

"Good God, Lacey." He runs his whole hand down the front of his face and swipes across his mouth as he draws in a breath.

"But if she needs treatment, I mean, if she's really sick—and we don't know that yet—well, I figure Hopkins is the best, right?" She moves to the counter so that her back is to him.

"Jesus," he says. The window beyond where Lacey stands frames a gray day.

"I didn't take on any classes this summer, figuring we could stay here and be close to Hopkins and all, you know?" She doesn't look at him but starts wiping the counter with the dishrag instead. "If they're right, if it's what they think. Of course, *if it is*, she may need to start treatments right away." She drops the rag in the sink. "There are still a couple of tests they have to do to be sure."

"Jesus, why didn't you tell me?" He stares at her back. "Why the hell do you do this?" he says, surprised at his own anger. "Blood cancer."

"It might be mono. They might be wrong. That's why we need more tests. She's awfully run-down and she never eats her lunch at preschool. I'm sure she's just anemic or something."

"Why is it you don't tell me things?" He gets up from the table as she plops herself at a kitchen chair and sighs heavily.

"I'm telling you now, Willy. Give me a break."

She whips her hand across the table and sends stray Cheerios flying across the kitchen where they clatter in the corner like a brief burst of rain.

"Christ, Willy," she says softly.

He turns to her, his backside leaning against the sink, his head moving slowly side to side as if he just can't understand her—just can't make sense of it all.

"It's just that every time I try to say it or try to tell someone, I think my insides are coming up," she says.

Willy blinks. She never did have a strong stomach for bad news. The one time he had tried to sit her down and tell her that he didn't suspect May was ever coming back—she was seven years old, and May had been gone a good while already—well, he had tried to tell her, if only because everyone said he should. But she had got a look on her face like she just drunk curdled milk and run from the room before he ever got all the words out. And so May's leaving had just hung in the air between the two of them.

He watches her look around the room now, like maybe there is a corner she can slink away to. Truth be told, the thought of that little girl being sick doesn't do his stomach much good, either. He turns back to the sink to dump the rest of his coffee and hears the small crunch of Cheerios under his boots.

"We better clean this up and get going," he says. He takes her cup from the table, dumps the coffee in the sink, rinses the two cups out with cold water, and settles them snug in the back corner of the sink. "This is just one of them things," he says, turning from the sink to face her. "One of them things you got to look square in the eye and take care of."

"I know," she says, her voice a tiny trickle.

But he knows she doesn't, not really. She is more like him in that way, looking to all the world as if she needs nobody and can manage just fine. Everyone thinking she is so independent, strong, stubborn even. But Willy knows. She already has that fearful sort of glazed-over look in her eyes so that he knows she isn't really seeing things for what they are. They are an awful lot alike in that way. Not wanting much to think about the future, and sure as hell not wanting to turn around and take a look at the past.

CHAPTER 4

Now That We Know

Lacey lifts Tasha up onto the examining table just as she has been told to do. The paper gown is folded in a neat square beside her on the table. Tasha is sleepy from the cocktail the nurse gave her twenty minutes earlier, but not so tired that she will lie down and actually sleep, just tired enough to be dead weight when Lacey lifts her.

The examining room is small and close, and Lacey notices Willy pressing himself into a far corner as if he can back right through a wall. He's been quiet throughout the morning, not asking questions and just following Lacey through the hospital, through registration and blood labs and X-rays.

At one point Lacey stopped to let Tasha look out on a courtyard where daffodils had sprung up, bathed in a light rain, small yellow sentries in perfect rows. The flow of the crowd carried Willy right past her for a few yards, and when she looked after him she could see that he was shedding crumbs of dirt from his boots as he walked. He'd always done that, always trailed a little of the farm with him wherever he went. Once, when she was ten or eleven years old, she'd lost him in Hutzler's department store. She had come out of the dressing room expecting to find him waiting, only to find that he had vanished and flecks of dirt led her around a display of peasant-style tops, past a trio of mannequins in plaid and paisley bell bottoms and tube tops, and into housewares where the trail ended at a display of waffle irons.

"Belgian or regular?" he had asked her.

"Regular," she said.

"Agreed."

"I couldn't find you," she said.

"I was right here."

That's the way it was with the two of them. He was there, just as he is now, quiet, but there just the same. If the man was nothing else—he was *there*. He is *here*.

Lacey pulls Tasha's sweatshirt up over her head and wrangles her out of her leggings—no small feat considering that she can't coax her to stand as she does it. Tasha leans against Lacey, draping her arms around her neck.

Willy steps up to the table and takes the sweatshirt and leggings, tossing them over his arm and stepping back to make room for the technician who is wheeling in a metal cart that she sets next to the end of the table.

As Lacey unfolds the paper gown, there is a soft knock on the door and Dr. Oren enters.

Dr. Oren is short, with a childishly round face made all the more disconcerting by the streaks of gray that run through his hair. He isn't at all what Lacey expected. For one thing, he is small. His hand when he shakes hers is too soft and not much bigger than her own. He doesn't make eye contact either, at least not with her, but he does smile at Tasha and Tasha smiles back, even shows him her bandaged forearm where they drew blood earlier that day, and he admires it in an earnest way that seems to satisfy her. But still, he isn't at all what Lacey was expecting, had been hoping for. And just what had she been hoping for? She was hoping for a hero, had been planning on it, in fact.

"Can you lie down for me, Anastasia?" asks Dr. Oren.

"Tasha," Lacey says. "She goes by Tasha."

"I have a princess's name," says Tasha.

The room feels crowded now, and hot, far too hot, and Lacey can feel the sweat on the back of her neck where her hair sticks to it. Watching Willy shuffle from foot to foot in the corner, she wishes for a minute that she hadn't brought him along. She had a hunch that his being here would require something of her that she just didn't have to give, some effort or reassurance that she wasn't going to be able to dredge up easily. But then Tasha, who is lying on her back, turns and reaches toward him and he comes up out of the corner quickly, clearing his throat, and says in that soft lion's purr of a voice, "No worries, sugar." And Tasha settles back down, even letting her eyes close for a few seconds. He pats her hand and steps quietly back again.

Dr. Oren nods, almost imperceptibly, to the technician who then says, in a bright, happy voice, "Can you turn on your stomach, sweetie? Now let's get this pillow under your hips."

Lacey helps hold Tasha while the pillow is slid under her. Her bottom, clad in pink panties, rises in the air.

Dr. Oren rubs his hands together quickly, like a mad scientist, and Lacey realizes he is just warming them before touching Tasha's hip and the realization of what he is actually doing strikes her as so thoughtful—so *aware*—that she lets out her breath unexpectedly and only then realizes that she has been holding it and perhaps that is the reason for the light-headedness she feels now.

"This is the iliac crest," he says, smoothing his hand over the top of Tasha's hip bone and along her backside. "This is called a bone marrow aspiration, Tasha," he says. "Pretty big word, hmm? This is your hip bone here."

Lacey watches him spread the fingers of his hand across her back, touching Tasha's hip bones with the tips of them and all the while Willy is nodding along with the doctor's explanation. In the heat of the room she can smell a dampness from herself, a heat rising out of the collar of her own shirt.

The technician peels back the paper on the cart she has wheeled in to reveal shiny metal tools, syringes and tubing. Dr. Oren dons thin rubber gloves, snapping them at his wrists.

"Your hip bone is really hard, just like all of your other bones. But inside the bone is soft and mushy. Now we're going to take out a little of that mushy stuff and take a look at it to see how we can make you feel better."

"I'm not sick anymore," says Tasha hopefully. "Am I, Mommy?" In a quieter voice Dr. Oren instructs Lacey to move to the head of the table and hold Tasha's arms and shoulders down firmly. "I was just a little bit sick but now I'm not!" she says, her voice rising and her wide eyes following Lacey as she moves around her.

Lacey watches as Dr. Oren prepares to swab Tasha's back. "This will be a little bit cold," he says.

Tasha startles, "Ohhh," and tries to roll over on her back. But Lacey does what she is told and holds her in place. *Shhhh, shhh,* hushing her as best she can as Dr. Oren places sterile towels around the site he intends to go into, leaving just a pale patch of thin skin to work within.

"This is Xylocaine, Tasha." But he keeps the needle well away from her sight. "This is a special medicine that will make this part of your back numb. Hold very still and let me do this quickly."

Lacey tries to focus on the side of Tasha's head, on her small ears, the flutter of her lashes, the breath that comes between her teeth. The needle goes in and Tasha yelps, kicks her legs back, and then relaxes. The needle is withdrawn and Dr. Oren begins to massage the site. "Not so bad, hmmm? Can you feel my hand back here? No? That's good."

"I want to go home," she whimpers.

Quickly, Dr. Oren explains in a clipped but quiet voice that the very large needle he now holds in his hand has a plug in it and that once he inserts the hollow needle into the skin and through the bone, he will withdraw the plug and attach a syringe. Tasha's liquid marrow will then be aspirated through the syringe.

"It's uncomfortable," he says quietly.

Lacey is confused. "I thought she was numb?"

"Not completely." He nods to the technician who moves to the opposite end of the table from Lacey and cups the back of Tasha's calves in her own hands.

Tasha doesn't even flinch when the needle goes in. Lacey could swear she hears it crunching through the bone and she loosens her grip to stroke Tasha's hair. Such a good girl. Dr. Oren removes the plug and still Tasha doesn't seem to be aware of it, but he looks up sternly to Lacey and nods at her with a flick of his head and back to Tasha, redirecting her to hold firmly to Tasha's shoulders and arms.

Lacey kisses her head, keeping her face close to Tasha's.

The syringe is attached and the aspiration of the marrow begins.

Suddenly, Tasha flings her head up from the table, clunking Lacey's chin so hard that Lacey's teeth slam together. Tasha screeches and Lacey feels herself going weak in the knees, but she drops her head back down to Tasha's. She tries to tell her it will be okay, she is doing a great job, she is so brave, but the words can't move past what feels like a rag lodged in her throat. Unable to move sound or breath or saliva around it she can only drape herself over Tasha, her face pressed into her daughter's, so close to Tasha that she is breathing Tasha's exhaled breath, tasting her tears, while her own knees turn to Jell-O and her arms are useless in their effort to still her, mere flaps of skin fallen down over her daughter's own small arms and shoulders.

"Almost finished here," says Dr. Oren. "You're doing great."

Lacey has always believed that if called upon to be Super-Mom, she would rise to the challenge—pull a car off of her daughter in a burst of adrenaline, fight a rabid dog with her bare hands, perform an emergency tracheotomy with a kitchen knife. But now, the truth is hitting her from behind. She is useless. She is no hero, either. Tasha writhes under her arms, twisting, begging to be let go of. The needle now sliding out of Tasha's back, slowly, too slowly, makes a queasy feeling rise up in Lacey's stomach.

Lacey looks up through her own blur of tears to Willy. He stands in the corner with Tasha's clothes slung over his arm, watching the needle, staring right at it as if he and the needle have come to some damn sort of understanding.

Even with the needle removed, Tasha's breath is still jagged and she tosses her head side to side. Lacey presses closer. "It's over, honey. I'm right here. Right here."

Tasha is bandaged and congratulated all around on her bravery. She sits on the edge of the table, whimpering more quietly now as Lacey wipes the shiny trail of tears and snot from her face with the hem of her own shirt before dressing her, careful to roll the waistband of her leggings down away from where she is now bandaged.

The metal cart is wheeled away before Dr. Oren suggests they take a seat in a waiting room down the hall to wait for the results.

They find the room easily and a plaque over the door tells them they are in the right place: FAMILY WAITING ROOM. It is carpeted and a television is muted in the corner. Willy takes the bag Lacey has over her shoulder from her and waits until Lacey and Tasha get themselves situated before setting the bag back down by Lacey's side and taking a slow seat across from them.

Tasha proceeds to doze on and off on Lacey's shoulder, and Lacey adjusts her on her lap every few minutes as best she can, holding her head with one hand and hefting her higher in her lap with the other. Her breasts are damp with sweat where Tasha has fallen against her and she feels a rush of cool there when she moves her.

Eventually the door opens, startling Willy who sits up anxiously in his chair. The young woman introduces herself as a social worker. She explains that the *team* will be in shortly with the results, and in the meantime they have a volunteer who will take Anastasia to the playroom while the family meets with the team.

"No," says Lacey. "She's asleep, you can see. It's been a long day."

"Of course," the woman says, but if she should wake up, they can arrange to take her to the playroom. She goes on to explain that with some kids the medication can really knock them out for a time. "We'll be with you in just a bit, maybe another half hour or so," she says, leaning down to glance appreciatively at the sleeping Tasha before leaving the room.

Willy and Lacey talk quietly, one or the other of them commenting as to how well Tasha had handled the procedure, how brave she was, how tired she looks now.

Finally, with nothing more to say other than the very thing neither of them wants to talk about, Willy looks to his watch and offers to go get them something to eat. Lacey isn't hungry. "You go, though," she says. "You must be starving."

"I'll bring you back something. You got to eat, Lacey, and she's gonna be starving when she wakes up." But just as he stands up, the door opens, and Dr. Oren and his team come into the room. Willy moves over to sit beside Lacey, and Dr. Oren takes a seat on the edge of the sofa across from them. He introduces the team that includes another oncologist who looks young enough to be an intern or even a student; the hematologist, a woman at least eight inches taller than Dr. Oren and who wears extremely sensible black running shoes with stockings; and the same social worker who had been in earlier.

"She's still asleep?" asks the social worker.

Lacey nods and kisses the top of Tasha's head.

Dr. Oren begins by confirming the diagnosis that has been shimmying around the edge of Lacey's world the last few days—acute lymphocytic leukemia.

Willy takes Lacey's hand and squeezes three times.

I love you.

I love you, too, she squeezes back four.

Lacey was five when she had "invented" the code. May was forever telling Lacey how much Willy loved her. And Lacey had no reason to doubt it. But while May had showered her little daughter with kisses and hugs and *I love you,* Willy had been more reserved. He was awkward with her, and part of it was due to the fact that he wasn't her father and had only been married to May for a few months.

But Lacey was bold and never one to beat around the bush, so one day she had followed him on his way up to the barn and when she caught up with him, she had slipped her hand in his and squeezed three times.

"Know what that means?" she asked.

"What *what* means?"

"That." And she had squeezed again, three times.

"Nope."

"Means I love you."

Willy had squeezed back four times. "And that means I-love-you-too."

Dr. Oren is explaining that they want Tasha to start treatment right away.

"The counts are concerning. We're having a room prepared right now, shouldn't be too long."

No, says Lacey, or thinks she does. But Dr. Oren only continues, talking strategies and goals, protocols and trials, *with all plans subject to change based upon the course of the illness.* None of it is sinking into Lacey's head.

She shifts Tasha again in her lap, and everyone quiets for a moment to make sure she remains asleep. Dr. Oren leans forward and then continues.

"The goal is to achieve complete remission—the disappearance of all signs of illness and restoration of normal bone marrow function. Should that occur, we would move to *Phase Two*"

Still, she finds herself trailing behind his words and unable to catch up with them. *Yes,* she finds herself thinking, *yes, I understand all of this, but what about my daughter, what's wrong with her? There has been a mistake. Nothing you are saying could have anything to do with Tasha. My God, just look at her, she's perfect! She takes my breath away.*

Dr. Oren goes on to explain that 95 percent of patients with ALL achieve an initial remission. He says this last clearly, enunciating his words and actually looking Lacey in the eye for what she thinks is the first time today. It is as if he has practiced this before (said this important thing to how many mothers?), but she is, instead, snagged on the acronym, afraid she is expected to get too familiar with the disease.

"Seventy percent are essentially cured," he goes on to say. "And the cure rates are even higher in children, more than ninety percent. All that is to say, we expect a positive outcome with treatment."

Again, she is tripping over the language—*essentially* cured? And of course, Tasha will be cured so what exactly is the point of a *Phase Two*?

He mentions *blasts* and *white cell counts* and *red cell counts* and *hematocrits*, but none of it is sticking with her. She has never had a head for numbers anyway, not without context. She loves words, but not the ones she is hearing now.

"So we will get her settled here tonight . . ." Dr. Oren is saying.

"Oh, no, no," says Lacey quietly, shaking her head back and forth. "Not tonight. She can't stay tonight." She leans back pulling Tasha tighter to herself.

Dr. Oren looks to the social worker who, as if on cue, sits down now on the other side of Lacey, leans in toward Lacey and Tasha just a bit, but knows better than to try and touch either of them. "I know this can feel very sudden," she says.

"No, you don't understand," says Lacey. But then she can't explain. The room is quiet. They all look at her, even Willy, waiting. "You don't understand," she says again. "*I* don't understand," she admits. "I don't understand why this happened."

"We just don't know the answer to that," says Dr. Oren patiently, kindly.

She knows he has misunderstood her question. She should rephrase it. *Why Tasha?* But she doesn't. She knows how selfish it sounds anyway—and such a cliché—that whole why-me thing. Shit happens. And besides, she knows he can't possibly know the answer, anyway.

"Please," she says now, trying to focus, trying to make sure she conveys that she is a reasonable person and not a nut trying to escape with her child. "Please, I need to take her back to the farm tonight, just until morning."

Tasha lifts her head and drops it back down, snuggling into Lacey's neck.

"I can't just leave her here." Lacey wants the world to stop and rewind. She needs to get back to before, before she knew this, before this day. She needs a do-over. She needs to start over with Tasha pink and healthy and a plan, a plan that acknowledges this wretched possibility but allows her to head it off in the same way she keeps her safe in the car with a properly installed booster seat, does background checks on babysitters, in the same way she checks the house for radon, makes Tasha hold her hand crossing the street, wear a helmet when she rides on the back of Lacey's bike.

"We can arrange for you to stay in her room, of course," the social worker is saying, as if this is the solution Lacey is looking for.

"No," says Lacey. "You don't understand. I need to take her home tonight." The world needs to stop. She needs to think. "Just for tonight. Please. Let me take her home tonight? It's been a long day. I need to explain this to her and . . ." Tasha begins to rub her head back and forth under Lacey's chin, smacks her lips, and opens her eyes with a few quick blinks before looking around. Lacey reaches into the bag at her feet and pulls out a boxed juice, sliding in the skinny straw while Tasha squirms on her lap.

"Her father arrives tonight."

"Daddy's coming tonight?" says Tasha, craning her head around so that she is inches from Lacey's nose and looking straight into her eyes.

"Yes. Daddy is coming tonight." Lacey looks at Willy beside her and notices he is looking at the faces around the room and then settling his eyes on Tasha. He stands.

"Hey, buttercup," he says, reaching down and putting his hand on her shoulders, turning her gently from Lacey. "You want to walk to that vending machine I saw down the hall? I got some quarters here and we could find something to go with that juice?"

She is still sleepy from the cocktail they gave her for the procedure, and she stumbles when she slides from Lacey's lap, but Willy catches her in his arms and rights her quickly. He nods to the others as he ushers her out through the door, as if to say they can carry on now.

"You said her counts weren't too bad, right? That's what you said, thirty percent, right? That's not real bad, is it? And the other one, the white one?"

"Normal white cell count is ten thousand, Ms. Cherrymill," says the hematologist in the sensible shoes. She is just far enough across the room that Lacey can't read her name tag and not knowing her name feels as though it puts her at a disadvantage. "And her hematocrit count is only twenty-four."

"What does that mean—hematocrit?" She should have been paying attention. She should have done more research. "I have a master's and a PhD. I should know these things, but I teach English literature. God—I should have gone pre-med." She is surprisingly aware of just how inappropriate she must sound, but she can't stop herself. "I used to say that all the time. I used to say that pre-med should be a prerequisite for motherhood." She looks around at the somber faces, watches. Their eyes all fall away, as if they can't bear to witness her pending breakdown.

Patiently, Dr. Oren leans forward and says that he understands how difficult this can be.

"Ask any of my friends," she says, ignoring him and knowing how pathetic she must sound. "I always used to say that." In her mind she is slipping out the door with Tasha in her arms. There are things she has to do, things to think about that cannot be thought about here, in this room, with these people looking at her. There are second opinions and third opinions, definitely another opinion. And doctors and insurance and trials and statistics, experimental medicines and drug protocols and ports and non-traditional medicines and . . .

"It would not be advised to take her home tonight," Dr. Oren says clearly.

"Her father," Lacey starts to say. She starts to say that he is coming up from Virginia that night, but instead she says, "You should have seen the look on his face when she was born. He was convinced that she could see him, but of course, you know, babies can't really see well when they're born, but he would have sworn that she looked right at him and that she turned to the sound of his voice—which is possible, I suppose, but not likely."

Though it was true that even as a newborn Tasha's infant eyes would track her around the room, and she would break into a squall if Lacey moved out of her sight. Those squalls, they would always make her milk let down and her breasts would sting, and then Tasha would tangle her fingers in Lacey's hair when she nursed. Always finding ways to cling to her, even on her first day of preschool, and it had ached so to leave her there. But then she would come to pick her up and find her squatting on her haunches in the play yard, not moving for the longest time, watching a bug or a toad in the grass, waving Lacey over with her hands to show her the bloat of a toad's neck or the throes of an earthworm. And now, now she is here with Tasha's fevered brow, her bleeding gums, and the parade of bruises that mount her shins and pepper her arms.

"Please." Lacey begins to cry, and she hates herself for it. She slashes the first tears from her face. "I have to take her with me. Just for tonight." She knows she isn't making any friends this way. Does it matter? Does it matter if they like her, if they like Tasha? "I'm not ready," she says. "We're not ready."

Everyone around her takes a collective breath.

"Of course," she says, sucking in air that is too thin, swearing off the tears and trying to sound reasonable, strong, in charge, "I want to do the right thing." She looks around at all of them, concedes by dropping her shoulders and asks softly, as if she is pleading with the jury. "Please—does it matter, would one night matter?"

"No one is ever ready for this," says Dr. Oren. The others nod in sad agreement. He puts his hands on his lap and then stands. "I want her back here by eight-thirty a.m. to admit. If her fever spikes over 101 degrees, I want her back here tonight."

The door bursts open behind Lacey and everyone in the room startles. "Here they are, Willy!" Tasha runs to Lacey's side just as Willy comes sheepishly to the door, shrugging his shoulders by way of apology.

"Willy couldn't find you," she says to Lacey.

"I'm right here," says Lacey as brightly as she can, touching her hand to her face to make sure all evidence of tears has been dried off. "I've been right here!"

Tasha dives into her lap face-first and then lifts her head to Lacey. "Can we go now?" Tasha swings her little foot behind her. "And where's Daddy? Hmmm?"

December 23, 1972

I told Lacey all about the virgin birth, about the manger and the star and the three wise men. She asked me if that was how she came to be here, too. Well, you would likely think so, I thought to myself. In a manner of speaking, is what I told her. I do love that story, though. Mama used to tell me the story every Christmas Eve and I always listened like I was hearing it for the first time.

Sometimes I'd ask to go out and see that star for myself and Mama would walk me outside where the wind would be whipping the scrubby pines so they looked to be bowing down and I'd search the cold black sky for the brightest star. Back home on the island the sky is deeper and blacker than it is here in Maryland so that you could feel yourself getting lost in it, not knowing how near or far the blackness is, and though you couldn't exactly hear the ocean behind the dunes, you could feel the rhythm of it pounding the very ground you'd be standing on and rising up through your body to your heart. Mama's hand was always warm in mine, soft and giving, like bread dough just risen. We would look up into the night until it would breeze up and a wind would run through me, setting a quiver to my whole body. She would feel it too and she would put her hand to the back of my head and show me to the inside.

It's true that Daddy would be drunk. He didn't need much of a reason to put hisself in that way. But it was different then, with Mama there. She would laugh to watch him sleeping in that old chair and she would tell him to come on along with her to bed or Santa wouldn't bring him nothing.

CHAPTER 5

A Reprieve

Tasha has fallen asleep in the back of the car. Lacey adjusts the rearview mirror so she can keep an eye on her as Willy squirms in the passenger seat and looks back at Tasha over his shoulder. He speaks softly, not wanting to wake her, and Lacey can't help but remember how much she has always loved the sound of his voice, thick and deep so that his words wrap around her like a warm quilt, and it makes her want to curl up to the sound of it.

"She's a pretty little thing, Lacey," he says now. "Like a little yellow sunflower." He twists a little more to look at her. "Smart, too, huh?"

"Real smart."

"Like her momma," he says. "Looks a lot like her daddy."

"She does. She looks a lot like Mac."

"Speaking of Mac?" says Willy.

"I know," says Lacey quickly. "I know, Willy, I should have mentioned that he was coming." She is easing off the beltway and coming to a light. She cracks the window as the car slows and the wind rushes by, sucking the car's warm air out with it.

Willy is slowly shaking his head side to side. "Yup, could've mentioned that earlier."

Willy looks out the window. She knows he is chewing it all over in his mind. "Suppose I just didn't realize he was still in the picture," he finally says.

"There is no *picture* here, Willy. He's her father. Look, Willy, he can stay in a hotel, but I just thought it would be better . . ."

"No problem here," he says. "Always room at the inn."

Lacey can see Tasha in the rearview mirror, curled up in the booster seat. Lacey's coat is balled under her head for a pillow, but she wishes she had thought to cover her with something. She rolls the window up.

The car is headed north over the reservoir, and there is a mist rising from the water below as they drive. Fittingly, it has been raining off and on all day, and now, though the rain has stopped, the late afternoon is soupy and thick so that it seems much later in the day. This is a new bridge. The old bridge had been closer to the water, and Lacey remembers that she used to be able to see the run of it beneath her as she drove over it, and she recalls the sound a car made on the grated metal, a hum that bounced off the water below. She would always know whether she was coming or going when the bridge sung underneath her. Now, it just sneaks up on her and she hardly knows she is crossing over. She wants to put the window down again, let the cold mist smack at her face, but of course, she can't, won't. She knows the air always feels different on one side of the bridge or the other. They are crossing now to the other side where it will be greener and wetter and scented a bit like overripe fruit.

"How long has this been going on," says Willy softly, tossing his head toward the back seat.

"A few days. I don't know much more than you do right now. I thought she had the flu. She's had a low fever off and on the last week, nothing too high," she assures him, remembering again that she will have to watch out for a fever tonight per Dr. Oren's instruction. "Ninety-nine, a hundred one morning so I kept her home from preschool."

She answers him quietly, certain that Tasha is asleep but careful not to wake her. They wind their way along the now-narrow road where it is darker and the late pale sun struggles to filter through a damp and heavy canopy of trees.

She looks over her shoulder and knows that Tasha is deep in sleep. In a hushed voice she tells him that the next day Tasha had seemed just fine, but then the school nurse had called around noon to say she had a nosebleed that they had had trouble stopping and it might be best to come pick her up.

By the time Lacey picked Tasha up from school that day, she looked exhausted. They'd cleaned her face, but muddy red flecks clung to her ears and the back of her neck and her favorite purple sweatshirt was crisp with dried blood.

"How about a nice, warm bath, sweetie?"

She was so tired she only nodded and curled up on the sofa while Lacey ran the water. Lacey dumped in half a box of bubble soap, hoping to make her smile, and then eased her off the sofa and began to lift her sweatshirt over her head, but as she touched her tummy Tasha had flinched and pulled her hands down to push Lacey's hands away.

"What's the matter?"

"My tummy hurts—"

"You feel sick?"

"No."

Lacey had pressed gently on Tasha's tummy and sides once more.

"Ow, stop it, Mommy!"

The teakettle was whistling so Lacey gave her a few minutes alone in the bathroom while she fixed a cup with too much honey and lemon. She would share it with her, and Tasha loved her tea sweet. When she came back into the bathroom, Tasha still had her socks on and her chest was smeared reddish brown with a thin stain of blood.

"Take your socks off, too."

As Tasha bent over to remove her socks Lacey had noticed tiny blue bruises marching up her spine, but she didn't say anything.

"Enough bubbles?" They were popping and snapping like breakfast cereal.

Tasha was not impressed. Once she was in the tub, Lacey slipped out of the bathroom to make an appointment with her pediatrician. They asked if it was an emergency or if she was ill. Not really, she said. All the symptoms were so vague. No, she just seemed a little run-down and was due for a checkup anyway. But then, seeing the bruises in her mind's eye again, she changed her mind. There had been a bad nosebleed, she was covered in bruises, something wasn't right. They said they could squeeze her in on Thursday, three days away.

Over the next few days, Tasha slept more than usual, got a second nosebleed, and sprouted tiny blood blisters on the bottoms of her toes. She complained of a sore throat and Lacey handed her lozenges like they were candy.

The doctor's appointment started smoothly enough. "We'll draw some blood," said the doctor. Her regular pediatrician had an emergency and they were seeing her partner. Lacey felt oddly relieved knowing that no matter what this man suspected, she was entitled to the second opinion of her regular doctor.

"She may be a little anemic," he said. Anemia sounded good to Lacey. A few iron pills, maybe some high protein shakes made with ice cream and eggs and chocolate syrup. She could certainly handle a little anemia. He pushed his thick hand, knife-like, into her belly and Tasha startled and pushed his hand away. "Or she may be battling a virus we've been seeing and if she's a little anemic, she may not be able to kick it. We'll run a couple of tests and nail this," he said. "In the meantime, sweetheart, eat your vegetables and stay away from those gummy bears! How long has she had this tenderness around here?" he said, smoothing his hand over the side of her belly.

"The last few days," Lacey said, still hooked on the idea of anemia. "But it doesn't seem too bad. She may have strained a muscle."

"I don't think this is muscular," he said, laying her down once again on the examining table and pushing four fingers into her side. Tasha squirmed on the table and pulled her knees up to her chest while trying to shove his hand away. "Easy, easy," he said, pulling her into a sitting position. "Well, let's run that blood work. Let's see what's making your tummy hurt, Tasha."

Lacey couldn't even look at him. She tossed Tasha's shirt over her head, snapped her leggings, quickly threading her legs through them, and swept her off the examining table.

"The lab will draw the blood," he said. "We'll phone you tomorrow."

She brought Tasha home tearful and sporting a glow-in-the-dark bandage on her arm. Within a few hours, the bruise from the needle had spread beyond the boundaries of the bandage and was creeping in a widening blue-black circle across the tender inside of her forearm. Lacey mixed up a batch of Aunt Virgie's bruise paste from the few herbs that grew on her windowsill and slathered it on Tasha's arm and also on the bruises she was now noticing on her wrists. *She's always bruised easily*, she had told herself. Tasha's so fair, more like Mac than like Lacey. She was betting that blonds bruise easily, though she couldn't remember Mac ever having said so.

The next day Tasha woke up cheerful and eager to go back to school. No fever, no reason to keep her home. Lacey was relieved, certain the blood draws would show nothing alarming and that she was on the mend. But the call came that afternoon from her regular pediatrician, Dr. Helen. "I've had the lab run the tests twice," she was saying, "and preliminary results suggest we're looking at *acute lymphocytic leukemia*. We're going to have to run another test, and it's going to be a little uncomfortable for her, but we'll need to confirm this with a sample of bone marrow from the rear hip bone."

Lacey sighs now, having told of the events in their entirety for the first time. Willy is quiet, not looking at her but glancing over his shoulder as she speaks. She is pulling up to a four-way stop. Rain is falling again and drumming on the roof of the car in a way that is almost soothing, the windshield wipers swishing efficiently and throwing off sheets of water. "Like I said," she says to Willy softly, defeated, "I just threw up."

Even after throwing up, the first thing she had thought to do was call Mac. But then, before she had the number punched in the phone, as she was pulling together the words she would use to tell him about this horrible thing that was happening to the three of them, she felt a spasm in her gut that had sent her flying to the sink again. The phone clattered to the floor and, just to let fate know how pissed she was, she left it there spinning and stepped out the door. She could hear it beeping as she stormed down to the water's edge and the sounds hung like a warning in the air. She startled a fat water snake in the reeds beneath the dock, watched him slip silently into the water and move across the silty river bottom without even a ripple left to mark his departure.

She kicked her toes into the banks of the river and then walked out on the dock. At the end of the dock she felt a strange compulsion to keep on walking and wished the dock was a bridge from one side of the river to the other. She wanted to be on the other side of wherever it was she was finding herself. She turned and stormed back to the house, replaced the phone in its cradle, and headed back out to pick Tasha up from preschool.

Tasha had scrambled into the car and scooted across the seat to hug her. It was one of her fast and furious hugs, the kind that comes with quick kisses and giggles, the kind of hug Tasha tended to peel herself from almost as quickly as it's delivered. Tasha climbed between the front seats and into the back where she got herself settled in her seat and began rummaging through her bookbag for the valentine she had made for Lacey back in February. She had liked it so much when she made it that she had asked the teacher if she could put it on the bulletin board instead of giving it to her.

"It has real candy on it!" Tasha said, stretching forward to hand it to Lacey as they pulled out of the school lot. It was made of red construction paper and candy hearts were glued in a random smattering across the front and back of it. A parade of letters—applied almost as randomly—came close to spelling *to mommy love tasha*.

"It's beautiful!" Lacey said, and it was.

Tasha reached for it and took it back into her lap, picking the stale candies off of it as they drove.

"I forgot to make one for Daddy."

"We can make one tonight."

"It won't be as pretty as this one," Tasha said. "But that's okay. Katie Morgan made one card for her whole family. That's because they all live in the same house. Some kids get to do that, you know, Mommy?" Lacey knew Tasha didn't really expect her to respond. In fact, she tended to get bored if Lacey went on and on, explaining their family. It was likely Tasha had no memory of when Mac had once lived with them. She'd been so young when he left, and in that regard, Lacey felt fortunate that she hadn't had to deal with the guilt of Tasha remembering his departure, of Tasha knowing one kind of family and then adjusting to another kind of family altogether. "When Ashley Carter has her six-year-old party she has to start making two cards, too," she said.

Lacey had no idea what she was talking about and tossed her the I-don't-get-it look in the rearview mirror.

"Because her daddy's getting his own house with a different phone number before she has her six-year-old party."

Lacey nodded and then reached back, felt for Tasha's hand, and took it in her own. Tasha's hand was sticky with a pastel rainbow of melted candy hearts, and she held it tight, too tight, so that Tasha asked her to let go. But even after Lacey had dropped Tasha's hand from her own and tried to put it back on the steering wheel, she couldn't manage to uncurl her own fingers. She had driven on with a white knuckled fist, gripping at nothing.

"Willy," she says to him now, "I just have to say this. I have to say it to somebody, and lucky you—you're the one."

They are pulling into the long gravel drive of the farm, past the pond, prickling with the rain, past the metal barn, and up to the embankment framed by a low stone wall and a row of wild hedges. She puts the car in park and turns to Willy, who looks to her expectantly, brows raised.

"I'm not like May," she says. "I'm not. I won't let her go." She clenches her teeth as the tears fall and sucks in a rattling breath to stop them.

"She ain't going nowhere," he says quickly, taking both of her hands from where she wipes the tears from her face. "You hear me?" He wraps both of his hands around hers, paws pressing hard and holding. "You ain't a runner, neither," he says. May's name hasn't been mentioned in years. The mention of May, Lacey realizes, likely feels like a blow from behind to Willy, but he must have knocked it away to focus on Lacey herself, just as he tried so hard to do some thirty years ago.

Lacey turns off the engine, letting it grind down, leaving only the sound of their syncopated breath.

December 24, 1972

Daddy phoned today. I believe he would of had to walk clear down to the coast guard station to make that call. Aunt Virgie wouldn't let him talk to me. I think I will write a letter to Sugar Lee and see if she will check in on him some. Her house peeks out over the scrub not far from ours and she can keep an eye on him. I also may tell her not to check in on him when he has been at the bottle, and maybe she should think of locking her door at nights. Our two houses look just alike and Daddy gets confused sometimes. Ain't nobody else round for a long ways as just about the whole of the island lives in the village and we are the only ones so far out from things. She'll know when he comes and goes as we share the little trail of a drive that runs down past her house. Her daddy is the real owner of our house, but Mama never had to live to see that.

Sometimes Daddy gets real bad with the drinking, and he gets a little confused. He'll stumble into the house and he'll see me set at Mama's worktable, threads dangling all over the place, scissors snapping, and he'll call me Ruthie.

I'm so sorry, Ruthie, he'll say, but I had to sell it. I had to.

I know it weren't worth much. But Mama would be sad to know it. It was her daddy's land and she was proud to be housekeeping on it.

I tell him, It's me, Daddy. It's me, May.

He says he never wanted to sell it. But the work's been slow and a man's sometimes gotta do things.

That's when he starts to cry and tries to wrap his arms around me from behind as I'm sitting in the chair.

I always stand up quick, but his hands come fast up the front of me, moving in heavy circles, and he burrows in my hair. Sometimes I am quick and I move from him afore he has the chance to breathe me in, to press his crying mouth on my neck. You sit down, Daddy, I tell him. You sit now. He will cry afore he falls asleep—if he don't come looking for me again. I usually slip out real quiet and go to Sugar's.

I don't know how it got this way. There was a before, when Mama was alive, and then there was an after—a sour tasting, vomit-filled kind of after— and I am in it. Here's what I do know. I can't say it out loud, and I can't even whisper it. I want to write it so teeny tiny I won't never be able to read it back to myself. But here's what I do know. I liked the feeling of my bosoms growing out. I like the tender-sore way they felt and the way they popped up under my under-shirt like little surprises. And I liked the way my feet felt in Mama's good patent leather Sunday pumps, the way the pointy toes and heels stretched the muscles in my calves and made them feel long and tight. And I liked the way I smelled on a summer night with the heat so thick it felt like velvet and a salty-wet smell coming from me that made me feel like I am the surf waiting to crash into the shore. I liked those things about myself when they started to come upon me. With Mama so soon gone, it felt good to see a part of her coming to bloom in me.

I did not know that my liking the feeling of being a woman was a secret.

I swear, I didn't know these things.

January 1, 1973

Daddy phoned again today. He says he misses me terrible and that he will have a talk with Little Jim. Nobody hurts his baby girl, he says, and why didn't I come straight to him instead of running away to Aunt Virgie's. I told him about the Silly Putty and also some little dolls I got Lacey for Christmas. I didn't ask what he did for Christmas dinner, but he volunteered that Lucy Clearwater, the widow with the harelip, which ain't bad to look at it, who lives closest to the inlet, had him over for a duck dinner. She is a fine cook, he says to me. But he has not seen her since that time.

I told him Aunt Virgie fixed a feast and Clint and Lyle were here, too. I told him Lacey really likes the boys and they dote on her. They bought her real nice gifts, girlie things like nail polish and a pocketbook.

Daddy says he is glad I am having such a fun time, but it is time to quit this foolishness and come on home. And this time, he tells me, I should bring the baby, bring Lacey. As a matter of fact, he is insisting upon this, he says. He never should have let Virgie take her away and she belongs home with her mama who belongs at home also.

She's not a baby anymore, I says to him. She is three years old now. And he says he wouldn't have any imagination about that because he has never seen her, not even since she was born and Aunt Virgie came for to fetch her.

The whole while he was talking to me Lacey was sitting under the kitchen table making a mess of trying to paint my toenails. When Aunt Virgie asked who I was talking to, Lacey shrugged her shoulders to her chin and scooched deeper under the table.

He says if I ain't coming home he might just head on down to Florida. He is forever talking about going on to Florida where a man can buy a boat cheap and the fishing is good.

Auntie said I had to hang up the phone. But Daddy just kept saying in my ear to let him talk to her, let him talk to his damn meddling sister.

He wants to talk to you, I said to her. But she said she wanted nothing to do with him. Then he yelled so that she could hear him even though the phone was up against my ear—For Chrissake, put that woman on the phone. You tell her she owes me respect. You tell her that. You tell her she needs to be respectful of me. But it was more like he was begging for it than demanding of it.

I held the phone up to her and his voice came through tinny and small and just sort of trickled into the kitchen.

May? I could hear him saying. May, baby? You there, baby?

Auntie took the phone from my hand and twitched as if she was gonna put it to her ear, but then she slammed it back down in the cradle so loud Lacey jumped and painted a big frosty streak of pink across my foot.

I can't stand knowing that he is crying right now. I know he is. If I was there right now he'd be crying over me, pulling me to him and telling me how sorry is—sorry about Mama, sorry about the house, sorry for the way the drink's got hold on him, and maybe even sorry for what he oughta be sorry for. His snot would be running on my shoulder, and then his big old hands would start moving down the back of me, pressing harder while I hold in my breath and think I got no reason to breathe.

I would likely twist carefully away and say it's okay, Daddy. Please don't cry. I'll fix you something if you just set down here. He would tell me how bad he is and how he is cursed and will surely go to hell for the sins he has committed, but that I am not to worry. He will tell me he misses Mama and didn't know she had the cancer and I have no idea what it is like to be a big healthy strap of a man with no missus to tend to his needs. It ain't natural, he'll tell me. It ain't right.

I might hand him a beer and turn on the TV for him. If it is a good night he will drink straight through the night, even if he wets himself, and in the morning he will wash up and not even have a recollection of what was spoke. While he is washing up I will Lysol the vinyl of the chair cushion as it is beginning to smell sour these days.

But I'm not there. I am here. I am writing this as I sit on the davenport with a nice bright winter sun coming through the window behind me and it is making me warm and sleepy. Lacey is curled up next to me like a fine fat cat and I twist her curls around my fingers and try to think only of how happy I could be here.

January 18, 1973

Happy birthday to me! I am seventeen today and Uncle Price says I am a lovely young woman. He doesn't know me very well, but Auntie says he cares very much for me. Aunt Virgie says he is sorry he didn't know about Lacey afore her sudden arrival else he would have helped make arrangements.

Truth be told, I weren't exactly sure about her coming until she was nearly right there. Miss Bunny and Sugar brought her into this world and I will always be grateful, for I thought surely I was dying and that Daddy had put the cancer in me like what Mama had.

Now perhaps that sounds ignorant—me being so dumb as to not know these things, but bearing in mind that Mama died when I was turning thirteen— and as I had never had the bleeding yet and knew nothing of these things—nor did I think to ask—well, I only knew that Mama had a bad cancer that grew in her woman's parts so as to resemble a baby. So when something began to grow in my woman's parts I could only think I had Mama's cancer. Only now I was beginning to suspect how it got in her. I learned about my woman parts after Lacey was born, which is pretty ass backward if you ask me. Miss Bunny told me everything while I lay back in one half of Sugar's bed with Sugar and Lacey tucked around me and waiting for Aunt Virgie to fetch down from Maryland and figure what we were going to do. Sugar is my best friend. Sugar Lee Lane. And she is sweet as her namesake.

After Lacey was born we had to wait for Aunt Virgie. Sugar's mama, Miss Bunny Lane, sent Sugar to tell Daddy about my new baby and that I would be staying up the path with her for a while. Sugar said Daddy only told her real sad-like that he knew it was coming soon.

I was real confused when Sugar told me that cause I couldn't figure on how he knew it was coming and I didn't. Like I said, I was ignorant.

Miss Bunny taught me everything I was to ever know about birthing and babies. When I was crying and cussing words I didn't even know I knew, she was talking soft in my ear and breathing with the pain like she was taking it from me. She told me how to push and how to find the pushing part of myself, and all the while she told me I surely would not die.

Sugar looked real scared, though, and her eyes, which are blue and sparkly, got real wide and glassy and a couple of times I saw her lip tremble. That's when Miss Bunny would send her from the room for towels, a blanket, scissors, cool rags, a hot water bottle, and such things.

Afterward Miss Bunny taught me how to lift my bosom up to reach the baby, pinch my nipple to slide into her mouth, and how to cradle her along my arm. She taught me how to bring the baby back to the breast when she slipped off by tickling her cheek with the tip of my finger. Like a little blind kitten she would open her mouth and turn her head back to me, making little sucking and smacking noises.

It took four days for Aunt Virgie to fetch down, and every day I fell deeper and deeper in love with Lacey.

Auntie asked me who the daddy was, but I never said nothing back. She didn't get mad, just said it would all come out in the wash and she was taking me and Lacey back up to Harford County, Maryland. Daddy didn't like it much that we was going, but he didn't give us much fuss, neither. It was shame that kept him quiet, but I didn't recognize the face of it at the time.

I stayed with Lacey up here till she got fat and sassy and didn't need milk from me no more. Then I knew it was time to go back to Daddy. Aunt Virgie said I could stay with her but Daddy was calling all the time telling me and Aunt Virgie both that I needed to come on home to the island. After thinking long and hard on it Aunt Virgie said I should leave Lacey with her, that I could come see her anytime I wanted, but this way I could go back to school and all. I knew it would be real hard to take care of Daddy with Lacey around, and I didn't know what I could do with her while I was at school, so it seemed the only right thing to do to leave her with Aunt Virgie who is good with her and Lacey loves her like a mama maybe even more than me.

I didn't want to go, but it didn't seem I had no choice yet. Up here didn't feel like it was my real life. It felt like I was just playing at being a mama to Lacey when all along I should have been taking care of Daddy. Mama would have wanted that of me. At least that's what I thought then.

When I got on the bus to go back my stomach was all cramped and tied up in knots. I got a window seat and pressed my head against the glass looking out for Auntie and Lacey. Lacey was hefted up in her arms just smiling and blowing little spit bubbles, hardly knowing I was leaving her. I blew her kisses through the window and smooshed my forehead up against the glass so tight I thought it would burst through. When the bus pulled out from the curb it groaned and screeched and a black smoky smell stung in my chest. I dropped my head to my knees, sick I think, with the knowing that I was heading back to the last place on earth I wanted to be.

CHAPTER 6

A Full House

Willy carries Tasha in from the car and is surprised by the way she snuggles against his chest, even as she continues to sleep. He settles her on the sofa where they can watch her from the kitchen and goes in search of a blanket. In the hall closet he finds an afghan of bright red and yellow knit squares that May had made for their bed. After May disappeared, he had slept with it for a very long time, right up until the next summer, until Virgie had washed it and then May's scent was gone from it and he had no need of it anymore. He presses it against his face now and takes a quick deep breath, but knows it will smell only of wool and cedar.

May was always making things. Nervous fingers, she used to say. She made doilies and afghans and needlepoint pillows. She did smocking on Lacey's dresses and darned Willy's sweaters. If you could put a needle to it, she could do it. Her mother had taught her, she said. They had pretty much lived off of what her mother made selling needlecrafts to the few tourists that visited the island in the summer. May's father was a waterman, though apparently not a very good one. He didn't have a boat of his own and was only hired out as help to other watermen when they needed him. He barely put a roof over their heads. Anything that went on the table was either hunted or fished for—or the result of May's mother's needlework. May's mother died when May was about twelve, and things must have only gotten harder after that. She didn't like to talk about it, and that had been okay with Willy. He figured he knew what he needed to know. He'd seen her bruises the first time she came down the back steps in the hardware store. They were old bruises with a greenish cast that blended into the pink of her flesh and he was surprised, even frightened, by how he had wanted to touch her the moment he saw her. He'd wanted to put his fingers to her face and touch where she ached and lift the pain from her.

Willy was enchanted, he would have said, like a spell had been cast on him. He was nearly thirty-eight years old the first time he saw her and May was only seventeen. And while she seemed, on the one hand, to be a child, there was also something about her that was knowing and older. She didn't have about her the sense of reckless silliness that he noticed in teenage girls.

She was such a young mother that it had been hard to believe, the first time he saw them together, that Lacey was her daughter rather than May's sister. He once watched them sitting together in a patch of sunlight behind the store. May sat with her knees pulled up against her chin, her feet tucked up to her bottom. Her skirt rose over her knees and fell in a tangle around her ankles, but when she leaned forward and down to giggle into Lacey's upturned face, she spread her knees wide and her skirt rose from her ankles and Willy could see the undersides of her long thighs. She seemed as unaware as any child would be as to what she had revealed, and Willy turned away quickly and walked to his truck, embarrassed for her by what he had seen.

Willy had no experience with women, though there were women in town who set their sights on him. He knew that, but they made him nervous. He couldn't say just why, though it was something he had given thought to. Maybe, he once figured, he had grown up so used to all the men at the farm, it having been only his own father and a loyal group of farmhands, so that he just never got used to women being around. His own mother had passed on when he was a small boy and he had hardly no memory of her at all. Men were easy, the way he saw it. The way they said what they wanted of you and you did it. The way you always knew what was expected of you because they said it outright—*open the paddock gates, clean the stanchions, fetch a clean bucket, mend the fence on the south side of the upper field, change the oil in the tractor.* And then, after the hands left at the end of the day, it was just him and his father. *Put the potato water on to boil, set the dishes out, turn the lights out when you come on up for the night and don't forget to stoke up the stove.*

Tolly Martin, the cashier at the pharmacy, had invited him to Easter dinner one year. It had been a small affair, just her and her widowed mother, but he had made himself sick with worry on the way over to her house and by the time he arrived he had no appetite for the ham or conversation and the evening had passed too slowly in awkward silence with Tolly hopping up and down from the table and refilling his plate with ham and potatoes and a gloppy stew of green beans and mushrooms—which he detested. Her mother had prattled on at length about how hard Tolly had worked to prepare the meal and what a good job she had done with the cornbread— an old family recipe, she said. Willy relished a good cornbread, but hers was dry as dirt, and he mentioned instead that his own mother had used bacon fat in hers and that's the way he and his father had made it for years. She might try it next time. Tolly, likely frustrated by the awkward silence thus far and then startled by his suggestion, had burst into tears and run from the table. That had been years earlier and he still had to steel himself to face her when he made a purchase at the pharmacy. Women. They said they wanted one thing when they really wanted another.

Reesie Harms, the sister of one of his farmhands, had been picking up her brother at the end of the day for years and always made a point of seeking Willy out and making conversation with him, even knocking on the back door if he wasn't up at the barn to ask if she could use *the little girls' room.* She brought him canned peaches and tomatoes and once offered to patch the fraying elbow of his old denim jacket. She had stood in his kitchen, rearranging the jars of canned tomatoes she had just gifted him, as if there needed to be some order to them, moving them forward and back and swapping a smaller can on the right side to the left side. He had shrugged off his jacket and handed it to her and she had promised to return it in a few days' time.

When she returned it the very next day, she sought him out in the barn, holding out his jacket like an offering. He took it from her, admiring the neat stitching around the patch and the fact that she had done it so quickly. "What do I owe you?" he asked her.

She waved her hand through the air, telling him it was on the house. He thanked her and slid the jacket on, testing the patch by bending his elbow and lifting it to examine the patch again.

She stood before him smiling, expecting something, so he said thank you again and commented as to how long he had owned the jacket. Still, she stood awkwardly beaming in front of him.

"Maybe we could go to the movies?" she said suddenly. "I've been wanting to see *The Way We Were*. I just love Robert Redford. And Barbra Streisand, too, but I don't think it's a musical. I don't think she sings in it. Have you seen it already?"

Willy's heart sank. He would have rather paid her. The date was disastrous from the start. The closest theater was nearly a forty-five-minute drive into Towson, nearly to downtown Baltimore. When she got in his truck, she brought with her such a heavy scent of musky perfume that he had to roll down his window, and she spent the long drive holding her hair behind her head as it kept whipping up into her face. By the time they arrived, she was clearly irritated with him. She stepped down out of the truck with a heavy sigh, her dark hair stiff and frayed around her face and her eye makeup running at the outer corners of her eyes, vampire-like, creating gray-black smears across her temples.

He offered to buy her popcorn and she waved him off, so he bought himself a box and, looking back, remembers that he never offered his box to her as they sat watching the movie. The movie he remembered as long and impossible, and he kept thinking it was over when it wasn't at all, nearly rising out of his seat only to be swung into another scene. The lovemaking scenes were hardest of all and he stared hard at the screen, afraid to move or even chew the popcorn in his mouth, just sucking it into softness and squaring his eyes with the screen.

In the years since, she still picked up her brother at the farm, but stayed in her car instead, seldom so much as tossing him a wave when he was in the barnyard. She eventually married the high school shop teacher. Her brother made a point of telling Willy whenever she had another baby, three in total, by the time Willy met May.

What unfolded with May was not really a courtship in the formal sense of the word. She was too young for him, for one thing, but he was taken with her and sometimes dropped off little things he would come across, never making the gifts too personal, no fancy perfume, which he now abhorred anyway, but usually something he spied that reminded him of the two of them—crayons and coloring books, a pen for May that wrote in five different colors (for he had seen her more than once writing in her little leather book), small mittens for Lacey when the weather turned cold, a packet of sunflower seeds for May—and sometimes Virgie invited him to stay for supper.

Most times Virgie sat him at the head of their small table, sort of an honorary placement for a special supper guest, but one night late in February he was instructed to sit to the side, next to May.

Outside the kitchen window, the sky was darkening, but the floodlights from the store spilled a sphere of light across the lot that extended into the small yard. A light snow had started. Lacey kneeled on a chair by the window, her nose pressed against it, and watched the flakes drift through the light. When Virgie called Lacey to the table, she didn't appear to hear her at first and May rose from the table, gently put her hands on Lacey's shoulders and turned her from the window. Lacey tried to take the seat next to Willy, but Virgie stopped her and pointed instead to a chair with a fat phone book set on it at the end of the table. Willy offered a hand and she climbed up the rung of the chair and settled onto the phone book, squirming her bottom back and forth to settle herself.

May had her own caramel curls pulled back in a thick knot, and stray ringlets trailed at the back of her neck and tangled at her temples. Her bruises had long since healed but she now bore a small scar on her lip and a longer one at the outer corner of her left eye. Every so often, when she seemed to know Willy was looking at her, she would reach up with thin fingers and pull strands of hair down along the left side of her face.

May was quiet, but he liked that about her, too. She wasn't given to gossip and cared little for the comings and goings of the community. Everything she did say became all the more important because she wasn't one to ramble on endlessly about silly things that Willy neither cared about nor understood.

She liked cows, she said. They had a few on Ocracoke, not many, but she liked their eyes and the way their ears twitched, and especially she liked the way they acted like they didn't care beans about who you were or what you were up to, but if you watched real close, it was their ears that followed you around when you moved amongst them, not their eyes.

She wanted to know if he had a pond on his place. She'd like to learn to swim, she said, or at least make sure Lacey learned. Did he know how to swim?

"Well, sure," he said. He had assumed she knew how to swim seeing as she had grown up on the water like she did.

She told him that watermen didn't swim. That's just the way it was. And she hardly knew a handful of Ocracokers who could do more than flop and splash in the water for very long before sinking. It was a funny thing, now that she thought of it, but that's just the way it was. Only the tourists knew how to swim. She loved to watch them, she said. But most locals didn't swim, didn't know how, and didn't care to. They weren't interested in being in the water, just on it. The sound side was shallow, she explained to him, more like a big warm bath in the summer months.

Yes, she had always wanted to learn how to swim, but even if she couldn't—couldn't do it, that is—at least maybe someone could teach Lacey. Lacey had climbed down from her chair by now and was squeezing herself between May and Willy. May ran her hand up Lacey's small back, fingered her curls.

"Maybe this summer I could teach you, May? I bet you could do it."

She said she doubted she could, but that she would try real hard. And then she scooped up an anxious Lacey who had begun tossing herself repeatedly across May's lap, grabbed her tiny jacket from a hook on the wall, and began to work the child's stiff arms into the sleeves. Lacey needed some run-around time, May explained, and she headed down the steps with her.

Price excused himself as well, saying he had some things to check on in the store.

Willy offered to help Virgie, but she insisted he stay seated with his cup of coffee at the table.

"She's a nice girl, my niece?"

"Yes, ma'am, real nice."

They could both see her in the small backyard behind the store. The snow was thicker now, falling in fat clumps like wet down. Four-year-old Lacey rode on May's hip as they walked through the backyard, trampling through Virgie's herb garden and brushing the snow from the stiffly feathered rosemary that still rose bright and deeply evergreen from the ground.

"Her father, May's father, is my brother," said Virgie. She pulled an apron over her head and down over her massive bosom before tying it behind her back. She was a large woman and when she moved you could hear her breathe. It wasn't a tired sound. It was industrious, the sound of someone with things to do and a passion to get them done.

"Little Lacey," she said. "She's smart as a whip." She looked straight at Willy, cleared her throat, and took one of her big breaths that made her breasts rise up tight under her apron. "It worries me some to have her growing up here without a daddy."

Some of Lacey's toys lay scattered around his feet. She had dragged everything out to show him earlier. He picked up a small doll whose eyes opened when he lifted it from the floor and closed again when he set it on the table. He kept lifting the doll upright and setting it down again, watching the eyes open and close and wondering just how it was weighted inside to do so.

Virgie turned her back to him and ran the water in the sink. "You're a good man, Willy," she said. "And you been alone for a long time now. Confirmed bachelor, hmmm?"

"Never thought to confirm it," he said, smiling. "Never thought about it much at all." But he had. He had thought about it a lot. He was lonely but used to it.

She turned from the sink and looked at him. The water was running hard and he wasn't sure he was hearing her right. "You know, May's eighteen now, a grown woman." She looked out the window to where the two of them walked, looking to all the world like two sister-fairies in the glittering snow.

Six months later, at the age of thirty-nine, Willy brought home his bride.

Willy tucks the afghan around Tasha and instinctively puts his hand on her forehead. She is too warm. Even now, years later, he knows the feel of a too-warm child.

"Little fever," he says, coming into the kitchen. Lacey looks up from the table. "Not too bad, though," he says. "She'll sleep through it."

"I better take her temperature. Where's the thermometer?"

"I'll get it. When do we expect company?"

Lacey isn't sure but figures not before eight o'clock. "Want me to make something for dinner?"

"No, you rest. I should've gone to the grocer," he says, looking in the icebox. "How about breakfast for dinner?" He turns to her from the counter and watches a tired smile spread across her face.

"Sure, Willy."

"I'll get that thermometer." He heads up the stairs.

When he comes back, he hands her the thermometer. She says she hasn't seen a glass thermometer in ages and isn't sure it's a good idea to put it in Tasha's mouth. Willy is confused but she explains that the new thermometers are made of plastic and have LED displays that state the precise temperature.

"I could take it under her arm and add a degree, but I want to be careful to get the exact temperature," she says. "Because of what the doctor said about having to bring her back if it spikes."

"I could run in to town," Willy offers.

No, she will call Mac on his cell and ask him to stop and get one. Not a problem. She takes her phone from her purse and slips out to the sunroom, shutting the door behind her.

Willy pulls eggs and scrapple from the refrigerator. When Lacey was a young girl, he had sometimes let her pick what she wanted for dinner for the two of them. Usually it meant a celebration. She could pick for her birthday, or if she got an especially good grade in school, when she won first place for her chickens in the state fair, when she won a swim meet, or when she made the National Honor Society (even though she said she didn't care about that). Once in a while she picked spaghetti, and once she picked meat loaf, but only because she knew Willy loved it and she really wouldn't have won the spelling bee if it hadn't been for Willy and the herd, seeing as most eight-year-olds couldn't spell *homogenized* unless they were growing up on a dairy farm. But sometimes she picked breakfast.

"Breakfast?" he'd said the first time she suggested it. "Breakfast for dinner?"

"Yeah, Willy. You know, eggs, scrapple, or pancakes, or something. Breakfast."

"But we already ate breakfast." But she just looked at him like that had nothing to do with it. "Breakfast it is," he'd said.

Now it was their comfort food, an easy dinner that was bound to make them feel better, or so he hoped.

Lacey comes in from the sunporch, tucking her phone in her pants pocket.

"Think she'll wake up and eat with us?" he asks, nodding toward the parlor where Tasha is sleeping.

"Oh, sure, she loves breakfast for dinner." But there is a look of worry on her face.

"What?"

"Listen," she says, "I didn't plan this, but Mac has Kat with him."

"Who?"

"Kat, his daughter. Couldn't be helped, Willy. I'm sorry for the trouble. I didn't realize he'd have to bring her. It's her spring break and her mom is traveling with friends."

Willy waves his hand through the air, no big deal, but it is. "Plenty of room," he says. "It's fine." He pulls a pint of milk from the icebox. "Can't be helped."

"Daddy, Daddy, Daddy!" Tasha screams when she hears the crunch of tires in the drive. Willy takes a deep breath and looks to Lacey to see what is expected of him. Tasha, who had woken only moments earlier and had sat dazed at the kitchen table, now scoots off the chair and runs out the door. Lacey catches the screen door just before it slams and holds it open, waiting for Willy to follow and grabbing her jacket from the hook at the same time.

Though it has been raining off and on all day, the outdoors feels no wetter than the indoors. A silver-gray mist has settled over the pond, and the filigreed bramble of shrubs along the far bank wiggle in and out of the fog as the spring winds move through. Mac throws open the car door and Tasha scrambles into his lap.

"Hey, princess!"

Tasha tangles herself so tightly around Mac he can hardly swing his legs out of the car. When he does manage to pull himself out of the seat, he rises with Tasha's legs wrapped around his waist, her arms around his neck, and her nose smooshed up against his. Lacey feels a small pang—not too terrible—in her chest, remembering when she and Mac used to sleep so wrapped around one another that even their toes hugged.

The passenger side door opens and fifteen-year-old Katyana comes up out of the car like a black rose in bloom. Dressed head to toe in shades of black, she is the picture of adolescent gloom—and beautiful in spite of her best efforts to look like death warmed over. She wears fat black boots and a long skirt with a cheap shimmer and a hem that curls up at the ends. Her hair is as light as Tasha's, but cut close and shaggy. Kat is fair, like Mac and Tasha, but her skin seems thinner, stretched taut across her chin and forehead so that there is a cast of blue beneath it, a pale blue flush that runs like a ribbon through her temples and round down to her neck. She is tall and lanky, like her father, but not wiry, not tough and sinewy like some girls—though Lacey guesses she would like to be tougher. Her hands, Lacey notices as the teenager takes her backpack from the car, are paint splattered, the left more than the right, smudged in deep reds along the heel and her pointer finger nearly black to the knuckle. Lacey knows she likes to paint, but whether she is any good or not, Lacey has no idea. In the room she shares with Tasha at Mac's house, she is said to have painted a fantastical jungle mural that at first frightened Tasha but that she has since grown accustomed to, claiming she and Kat have named the animals. Tasha described in great detail a black panther lazing in the crook of a tree, a bright green viper twining the branches—and what was to become Tasha's favorite—a vine-swinging monkey. Thankfully, once named, Tasha had befriended the wall of creatures, reporting to Lacey that when the rain forest dies—as Kat says it surely will—they are going to paint *all* the walls of their room so that all the homeless jungle animals can come and live with them.

Mac awkwardly hugs Lacey with Tasha still hanging from his neck, pressing the girl briefly between the two of them.

"I'm squishing!" Tasha squeals and slides down from between them.

Katyana scuffs at the stones in the drive and pretends not to notice Tasha's obvious delight in seeing her. "Hey, jerk," says Katyana, not terribly unkind in her tone, but it irritates Lacey just the same.

"Hey, jerk!" says Tasha.

Lacey sighs and catches herself.

"What's up?"

Tasha shrugs and then announces, "I lost a tooth!" She pulls down her bottom lip and thrusts her tongue at the tiny gap.

"Cool."

"How come you're here? You never been to Willy's before."

Kat shifts her shoulders, glares at Mac, and says nothing.

"He has chickens," says Tasha. "I'll show them to you, but they stink."

"Won't that be special," she says, heaving her backpack onto her shoulder and slamming the car door.

"Nice to see you again, Willy," says Mac. The two shake hands and step back from one another. It has been more than four years since they've seen each other. "I don't think you've met my daughter Katyana?"

"Another one," says Willy, nodding.

"Kat just started senior high school this year, Willy," Lacey offers, almost as an apology. "You look great, Kat."

Kat kicks another stone across the driveway.

"And I like your hair that way. Nice. She looks good, Mac."

Kat mumbles something about having to pee.

"Honest to God," says Mac, "we must have stopped five times on the way up." He smiles at her, but she scowls and turns her eyes toward the road, eyeing an escape.

"Come on in," says Lacey, but she doesn't move. She feels herself wanting to move, wanting to turn and walk away, away from it all, but she stands rooted, unable to lead them to the house. "You look great, Kat," she says again around Mac's shoulder. "Really, and you, too, Mac. You do. You all look great." Kat always does this to her, always throws her off-kilter. Lacey doesn't know why, can't quite put her finger on it. A part of it, she is sure, has to do with the fact that she feels guilty. But she shouldn't, she reminds herself now. She had nothing to do with Mac and Diane splitting. But still, she knows something of what it is like to be left behind, and so while she was not the one to pull Mac away from his marriage, she may well have been the one that kept him from going back to it. Somehow or other she feels accountable to Kat, and the fact that Kat only tolerates her at best makes it all the more complicated.

"We're having breakfast for dinner," Tasha announces. "It's a tradition, right, Mommy?"

"That's right."

"A *family* tradition," she says, slipping her hand into Mac's.

CHAPTER 7

The House

Lacey is in her old room, stretched out with her limbs spread as if she is preparing to make a snow angel. It is an act of contrition. She will do anything for sleep, but sleep appears to have forsaken her.

The house is filled to overflowing with all of them here—the girls next door, sharing a bedroom just as they do at Mac's house, and Mac bunked in the sunroom. When she had first climbed into bed, she could hear the girls chattering next door, just the sounds of their voices, but not their words. She strained to decipher what was being said, but the heavy door between their room and her own was shut. She wondered, when they slept at Mac's, did they stay up talking late into the night and just what did they find to talk about? Sisters are a mystery to Lacey, though she thinks maybe a sister would have made the difference in her own life, would have changed something about the shape and dimension of the hole May had left behind that Lacey had backfilled with her career, her classes, her devotion to Tasha.

But now the house is silent, reminding Lacey yet again that sleep eventually comes to everyone but her.

She tosses the covers off and pulls her robe from the back of the door. The floor is cool and gritty on her bare feet. She wonders if she will have time to sweep before they head to the hospital in the morning. Tasha is packed, but Lacey knows she will need things from home. Just what, she isn't sure yet. She isn't sure about anything.

She pads down the lit hall—having promised Tasha she would leave the light on—toward the bathroom where she intends to brush her teeth for the second time that night, splash her face with warm water, reapply the moisturizer that had promised a dewy, youthful complexion but so far has failed her as well. She thinks maybe reliving her evening rituals will encourage sleep.

Kat and Tasha's door is slightly ajar and she thinks to shut it so she won't wake them but instead she creeps in, the light from the hall spreading across the room, and stands like a voyeur at the foot of their beds. Tasha has tossed off her covers, and as Lacey steps closer she sees that beads of sweat jewel her forehead and upper lip. She pulls Tasha's covers up and Tasha kicks them back down. "Mommy," she says, sweetly, her eyes not fully open. "It's too hot," and she pulls at the neck of her nightie so that it slips over her shoulder and halfway down her upper arm, pinning her arm to her side.

Lacey puts a hand to Tasha's damp forehead and feels the heat coming off of her. From the bedside table she takes the thermometer that Mac had remembered to pick up on the way and asks her to open her mouth. Tasha opens her lips just barely, claws at the hair that has fallen across her neck.

When her mouth closes over it, Lacey whispers, "You're drenched." She pats her small chest and feels the damp coming through. Tasha opens her eyes fully and nods, blinks.

The thermometer registers 99.6 and Lacey tells herself this is not so bad. She picks up Tasha's sweatshirt and socks from the floor and scans the room for her pink duffel. It is half under the bed and holds more markers and pads of paper than clothing. She moves her hand around inside the bag and comes up with a yellow cotton nightgown. Settles beside Tasha on the bed in order to change her. Tasha sits up just enough for Lacey to get her flannel nightgown off and switch her to the fresh one. She is asleep again the moment she puts her head back down. Lacey kisses the moist crown of her head, can smell the sweat.

Glancing over at Kat, she cannot imagine Tasha growing to such heights as to take up the entire length of a bed. Kat makes two quick and oddly sensual smacking sounds with her lips and tongue and stretches her long legs beneath the covers but does not seem to wake.

Lacey stands and wraps her robe tighter around herself and leaves the room, knowing, as she considers slipping downstairs for a smoke, that the old creaky floors are likely to give her away.

Yes, she would like a cigarette. But her teeth are clean and there is still the struggle with sleep that lies ahead. The smoking is a filthy, dirty, smelly habit, and she knows it, knows she will have to fully quit someday, that there is no such thing as a *social smoker*, even though she told herself that's what she was for years. When that didn't work out, she changed to a secret smoker and gave up the social side altogether. No one at the college really knows about her nasty habit, and right now she is very grateful that she has not quit yet. Sometimes a cigarette is the very best part of her day—or night. Tasha has caught her a handful of times. She hates it. Of course. She says Lacey will die from it. This is all weirdly laughable right now.

She hangs up her robe and squares off with the bed, warning it that she has come to do business. But once under the covers, she fails to find the sweet spot and reconsiders smoking out the window.

Mac quit when she was pregnant with Tasha. It was a noble gesture, and Lacey thinks perhaps made him feel better about leaving Diane and Kat, though she heard he had started again when he left her and Tasha.

She thinks of Mac asleep in the sunroom. It's cold in there at night, but he always liked it cold. He sleeps in his boxers under layers of blankets and he's one of those guys who never owned a bathrobe but just slides his legs into a crumpled-up heap of denim every morning. He pulls a shirt from the back of a chair only if it's cold enough. Otherwise he heads for the bathroom in his jeans, breathing bigger and bigger as he comes to life. He's never worn slippers, and his feet are often bare, the blond hairs curling like spun sugar on the tops of them.

This evening, after breakfast-for-dinner, after she had tucked in Tasha and before she turned in for the night, he had lifted her hand from the table and held it in both of his. "She's going to be okay," he said. "You know that, right? You're not in this alone."

"Yes, Mac. I am very alone." She had said it quietly, almost a whisper that she thought belied the anger his words had stirred in her. He let loose of her hand so that it fell back to her lap.

"Good night," he said. "Try to get some sleep."

"Mac?" she said to his back as he crossed into the sunroom. "I know you love her—it's just different for you is all."

"It's different for everyone, Lacey. That's the nature of the beast."

In the predawn hours of the morning, having banked only a few hours of sleep, Lacey lies still and listens to a wind that has begun to kick up. It makes a whistle in the gables and it is as if the house takes a breath. After May left, Lacey recalls she spent an inordinate amount of time listening to the house. She would lie on the cool linoleum in the kitchen with her ear suctioned to the floor and listen to the sounds that ran through it.

On a hot summer day, the house would creak as though it were stretching its bones, and as the cool of the evening came it seemed to pull back into itself, folding a cloak of dampness around itself and shifting its timbers with a knowing sigh. In the fall the floors clicked and clacked with mounting urgency as the days became shorter. Mice darted through the kitchen and pantry, hugging the floor moldings, and shot through impossibly small crevices that led to the basement rafters just beneath the kitchen floor. The occasional squirrel or raccoon might make its way to the cellar as well, and then the scuttling of mice gave way to the rattle and bang of the larger animals. With the first heavy snowfall the house could be felt gasping for a breath. With a shimmy and a tired creak, it would heave under the weight of the snow, but then straighten its frame again, braced for the long cold days ahead.

This house, she thinks now, has breathed along with all of them for as long as she can remember. It *is* all of them. It is Willy and May and Lacey, even Aunt Virgie.

After May left, Aunt Virgie began coming on Tuesdays to clean. She dumped the ash from Willy's pipe and waxed the insides of the ashtrays so they wouldn't hold odors. She aired the house by opening all the windows on even the blusteriest day. The windows were squeaky-cleaned with vinegar and crumbled newspaper.

When Uncle Price brought her on Tuesday mornings, he always came in for a cup of coffee and toast and then he'd help Auntie flip the mattresses before leaving to open the store. First there was Willy's double mattress, which was light but clumsy and often required even Lacey's pitiful assistance to maneuver. Uncle would help with Willy's mattress only if Willy was already outside tending to chores. Lacey suspected, even then, that he felt odd about being in the room Willy and May had shared. Uncle Price always stalled with a second cup of coffee or small talk until Willy was well out the door. And Aunt Virgie never asked Willy to help. Seems she took some kind of pity on him and she, too, couldn't confront the marriage bed in his presence.

Next they would move on to Lacey's room where Auntie would cluck and fuss over her lack of tidiness. Truth was, Lacey kept her room fairly orderly right up until the night before Virgie's cleaning day, when she would purposely leave clothing tossed about, books spread open on the floor, and the bed rumpled. She welcomed the fussing. It reeled Lacey in, made her feel there were some limits to where she could go and how far. Virgie would bend over with a heavy sigh and retrieve discarded socks and towels, chastising Lacey in a vague sort of way, and Lacey would be quick to snuggle under her bosom as she straightened up and let her heavy arms fall down over her. "What am I going to do with my messy, messy girl?" she would ask, hugging her quick and hard before handing her a pile of dirty clothes and sending Lacey off to the hamper while she and Uncle Price flipped the mattress.

Lacey swings her feet over the edge of the bed to the gritty floor, stares at the bent screen against the window, and wonders if the house can actually feel the neglect, if it could be angry. She is certain it should be. It's a house that once, or so she thought, was tended to just as lovingly as Lacey had been at one time, and then abandoned. She shakes her head. It's a ridiculous idea, but she wants the house to love her again, to care for her, to heal them all. And even though May's leaving had been a hurt they all reeled from, there had always been Aunt Virgie and Tuesdays, magical Tuesdays when everything felt clean and new.

Aunt Virgie put pine needles in the vacuum cleaner bag so that the house would smell like a forest. And she always cooked a two-day meal. Something would get to simmering as soon as she arrived in the morning and it wouldn't get turned off until she left that evening. On steamier summer days she wouldn't want to put anything on the stove so she'd make an enormous platter of tuna salad with chopped sweet pickles and a molded Jell-O salad with chunks of peaches and sliced grapes from her vines. Lacey liked to squish and swoosh the gelatin in her mouth until it turned to juices and left torn bits of fruit sieved to her teeth. Whatever was made on Tuesdays was, at the least, enough for two night's meals and maybe a lunch for Willy.

Aunt Virgie was made of magic and knew the answers to every question—every secret. Somehow Lacey always expected Aunt Virgie to tell her about May. Though she never asked. She waited, feeling certain that an explanation would come. The woman knew so many things.

"Why do you put a lettuce leaf in the oxtail soup and then take it out again?" Lacey asked, peering into the big steaming pot as she removed a hand-size leaf of lettuce from the top of the broth. "It absorbs the fat and grease from the soup," Aunt Virgie told her. "Why don't you throw out the sour milk?" Lacey wanted to know, pinching her nose as she unscrewed the lid from a two-quart ball jar filled with the thick globs of soured milk. "I boil it, sweetie, to wash the lace," she said. "Makes them pretty and white again." She had a small pile of hankies and a couple of Lacey's good lace church veils piled on the counter. Later that day they would hang to dry, crisp and white as sunshine on a cool morning.

"Why do you do that?" Lacey had asked as Virgie spread wax paper on the ironing board, sprinkled salt on it, and proceeded to press with a hot iron.

"Burns the starch off Papa Willy's iron," she said, moving the iron slowly, pressing hard across the salted papers until a pungent smoke would begin to rise from it. Then she would take the balled-up white shirts from the freezer and begin to work them flat with the iron, steam hissing from the board and falling over the edges in a rolling mist.

Aunt Virgie knew everything, how to get it, how to mend it, how to keep it. Certainly, she would tell Lacey how to get Momma back.

Lacey doesn't think of her mother much anymore, by design. She has worked hard to forget. She looks around the room now at all of the doilies, all of her mother's handiwork. It had been easier to forget once she left home for college years ago. It is harder now. It has become harder as a mother herself and it is even harder this morning. It is, in fact, excruciating. She thinks of her young daughter and feels the rip of it at her heart. She will not let go of Tasha, of that, she is resolute, and so she is confounded by the memory of her own mother letting go without so much as a goodbye.

If Virgie were here now, Lacey would ask her. She would ask her aunt how it was even remotely possible that a mother could walk away from her child. And then she would ask her how to fix it, how to fix everything.

Willy and Mac are settled over either side of the kitchen table like old adversaries, eating their eggs and looking up at one another when they don't think the other is looking. Willy nods to her when she comes in, tips his head to the coffeepot on the counter.

"What's the plan this morning?" he asks her.

Lacey tells them she will let Tasha sleep until the last possible moment. It's barely dawn, just a hint of light seeping into the kitchen.

Mac mentions that Kat will need to be woken soon. She'd sleep until the noon if he allowed it. And then she'll take forever to get herself ready and out the door.

Kat should stay here at the house, Lacey tells him.

"I don't know . . ." he says. He is surprised, Willy thinks, and hadn't considered this. Mac shifts heavily in his chair, pulls his hand to his chin, sits back, and repeats himself. "I don't know about that."

"It should just be the two of us, Mac. I don't want to make a big deal out of it."

"It *is* a big deal."

"I know that," she huffs. "But I think it will be easier for her if it's just the two of us." She is pouring coffee with her back to them but turns suddenly. "Just the two of us, Mac."

"That's ridiculous."

"Not."

"She's her sister."

"And she won't want to be there," says Lacey.

"Ask her."

"I won't. I'm telling *you*, Mac. It should just be the two of us."

Willy watches the two of them like he's watching a Ping-Pong match at the Whistle Stop Bar.

"She can stay here with me," Willy offers, as if that settles it.

"Perfect," says Lacey. "We'll need to take two cars, Mac. I'll be staying with her overnight."

"I should stay with her, too," he says, then appears to reconsider. "This is complicated," he admits.

"Yup," says Willy. "Seems like Lacey's got it figured out." He stares Mac down. Daring him to come up with a better solution. Mac looks at him, at Lacey, and resigns himself to his eggs.

They are all uncomfortably quiet for a moment, Lacey dumping her coffee after only a sip, Willy not willing to take his eyes off of Mac, and Mac brooding, his chin tucked into his chest.

Unexpectedly, Mac lifts his head to Willy. "Any family history of cancer on Lacey's side?"

"Mac, what the hell?" says Lacey. Willy watches her twist into a kind of anger he knows she can't kick her way out of, and he suspects Mac knows her family history—her lack of family history. "What is wrong with you?"

Mac looks sideways to both of them, sheepish, realizing his mistake. "What? It seems to run in families, you know." But Willy can tell that Mac knows he stepped over an invisible line.

"No," Willy fires back. "Must of come from your side."

"Oh, for crap sake—the two of you!" She slams her hand on the counter and shakes her head. "It could be anything," she says, resigned. "I mean, it could be environmental, toxins and stuff; could be all the shit that dumps into the bay and sludges on down to St. Mary's, could be the power plant at Calvert Cliffs." She storms over to the table, standing between the two of them and looking to them both, one at a time and back again. Willy leans back in his chair, hoping this has nothing to do with him.

Clearly, she is angry and it is building, making Willy wish he hadn't said anything at all, wishing he had let Mac hang himself. "Acid rain," she says. "Preservatives, shellfish? Microwave ovens, fluorocarbons, power lines? Goddamn nitrates, food coloring." She grabs Mac's nearly finished plate of eggs and toast and takes it to the sink and then, with a what-the-hell flip of the wrist, lets the plate crash into the sink where it meets the porcelain bowl with a clatter. "Could be radon . . ." Willy sees her shoulders rise with a deep breath. "Or the immunizations she got, or the sushi I ate when I was pregnant." She turns to them both and tears storm down her face and pool in the corners of her lips where Willy imagines she can taste them, hot and salty. But she doesn't stop. "Or maybe it's because I nursed her, or because I stopped too soon, too much protein, not enough—or stress," she says, more quietly. "It could always be stress." She whips her hands down her face, flinging off the tears. "It's probably stress." And she walks out the kitchen door and into what is turning into a cold, bright morning, leaving the two men sitting behind in the kitchen where they will sit for many minutes staring blankly at the walls and one another, each hoping that her outburst was the fault of the other.

CHAPTER 8

Checking In

The hospital is a city unto itself, peopled by the sick and hopeful. Crossing the threshold through the wide wall of glass doors, Lacey swears she can feel the underlying pulse of collective prayers, the bargaining of the masses. It is suffocating, and she sucks in each breath as if it is not enough. She realizes she is holding Tasha's hand too tightly and releases the pressure, hoping to appear less desperate in the way she clings to her daughter. Tasha reaches up to Mac's hand beside her and he smiles down at her, that smile meant to say *isn't this something*, instead of what Lacey is certain he is really thinking—that this is the *it* in their life that changes everything. He scoops Tasha up and perches her on his side, her legs wrapped around his waist, and carries her through the corridors as the three of them make their way to the registration desk. Stopping at the glass partition, Lacey turns and motions to a low couch designed with a Lysol-able fabric. Tasha squirms to be put down and Mac lowers her with his lips pressed against the top of her head. He leads her to the sofa and settles uncomfortably, his long legs bent at an angle that has his knees rising above his seated bottom—the couch is that low—and pats beside himself, inviting Tasha to take a seat as well.

Lacey tells the young woman behind the glass that she is checking in with *Anastasia Virginia Cherrymill*. She must spell it for her and in doing so she is reminded that she and Mac have given their daughter an impossibly long name that Tasha will certainly struggle to learn to spell. She gave

Tasha her own last name rather than Mac's, and Mac said he understood, but secretly she had promised herself she would change it once they got married. Although it was a promise she never spoke aloud, not wanting to hold it out as a bartering chip.

She recites addresses, phone numbers, parent names, date of birth. *She's only five*, she hears herself saying. The intake clerk doesn't seem to notice. Lacey feels a flip in her stomach, like a small kick, and her next thought is that she wishes Tasha could have stayed there, safely tucked beneath her heart.

In the first weeks after she was born, Lacey could hardly bear to put her down. She would nurse her and then, after, keep her snug in her arms, a doughy bundle swaddled in a bubblegum-pink blanket, Tasha's breath as delicate as butterfly wings, her lips still wet, smacking softly, once, twice, in remembrance of Lacey's milk before parting at the touch of her own tongue. Lacey thought she could drown in the smell of her, bottom heavy, curled and cupped in her arms, Tasha's blue-pearled eyelids fluttering. Lacey would think, *She dreams?* Of what—of all she knows, the reliable crook of Lacey's arms, the wonder in her voice, the feel of Lacey's breast against her face. She dreams, Lacey would imagine, of her too-new world. *She dreams of me.*

She looks over her shoulder to where Mac and Tasha sit, Tasha scooched against the back of the sofa and wiggling her feet over the edge of it, Mac running his hand over her shoulders in a way that suggests he is resisting the urge to pull her to himself. Lacey has no doubt that he loves Tasha just as much as he loves Kat. Maybe it's even easier loving Tasha than it is to love the sulky and surly Kat. Tasha can love her father back with absolute abandon. She wears her delight upon seeing him like a banner draped across her tiny body. Kat, on the other hand, plays a push-me-pull-you game of you-love-me-now-you-don't, staring at Mac side-eyed and hopeful when he isn't looking, but her face dissolving in a wash of disinterest the second he tries to catch her eye.

Mac and Diane had been separated for less than a month by the time he and Lacey had begun seeing each other. Mac didn't even have a place of his own yet and had been sleeping on the sofa of his good friend David (soon to become Lacey's department head), and then in Lacey's bed. By the time nine-year-old Kat understood that Daddy wasn't coming home, she also understood that Daddy had a *new friend* who was going to have a baby who would be Kat's little brother or sister. Of course, Kat still blames Lacey, maybe has a right to. After all, Mac and Diane might have gotten back together had Lacey not made it so easy for Mac to fall in love with her—and she did make it easy, asking nothing of him so that he found himself falling into something he never saw coming.

Getting pregnant was a complication, a fail precipitated by the expired condoms Lacey had dug out of her nightstand on a windy evening with the curtains beating against the window and the musky smell of the river ratcheting up their desperation for one another. Mac had surprised her by being elated about the pregnancy, but even before he had thrown his arms around her like it was the best news he'd heard all day, before he had pulled back and said, *Really? Really?* And then high-fived her like he had just scored the winning goal, even before all of that, she had felt that first nudge of something coming between them.

She quit smoking and gave up caffeine. She stopped eating tuna and shellfish, raw sprouts and processed meats. She bought an air purifier and threw out their mattress for fear of dust mites. She tossed out the Teflon pans, had the cottage checked for radon, sampled the walls for asbestos, switched to vinegar and water for cleaning the windows. She stopped swimming in the river and took to doing laps at the college pool instead. In the relinquishing of all these things, she knew herself to be separating from the world around her, setting up a barrier reef to protect the tender thing that clung to her womb.

They are handed ID badges and instructed to move on, up two escalators that delight Tasha, and down a long hall to a ward cordoned off with walls of cartoon murals, SpongeBob, magical ponies with wings and unicorn horns, fat friendly trolls, and fairies. Tasha reaches out and touches the wall, trails her fingers along the way.

A bald baby, maybe one year old, maybe older, is seated on its mother's lap. The sight of the two of them pounds at a soft spot in Lacey's chest and she cannot look at them, cannot see if it is a boy or a girl, if it is naturally bald or chemically bald, but she can hear the mother's baby talk voice as she plays with her child, a voice that surprises Lacey in that it doesn't belie the dread and sadness that saturates the room. Still, Lacey can't look and shifts her back to the both of them while she stands at the second registration desk. Though they have come up two full stories since entering the hospital, she cannot help but feel as though she is descending.

They are sent to a cubicle that is too small for the three of them, and she and Mac squeeze themselves into the two chairs, the arms of which are almost touching, and Lacey pulls Tasha to her lap. The intake questions are more detailed here, more personal, and Lacey is unprepared. *How old was Anastasia when she rolled over, started crawling, started talking?* Lacey can't remember, can't believe she can't remember. There is a baby book, a gift from her dearest friend Franny when Tasha was born, and it is filled with all these details. But it is far away in her little cottage, tucked on a shelf next to *What to Expect When You're Expecting* and *The Womanly Art of Breastfeeding*. She is forced to improvise and recall the details to the best of her ability, but Mac corrects her. No, she was eleven months, not quite a year, when she started walking, remember? He is right. And just how could that be, that he is right, that he remembers this and she does not?

Lacey couldn't tell Willy that Mac was still married when she had Tasha. In fact, the first time she had gone to visit Willy with Tasha (a bitter-cold winter day), she had insisted Mac stay behind, insisted she and Tasha would be fine. It was foolish of her—sleep deprived as she was and still aching from the stitches in her bottom and her milk leaking at the mere sound of Tasha's cries—to be on the road for hours with a nursing newborn. And while she knew it at the time, she wasn't up to what she feared would be a confrontation between Willy and Mac, should Willy inquire as to why they had not yet married. She can still recall arriving at the farm that afternoon, excited to present Tasha to Willy, but rising from the car and her milk-soaked breasts chilling in the sudden cold.

Mac said he wanted to get married, of course, but when his divorce finally came through, they both let the marriage idea hang in the air, a sheer sheet of a promise that flapped this way and that but still hung between them. There had been a shift of sorts, from the moment she had told him she was pregnant, and once Tasha was born, she had felt herself pushing against a current, away from him, as if she were a lifeboat with room for only herself and Tasha. The shift was small, barely perceptible at first, but slapping up against Lacey's consciousness at times. It had something to do, she was sure, with the way she was loving Tasha, loving her so hard it scared her, loving her so hard that there wasn't anything left to love anything else. The harder she loved Tasha, the more she realized she was the only one loving her that way.

She babyproofed the cottage to an extreme degree, corner guards and drawer locks, bolting the bookcase and the dresser to the walls so they couldn't be toppled, locks on windows that only allowed them to be opened six inches—no babies tumbling out of windows on her watch—turning down the hot water heater so that Mac was grumbling about lukewarm showers, locks on the stove knobs that made it cumbersome to light the burners, and all of this before Tasha was even crawling. Lacey was obsessed, Mac said, with the possibility of disaster. He joked that they could leave Tasha home alone for days with only food and water and she'd be just fine. It was a joke that Lacey didn't like, and it made her afraid of dying, afraid of leaving her.

Tasha was just over a year old when Mac moved out. There wasn't any one particular incident at the root of his leaving, but by the time it actually happened, by the time he was packing his bags and headed back to his friend David's sofa, it didn't feel like a surprise at all and in fact felt expected. They had run their course. It had been a good run for a while.

"I can't believe you're leaving us," she had said standing helplessly by while he packed a duffel. He had an irritating habit when he packed of rolling his clothes over in his hands into balls and stuffing them into the corners of the bag. She wasn't sure what was irritating her more, that he was leaving or that he was doing it so carelessly.

"Come on, Lacey, you know you don't want me here."

"That's not true," she had said, but as she said it, she went to the crib and picked up Tasha, still sound asleep from her nap, and held her to herself as she began to wake, blinking from sleep, her damp eyes drawn to Lacey's own as if what was between the two of them was all there was. Lacey held her tight, swinging her away from Mac as he packed as if to say, *You can take everything else, but this is mine.*

"You don't want me here," he said again.

She couldn't say that that was true. She did want him, or thought she did, but he didn't understand what this child in her arms was taking from her, how much she required of Lacey's heart, the diligence it was taking to keep her safe and protected from all the world would throw at her, all the leaving.

"That's ridiculous," she said. "You're Tasha's father."

"I'm talking about you, Lacey. What do you want?"

"If things are difficult, you should try to work them out, Mac. You can't just run away because things aren't perfect."

"And you shouldn't let me," he had said.

She couldn't look him in the eyes and watched his hands instead. Packing hands.

Something was expected of her, something that might change the course of what was transpiring, but whatever it was felt just out of reach, like a word one might search for and though it shimmies around the tongue, it can't be called up. She swung Tasha higher on her hip and let Tasha's hands play at her face, the tiny tickle of it drawing her farther from Mac and deeper into the well of only the two of them.

"I'll be at David's," he finally said. "I'll call you."

His leaving left a hole in her heart for a time, but slowly Tasha nudged herself into the empty space he left behind, and Lacey couldn't feel it so much. It made her wonder, though, had she ever loved Mac enough? Maybe it had all been about the fact that he loved her. Maybe she simply loved being loved, but in the end, it divided her loyalties and ultimately asked too much of her.

Mac is wandering the small hospital room, his shoes squeaking across the floor as he paces from the window to the bathroom. They are both trying to settle Tasha into a hospital bed that she doesn't want to get into. There is too much to explore in the room, the small blue plastic pitcher and matching cup, the wall-mounted television, the buttons on the bed. Maybe, Lacey thinks now, watching Mac pick up the remote attached to the bed by a thick cord and aim it at the television, maybe she could have stopped his leaving years ago. She could have cracked open her heart to him a little more and let him in a little deeper.

She snags Tasha from the windowsill, lifts her shirt over her head where it drags across her forehead, and releases with a swoosh and a feathery tumble of blonde hair. Mac hands her the hospital gown and she coaxes Tasha's arms into it. They are preparing to have a port installed, and Lacey struggles with how much to tell her and how to tell Tasha about something that she herself knows nothing about.

Yes, Lacey thinks now, the three of them standing so near one another and pressed against this daughter of theirs, yes, she could have stopped his leaving, but doing so would have required something of her she couldn't spare then and is certain she cannot spare now.

January 21, 1973

Daddy called and said he was gonna borrow Little Jim's truck and come and fetch me back. He says me and Lacey gotta come home.

Sugar wrote me a letter and told me sometimes Daddy doesn't come out of the house for days and days, and then when he does come out he walks the quarter mile to the Methodist church graveyard where he sits on the yard's big old monument across a ways from Mama's grave and talks to her—loud, too, Sugar says. Cause he done it once on a Sunday and all the people in the church heard him wailing and shouting like a wildcat. She says he's been heard going on and on about being a sinner and why'd she go and die on him like this—leaving him in a unnatural state that could only lead to problems. He might as well just cut his losses and head on down to Florida. She says he tells Mama I been nothing but trouble for him and there are times he cries so hard he just tumbles down off that monument and falls to the earth just carrying on and on about the heartache he's been bearing.

Some of this crying he did afore Mama ever died. I remember one time he didn't come home all night—which was not too uncommon—but this particular night Miss Bunny come by to report that her husband, Mr. Lane, had seen Daddy heading off in Loony Junie's Chevrolet, and he had felt it was his Christian duty to tell Miss Bunny to tell us so. Loony Junie is three-quarter crazy and loves her menfolk. Men say she'll do everything and anything and you don't even gotta pay her. At the time I didn't know what that meant—like I said, I was a little ignorant of these things, but I have since come to know what is meant specifically as Little Jim has told me some things.

When Daddy dragged his sorry ass back the next morning, Mama said, Well, lookee here, ain't you a sorry ass dragging your sorry self back home. He said he was full-up apologizing. Liquor caught up with him last night and he never did get home is all.

But Mama weren't having none of it. She lay a cussing on him and she told Daddy she was leaving him and taking me with her and she started throwing all her belongings in a box. I got no idea where she thought we was going. Though I suppose we could have took the ferry off the island and headed up to see the other side of her people in Kinakeet. Daddy got a look of sadness in his face that near hurt to look at.

I'm begging you, Ruthie, he said. But she kept throwing things in the box. She put in her panties and her slip, then her other housedress, followed by her nightie and a pair of pink slippers. She grabbed her special soap from the bathroom and wrapped it in paper and took her sweater off the hook in the bedroom. She even flung open the bottom drawer of her wardrobe and fumbled around in there coming up with a few dollar bills and a handful of coins. Lastly she grabbed the Bible next to the TV cause he obviously wouldn't need it knowing now where his sorry soul might one day repose, she said. Then she told me to get my things cause we were leaving.

I reminded her real quick that he was sorry.

He followed her around the house, begging her not to go, right on her heels, trying to reach out and touch her, but she shrugged off his hand whenever it come down on her shoulder.

I will follow you, he says to her, right on into the ocean. Ain't nowhere you can go I ain't gonna come and get you. You hear me, Ruthie?

But Mama don't pay him no never mind at first. She just kept looking round the room like she was trying to figure out what it was she was forgetting. He says he flat out ain't going to let her go is all. That's all there is to it. She says if he wants to follow her that is fine with her cause she will walk straight out into the ocean and drown them both.

I'm a coming on after you, he says.

Now I am scared and my knees are knocking and I'm thinking on whether Mama's gonna walk me into the ocean with her. She can hold my hand so tight sometimes and just pull me along beside her and I'm thinking she will just take hold of my hand like that and drag me on down to the ocean.

He says he will do it, too—walk right into the surf. He was starting to cry and he was really begging now, too. Please, he was saying, please, Ruthie. It was just Loony Junie and she don't mean nothing.

It means something to me, says my mama, and she turned round real fast so he nearly run right up against her. She was spitting nails kind of mad, but then right away she sees his hurt sad face and her own eyes start filling up with tears and the next thing I know the two of them is standing in the room just a crying and holding each other up. Every time Mama would sniffle, Daddy would start to cry more and say how sorry he was and he would follow Mama anywhere, even to the bottom of the sea—but it was only Loony Junie and she don't count for nothing.

January 23, 1973

Daddy has not come for me yet. Aunt Virgie has told him he best not do so. That I am best off here. I am surprised that he listens at her cause he don't listen too good at nobody. Why I find myself feeling sorry for him is a mystery to me.

Maybe I ought to explain about Daddy's eyes. Daddy has the kind of eyes that tell you just what he's feeling—not what he's thinking necessarily, but exactly what he's feeling. His eyes are brown as earth and you can't help but wonder if they got some special power over you when he looks at you. His eyelids are heavy and his lashes are thick so that sometimes he has a dreamy look that reaches far away and makes you think you need to go with him. And when he's wanting something, when he's nearly aching for something, like he was when Mama turned around that night and couldn't help herself but to go into his arms, his eyes get even darker and damp, like fresh-turned soil, and it is very hard not to try to soothe the hurt in him, even if it hurts a body all the more to do it. You see, he has this way of making you think that you are the only one that can ease the pain that's crawled up inside him and what's more, it's likely you are what caused the pain in the first place.

And so, I am hoping very much that Little Jim will not give Daddy his truck and Daddy won't try to come and carry me back. I am hoping he is fearful of his sister and knows that she will not let him. I know I will not let him carry Lacey back. I know that. But I am a little worried about me. I don't say no to him so good and I would surely hate to leave this place and could not bear to leave Lacey.

CHAPTER 9

The Cottage

The parking lot is more like a small expanse of bad lawn covered haphazardly in crushed oyster shells. Tufts of weeds struggle through the layer of shells, and cars are parked in no apparent order, some of their noses practically touching the front of the building. "Bailey's Bar and Grill" is hand-lettered across the top of the sign, and below that it reads "cottages for rent, ice, tackle, bloodworms."

Tasha has completed a grueling seven days of treatment. Lacey was warned that Tasha would get worse before she would get better, but she hadn't been prepared for the way treatment would draw the color from her face, the way it would make her small lips crack so that she would wince if she risked a smile, which she did less and less each day. She hadn't expected the vomiting, the diarrhea, the headaches that left her silent and glassy-eyed.

Lacey hadn't wanted to leave her. Almost didn't. But spring break officially ends tomorrow and there are some things she needs to get from the cottage, lighter clothes for one thing as the weather has suddenly begun to warm and she had only packed for cooler weather. And Tasha needs some toys, a second bathrobe, puzzles, her own pillow. There is mail to pick up, and perhaps most important, she needs to meet with David, her department head, to make a plan to cover her classes.

Mac will sleep at the hospital tonight. Before she left, she started to go over their bedtime routine. The book du jour is *My Father's Dragon*. Then

Lacey always tells Tasha that she loves her and then Tasha will ask Lacey *how much?*

"More than you know."

"I know a lot," Tasha will say, but not with the wide grin of just a week ago.

"Well, I love you a lot more than that."

Lacey wanted to tell Mac because she thought it was important that they stick to the routines she knows, especially in a strange place like a hospital where it's hard to even know day from night. But he was quick to remind her that he has put her to bed hundreds of times, and they have their own routines that work for them.

She reaches for her phone now on the seat beside her. She thinks to call him but then thinks better of it. Still, she hopes he reads her the right book. She is so tired.

Eight cottages are scattered behind the bar, each with a view of the river and dock. Southern Maryland College is fairly rural and there's no town, per se. Faculty and the students who choose to live off campus usually rent old tenant houses or fishing cottages that are just barely winterized.

Three lacrosse players rent the one closest to the bar, which Lacey is sure they consider a bonus. Their music is loud and their hours are obscene, but they are friendly with Tasha and Lacey appreciates that. They think nothing of running out to their cars to grab books or whatever while wearing nothing more than a towel. One cottage is rented to Old Jenny, who makes crab pots in the back room of Bailey's for two bucks apiece, and one houses a fifty-something fishing guide who keeps pretty much to himself. His name is Logan, but everyone calls him Log, due more to his build, she assumes, than a shortening of his name. He is built from head to toe like the thick trunk of a tree and his skin is ruddy and creased from years on the water. He keeps his boat at the dock, where he spends most of his time. He is always hosing something down or slicing something up. Another is rented to Cade Clipper, the college's lacrosse coach. They are friends—good friends—and while she very briefly entertained the idea of flirtation two years ago when he first came to the college, it took her all of five minutes at David's new-faculty welcome cookout to come to her senses. She had watched the women watching Cade and something in the way their eyes danced in their heads when he spoke to them, blinking and looking away, the tossing in of a breathy laugh—the kind that draws attention to itself in the way it lands awkwardly before the joke is finished—and the way their hands played nervously along the rims of their drinks or the twist being wound at the end of their napkins, had made her resign herself to friendship. Lacey couldn't afford to compete for a man's attention. Didn't like the anxious way it made her feel, the puzzling out of innuendo, or the way it all required a vulnerability that itched at her core. Better to be friends.

She grabs her bag from the back of the car just as Log heads down to the dock. His cat, a loathsome creature she is always shooing away from Tasha, trots behind him and then leaps from dock to boat in an effortless arc.

She hoists her bag on her shoulder and walks down the path that winds around the side of the bar, past the dumpster that always reeks of fish and grease and stale beer, waves to Log when he turns and nods to her, and heads for her cottage, which sits like a tiny jewel against the backdrop of the river.

Lacey loves this cottage. She especially loves the smallness of it. From the kitchen and her bedroom, she can look out to the dock and river. She's close enough to the water to watch the larger schools of minnows dimple the surface and to hear the water kitten-lap against the shore.

She lets herself in through the door of the screened porch and then through a second door into the kitchen and drops her bag to the floor. The herbs on the kitchen sill have turned brittle and there is a stink that reminds her that she should have taken the trash to the dumpster before heading north in the middle of the night.

It is almost eerie to be here without Tasha. The distance between here and Tasha is like a hole growing behind her. She leaves the door open to air out the kitchen and jiggles the screen door of the porch to make sure it is latched. It is always both amazing and aggravating to her that the mosquitoes will find their way through a screen, but somehow they do.

While Mac is at the hospital, Willy will be alone at the farm with Kat. Lacey feels guilty about the situation and can't imagine what the two of them will find to talk about. There will likely be a lot of huffing. Lacey is especially bothered by the huff of breath that precludes every response on Kat's part, as if it is a great bother to answer anyone directly, like she is being pulled from another place with their questions—Tasha asking if Kat likes Tasha's new shoes, her hair-tie, her overnight bag. And when the questions come from Lacey the sigh is even heavier, the blow of breath a billow of barely hidden anger. School is fine, okay. The ride was boring, and no, she is not looking forward to the weekend, all delivered on the edge of a heave that drops her thin shoulders and flutters her lips.

Mac is heartsick. She has seen him fight the urge to crumble when he watches Tasha gagging as she spits up on herself, her eyes tearing and the foul smell of it filling the room. "That's okay, princess. It's okay," he says, holding the plastic bin at her chin. Lacey will change her gown and Mac will wipe Tasha's face with a cool cloth and if his eyes catch Lacey's she will see the way the brows twist, locking his tears behind his eyes and forbidding them to fall. Then he will go to the bathroom to empty the bin and rinse it in the sink, and under the sound of the running water there are deeply swallowed sobs. Once she went to him, shut the door, closing the two of them in the cavernous echo chamber of the bathroom, smoothed her hand up his back, and let him lean down to her shoulder and cry while the water ran. She had felt especially strong at that moment, surprising herself that she was able to, if not comfort him, at least give him a place to tumble down in his grief.

The last week has been a nightmarish reckoning with the illness. This very morning before Lacey left, Tasha had her second bone marrow aspiration. Lacey wasn't surprised to see the way Mac's face wrinkled when he watched the needle move through her back, the way he shoved his hands so deep in his pockets, in an effort, Lacey was sure, to keep from reaching out and stopping the procedure, that his pants slid down the front of him and his shirt came untucked.

Tasha is going through Phase One of treatment, known as Induction. It is to be the most intensive and aggressive phase of treatment for the purpose of killing abnormal white cells. The idea is to get rid of the little bastards and do it quickly. Induction will last about four weeks, and Lacey has been told that Tasha can expect to spend at least the first two weeks in the hospital.

There have been so many decisions to make—clinical trials, ports, catheters, various drugs, anesthesia. And then there is the whole protocol thing, explained to Lacey as the *recipe* for Tasha's cure. She made a copy of it to leave with Mac and carries her own copy with her. Lacey is never without it. Can refer to it at any moment, though she believes she hardly understands it. Vincristine, Lasparaginase, methotrexate administered intrathecally, subcutaneous port, EMLA cream. But even now she thinks that if she could just understand it, could just figure the whole thing out, then she could take over and get Tasha cured lickety-split. And if she doesn't, if she fails to understand, she is standing idly by, like the town idiot, and watching her daughter die.

There has been talk of bone marrow transplants, but only *if it comes to that*. And everyone has been tested—even Kat. But *everyone* is a small group, only Lacey, Mac, and Kat. There is no one else, nowhere else to look. Mac, too, is an only child and his parents were gone well before Lacey met him.

She reaches into the zippered pocket of her purse and carefully draws out a triple-folded piece of paper she has stowed there, opens it carefully, and touches the pads of her fingers to the blonde hair that lays in the folds, careful not to sigh in a way that will carry the contents away.

She can't believe how quickly the chemo has made Tasha sick. It's hard to believe that the stuff that is nearly killing her is supposed to cure her. Already the first tufts of hair have started to fall out. They told Lacey and Mac that it could happen quickly, or not at all. But Lacey's heart still snapped in two when the first silky clump slid from Tasha's scalp. Her hand began to shake and she lifted the brush to the crown of Tasha's head and pulled down slowly, tenderly, barely letting the bristles touch her scalp, so careful. And still, again and again, another swath of her hair sifted from her head. Lacey pulled it from the bristles and folded a scrap of paper around it. It meant something, this beautiful piece of the *before Tasha*, and she meant to hold on to it.

"Sweetie, you know how we talked about how getting better might make you sick for a while?"

Tasha was tired and didn't answer, just nodded. "I don't want to go to the playroom. I want to stay here. Watch TV with me, Mommy."

"You don't want to go play with the other children? You sure?"

"Stay here, Mommy."

"Tasha, honey, your hair is starting to fall out—a little bit. Remember we talked about that?"

"I know, Mommy. I put it in the drawer so we can glue it back on later."

Tasha slid open the nightstand and there tucked in the corner was a tiny blonde bird's nest. Lacey's throat tightened as though fingers were wrapping around her neck. "Oh, honey." She lifted the nest of hair and tucked it into the folded paper.

"We can fix it later, Mommy. I'm so tired."

"Okay, honey," she whispered, still trying to find the full power of her voice. "We can fix it later."

Lacey walks into her bedroom and tucks the paper in her top drawer, next to trinkets she treasures, Tasha's newborn ID tag from the hospital when she was born, a cheap gold-filled 4-H medallion she won at the state fair for her chickens when she was nine, the pink beanie Tasha wore home from the hospital, ticket stubs from her first Grateful Dead concert at Towson State that she went to with Franny twenty—she can't believe it—years ago, her swim goggles from when she won her first meet, and three copper-colored chicken feathers from Huey, the nastiest rooster she ever owned.

When she looks up from the drawer and out the window, it is nearly dark and Old Jenny is making her evening walk down to the dock. She always carries a lit cigarette in her hand. Lacey thinks she smokes them all the way down to the filter. Log is coming off his boat and he has said something to Old Jenny that has made her laugh so hard that the smoke is pouring out between her teeth like a fog. When she's finished with this one, she'll flick the butt into the water and light another, cocking her head to the side, closing her eyes while her lighter flares. The smoke hangs low and floats back in through the window making Lacey wish for one.

Back in the kitchen, she digs in her overnight bag and comes across one last wrinkled cigarette in a crumpled pack. She has to smooth it through her fingers before lighting it. Her throat is raw, and the cigarette only serves to remind her that she is a lousy parent who probably gave her child leukemia from secondhand smoke. She snuffs it out quickly in a saucer—and immediately wishes she hadn't.

From the kitchen window, she hears the first shriek of a screech owl. It is synchronized almost perfectly with the last drippings of sunlight flushing down the horizon. It's the kind of sound that gets under one's spine and travels. Willy always said the sound of a screech owl meant a death had happened. He said he heard one the night Aunt Virgie and Uncle Price went to the church supper.

It was hot that night. Lacey was twelve and she lay spread eagle in her bed in nothing but her gym shorts and a tank top, the covers and spread kicked to the end of the bed, the air so thick she felt wrapped and tangled in it. She was reading *Love Story*, having recently found it on the shelf in Willy's room, surely having been left behind by her mother, just like everything and everyone. She and Willy had expected to go to the supper that night, but one of the heifers looked to be coming down with scours. In the heat wave, it was likely to pass through the barn quickly and Willy had called on Doc Asher earlier that night to have a look and get ahead of an outbreak.

Willy had the big old attic fan whirling, but the air it sucked into the house was thick and steamy and offered little relief. It had been unusually hot the last week and a half, so hot in fact, that the cattle wouldn't eat. They just stood flank-deep in the stream, pawing the water and swishing their tails at the horseflies. Flies buzzed through the house, tinging against the screens as if their wings were on fire. The refrigerator hadn't stopped running, but the engine had worn itself down to a sort of grinding sound that suggested a certain lack of efficiency. The whole house seemed to hold its own hot breath in against itself, waiting for a breeze.

Lacey was three quarters through the book and had never seen *fuck* in print so many times. It was glorious, the way it could bounce off the pages so fast that it began to feel like a normal everyday kind of word. She practiced in the sticky dark, inserting it in the middle of sentences as if it meant nothing. *So fucking nice to see you again. How fucking are you? Where the fuck is the sugar bowl? Pass the fucking salt. Nice fucking weather.* She liked the *feel* of the word, the way it started so soft and ended so abruptly and the way in which delivery meant everything. If you said it gently, as if you hardly noticed you had said it, as if it was just another word, it had twice the power as when it came out of your mouth with a slam. It was just that kind of word. She was going to conquer it, own it in the same way Ali McGraw had in the movie. It was the word that would tell the world not to tangle with her, that she could hold her own for she would deliver profanity with a kind of grace and defiance that would surely endear her to preppy boys from all corners of the county.

The heat continued to stick in the same relentless way it had all day and as she read, she kept flipping her pillow, searching for a cool spot. Earlier that afternoon, after a futile effort to cool off in the lukewarm pond, she had tried to ride her bicycle into town, but the front tire had popped on the hot asphalt and she had to walk her bike the rest of the way.

In town she stopped to see Uncle Price and ask if he could fix the flat. He sent her upstairs to Auntie while he worked on it. Auntie had stuffed a ham for the church supper that night and was trying to figure out how to get it in the refrigerator. Ruffles of green kale stuffing ran round the ham and a syrupy sweet sauce sloshed in the bottom of the pan.

No matter what she moved or rearranged in the refrigerator, Auntie could not seem to find a place for that ham. Finally, she covered it with baking foil and left it to sit on the counter. Beauford, their old collie, eyed the platter from where he lay stretched out on the linoleum, but the heat kept him weighted to the floor.

"It'll have to do," Virgie said with a heave of her chest before popping open the snaps on her housecoat and heading for the back bedroom. She motioned Lacey to follow. "Come and keep me company, darlin'." Another fan whirred in the bedroom window, but the air it caught came from the asphalt roof a floor below so that it was hotter still and filled with dust. Lacey flopped back on the bed and pulled her shirt up to just below her new breasts (or what were almost breasts).

Virgie turned her back to Lacey and let her housecoat slide down her arms. Her back was wide and her skin rolled and folded on itself. Lacey watched her back rise with her breathing. Aunt Virgie had what they called *angina*, which Lacey was made to understand simply meant that she some-times thought she was having a heart attack, but she wasn't. Sometimes she would stand still, put her hand open-palmed on her chest, and take a particularly deep and steady breath that almost looked like it was hurting coming into her lungs. She did that now, claiming the air was too damn heavy to breathe.

Lacey ran her hands over the nubby summer spread. It was light cotton, cream colored with a crocheted hem that she knew her mother had made. "Where do you think Momma really went?" she asked.

"Lord, child, I am too hot for this constant conversation."

It was a strange thing to say because Lacey couldn't remember ever having asked before.

"Do I have any people? I mean, I have you and Uncle Price and Clint and Lyle—and Willy, I guess. But what about Momma's other people?"

"Why do you need other people when you got us?"

"Come on, Auntie. What about my Momma's mother? Or her father?"

"I told you, her people come from down around Ocracoke. They were water people, but there ain't none of 'em left to speak of. My brother, that would be—he would be your—he was May's daddy, so he would be your grandpa, well he wasn't much good, Lacey." She picked up a bottle of Jean Nate and spritzed herself several times around her neck and over her shoulders so the scent fell heavily along her back and left a slick sheen.

"And Ruth, God rest her soul, that was my sister-in-law and the mother of your momma, she was an angel on earth, but a sickness took her when your momma was only about thirteen years old, about your age. Duane got bad after that. Without Ruthie loving him, he just didn't seem to believe he had any reason to be good, I suppose."

"What do you mean?"

"He drank too much, Lacey. There was an accident and he drowned. That was a long time ago."

Lacey sat up a bit, propped herself on her elbows. "What happened?"

"No one really knows for sure. That was some time ago, Lacey. He'd been missing for a while, from what we knew, then he just washed up on the shores of Kill Devil Hills."

"That's sad." Lacey flopped back down on the bed, flapped her shirt, pulled it open at the neck, and blew down the collar. "Where's my father?"

"You keep asking me and I keep telling you. Willy is your daddy."

"My real father." But they had been over this a million times and it always circled right back to Virgie telling her that she had a daddy and it was Willy and he was a fine man and why the heck did she need another one. Lacey knew the routine and wasn't up for another round.

"Did Momma love Willy?" she asked.

"Damn silly question."

"It's not."

"Of course she loved him." She picked up the talcum powder and dumped it across her chest so it sifted down the gully between her breasts and fell to the floor. "Woman can love more than one man, you know."

Lacey thought it was the heat at first, thought that maybe the sounds weren't moving properly through the thick air. "What?"

"You kind of love 'em in different ways, is all." She set the powder down on the nightstand and pulled a lime green shift from the hanger. "One might be a good kind of love, you see, and one might be a not so good kind. But when you're in it, well, it's hard to tell one from the other—right from wrong."

Lacey felt suddenly sick, like the heat had soured the contents of her belly. She sat up to the edge of the bed. "Which kind was I?" Lacey asked quietly, asking so quietly, as if maybe she didn't want to be heard at all.

"Oh, baby," said Aunt Virgie, lifting each breast one at a time into the cups of a massive white brassiere. "You were always the right kind. Your momma had a heap of troubles such as you can't imagine. But she always loved you best of anything—always loved you best."

But it still made no sense to Lacey, how she could be loved best and left.

Late that night, in between practicing her curses and wishing for a breeze, she thought of May. She thought of her mother, wondered what she had thought of *Love Story*. If it meant anything to her, anything at all, if love really did mean *never having to say you're sorry*, because that just couldn't be true. Lacey knew she and Willy were owed an apology. And when she puzzled over what Virgie had said, she couldn't help but wonder what kind of love could be so bad, seeing as she was soaking up every kind she could get.

Eventually, the curses she practiced lulled her into a restless sleep so that while she never heard the screech owl, she remembered tossing and turning through the night.

Willy heard it. He said it was nearly dawn and that it woke him from a sound sleep.

The food poisoning was traced to the ham. Seemed like half the town was hospitalized by morning. Everyone seemed to recover in a few days, except for Aunt Virgie. Her heart couldn't take the strain and she passed that very night. Uncle Price was getting better, or so they thought, but five days later, with Aunt Virgie barely in the ground, he had a stroke in his bed and he was gone.

He was buried next to Aunt Virgie, and as they left the graveyard, Lacey remembers looking back at the two mounds of dirt, side by side, the dirt on Uncle Price's side being slightly darker, moister than the dirt on Aunt Virgie's side that mounded in the same way but was dry and bore a long crack in it. It seemed right that they should be together, but it didn't seem fair to her and Willy. Lacey remembers Willy putting his arm around her as she tucked her head under his chin. As if he knew just what she was thinking, she heard him say softly, "We're gonna be just fine."

Price's Hardware became the property of the nephews Lyle and Clint and they were bound and determined to do right by it. They changed only one thing and that was the name. Price's Hardware became known as Price-*less* Hardware and all the town believed Uncle Price would have found the humor in that.

Old Jenny is tossing her third butt into the river and will probably head for the bar. Log has pulled the tarp over his cabin and tried unsuccessfully to coax his cat from under a shrub.

Lacey watches as the screech owl swoops down over the water, dipping its talons and then lifting upward again, but now with a small wiggling snake in its grasp. It flies to a piling and proceeds to shred its writhing dinner. Log's cat bursts out from under the shrub and streaks across the lawn, past Log's ankles, hungry for the safety of his cottage.

CHAPTER 10

Phone Calls to Home

The next morning, Lacey wakes. That she has slept surprises and confounds her. Even makes her feel a little guilty. But the sleep was deep and dreamless, and for that she is grateful. She goes to the kitchen and calls Mac at the hospital, the phone wedged between her ear and shoulder, the cord trailing her around the small kitchen as she makes her coffee.

He tells her Franny and her husband, Duffy, had come by the hospital the night before and brought Tasha some *Highlights* magazines, and a neighbor of Willy's is rumored to have brought a giant stuffed bear twice the size of Tasha to the house.

"Willy won't bring it to the hospital," he says. "Says it's so big it would have to ride in the passenger seat, and he'd look like a damn fool driving around with it in his truck."

"What neighbor?"

"Hmmm, Carlotta *something*."

Lacey has no idea who the neighbor is, never heard of her. She asks to talk to Tasha and Mac tells her she is eating her breakfast. Lacey says never mind—let her eat. The eating, that's a good thing, and they both agree.

The doctors haven't been in yet, but he expects them soon—and yes, he read *My Father's Dragon*. He shares this last bit with a self-deprecating laugh, as if he has admitted to a small defeat. They will go to the playroom once the team has come by, and he wants Lacey to know he can stay another night if need be but has to get on the road early. Kat will be missing her first day back at school as it is.

Again, Lacey finds herself grateful—and guilty, of something.

She assures him she will be back that evening, as soon as she meets with David to work out her classes. She's waiting to hear back from him but hopes to see him earlier today rather than later. She will keep Mac posted. Hugs and kisses to Tasha.

She throws on a long skirt, flip-flops, and a light cotton sweater that is stretched too much and falls low on her hips, pours a cup of coffee, noting the lift in her own mood, and steps out through the screened porch to settle herself on the stoop and gaze out to the river. Log's cat scrambles out from under the crawlspace, stops and sits to lick his front paws, and ignores her completely. She is certain he shits under her cottage. Sometimes she can smell it.

A massive great blue heron stands stock-still in the shallows. They nest together in the tallest trees at night, calling one another home, but in the morning they disperse and she never sees more than one at a time in the water. Slowly, it lifts a leg, one and then the other, a ripple-less wade of a few feet, its head lowering slowly as if to avoid making a shadow over the water.

The cat trots off behind the cottage and reappears a moment later, weaving in and out of Log's thick legs as he heads to his boat. He stops to say good morning, telling her he has heard about Tasha. He's damn broke up about it, he says. A large sloshing bucket, likely full of minnows, hangs by his side.

Lacey nods, thanks him, tells him she is sure everything will be okay. A wet breeze shimmies down her shoulders as the cat wanders from Log's ankles to dance in a figure eight in front of her.

"How you holding up, Mama?" he says. He always calls her that.

"Okay," she says, because what else can she say. "We're okay."

They are quiet for a moment, both watching the heron without saying so. They both hold their breath as the monstrous slate-blue bird lifts each leg without a ripple and dips it back into the water. It doesn't make a splash when its beak slices through the surface of the water and comes up with a wiggling sliver of silver fish. It never ceases to amaze Lacey—the grace and athleticism that comes with a small death. When it rises up into the air, they can hear the power of the wind being sucked and pushed beneath its wings.

"How long you here?"

"I'm heading back tonight," she says. They both track the flight of the heron across the water.

"How's the fishing?"

"Perch is good. Got a nice rock last week—thirty-five pounds—good for spring. Crappie should be in soon." He nods to the bucket of minnows at his side. "We'll see."

She nods.

"If I get another good rock, I'll save you some."

"That would be nice," she says. "Not sure how often I'll be back."

"It'll keep good in my freezer." He keeps a large freezer chest on his screened porch. In the dead heat of summer, she can sometimes hear it hum and shift to a groan as the day heats up.

"Okay, Mama," he says, a little awkwardly. "You take care of yourself and the girl. I'm gonna say a prayer for you both."

This last part surprises her, but she thanks him with a smile, not sure what else to say. He heads down to his boat and she watches the bulk of him, the wideness of his steps next to the delicate prance of his cat, tail high as he moves down the dock. Once Log starts the boat up, the cat will jump from boat to dock and retreat into the shade, stretched out on his belly with his paws long in front of him to await his return.

She is snagged on his offer to pray. Others have offered prayers as well. Franny in particular. Franny, having converted wholeheartedly to Catholicism once she married Duffy, lights candles for Tasha. She actually buys prayers in her church. Seems you can buy cards that can be exchanged for prayers, like a coupon, Lacey thinks now.

While she doesn't mean to spurn a prayer and she knows it's a kindness being offered, the very idea of prayer has a kind of helpless and hopeless feeling to it. Lacey thinks of prayer as a last resort, and she doesn't want to be in that place, a place where the only thing left is a plea to God. There is a helplessness to prayer that she cannot reconcile. And so, watching Log's boat rip out to the mouth of the bay, she says a prayer of her own: *God—I'm just not yet ready to call on You. I'm still trying to work this out on my own—and please don't stick Your nose in this until we really need You. So far we're hanging in there. Just don't go making any big decisions up there about what's going on down here. You can go take care of whatever other issues are cooking up—war and famine, that kind of thing, and I'll be sure to let You know when we need a consult. Thank You very much for Your time.*

It can't be said that she doesn't believe in God. She does. She just doesn't trust Him.

CHAPTER 11

The Neighbors

By the time David finally calls, Lacey has cleaned the cottage top to bottom, even wiping down the bookshelves and changing the bedsheets on both her own bed and Tasha's. She recovered a pair of slippers tangled in her daughter's quilt as well as an open felt-tip marker that had bloomed purple against the sheet. She dug out puzzle books and a favorite paisley smock of Tasha's, some long- and short-sleeved T-shirts, and reached for a cluster of Tasha's headbands and hair clips before realizing her mistake in that regard. She has packed everything in her already overburdened bag and set it by the door.

Still waiting, she begins cutting back the herbs and watering the now nearly balded pots in the hopes that something might flourish again when the phone finally rings. David can see her in an hour. Will that work?

She had planned to stop at the pediatrician's to pick up some paperwork and she wanted to find Old Jenny and get a few crab traps from her for Priceless Hardware. Lyle and Clint had stopped by the hospital the week before and while Tasha slept, they had gotten to talking about possibly selling them in the store. Clint, a little thicker in the jawline than his twin, had perched awkwardly on the windowsill, the bulk of him blocking the light, but Lyle, owing to some back surgery, had paced the floor in front of him. Lyle was explaining the changes over the years, the reasons Clint needed to *get with the program*.

Clint was hunkered down in the window, scowling, but admitted that

Lyle had been right all along. Yup, Lyle had a better sense for change, to be sure, but maybe was going too far with the crab traps.

Their customers these days wanted things they had never sold before, Lyle explained. They were different these days, unlike the farmers they had serviced for so many years. Retirees and young families with boats and fancy dressage horses. They had slate walks and bluestone patios, fancy shrubs to tend to, and needed to find ways to take care of their lush lawns while they boated on weekends down around Annapolis or traveled to the ocean for the summers. He and Clint had argued over the opening of the garden center section of the store but in the end, Lyle had persisted and Clint had grudgingly gone along, only to find that the garden center was a huge and growing success.

"Crab traps—jeez," Clint had said again. "Next thing you know, we'll be selling bait." But he had to admit that the garden center had been the right thing. He wanted to put his foot down at the selling of lawn ornaments, but Lyle had won that argument as well and so now a small section was devoted to bird baths, concrete rabbits, and painted gnomes. "Damnedest things, those little trolls."

"They sell," Lyle said. And that, for the moment, had settled it.

All three crab traps are not fitting in the back of Lacey's car, so Jenny uses her gnarled fingers and a pair of needle-nose pliers to break them down a bit and show Lacey how to put them back together again.

"Jesus, Jenny. You only want two-fifty apiece for them?"

"Half dollar more'n I'm gettin' here."

"You're kidding. How many can you make in an hour?"

"Not quite four. No taxes." She coughs hard so that it rattles in her throat and then she spits on the graveled lot. "Beats working at Taco Bell."

Lacey has to concede that point. "I'm giving you ten apiece." Lyle and Clint would still consider it a deal. They'd sell them for thirty dollars apiece.

She watches Jenny stuff the money down her bra. "Heard about your little girl."

"Yeah, well."

"Got a good doctor?"

"I think so."

"Had me some cancer once. The woman's kind. Get a good doctor."

"She has a lot of doctors. I think they're all good."

"They can cure everything but stupidity these days." Old Jenny slips her needle-nose pliers into her back pocket and pulls her cigarettes from her front one. It's a new pack and she slams it twice against the heel of her hand before opening it. "Gonna get me a beer and shot of Jack." She nods toward the bar. "Care to join me?"

"I've got errands to run, and then I need to get back north."

Old Jenny nods again and clears her throat before wandering into Bailey's, just as Cade is coming out the door.

"A little early for you, hmm?" Lacey says.

"What? Oh, no." He smiles sheepishly, looking back over his shoulder at the bar. "Just paying the rent. How's Tasha doing?" He is wearing a red T-shirt, ripped at the collar so that one freckled shoulder is visible. His skin is slightly pink with sunburn. His hair is a color that suggests he might have spent time as a redhead when he was little.

"She's mostly bored, you know. And tired." She doesn't know what to say, doesn't know how it's going, given that Tasha seems worse, but Lacey was told to expect that. "It's rough, but we're getting through it. I'm trying to make arrangements for my classes and—well, you know. This is all a mess."

He kicks at the gravel with his tennis shoe and sends a piece of oyster shell sailing across the lot. He has freckled knees, too. He is wearing what Tasha and Lacey know to be his favorite cap, if only because he is never without it, a pine-green baseball cap with a small logo of a dancing bear with a lacrosse stick. "David told me about it. The guys were upset to hear about it, too." He nods to the cottage Jonny, Kane, and Marcus share. "Hey, I've got something for her," he says. "Didn't know when I was going to see you, but I was going to try and mail it to the hospital. I'll bring it by tonight."

"That's sweet, Cade. But actually, I'm hoping to get on the road after I meet with David."

"Right—your classes. David's been working on that." He starts to say something more but stops.

Lacey is aware that David is a huge lacrosse enthusiast, hardly misses a practice let alone a game, but she is surprised to think David has discussed Lacey's classes with Cade.

"If you've got a minute?" He starts walking toward his cottage. "I've got it on my kitchen table."

"Sure." They walk over to his cottage together. He smells like grass and sweat and a little bit like the beer he said he didn't have a minute earlier. Though squarely in the middle of his forties, he could pass for a student in his gym shorts and baseball cap.

When he steps inside his cottage, Lacey waits outside. These cottages are so tiny and she is self-conscious about cramming her way into the kitchen with him.

He comes out with another cap, complete with dancing bear lacrosse logo, just like his, but pink.

"Oh my gosh, she'll love it!"

"I hope it's not too big." He is clearly pleased that Lacey likes it and he smiles one of those big preppy smiles, the kind she used to be afraid of when she was a teenager.

Lacey reaches out her hand to take it when he turns it over and shows her that the entire inside of the cap is filled with signatures and get-well messages from the lacrosse team.

"The whole team signed it," he says. "We were up in New York for a game and one of the guys saw it in a bookstore. It was their idea, really."

"I don't know what to say—"

"We miss her. Jonny and Kane and Marcus." He hefts a shoulder toward their cottage. "They don't have anybody knocking on their door anymore to return stray balls. And the guys are missing their biggest fan at practice."

Tasha used to spend time watching the guys at practice in the afternoon while Lacey ran on the track. She'd sit with the trainer and hand out paper cups of water and run around collecting stray balls. But still, Lacey never imagined they would notice her absence.

"Really, Cade, this is so thoughtful."

Suddenly she finds herself on the edge of a crying jag. "It's very sweet," she says, then sucks in her breath and holds it, holding everything.

A hand comes down on her shoulder.

"You okay?" He leans down and looks into her face.

"We're fine, we're going to be fine."

"I know that," he says. "But are you okay—right now?"

She can't answer him. The floodgates are building and she can't risk it.

"Really, you shouldn't drive right now."

"I'm okay," she finally manages. "Really."

He draws her in for a very gentle hug that is all too short and ends with his hand running over her shoulder and a small pat that tells her it is time to buck up and go back to taking care of business.

"I'll walk you to your car," he says. He puts an arm around her shoulders and walks with her, their feet crunching and popping across the oyster-shell lot. "I'll take care of your paper and mail while you're away," he says. "I'd like to help—with anything, whatever you need."

"Sure. That'd be great. You don't need a key. I never lock it," and suddenly she is struck by her own carelessness. *I live behind a bar*, she thinks, *for God's sake*.

"Take care. Drive safe," he says at her open window. "Seriously, the last thing Tasha needs right now is for you to get hurt because you're tired and distracted." When he leans in her window, she notices the way in which his brows and lashes have lightened from the sun, just as they do every spring, from hours spent on the lacrosse field.

Lacey buckles her seat belt. "I'm just going to run errands. I still have to meet with David," she says. "I'll be fine. And thanks for the hat."

She parks in front of Potomac Hall and heads up to David's office. The door is open, and he sits mired behind a pile of papers. Stacks of papers and folders stand in precarious piles ready to topple on the floor. The windows are closed, probably because the slightest breeze would whip the whole place into a whirlwind of papers.

"Lacey! Good to see you." He pushes his glasses back up his nose and stands to tuck in his shirt. "Come in, come in." He motions to a leather chair covered in books and CDs. Lacey wonders if he actually expects her to sit on top of everything, but she scoops them up and turns to look for a place to set them back down. There is a two-foot-tall stack of papers on the floor beside the chair. In spite of email communication, David has always been one to print everything, even the papers his students submit electronically. He has a need, he once said, to touch the printed page.

"Here," he says, sliding more paperwork from the corner of his desk to create a small space that might or might not be room enough for everything.

They spend a few minutes discussing Tasha. David wonders how Mac is holding up. Mac and David are friends, and yet it sounds to Lacey as if they haven't spoken since all of this began. It surprises her some, but then, it is her observation that men don't discuss these things as easily as women do. She suggests he give Mac a call. He could use a friend right now.

David has been her department head for three years now, replacing Dr. Craylee, who Lacey had always both admired and respected, but who had decided for whatever reason to step aside as head and focus on only a class or two per semester. It was a surprise to Lacey when David was made department head, not because he was inept in any way, but because it came so suddenly. He's only nearing forty, but like Lacey, he had come in fresh out of grad school and their friendship, their shared complaints about faculty and enrollment and the arrogance of undergrads, had aligned them in a way that she feared his new position might change the balance of. It had, but just a bit. Underneath it all there is still a friendship that she values.

Still, she is anxious. An extended leave in the middle of the semester is always a problem, and she is not tenured yet. She worries that this is not something that will be overlooked in the future.

"Well, now," he says, tapping his fingers together. "I think we've worked something out for you." He smiles, but it is a weak smile, a smile that suggests he is going to feed this to her in pieces. "I'm going to take your Construction of Modern Poetry class and your freshman English. I can teach that with my eyes closed."

"Oh, David, that's great. Thank you." She is relieved. She digs in her briefcase and pulls out the syllabus for her poetry class, but he waves it away. He has it in his electronic files, has printed it already, he tells her.

Not a problem. Of course, he does. She knows that, but something about handing off the hard copy would have been satisfying. He reminds her that he has taught it before. It stings a little, but she doesn't acknowledge it. Though he notices the look on her face and shifts gears.

"You'll get through this," he says kindly.

She nods, but not necessarily in agreement. "It's some shit," she says.

He sighs, *Yes, yes, it is.*

"My American Lit class?"

"That," he says, "is proving to be a little more difficult." There is a ding from his computer and he swivels to it and begins to peck away at the keyboard. "Give me a minute—sorry—just a second."

She listens to the tap of the keys, the squeak of his chair when he swivels back to her.

"Okay," he says, his full attention back on her again. "We do actually happen to have someone on the faculty who may be qualified—it's not a perfect solution, but with only eight weeks left in the semester . . ."

"Who is it, David? Who will take my class?"

"It wasn't easy to find someone qualified. In fact, it wasn't easy to find someone whose schedule would work with your class schedule, either. But I think we've come up with a reasonable solution. Of course, you'll need to maintain contact with him. You'll need to meet as soon as possible."

"David, who did you find?" She is hoping it is Dr. Craylee. That would be the most logical choice. Surely, he has the time to pick up her class. American Lit would be a no-brainer for him.

"And he'll work from your syllabus, of course."

"David."

"Mind you, it's not a perfect solution, but it's a solution of sorts."

"Damn it, David—"

"Cade Clipper."

Lacey would later swear he flinched when he said it. "Cade Clipper—our lacrosse coach? Are you out of your mind? What the hell does he know about American Lit, David? This is a joke, right?" She sits back in her chair with such force that the tower of papers at her side flutters and paper wafts down to the floor. "He's a lacrosse coach."

"He has his master's in English," he offers, almost pathetically.

"I know, I know that," says Lacey. "But he's a lacrosse coach!" Lacey knows Cade's academic credentials. He was working on his master's in English at the University of Maryland and also as an assistant coach for their Division I lacrosse team, which just happened to take the championship two years in a row. Once he finished his graduate work, he was reluctant to give up the coaching and finally embraced it when he was offered the position at Southern Maryland College running their Division II men's lacrosse team. He was coming up on his third year and already he had built a hell of a team. Still, that didn't mean he could teach.

"He was a TA at Maryland when he got his master's," David offers.

"Oh, well that changes everything," she says sarcastically.

David leans back in his chair. "No, Lacey. It is not ideal. But it is a workable solution." He pushes his glasses up his nose and then threads his fingers in finality. "We can make this work. And as for the two independent studies you're directing, I'm assuming much of that can be handled by email?"

"Of course," she says. "And I'll try to make a few trips back."

They sit in silence for a moment. "Craylee has some health issues right now, if that's what you were thinking," says David.

This admission startles her. It hadn't occurred to her that anyone else in the world was sick besides Tasha and she feels chastised. All she can say is "Oh, I didn't know."

"Of course not. I'm telling you this in confidence. I tried. He just can't."

"I didn't know. I'm sorry," she says again. She looks around the office, hoping to find an answer hidden among the piles of papers, the stacks of notebooks, the volumes on the shelves. "I'm fond of him. I hope he will be okay."

"He won't," says David, shaking his head gently. "It's dementia, likely Alzheimer's. He came to me privately. He wants to finish the semester but I'm not sure that is workable, either."

A Frisbee crashes into the window behind him, and they both startle in their chairs.

"Shit," says Lacey, not sure if she is referring to Craylee or the slam of the Frisbee.

"He's struggling with his one class. I've had a complaint recently and may have to take over his class as well."

"Wow—he is a bit of a Mr. Magoo, but I never thought . . ."

David scowls, not so much at her, she hopes, but at the situation.

Leaving the office, she turns and asks, "David, when was Cade informed of this?"

"We talked a few days ago. He's looking forward to it. Be sure to send him your notes and syllabus, Lacey. Then get back to Tasha. We will manage here."

She has been sitting in her car in the parking lot for too long. There is a numbness in her head that she is almost getting used to until she finds that she has allowed time to pass—the sun has moved, the wind has shifted, the engine has ground down—and she has no idea how much of it she has lost.

From her car she uses her cell phone to call Mac at the hospital. He doesn't answer and she leaves a message. *Call me. I may not make it tonight.*

Another Frisbee whirls past her windshield as she shifts into reverse. She waits. It has landed a few feet from her car, somewhere, and she doesn't want to run over it. Five shirtless boys swarm down the embankment and move around her car as if it is not running, as if it is not running and sticking three quarters out from a parking slot. She waits with both hands on the steering wheel. The boy with his gym shorts hanging lowest on his hips and a wide red strip of red boxer fabric blooming at his backside lets out a loud hoot, stoops to retrieve the Frisbee, looks into the distance, and whips the disc in a graceful swoop, coming up on his front leg like a dancer, before pumping his fist in the air.

They move on, shirtless boys without a care in the world. But just as she has pulled out in reverse and is shifting into gear to move forward, her phone rings on the seat beside her.

Mac tells her everything is fine, just fine.

"What does that mean—fine?" She doesn't mean to sound irritated, but she is. *Fine*, what is that? She's not fine. "What did the doctors say this morning?"

"They just said everything is as they expected. Everything is okay, Lacey, and she's tired now, but she had a good morning."

She is frustrated. He isn't paying attention, doesn't know what questions to ask. She needs to be there. But she knows she cannot explain this to him.

He goes on to say that Willy will stay with Tasha tonight. Mac is going to stay at the farm with Kat and they'll be leaving the next day. Lacey is not sure if this is a good idea or not but she doesn't say so. He and Kat will come by the hospital mid-morning to say goodbye. He'll be back in a week. She listens to all of this and can only think of how little control she has over everything. She wishes she could clone herself and be everywhere at once.

"I'll leave first thing in the morning," she says, "but I may miss you. Are you sure Willy is okay to stay the night with her?"

He insists Willy is fine with it, and besides, he doesn't think that Willy really feels comfortable in the house with Kat.

This, she is sure, is true. Kat slinks around the house like a ferret. Lacey knows it makes Willy nervous. He goes on to tell her that he—of course—wants to come back as often as possible but can't neglect Kat and his every-other-weekend custody arrangement. It's complicated, he tells her, but she can count on him.

She is struck suddenly by how hard this has been for Mac, too. How hard it has been the last week to balance Kat and Willy and, of course, Tasha.

"Thanks, Mac," she says.

"For what?"

"For everything. For being there for her."

"She's my daughter, too, Lacey."

He may have been angry when he said it. She couldn't be sure.

"I know, but—"

"No, you don't," he snaps back at her.

Yes, he is definitely angry, and she isn't prepared for it. Two bicycles zip in front of her and though she hasn't moved, she is startled by it and hits her horn. They are too close, everything is swarming around her, and then to have Mac snapping in her ear . . .

"You just don't get it," he is saying. "She's my daughter, Lacey. I love her. I am not going to tuck my tail and run."

She almost reminds him that he had already done that once, but at that moment it dawns on her that seeing as she doesn't want him back, it wouldn't be fair to punish him for leaving in the first place.

"Don't snap at me, Mac."

"Damn it, Lacey. You always act like you're in everything all by yourself. You don't have to lean on me. God knows, you don't have to lean on anybody. Suit yourself in that regard. But don't for one second think I wouldn't be here for Tasha."

"I get it, Mac." And she does. She understands. He isn't getting in the trenches for her. He is there for Tasha—as it should be.

"It's not about you anymore, Lacey. It hasn't been for a long time. I have two daughters to raise and that's all I'm trying to do."

He isn't angry anymore. She knows he is just trying to tell her what she should have understood all along.

"You're a good father, Mac."

"I know," he says. "And you're a good mother."

They are quiet for a moment and she thinks maybe the call has been dropped. "Mac? You still there?"

"I'm here," he says.

"I'm sorry, Mac," she says. "I'm really sorry. I'm sorry for everything. I'm sorry I'm not there, and I'm sorry she's sick." Her throat tightens and her voice comes out small and squeezed. "I'm just so sorry, Mac. I'm sorry I let her get sick and—"

"Lacey, *stop*," he says.

"And I'm sorry I didn't love you enough."

He is quiet for a moment and she searches the glove compartment for a tissue because her nose is running.

"That's okay, Lacey. I'm okay."

CHAPTER 12

Another Night

When she gets back to the cottage, she grudgingly pulls together all of her notes, books, and paperwork for Cade. She feels foolish about their talk earlier while all along he had known he was taking over her class.

He is still at lacrosse practice, and she sits on the back steps and thinks about how she will approach this with him. There's something about having the lacrosse coach take over her classes that trivializes what she does. She takes her classes seriously, even when her students don't.

It is well after dark when he comes home. She has just eaten a peanut butter sandwich but the milk was soured and so she is washing the peanut butter down with water when she hears his screen door slam. She gathers the things she has prepared for him and by the time she comes out the door, Springsteen is blasting from his cottage.

He comes to the door, surprised to see her.

"I thought you had headed back up north." There are dark crescents of sweat under his arms and the neck of his T-shirt is puckered, loose threads trailing.

"Obviously, you and I have some things to discuss." She hates the iciness in her voice, but it creeps in regardless of her intentions. "*Moby Dick*," she says holding out the tome for him to take.

"Hmmm?" He takes it from her and pretends to drop it, hefts it again and flips it in his hand to look at the cover.

"We're wrapping up *Moby Dick* right now in my American Lit class."

"Great, I loved *Moby Dick*."

"You're lying," she says, and she can't help but smile. "No one likes *Moby Dick*."

He looks at her for just a moment, maybe to see if she is serious. "No," he finally says. "I did. The whale is cool."

"And wait till you get to *The Scarlet Letter*. That pisses all of them off."

"Looking forward to it."

"You'll have to undo everything they learned about it in high school."

"Noted." He moves to the side and sweeps his free arm to usher her in.

The cottage is just like hers, in reverse. A small kitchen she walks through, the same too-small sink, lack of counter space, a tiny metal table for two pushed up against the wall, a pile of clipboards stacked on it. In the living room there is a dark sofa, maybe faux suede, too large for the room, wrapping along two walls. A tangle of laundry sits in a heap at one end of it. He drops *Moby Dick* on a narrow stone coffee table and scoops the laundry in his arms, heading with it to one of the two small bedrooms.

"Sorry," he says. A sock sifts from his arms to the floor at the threshold to his bedroom and he catches it on the toe of his shoe to kick it into the room. She can see that the bed is unmade as he dumps the clothes on it and comes back into the main room, shutting the door behind him.

She hadn't thought to ask him if this is a good time and while she realizes she has caught him unaware, she still isn't asking. He turns down the music so Springsteen is only a whisper.

"Look, Cade. I don't mean to be pissy about this. I appreciate that you are willing to do this, but . . ." She drops a pile of papers and a stack of paperbacks to the coffee table, puts her hand on her hip. She shakes her head, drops her chin, takes a breath, and looks back up at him. "Do you know what you're doing? Do you know how to teach this stuff? Do you know the works? Have you read *any* of it?" She notices now, without his cap on, the start of balding above his temples, the very slightly receding hairline carving out two pale half-moons of scalp usually protected by his cap.

He doesn't say anything, walks over to the table, and picks up the first book.

"Yup," he says. He has Brown's *The Power of Sympathy* in his hands.

"Actually, we've finished that already. Like I said, *Moby Dick*. I gave them all of spring break to get through it. Most of them will try and bluff their way through it anyway."

He bends down and picks up a slim paperback, *The Old Man and the Sea*.

"The class is broad, an overview, I favor the shorter works when I can. *The Scarlet Letter* is next because . . ."

He cuts her off. "Because Melville dedicated *Moby Dick; or The Whale*," using the original longer title, "to Hawthorne."

"Right," she says, not impressed. "They can read it quickly. Then *The Jungle*, then Cather, Hemingway, Hurston . . ."

"Got it." He puts his hand up.

"Is this a good time?" she finally asks.

"Works for me. Have a seat."

The huge sofa, she knows, is too soft and deep, and she tries to perch on the end of it but fails, almost tumbling back into it. "This damn bachelor's sofa of yours." She scoots up to the edge of it, pulls a hair-tie from her wrist, and wrangles her hair back into a mop of a ponytail. She begins flipping through her notes that she will be leaving with him. "I emailed you and I also made copies of everything," she says. "So call me any time to review."

She gives him a quick overview of what has been taught thus far, the connections she is trying to make between the works, the historical signif-icance of each. And there are handouts, excerpts from important works that, while she would like to assign the whole book, she realizes they won't be read. When she began teaching years earlier, she had been optimistic and had failed to realize that most students didn't read the way she did, as quickly, as voraciously. It was a hard-learned lesson with three quarters of the class muddling through on a cursory read at best, and so now she has resigned herself to supplementing with handouts because there are works she just can't entirely skip, *Native Son*, *Invisible Man*, and short stories that rocked her as a teenager, Shirley Jackson, Flannery O'Connor, Bradbury.

Cade sits on a wing of the sofa, his knees close but not touching hers, sifting through her handwritten notes, flipping over the pile of books. He's actually looking forward to this, to all of it, he tells her, to reread-ing the works and immersing himself in some of his favorites.

She is somewhat familiar with his bookshelf, as they have exchanged favorites over the years. She squints now to see the titles but fails to make out anything more than *Gray's Anatomy*, some Grisham titles, and possibly, maybe, *War and Peace*. He sees her looking and smiles. "Check it out, if you want," he says with a small, surrendered laugh. "You know I have very eclectic taste."

This is true. She knows he is a huge Denis Johnson fan, as he had presented her with a signed paperback copy of *Train Dreams* at Christmas, joking that he bought it off of eBay and there was every possibility it was a forgery. But he also loves everything Harry Potter–ish and claimed to have bonded with the red-headed Ron. She had once teased him about the Grisham titles. But evened the score by telling him she still had *Love Story* on her shelf.

He nods to the shelf, inviting her again to take a look. He knows she can't resist scanning a bookshelf, even one she has perused before. She gets up self-consciously, pulls her T-shirt down over the waistband of her skirt, and walks to the shelf, leans in, and—sandwiched between Jones's *The Known World* and *Harry Potter and the Sorcerer's Stone*—spies *Billy Lynn's Long Halftime Walk*. She puts her index finger to the tip of the spine, pulls it out.

"Great book," he says. "You can borrow it if you want."

She flips to the inside jacket flap. She has it on her shelf, she is certain, but has not read it yet. There are always books she is meaning to get to.

"Here's the thing," she tells him now, sliding the book back into its place on the shelf. "They will always begin by telling you if they *liked* it. And the rule in my class is that I don't give a damn if they *like* it. Like it— hate it. None of that matters. In fact, I begin the semester by telling them I don't even want to hear whether or not they like it. These are historical documents that track the sentiment of our nation, challenge what was status quo, and ask questions that deserved answering. I'm much more invested in how the works make them *think*."

Cade nods in agreement. He gets it, he says. And still, she is certain now, he will screw this up. But if she stays in touch and coaches him along the way, there's a chance, albeit a slim one, that he can muddle through this.

It is after eleven when she gets up to leave.

In his kitchen she reminds him of his promise to stay in touch, and he says of course, not to worry. As she hefts her now-lighter briefcase over her shoulder and steps out to the lawn, he comes out behind her, moves up beside her, saying he has some equipment to get from his car and he will walk with her. The patchy lawn between their cottages has been recently cut and blades of grass feather to her feet and tangle in her flip-flops and toes.

At her door he reaches out and draws her into a hug, their second of the day, and she allows herself to relax into it, breathe deeply the still sweaty scent of him, feel the draw of his scrubby day's beard along her cheek. She catches herself thinking how long it has been since she has felt a man's arms around her for anything more than a cheery hello or a friendly goodbye.

Once inside, she kicks off her shoes and looks around for any last-minute items she might take with her. There are photographs on a trunk in her living room and she lifts one of her and Willy at her graduation from Columbia. He has a hundred-watt smile on his face and it belies just how trying she knew the visit was for him—hotel reservations, the long drive with a map spread across his lap, his frustration with parallel parking when they went to dinner afterward in his big old truck that he insisted on driving. And then there was the confusion with his room key, which, he pointed out more than once, was not a damn key at all but more of a credit card that he had to wave around like a monkey to get the door to his room to open.

She smiles and sets the photograph back among the others, picks up one of Tasha and Kat that Mac had sent her, the two of them sitting side by side at a picnic table with ice cream cones, a giggling Tasha dripping pink down her wrists and Kat watching her side-eyed and smiling. Tasha adores Kat, suffers her moodiness in silence, and is patient in a way that amazes Lacey, given how hard Kat seems to work at ignoring her.

Lacey doesn't often see the two of them together but when she does, she is always bothered by the way in which Kat manages to ignore Tasha's questions, turn her back to her when she is talking to her, roll her eyes at Tasha's entreaties to play with her, look at a drawing, or sit next to her at the table. But the photograph had captured a moment, however rare, in which Tasha had, for whatever reason, drawn a smile out of Kat, and Mac had sent it to Lacey as proof, she is certain, that there is some small affinity between the two of them.

She puts the photo down and scoops up another, Tasha as a one-year-old, still fat and doughy, cherubic, smashed between Lacey and Mac in Lacey's arms but Mac with his arm around the both of them. It had been taken at her first birthday, only weeks away from Mac's leaving. They look happy, at first, but when Lacey looks at it more carefully, she recognizes the firm set of her mouth, as if something had been decided in her head the very moment the picture was snapped. There had been a distance between her and Mac all through the long day, and Lacey was frustrated with him, with the way he was so busy tending to everyone's needs and hardly noticing Tasha, not noticing that she was cranky or that her diaper was wet or that the constant swirl of people in their too-small cottage staring at Tasha and poking their fingers at her was setting Tasha on edge and making for a nervous baby who shied away from each new face and snuggled deeper into Lacey's neck. She wonders now if the photo captured the very moment she had realized that she was the only human being up for the job of loving Tasha. Well, maybe not loving her—maybe just up to the demands of caring for her properly, knowing what was too much or too little, dangerous and safe, right and wrong. Still, she touches the photo and remembers when, in spite of a myriad of worries, the very thing that has finally caught up with her was never on her radar.

February 13, 1973

Little Jim fetched up here today. Could have knocked me over with a feather. Lyle says he just walked into the hardware store like he come all the way up from Carolina to buy a pound of ten-penny nails. He started asking about me, and Uncle Price sent Lyle up to get me. Lyle says to me, there's a man downstairs asking after you. I thought for sure it was Daddy and I didn't know what to do. Aunt Virgie had just headed off to her church ladies' meeting and Lacey was set on the floor looking right up at me, like she was wondering if we was going somewhere. I picked her up and held her real tight so that she squirmed in my arms and pushed herself back from me, wanting to walk down the steps holding my hand, like she does now, but I wanted her closer and wouldn't put her down.

I come down the steps real careful, holding on to her. And then I saw Little Jim standing at the counter and watching me. He stood there, leaning his elbow on the counter, one leg crossed over the other, a little half smile dancing at the corner of his lip, like he had all the time in the world. My heart got a little flutter going in it, seeing him there, but then I reminded myself of the truth of Little Jim—that you just never know him until he's gone and done something hurtful that you recognize as being all too familiar now that you think about it. When I got closer I could see his little toothpick wiggling in his mouth and I remembered the time he kissed me quick with a toothpick in his mouth and he cut my lip real nasty so it bled and dripped drops of blood down the front of my shirt. He laughed when he did it and he licked the blood off my lip, like getting wounded from kissing was a normal kind of thing that I would have to get used to.

So, is this the baby who ain't got no daddy? he said to me. Lacey tucked her head into my neck and wrapped her arms around me, tossing her head so that her curls flipped across my face.

I didn't say nothing. This conversation was exactly what earned me a beating once before. He said he's real sorry about hurting me but there's something I gotta understand here. He tried to bring me close by sliding his hand under my hair and taking hold of the back of my neck, but I slipped quick out of his touch with two steps back and then Uncle Price cleared his throat from behind the counter, which made him drop his hand into his pocket instead. He said if I'm going to be his girl, it's only right he know who the daddy is.

I didn't say a word, but I watched the toothpick in his mouth real careful.

Damn it, May. I come all the way up here to make things right with you and you ain't got the courtesy to answer me straight.

I told him he shouldn't of hit me like he did. And he said I got no right to keep secrets from him. He's got rights, he said.

I could see the bulge of the fingers of his left hand flexing inside his pocket and I took another half step back so I was flush up against the shelf that held the rodent traps. It struck me as funny somehow that I felt trapped between Little Jim and some rat traps.

He put his curled-up fist on the counter, all the while looking hard at me. His voice low and mean so I couldn't be sure what Uncle and the boys could hear.

Then he said, Who'd you whore around with, May? I done ask every last man on the island and no one's got a clue who the little bastard's daddy is. I go all along thinking you was saving yourself for me and done find out you got a baby from long time afore I ever even come along. That ain't right, May. That ain't right.

Stop, I said. I wanted to push him back but I was keeping both arms wrapped around Lacey, covering her ears but she kept turning her head side to side, shaking my hands off.

He wanted to know how old she is. She's three, I told him, and she's not yours so <u>back off</u>, I said. And it weren't too often I stood up to him but nobody is going to call Lacey a bastard. His eyes went real wide and his tongue worked around his lips and truth be told, I was scared but more for Lacey than me because he was glaring at her like she was the root of a problem he meant to solve.

But afore he could make a move, before he could mull over in his mind how he planned to deal with me, Uncle Price and Lyle swooped out from behind the counter and a shelf of insecticides and got between the two of us.

That'll be enough now, son. Move on out, said Uncle Price.

Little Jim jumped foot to foot like he has a way of doing.

He said he weren't going nowhere, and started swinging his right arm wide as if he needed to clear some space. But in a few seconds' time Clint come out of the storage room and when Little Jim looked from Lyle to Clint to Uncle Price he got the message that he best move on. He had a few choice words for me on the way out the door, but nothing hurt in that nasty way like calling Lacey a bastard did. Lacey buried herself deep in my hair and her fingers clawed at the back of my neck. The shame was crawling up the front of me and there was a heat in my chest and face and all I could do was hold her tight to me and run up the back steps into the apartment where I spent some time feeling embarrassed and sorry for myself and crying in that sorry way but never let go of Lacey. She just took her little hands and wiped away the tears, turning over her little hands to look at them like they were fine jewels on her fingers.

February 16, 1973

Aunt Virgie has been acting real funny around me and Lacey lately. I could hear Uncle Price whispering things to her after Little Jim was run off. And every time I come in the room lately they change their tone of voice so as to seem casual. Finally, this morning, Aunt Virgie had me sit down at the table with her for a girl-to-girl chat. That's what she called it. She said she was a bit confused and it was high time I helped her make sense of all this. If it weren't Daddy who beat me so bad, who was it? And if Little Jim weren't Lacey's daddy, then who was?

She put a cup of steaming tea down in front of me, and a little pitcher of cream. Her teacups have bright red roses on them and are almost too pretty to drink from. But I was feeling a chill all through me and so I sipped at the tea and tried to keep my hands from shaking by wrapping them around a cup.

I had kept all the truth of everything inside myself for so long that I had clean forgotten that without a truth, Aunt Virgie and Uncle Price were likely to have made up their own. It just never would have occurred to me that Aunt Virgie would of thought Daddy was the one who beat me. No. He never did. That's a different thing altogether, the way things are with Daddy. And as for Little Jim, he didn't even have no interest in me at all when I had Lacey three years ago. He was older than me and back when I had Lacey he was just one of them boys who had already left his schooling and was looking to make his own way on the boats.

I explained how Little Jim had done what he done. How we were sitting in his truck watching the ferry come in and how he heard rumor that I had a baby up north but he knew that weren't true as I was saving myself for him. And then he smiled that funny smile of his that tricks you for a second into thinking it's safe to tell the truth.

Well, Little Jim, I said to him, and I ran my finger up his arm as I said this. Truth is, I do got a little girl up in Maryland, but she's hardly a baby no more. I told Aunt Virgie how I had been stupid enough to smile wide as the whole world when I said it cause I never get to speak much of Lacey and I'm real proud to be her momma—even if it is something of a secret and a sin. Little Jim kept on smiling at me but I already could see there was something different going on in him, something working its way round in his mind and likely to come out all twisted and mean. Right away he wants to know who the daddy is and he starts out asking real nice, real casual, like it almost don't even matter to him.

Don't make me tell you this, I says. And when I tell him I can't tell him he starts getting hard in his jaw and his fingers wrap real tight around the steering wheel.

The wind gets to kicking up off the water and I can hear the sand smatter against his truck and I am taking this all in as a warning.

He stretches his fingers and rewraps them around the wheel when he says he's only going to ask me this one more time. I am watching his hands careful now, but I'm not moving fast enough. He snaps his hands around my wrists and starts to twist them so I almost begin to wish I could tell him but I ain't never said it and I ain't going to.

Nobody is what I say. She ain't got a daddy.

Then he slaps me real hard with the back of his hand across my jaw and funny thing is, I remember thinking it didn't hurt so bad. But then quick as can be it comes back across the other side of my face and a numbness is coming over my jaw so that I don't think I could of formed any sensible words if I wanted to.

Who is it? He's wanting to know. He kept at me and called me names with his face spitting up close to mine so that I could feel the ugly words hitting me like stinging bursts of air.

I don't know, I says, and I don't know exactly why I said that except it felt more right than the truth. Afore I knew what was happening blood was splattering in little red droplets across the seat and he was pulling me to him by my hair. He had a right to know, he said, and I was going to tell him if he had to beat it out of me.

Blood was smearing all over his shirt and down his pants and I was pretty sure it was coming from both my lips and my nose. I couldn't breathe so good and I tried to twist myself out of his hands that was tangled up in big wads of my hair. I was drowning. I could feel blood pooling all thick and salty in my throat. When I yanked my face free, he ripped clumps of my hair from my head. I believe that was when he saw the blood smeared across my face and when he saw my lip cut a half inch deep—and maybe my eyes were starting to swell shut already. But I believe it shocked him some. I don't believe he felt remorseful of it, just a little surprised. I remember he sucked in air, like he was reevaluating the situation, and then he spit more ugly names at me, but I never did tell him what he wanted to know. Even after he slammed my head against the window and kicked me in the back when I tried to get out of the truck. Even then, I didn't tell.

I walked three miles back home. It was hard walking, and cold. I was spitting blood and my eyes was swollen so I couldn't see so good. I stayed off the road and tried to stay behind the dunes so Little Jim wouldn't find me on the road. Every so often the wind would kick up some and I would get a spray of salty sand in my mouth.

Daddy weren't there when I got home. He had work that day on Claggat's boat. I washed my face, which I hardly recognized as my own, and I tried to figure out what I was going to tell Daddy. Daddy would likely kill him. I knew that. And drunk as he would get afore he took to killing him, it's most likely he wouldn't even remember doing it.

I knew I had to get out of there. I had to get to Maryland and fast, afore Daddy got home the next morning or Little Jim came looking for me again.

It was kind of a funny situation I was finding myself in, I explained to Aunt Virgie. I couldn't let Daddy know Little Jim beat me, cause Daddy would surely kill him. And I couldn't let Little Jim know the truth about Lacey, cause he'd kill Daddy. And in all that mess—of one wanting to kill the other—no one would really be doing it for the reasons they would claim. No one was watching out for my honor. They was just men watching out for their property and willing to kill each other on account of who owned the parts of me.

I had a few dollars from some smocking I had sold and I set out on the road again to get to the ferry. I knew I'd have to wait there the whole night for the morning ferry to come in with the garbage truck and the postal so I had plenty of time to make the long walk again. The wind was whipping sharp off the water and my head was pounding so hard I just couldn't walk by way of the shore no more and so I took to the road, prayerful that Little Jim would not be on the road afore I got to the ferry. But not far along Loony Junie come on up the road and offered me a ride. She seen me beat the way I was and wanted to take me to see Miss Carolee, the midwife who also does some good nursing, but I said no but that I would gladly take a ride to the ferry. She said she wouldn't tell no one and she sat with me at the ferry till the 6:10 came in. I am grateful to her for that kindness.

After I explained this to Auntie she just set still for a real long minute, looking me over with them big watery eyes of hers and her lips smacking real quiet. Then she reaches across the table and sets her hands around mine. She has nice plump hands and they feel real good wrapping around my own. You should of told me before, she says. She's crying real tears for me now and for the first time I'm thinking maybe I'm worth crying for.

Aunt Virgie says that I am never ever to go back to the island. Furthermore neither Daddy nor Little Jim are ever coming to carry me back, not ever, she says. He is no longer her brother, she says to me. He is dead to her.

CHAPTER 13

A Night in the Hospital

Next to Tasha's hospital bed is a blue vinyl chair that, in theory, is meant to recline and resemble a bed. Willy is spent, having struggled with the chair until he eventually managed to pull it apart enough to create a lumpy facsimile. An aide gave him a coarse white sheet, which he now drapes over the chair, but when he tries to lie down he finds that the sheet shimmies and slides all over the slick vinyl. He tries tucking the sheet in the creases, where the seat meets the back of the chair, for example, but the slightest movement on his part pulls it free of the crease and sends him slipping and sliding. He is further confounded by the fact that the back of the chair refuses to lie back perfectly flat but remains at a slight incline so that the crinkly pillow they provided him slides from his head to his waist every time he lifts his head even slightly to adjust the sheet.

"Damn," he mutters, pushing the pillow back up under his head. He pulls the blanket up to his chin and tries not to notice that his bottom is pinched in the crease of the chair.

"Willy?" says Tasha.

"Yeah, honey. I'm sorry I woke you. I'm having a little wrestling match with this here chair." He sits up, grateful to be distracted from his struggle.

She lifts her head over the bed rails, which he knows she resents, having said on more than one occasion that she is not a baby, but the nursing staff insists the rails be up. She is alarmingly pale, her skin blotchy around her neck and chest, and her hair, what is left of it, is like tufted duck down.

"Is Mommy here?"

"She'll be here tomorrow, sweetheart. Why don't you get some sleep."

"I'm all the time sleeping, Willy. I want to be awake."

She turns more to her side and toward him and the sleeve opening of her hospital gown slips down to the center of her chest. He can see the rise, about the size of a small stack of quarters, beneath her skin and high on the right side of her chest where the subcutaneous port had been placed. An internal catheter lies beneath the skin and leads from the site of the port up to the collarbone and into her jugular. In seems cruel to him, to put contraptions under her thin skin, but it has been explained to him that in this way her treatments, chemo, any antibiotics she might require, transfusions, and so on could be fed through the port. Likewise, the many blood samples Tasha has to have drawn can be taken from the site of the port and reduce the number of "sticks" she would be forced to endure.

"Tell me a story," she says.

"Aw, honey, I don't know any stories."

"Sure you do, Willy. Tell me a story about Mommy when she was a little girl. Was she ever bad, Willy? Tell me about something bad she did."

"Nah, your momma was a good girl. She didn't do nothing much too bad."

"Never ever?"

"Well, there was the time she forgot to let the chickens back in the coop. That was a bad time."

"What happened to the chickens?"

"See now, chickens can't be running around at night like some of your other animals can." He sits up and the pillow falls again down to his back. "They haven't got any defenses, if you know what I mean."

"They have claws," and she drags a clawed hand through the air to demonstrate.

"The claws are pretty useless, and their beaks, too. Anyways, your momma was about probably nine years old and up until that time she had taken pretty darn good care of them birds. Course I didn't have much time for 'em, what with the herd and all. But one day she starts sassing at me about them chickens, pointing a finger at me and wagging it back and forth saying she had fourteen banties that morning and now there's only twelve and I best not be butchering her chickens."

"You killed Mommy's chickens?" she whispers, awed and horrified at the same time.

"Course, honey. You ever eat chicken? Where do you think that chicken comes from? Even them darn little chicken nuggets your momma says you eat. You don't pluck 'em off a tree, you know. Fact is, your momma's chickens got treated real good compared to the ones ending up in them McDonald's nuggets. Your momma's chickens had fresh air and a place to dust. They're ground-fed. That's the Ritz hotel for chickens nowadays. Mr. Perdue, he never ground-fed his chickens, you can be sure." He looks up to see her staring straight back at him. It was hard to tell what she was thinking, but she didn't appear to be especially bothered by the revelation.

"You probably just had to eat the bad ones, huh?" She nods her own head as she says it, certain that is the case.

"Well, anyways," he says, not answering exactly, and he clears his throat. "Anyways, I was always careful not to be butchering chickens when your momma was around, thinking as it might upset her some, but she knew what she was eating at the supper table, alright. But this day something just come into her. Had a bee in her bonnet, she did."

"She was real mad at you, huh?"

"Hopping mad. Anyways, she goes into the house, slamming that damn kitchen door so hard it bounced. Wouldn't come down to supper, neither. Well, she sat up there in her room all night, drawing pictures of chickens—even wrote a little poem about them, which I don't recall clearly, but it said something about—*I would not let my chickens die if only they could learn to fly.*"

"Chickens can fly, Willy. I saw them."

"Not too good, honey, and the one or two of your momma's that give me particular trouble, I clipped a wing a little bit to keep 'em grounded. So your momma was up in her room saving chickens when all of a sudden I hear them chickens squawking and carrying on like the devil hisself come to the henhouse. And your momma comes flying down the steps, hollering at me 'fore she even hits the last step. *Willy! You best not be killing my chickens!*" He smiles now at the memory, tucking his chin and shaking his head, chuckling softly.

"I was out the back door already when I seen what the hoopla was all about. Slinking out under the fence was a fox, and in her mouth, which—and I'm telling you the truth, here—nearly looked like she was smiling, she carried one of them chickens, wings flapping and feathers still flying. Your momma was beside me in a flash and she saw that fox slinkin' away with her chicken. We watched him head into the timothy and we could tell he was zigzagging through the hay, making off with that chicken. About twenty yards in, a cloud of feathers come up out of the field."

He stops for a minute, remembering how the moonlight reflected on those feathers as they rose and then shimmied down into the hayfield.

"'It's done then,' your momma said, and I suppose we both knew what she meant."

Willy remembers it all now, remembers watching the feathers fall from the sky and hearing Lacey sigh. She had leaned into him then, and her shoulders had begun to tremble. He had put a hand on her shoulder and without looking at her he had said, "Lacey, that chicken is fox meat on account of you." When she didn't answer, just stayed solid, leaning into him, he felt he had more to say. "You got a responsibility to these animals. Fact you kill 'em in the end don't relieve you of duty when they're living. They have a right, dumb as they are, to be clean and fed and safe. And you denied them that safety when you spent all your time sassing and sulking over me putting one of them birds on the table instead of locking 'em up in the coop for the night. This is what you call *biting off your nose to spite your face* and it ain't a real productive way of doing things."

"Did all Mommy's chickens get killed?"

"No, but she lost a few of 'em. Your momma learned her lesson after that, though, and she always remembered to lock up the henhouse. Your momma's real good with living things now, 'cause of that lesson. She helped me a whole lot with the herd, and she took real good care of Beauford when her aunt and uncle passed on and the dog came to live with us."

"Mommy likes to take care of things."

"I know she likes to take care of you."

"Willy, s'pose if I die, Mommy will have to get another girl to take care of?"

He isn't sure he has heard her right and is afraid to answer at first, afraid he'll be answering the wrong question. When he looks at her, she just watches him back, her eyes steady on him, her fingers twisting the corner of her sheet.

After a few seconds, she shrugs her shoulders, like maybe she didn't expect an answer anyway.

"You're not going nowhere," he says. "And your momma will always take care of you." He hopes he says it loud enough, strong enough for her to know it is true.

"Willy? Can we go see the chickens tomorrow?"

"Chickens are back at the farm, honey. You have to stay here and get better."

She rolls onto her back and appears to consider this a moment, crossing her arms across her chest. "I hate it here!" she says, kicking the covers down to the end of the bed. "Why did I have to get put here? Why did I? I hate it, hate it, *hate it*!" She shoves the small pile of stuffed animals that nestle at the head of her bed onto the floor and stares at the ceiling.

"Now why you gotta go and do that for?" says Willy. "No need to act up like this." He bends over and picks up the small stuffed pony that bounced off his knee before landing on the floor and sets it next to her on the bed. She looks to him, her eyes damp and fiery, a glittering rage.

"And I hate you, too, Willy. I do!" she says, sweeping her arm out from her side and sending the pony flying again. It bounces off Willy's chest and tumbles under the bed.

Willy runs his hand down his face, massaging his chin slightly before taking a deep breath and lifting his shoulders as if he might have something important to say. But before anything comes to him, he sees her small body ripple with tiny sniffles that are growing into full-blown choking sobs. Without thinking, he comes up out of his chair and picks her up from the bed. She weighs next to nothing but drapes herself in his arms and around his neck so that he feels wrapped in her.

"I don't feel good, Willy," she cries into his neck, rolling her head along his shoulder.

He feels the fluffs of her hair tickle his neck and tears drip under the collar of his shirt. Rubbing his hand up her back he feels the bones of her spine, like marbles, parading up her back. She seems to have trouble catching her breath and her words come in soft bursts.

"I feel sick," she says. "I . . ." And she lifts her head from his shoulder and sniffles. "I feel sicker than—than chicken pops," she says. And she drops her head back down to the hollow of his neck.

"Chicken *pox*," says Willy, understanding what she meant after just a moment. "That's bad," he says. "You must feel real bad, sugar."

"Real bad."

He paces across the small room with her in his arms, to the window and back and to the bed again, jiggling her ever so lightly just as he had Lacey when she was that age. He is amazed at how easy it is, how natural, how it all comes back. He rests a hand on the back of her head and feels a pang for her at the recent memory of her silky blonde locks. Shifting foot to foot with a rhythm that seems to quiet her, the warm breath on his neck becomes slow and steady and she relaxes in his arms. When one of her arms drops from around his neck, he holds her closer and promises her he will hang on good—if she will, too.

The next morning, after hardly having slept a wink, Willy sits next to Tasha's hospital bed sipping the flavored coffee that he'd gotten in the cafeteria earlier. It tastes like burned almonds. Lacey is curled up in bed with Tasha, her arms wrapped around her and her lips resting close enough to the back of Tasha's neck that she can kiss her without moving her head.

Lacey had crept in around eight that morning, and Willy figures she must have left the college around 4:00 a.m. He worries about the circles under her eyes.

Tasha is dozing again, having woken for breakfast and then falling back into her bed, exhausted from the effort and probably also from Willy's jabbering about how good them peaches look—for canned peaches—and did she want to finish her cereal?

Willy knows there will be test results coming back this morning, so he figures on staying. It's easier with two anyway, so one can take a break, grab a coffee, whatever, while the other stays with her.

Tasha doesn't like to be alone. That much is clear. Willy hates to use the bathroom in her hospital room—just doesn't seem right, what with the bedpans in there and all—but during the night when he went to use the one down the hall, she'd got to fussing so, calling for him and such, that he just resigned himself to the fact that he'd be using the toilet in the room. It was mighty uncomfortable just the same. That morning she had watched him go in and she'd called to him just as he was shutting the door. "Be right out, sugar," he'd said.

"What are you doing?"

He thought that was the doggone silliest question, especially given that she'd be hearing him pee, loud and clear, in the next few seconds. The bathroom was big and cavernous, and he was certain that his peeing into the bowl could be heard clear through the halls. This made it harder for him to start his water and pretty soon she was calling for him again and asking what was he doing in there. When he came out, she was sitting up staring hard at the doorway like she had never taken her eyes off of it.

Now they are waiting to hear from Dr. Oren as to the results of Tasha's latest tests. Tasha, to Willy's way of thinking, isn't tolerating the first round of chemo too well, even though the doctors keep saying everything is going just as expected, whatever that means. She complains of numbness in her toes and fingers, and the mouth sores have made it particularly hard to get her to eat anything. She is dizzy sometimes. Sometimes she cries and the crying tugs at Willy's core in a way that makes him angry—not at her, of course—but at the hospital and the doctors and the world at large. He doesn't like the feeling of it at all. There are headaches, or, as he has come to think of it, one long headache that she doesn't seem to get any relief from. There are nighttime medications they give her to ease them, but they only send her into restless sleep that has her turning side to side while holding her head in her hands.

But now she rests, snug against Lacey, who hadn't even bothered to kick off her shoes when she crawled into bed with Tasha. "Good morning," says Dr. Oren to the three of them. He comes into the room followed by his band of interns and parks himself, legs spread wide, arms crossed, at the end of the bed before reaching down and unhooking her clipboarded chart from the hook where it hangs. "How are you feeling this morning, Tasha?" The gaggle of young interns semicircle themselves and fan out behind him.

When Tasha doesn't answer him, just blinks and looks over the gathering of young doctors, he taps his pencil on the chart and continues.

"I have some good news," he says. "Just as we expected, she is responding to treatment in a textbook manner." A slow smile spreads on his face as he continues. "Meaning that she is responding in the same way that eighty to ninety percent of all patients who go into an initial remission respond to treatment." He jots something on her chart and hangs it back on the end of her bed. "This is exactly what we like to see," he says.

Lacey breathes a huge sigh of relief, and Willy slaps himself on the thigh. "Hot dang," he says, "I knew you could lick it, sugar."

"It's not *licked* yet," Dr. Oren cautions, but he is amused by Willy's optimism and brightens. "But her counts are good. I think we can finish this phase of treatment on an outpatient basis with Tasha coming in three times a week for her chemo."

"Well, this is great news, Doctor," says Willy. He comes up out of his chair to pump the doctor's hand. "Real good news."

Lacey wraps her arms around a smiling Tasha and smatters her face with kisses.

"I don't want her more than an hour's distance from the hospital," says Dr. Oren. "Not because I have any serious concerns, but just in case she has a latent reaction to any medications or treatments, I want to have her close by. Understood?"

Lacey just smiles and takes deep breaths from Tasha's neck. Willy nods his head enthusiastically. "Yes, sir. No problem with that. Just in case. Good thinking, just in case, Doc."

"Daddy will be sooo happy, Tasha," Lacey says now. "I'm going to call him and tell him we'll be bringing you home this morning."

"He'll be proud of me, won't he, Mommy?" she says quietly.

"Yes, honey, but Daddy is always proud of you."

"I know, but now he can be extra proud because I'm not too sick anymore. Right?"

"That's right, honey."

"Mommy?" Tasha pulls Lacey's smiling face down to the pillow and whispers in her ear, loud enough for Willy to hear. "How come I still feel so sick?"

CHAPTER 14

Back Home

When they got home from the hospital, Tasha refused to come inside. She wanted to be in the yard, she said. And no, she wasn't hungry. Why was everyone always trying to feed her, she wanted to know.

The ride from the hospital had seemed long, and Lacey realizes now that all the attention, pointing out landmarks that popped up along the way, funny billboards along I-83, the high school that Lacey went to, the ducks at the reservoir, and the constant chatter about all the things they would do back at the farm had worn Tasha out.

Lacey insists that Tasha at least wear her jacket, which she then sheds in less than three minutes and leaves tangled in the remains of a barbed wire fence. She leaves on the pink baseball cap that was a gift from Cade and the boys. Lacey watches her from the back stoop as she stands outside the chicken yard and uncharacteristically kicks dirt that flies through the fencing at one of the chickens dusting itself. Lacey calls her away from the coop. Tasha's counts are still low and she needs to stay away from the chickens for a time.

Lacey thinks she hears Tasha call the chickens stupid when she turns her back on them and wanders toward the pond instead. Lacey calls to her again, but she shuffles away from her. Lacey watches her from one of the Adirondack chairs and calls to Willy to join them outside. Mac and Kat are packing their things, preparing to head back to Virginia, and so it is just the two of them seated by the pond, and Tasha meandering the muddy edges.

Willy settles in with his pipe and bag of tobacco. The two of them startle in unison to see Tasha stumble, but she doesn't fall. Neither will say what the other is thinking—that she is not herself, that she seems dazed, a little *off*. She doesn't have any interest in the water's barely rippling edges. She just walks, having to stop now and again to pull up her feet, her sneakers sucking at the muddy bank as she disappears into the cattails, batting at the stiff stalks and kicking her toes at the stubbled new growth that sprouts in the sloppy earth. When she emerges from the cattails, spreading them with her arms and stepping as if through a portal, she shakes her head and rubs her hands down her face, turns again and heads back into the thick growth. Lacey watches the cattails shimmy and close behind her daughter like a curtain as she disappears once more, suddenly stepping out and reappearing a few feet farther down the banks, then closes her eyes and tilts her head back with her hands out to her sides as if she is feeling the world spin. Her legs are spread for balance. Dropping her arms to her sides, she trudges on, moving up the embankment to drier ground by pulling at the tough grasses that sprout in thatches along the side.

Tasha's walk is lazy and unsteady, her toes dragging and her head bobbing. She walks toward them now, lifting her head to look at them as if she is trying to gauge the distance to Lacey's lap. Lacey anticipates the hug she will get even before Tasha can climb into her lap, but instead, Tasha stops at the open doors of Mac's car and slides into the back seat on her belly.

Mac emerges from the kitchen door to carry his and Kat's bags to the car, setting two of them in the trunk and then slamming it shut and coming around to where Tasha now hangs her head from the car. He sets a third bag down in the driveway. Both doors are open now, and her head and arms still hang out of the car. She picks stones from the drive and tosses them at Mac's feet.

"So we still got some hospital visits ahead of us," Willy says to Lacey, drawing on his pipe and tucking the bag of tobacco in his shirt pocket.

She pats his arm absentmindedly. "And Phase Two, from what I'm told, is a journey into hell."

"We'll manage. What do you think about that big damn bear in the parlor?" he asks, his eyes going wide.

"It's huge!" says Lacey. "Where did it come from?"

"Neighbor lady, Carlotta something-or-other," he says. "I don't really know her. She brung it by a few days ago. I believe she bought a few acres off of Hurline's farm last year and built a house on it." He points with his pipe in the direction of the next farm over across the meadow. "She just left it at the door with a note."

"Sweet of her, I guess," Lacey says.

"Note said she's a nurse and happy to help out."

"We'll be fine," says Lacey.

"Course we will."

Tasha is tossing the pebbles up into the air now and Lacey can hear them pinging off the roof of Mac's car. She thinks to stop her and then decides Mac can handle it.

"When's he coming back?" Willy nods in Mac's direction.

"I'm not sure. He says he thinks he can get back most weekends, and he has the summer off." Lacey looks out over the pond. "And there's Kat," she says. "Every other weekend for the most part. It's complicated." She looks to him. "Is it that bad?" she says earnestly. "Having them here? I know it's not ideal."

"Nah." Willy shakes his head. "It's not bad, Lacey." He holds his pipe clenched between his teeth and runs his hands down his thighs like he is dusting them off. He sucks two quick puffs and pulls the pipe from his mouth. "He ever get married again?"

"Nope."

"Got a lady friend?"

"I don't know, Willy. We don't talk about things like that."

She looks out to the fields. "Looks like you got the timothy in." She loves the way a full field of timothy looks by midsummer, and it is something to look forward to. Now it is bare and striped in furrows but by mid-June it will roll with the evening breeze and unfurl itself like a sheet snapped in the wind. "You do the upper fields, too?"

"Doc Asher helped me with it, and I'll give him a quarter portion for his horses. He has time on his hands."

"God, he's not retired, is he? He's only, what, fifty-five or so?"

"He's not vetting so much these days—not so many large animals, you know, since the TB hit. Then, of course, there's all them farms got subdivided. He's got time on his hands. And he likes to fool with them horses of his."

Lacey leans her head back and closes her eyes, thinking back to the many visits from the doc, some routine, some for emergencies, but her favorite visits were birthing nights. The men would work late into the evening, sometimes straight through till morning, and the night would be filled with the sounds of their voices, the clank of chains and lead shanks, the soft shimmy of fresh hay being tossed. The next morning the kitchen floor would be tracked with mud and manure, puddled in places, the counter splashed with coffee and crystalline trails of sugar. But the best part of all would be the barn, suddenly filled with little calves nestled against their mothers, curled in butterscotch balls with their long-lashed eyes blinking, nuzzling at the teats with a foamy muzzle. The barn would smell damp and coppery, the cows dreamy and content; the men, exhausted and filthy, collapsed on bales and buckets.

"I did love birthing nights," she says.

Willy looks to her, surprised maybe. "Toughest nights of the year," he says. "Never got any sleep, sometimes for days."

Funny, it had never occurred to her how tired he must have been. She looks at him now and sees the lines in his face, the deeper ones that cut through his brow, the more recent deep sag of his jowls. She always thinks of him the same, but now she can see that he has aged, his shoulders are thinner, the skin around his eyes loose and crinkling, the hairline having retreated enough to reveal two inches of shiny pink scalp freckled with age spots. She wonders, too, what her mother looks like now. May was so much younger than Willy. Lacey tosses the thought out of her mind with a quick shake of her head. There is no room in her head right now for her mother.

She gets up from her chair, explaining that she will say goodbye to Mac and Kat. Willy heaves a small sigh and dutifully rises.

They stand, the three of them, a little awkwardly, by the car, Lacey and Mac discussing weekend visits and the necessity of staying in touch daily.

"Move over, princess. Daddy's packing," says Mac, finally hefting the one bag at his feet to place in the back seat.

"Take me with you, Daddy," she says, dropping her head even farther toward the drive below so that the pink ballcap slips off of her head and tumbles to the ground.

Mac retrieves it and holds it in his hand. "Sorry, no can do. You have to stay here and get well." He goes to pat her head, but as he reaches his hand to the downy fluffs that remain, he hesitates and twists his wrist so that his fingers fall down the sides of her cheek instead. He settles the cap back on her head.

She looks up at him, not blinking. "Did Kat have bad blood, too, when she was a littler girl like me?"

Mac sets the bag down on the floor of the back seat next to her.

"No, honey. She didn't."

"Just some people get bad blood, huh?"

"That's right," he says, and he leans over and kisses the top of her head through the fabric of the cap. "Go find your sister for me, okay?"

"I saw her behind the coop. She's smoking a cig'rette back there." She drops her head back down. "I think maybe she's gonna die, too, Daddy," she says with a small and resolute sigh.

CHAPTER 15

A Visitor

Two weeks have passed since they brought Tasha back to the farm. Her counts are up, and she and Willy spent some of the late afternoon in the coop, spreading fresh pine shavings, Tasha trailing behind him and asking the name of each banty. Willy was forced to make it up as he went along. Recalling the seven dwarfs to the best of his ability, he randomly christened them as she pointed to each one—Dopey, Sleepy, Bashful—and then moved on in the vein of fairy-tale princesses—Cinderella, Sleeping Beauty, and Rapunzel.

It is early evening now, still light but with the sky outside the windows fading to a dull gray. Willy flicks on a floor lamp in the sunroom where Tasha is curled on the sofa and the corner of the room melts into warmth. He has just gotten off the phone with Lacey, who that morning headed back down to the college for two nights. Tasha had been indifferent to her call and he knows it worries Lacey. She's just a little worn down tonight, he explained to her when Tasha handed the phone back to him and padded into the sunroom. Mac is expected in the morning, likely bringing Kat, and so it will be the four of them for the weekend.

He had worried that Tasha wouldn't eat but had found in the hospital that ice cream was acceptable to her and so he has stocked his freezer with several flavors. "What flavor, sweetie?"

"Pink."

"Pink ain't a flavor."

"Just pink."

"Okay, okay, pink-flavored ice cream it is." He fixes her a bowl of strawberry and brings it into the sunroom where the television is on. Lacey bought an old VCR player at a yard sale up the road and it came with twenty-five or more old movies. Mac set it up for Tasha and she has the movies jumbled in a box beside the sofa, but she tends to watch the same one over and over again. It is *Pollyanna*, and Willy can remember seeing it at the picture show many years ago.

He is about to settle on the sofa with his own ice cream when there is a knock at the front door. Hardly anybody ever comes to the front door, so when he goes to open it it sticks some and makes a sucking noise.

Standing at his door is a large woman with wide shoulders, big curves, and too much cleavage. Her hair, too, is big, shiny and black, rising high on her head and falling in a massive wave under her chin. She wears a leather patchwork jacket in shades of copper, black, and red. Something, Willy is certain, that was made for a younger woman.

"I would have called, but I didn't have your number."

Willy stares at her, his mind racing to figure if he is expected to know who she is.

"Carlotta Talucci, your neighbor down a ways." She thrusts her hand through the open doorway and into Willy's.

"Willy . . . Willy Cherrymill." He shakes her hand, not sure how long to hold it, but she pulls back quickly. She has a small animal cage in one hand and a mesh bag filled with large red fruit is at her feet.

"I won't stay," she says, but hopefully, like it is a question. She lifts the bag at her feet so that both her hands are full now and Willy wonders if he should be taking something from her, but he only steps back making a wide space for her to enter. "I just wanted to stop by, and I thought, if your little grand-daughter is around, she might enjoy a visit with Thumper. She's not allergic to anything, is she?" she asks, hefting the cage up in her right hand. "My rabbit," she says. "Thumper. Thought they could visit awhile if this is a good time?"

Willy doesn't know what to make of this intrusion and finds himself at a loss for words. She sweeps into the house, pauses, and turns to him.

"Pomegranates," she says, and she hands the mesh bag to Willy. "Ever had them before?"

Willy shakes his head, no.

"They're fun. I'll show you. I'm not interrupting anything, am I?"

Again, Willy could only shake his head. No one had ever brought a rabbit and pomegranates to his house before.

"I stopped by for just a couple of reasons. I wanted to introduce Tasha to Thumper, here." She hefts the cage again and spins it gently so that she can look through the small screened door at the extremely large rabbit inside. "And I wanted to remind you that I'm a nurse, I mentioned that in my note—retired—but not so long ago, so if you have errands to run or things to do, please call me."

"Well, that's awful nice of you," he says, running his fingers through his hair and certain as the day is long that he would never ask this strange woman to stay with Tasha.

"Well, maybe," she says, considering, "but to be honest"—and she looks him straight in the eye with her own big brown ones—"I'm just a bit bored." She laughs uncomfortably. "And taking care of people is what I do best."

"Well, sure, being a nurse and all," he offers.

"Retired." She straightens her back. "And widowed, just six months back. Helluva thing."

Willy is truly at a loss for words and they stand awkwardly for a few seconds before he hears Tasha stir in the sunroom. He can smell something, not offensive, fresh, like good soap, maybe lavender, he's not sure. "We was just about to watch a movie." He points to Tasha in the sunroom and Carlotta apparently assumes it to be an invitation and heads that way.

Tasha is sitting up with her bowl of ice cream in her lap, twisting her head around the corner to get a look at the visitor.

"Honey, this here is the nice lady who give me that big bear to give to you."

"Hi, what's that?" she says, pointing to the cage at the woman's side.

"A little visitor. This is my rabbit, Thumper. Thought you might like to visit with him."

Tasha squeals and puts her bowl on the floor at her feet.

"Is it okay if I let her hold him?" Carlotta asks Willy. She doesn't wait for an answer and puts the cage on the ground, squatting down beside it to open it and remove the rabbit—with some difficulty. The animal is about half the size of a bed pillow and obviously heavy. When she gets him from the cage, Willy notices that his ears hang down below his head, giving him a forlorn appearance.

Carlotta has Tasha pull up her legs and settle herself cross-legged on the sofa before placing the rabbit in her lap. Willy watches as a smile, the likes of which he hasn't seen in weeks, spreads wide across her face.

"Well there, now. He looks comfy with you, sweetheart," says Carlotta, standing up straight and beaming. Indeed, the rabbit has settled itself right snug in Tasha's lap, and she curls the whole of her small upper body around it as she strokes its fur. Carlotta leans back on her own wide hips and folds her arms, satisfied. "*Pollyanna!*" she exclaims suddenly, turning in the direction of the television. "I love this movie."

"Me, too," said Tasha. "You can watch it with us. Can't she, Willy?"

"Well, sure, I guess," says Willy, not knowing what else he can say. Carlotta smiles a plump and pretty smile that makes Willy, despite his best intentions, almost smile back, though he doesn't relish the idea of spending the evening with this strange woman in his house. "Uhm, would you care for some ice cream? We got several flavors here."

"Anything pink?" Then turning to Tasha, she says, "Won't this be fun?"

Willy is not so sure. He hears Tasha giggling on his way into the kitchen. He brings Carlotta a bowl of ice cream where she has settled next to Tasha on the sofa. He watches Tasha tip her head to Carlotta's shoulder, and by the end of the movie she is sound asleep against her bosoms and Carlotta has one arm wrapped around her thin shoulders and is wiping a tear from her own cheek with the other hand. Thumper is still, but Willy sees his little heart pounding in his chest even through all that fur. "This movie always did make me cry," she says.

While the tape rewinds, they sit in the very same awkward silence Willy has been afraid of. Something, he is certain, is expected of him and damn if he isn't at a loss as to what it is.

Carlotta speaks first, quietly so as not to wake Tasha. She tells him she cries at the drop of a hat these days.

"Hear tell you bought a piece of land off the Hurline farm?" he asks.

Eight acres, she tells him. Antonio, that was her husband, she explains, had always dreamed of having a little *farmette*.

Willy hated that word, *farmette*. Sounded like some kind of fancy dessert.

They had already moved out to the country from Little Italy in downtown Baltimore and had been living in their newly built home for less than a year when Antonio passed away. Nothing terribly tragic or awful, she tells him, other than the loss itself, but given what she has seen and tended to, passing in one's sleep from a stroke was about the best thing anyone could wish for. "It's been six months," she reminds Willy.

Willy doesn't know exactly what to say to that. He mumbles something about how sorry he is, but she is focused on sleeping Tasha, gazing at her with an odd appreciation. He's curious, however, is she growing anything, raising any animals?

"Just Thumper, here." She runs her hand down his silky fur and Willy watches clumps of it float to the floor. "He's an ambassador rabbit. I take him to various hospitals a couple of times a week to visit the kids."

"That's nice," he says. Though he isn't quite sure what all the fuss is about the beast. The rabbit just sits there, blinking off and on, occasionally chewing at nothing and wiggling his whiskers, but is absolutely motionless otherwise. Willy stares at it now, from his chair, thinking on it. "That thing *do* anything?" he asks.

"Not really. That's why Thumper is the perfect companion for sick children. Just lets them love him."

"Well, made her real happy tonight. She'll be disappointed in the morning when he's gone."

"I can bring him by anytime." She plants a kiss on the top of Tasha's head. He finds himself wondering if Tasha can smell her in her dreams.

"Your daughter, her mother," she says, with a side nod to Tasha next to her. "She's not here?"

"Yeah, well, Lacey had some business to finish up at the college where she works. She's a college professor, you know—*literature*, that's her specialty." He feels the pride over her rise as he says it. "She'll be back again tomorrow. And her daddy, too." The tape spits out of the machine, making a quick grinding noise. "They ain't together, you know." He doesn't know why he is telling her that. It seems kind of personal.

"Oh, the pomegranates," she says suddenly. "I almost forgot. Just slice them in wedges and let her pick the seeds out. You just suck the flesh off the seeds."

Willy couldn't help squirming when she said that.

"They're real sweet, but low acid, so it won't hurt her mouth sores. She'll have fun picking at it and she'll hardly notice she's eating anything. But they stain, so be careful where you let her eat them."

Later that night, after Carlotta has left and after he has carried Tasha to bed, he slips back down to the kitchen and cuts one of the pomegranates in half to have a look. He's never seen anything like it. The whole inside is filled with slick wet beads of bright red fruit. He tries to pick one out with his finger, but it pops out and shoots across the counter leaving a trail of tiny pink-red splatters. He works more gently at another one, gets it to his lips, and sucks the flesh from it, spitting the seed into the sink. A whole lot a fuss about nothing much, he decides. But then he picks another, and another, until his fingers and lips are stained red and he holds only a skeleton-like shell of the former fruit in his hand. *She's gonna like this*, he thinks as he tries like mad to wash the stain from his fingers.

September 2, 1974

   It's been a long while since I last wrote. After that time more than a year ago when Little Jim come to the store and I had to tell Aunt Virgie about him and about Daddy, too, I just lost the heart for writing anything down anymore. Seems I couldn't avoid looking at the truth once it came from my lips—but I sure didn't want to write about it.

I put this here book between my mattress and the box spring and I would see it every time I changed the sheets. I would think to write in it, but I just didn't have the spirit for it. Then yesterday I pulled the book out and thought maybe if I don't read what I wrote a ways back, well then I can start writing the happier stuff that is coming upon me lately.

Of late I have begun to feel good inside, like a quamishness is being cut out of me. I still have some worries now and then, like the fact that Little Jim has been seen in town at least two times that I know of yet. Clint saw his red truck at the Esso around the corner last summer. And I saw the truck driving up and down the street in front of the hardware store not but three weeks ago. Watched it go by, then turn around at the feed store and come back down the street again, cruising real slow and then pealing and squealing the tires when he took off for good—or at least I hope it was for good.

Daddy is fussing some at me, too. While I was not the one to tell him, he has recently been learned of the fact that I am going to marry Willy Cherrymill and it has made him hopping mad.

Let me tell you how I feel about Willy. Willy don't give me that kind of feeling like Little Jim did, where I could melt like butter in a hot fry pan just by the sound of his voice, but then he don't give me that fearful feeling neither, where you just don't know what lays around the corner and how bad it's going to be. But I surely do love that man. I love the way he looks at me, kind of shy, like he hopes I don't notice, and the way he touches my hand or arm and doesn't want to pull away, like he's touched nothing like it before in his life. I like his quiet, too, and the way he don't have to know things, just knows everything is what it is. He done never asked me about Lacey's daddy and I don't expect he will.

He's been teaching me and Lacey to swim in his pond and I do so like the feel of his hands on my waist when he holds me at the top of the water and tells me to kick and blow. I have not yet learned to swim on my own without his hands around me, but he never gets cross with me, just keeps on telling me that I will get it very soon.

He is a man set in his ways and all. I think that comes from the demands of animals, the way everything has to be done at the right time. Waterways are so different. Conditions change and we always changed with them. When the blues ran, Daddy had work. After a storm, things were quiet for a long while till the silt settled and the ocean healed over. But the ways of the animals is different. The milking and the feeding and the birthing—it's like its own clock, and Willy and the men answer to it with each minute that ticks off through the day and night.

I will like living on the farm. I am certain of that. And Lacey already acts like she was born to it. She's almost five now and it's hard to believe I missed so much of her growing up. And I'm just a bit sad to think she doesn't know the waterways of the island. She don't know how big the sky is over the ocean, and she don't know the true color of it, neither. She always makes the ocean blue in all her coloring pictures, and I ask her, why is the ocean blue? She tells me it's always blue and don't I know that? But she's wrong. Willy says all children color the ocean blue, and I suppose that comes from not knowing that it is also green and silver and gray and black, and shades in between.

My wedding dress is not white, but it is very pretty. Aunt Virgie made it for me and she said I could wear almost-white and the color we picked is called ecru. I never heard of that color before and I didn't really see the difference between off-white, eggshell, and ecru, which were some of the choices allowed to me. But I like this color. It puts me in mind of a cup of weak tea, something warm and good for your feelings, but not too strong. It's not a fancy dress, and that suits me good.

Tomorrow I will write more, but tonight, Lacey is sound asleep on the pillow beside me and her breath makes a pretty little whistle sometimes. When I put my finger to the palm of her hand and tickle it, she still wraps her hand around mine. Though she does it nearly every time, I am always surprised. I am so happy in my thoughts that I think I will just snuggle down next to her and breathe her in and think of how our life will be.

CHAPTER 16

The Start of Something

Lacey is back at her cottage in southern Maryland. It is evening and she has just arrived. She plans to meet with Cade, touch base with David as well as her two independent studies students, and get back on the road the next afternoon. She digs in her top cupboard for the pack of stale cigarettes she had shoved behind the cannisters a few weeks ago when she was thinking of quitting but hadn't quite committed to it yet. She finds the pack, slips a single cigarette from it and a pack of matches from a jar she keeps on the back of the gas stove, and heads out to the dock. The moon isn't full, but it is bright and rising in a clear sky, throwing enough light that she can watch the bats skim the surface of the water. Small silky ripples make their way to the dock and wrinkle around the pilings.

The door from Bailey's keeps opening and closing, alternately letting bar sounds into the night and then muffling them again when the door *thunks* shut. She settles cross-legged on the dock where the draping needles of a pine tree block her view of the other cottages just enough so that she thinks she can smoke her cigarette in peace without anyone noticing. It is fabulous—best part of the day, but over too soon.

A few minutes later, she hears a door slap shut followed by footsteps behind her and she turns to see Cade walking down the pine needle path from his cottage with cans of beer dangling from the plastic rings of a six-pack. He smiles and waves as he makes his way down the dock. When he settles beside her, he draws his knees up and rests his arms on them, offers her a beer. She shakes her head, no, then watches him peel a can from the plastic ring.

"I smelled smoke and figured I'd find you here," he says.

"Very funny." She eyes the sweating cans. "On the other hand," she says, extending her hand toward the six-pack. He offers the one in his hand to her, popping the tab back before he does so, and then pulls another one from the ring for himself.

"Your secret is safe with me," he says.

"It's only once in a while."

"Right." He smiles.

"I'm quitting."

"Yeah, you've mentioned that before."

She swings an elbow into his side playfully.

They sit in silence for a time, comfortable, not having to say anything, and she is grateful just for the company. Spring has settled in even earlier in southern Maryland, as it does, having something to do with the way the peninsula is cradled between both the St. Mary's River and the Chesapeake Bay. The trees are budding wildly, spindly dogwoods confettied in white blossoms, and the pines are tipped in pale-green new-growth needles.

She tells him Tasha is out of the hospital and outpatient for now, traveling to the hospital for treatments three times a week.

He wants to know how Lacey is holding up, and she tells him she's okay.

She doesn't mention the way she is struggling with blame, cause and effect, accountability. Lacey spent the better part of the ride down debating with herself, thinking that maybe she was the cause of everything—Tasha's getting sick, Mac's leaving, her mother's leaving—but eventually came around to thinking that while she may not have been the *cause,* she may have still, in some weird way, gotten what she *deserved.* It is an unsettling conclusion and while she can't be exactly sure as to why she deserves it, it has to make sense, and then she found herself even more angered by the fact that Tasha had become the collateral damage for Lacey's own sins—whatever they must be.

She wraps her arms around her knees and gazes across the river. "I wonder sometimes if these kids appreciate what they have here. You know, the tidewater architecture, the sailing, the sense of history."

"Some do and some don't, and some will someday." He sips his beer. "I still wish there was a decent restaurant somewhere—or an art museum. I'm a little tired of student exhibits where the name of the piece has to be six paragraphs long because that's how long it takes to explain the damn thing." He leans back against a piling and Lacey looks at him, surprised.

"Are you telling me our little college's lacrosse coach is into art?"

"I'm a coach, Lacey, not a Neanderthal."

She laughs appreciatively, but thinks it is possible she has hurt his feelings. "Sorry," she says sincerely. "That was snotty of me."

"It was." His jaw softens into a forgiving smile. "However, I'm also still a little freaked out about buying my milk and butter from a place that stores bait and bloodworms in the same refrigerator." He grimaces and shakes his head.

"Okay, I'll give you that. But really, you'll get used to it. Give it time. This place has a way of sneaking up on you and one day you'll wake up and it just feels like where you belong. And the things that you're missing—the nightlife or the shopping or whatever, won't seem so important." She smiles at him. "Didn't you read the brochure before you signed up? I do believe it specifically states that Southern Maryland College is a rural riverfront campus."

"They neglected to mention that it's one hundred and six degrees in the summer and that we serve as human Slurpees to the mosquitoes."

Lacey nods. The part about the mosquitoes is true. "And just how is it that they manage to squeeze through the screens?" she asks. "Have you noticed that?"

He says that he has and reminds her that he sprays his screens with mosquito spray. He'd suggested it to her last August when the mosquitoes had been especially voracious. She tells him what she told him then, that she didn't want that poison around Tasha. "I don't like using that stuff," she says.

There is a certain irony in it all that is not lost on either of them.

"Better than malaria," he says.

They both simultaneously sip from their cans and then he leans back on his elbows. She watches him squint and flick a small stone with his thumb, shooting it like a marble across the dock and into the water.

He turns to her and asks when she wants to get started in the morning and she tells him the earlier, the better. She wants to get back on the road as soon as she can. He says he understands.

When he sits up, wipes the sweat from his can of beer and pulls at the collar of his T-shirt, she can hear the threads pop and snap at the neck.

He points to the dusky outline of a muskrat sludging up the bank and then brings his hand back to the dock and leans back on his elbows again beside her.

"Oh," she says, "Tasha loves watching the muskrats!" And she looks over her shoulder thinking to call Tasha from the house, but catches herself and instinctively, without forethought, tips her head with a sigh to his shoulder.

His hand smooths slowly up her back, nudging her closer, she thinks, wants to think. He presses his lips against the side of her head and holds them there. There is a shift in the air between them, but she can't be sure if it is coming from her, blowing out of the depths of her recently ripped heart, or from him—a turn perhaps—in the way he is seeing her, an object of pity, perhaps? In spite of his warm breath in her face, a flood of caution warns her that she is misreading the moment. She sits up just a bit, trying to ignore the dark *thunk* of resignation that has just landed in her chest. He is just a friend, though right now she feels she needs something more, whatever that means. His hand slides down her back but then reaches for her own. He rubs a thumb across her knuckles.

"So how is she, really?"

"I don't know. Compared to what? Compared to before she was sick—awful. But compared to how she was a month ago—better, I think. It's hard to know, you know? Because the treatments themselves are so hard on her. That's the thing, Cade. Sometimes I think she's doing okay, and the doctors say she's doing 'as well as can be expected'—whatever the hell that means—but then other times, oh . . ." She looks up in the sky, noticing the way a milky cloud is filtering the moon. "It's like, when she feels really bad and she just isn't acting like herself, I get this feeling in the pit of my stomach that reminds me it could get worse. I think I'm not trying hard enough—like if I just focused more . . ." She pauses, knowing she has changed the trajectory of the previous moment with her rambling. "I sound ridiculous. I don't know if you can get this or not. It's probably just a mother thing."

"What is?"

"This feeling I have all the time, you know, like I'm not trying hard enough."

He tells her he knows that's not true.

There is nothing he can say that will change the way she feels, that everything rests on her shoulders and that *everything* is Tasha. She changes the subject, something she has a knack for. "Do you have any nieces or nephews, Cade?"

He reminds her that he, like she, is an only child, and so, no. She doesn't remember that he has told her this before and is surprised. She thinks now that she should have remembered something like that.

"Really?" Lacey says.

"Really, I'm an only child? Or really I told you?"

"I figured you came from a big family."

He looks at her, puzzled, and she rushes to tell him that she's not sure why, but she always pictured him coming from a big family.

"I boarded at prep school," he reminds her. "It was like having twenty-six brothers."

She remembers this about him. He had gone to a prep school in Connecticut, but his family lived in western Maryland, only an hour or so from where she grew up. He often told her stories about the crazy shenanigans he and his housemates got into, the pranks they played on their dorm parents, the way the boys had all bonded like brothers.

They talk until the mosquitoes begin to buzz in her ears and the air feels too damp around her neck and shoulders. When she says she has to go in, has to get some rest, *has to pee*, he walks her to the door and says he'll see her tomorrow. She flicks on the kitchen light and is running water in the sink when he comes back to her screen door.

"Hey, breakfast tomorrow?"

She smiles because she can't help herself.

"Don't tell me you're one of those women who don't eat breakfast," he teases.

"Oh, no. I eat breakfast, don't worry about that."

"I'm up at seven," he says. "Come by when you're decent." He winks and waves, stepping back into the shadows.

The next morning, she finds herself across from him in his kitchen at a small metal table, the kind you might expect to find on a patio, with a plate of pancakes steaming in front of her.

"I can't remember the last time somebody made me pancakes."

"My coffee's not bad, either."

"No kidding," holding up her mug for a refill. He obliges, pouring with one hand and flipping two pancakes onto another plate before sitting down across from her. The table is so small their plates touch.

"So, there's a rumor you might be taking the team to the semifinals," she says.

"Yeah," and a grin spreads across his face like a wave. "Depends on the next four games, but it looks good."

"If Tasha's well enough, I'll bring her to the games—in Baltimore, right?"

"Will her treatments be finished by then?" He puts his fork down and touches just the tips of his fingers to the tips of hers.

"I don't know." She pulls back her hand from his and lifts her coffee mug. "We just don't know anything. Maybe. Maybe not. It all depends on how things go." The dark hole of missing Tasha is creeping up on her again and she finds herself trying to nudge it away, to no avail.

"Can I tell you something, Cade?"

He puts his hands in his lap, giving her his full attention.

"Sometimes, not every day, but just sometimes, I think she might die." The next thing she knows she is seeing him through a blur of tears, and she doesn't know if she has scared him or not, because she can't see him through her suddenly flushing eyes and he is quiet. "I don't know what will happen," she whispers. "I've never done this before. I don't know what will happen." Her fork clatters off the edge of her plate, flipping drops of syrup across the table, and tumbles to the floor.

"Oh, shit, God, I'm sorry. Oh, damn." She scoots back from the table, her coffee sloshing across his plate. "I'm sorry, I'm so sorry. God, what's wrong with me?" But before she can get away, before she can jump up, he is there, kneeling beside her and picking up her fork.

"Hey. It's okay. No big deal."

"I'm sorry, Cade, really. I don't know why I'm acting like this. I didn't mean to go to pieces like this." She wipes at her face with her hands.

"No, no," he says softly. "I wish I could just tell you it was all going to be okay." He sets the fork back on the table and uses his napkin to wipe syrup splatters from the floor.

"Then you'd be a huge liar," she says, but not harshly, "because you don't know any more than the doctors and I do." She sniffles and tosses her head back.

"I'm here for you," he says quietly from where he kneels beside her. "Whatever I can do."

The way he has said it makes her want to believe it, makes her want to be the kind of woman who accepts such things at face value and also accepts the calculated risk that goes along with the acknowledgment of them. She drops her head. "I'm very sad," she says simply.

"I know you are." He is kneeling beside her, a napkin in his hand, syrup spotting his shirt. When he leans toward her, she collapses into his shoulder and sobs. His arms come up around her, holding all the pieces of her together.

It's okay to cry, he is saying. When he tilts his head back from hers, he wipes her tears with his fingers. She pulls her napkin from her lap, sliding it under her now-running nose and across her cheeks.

His hand goes to the back of her head, threads through her mass of curls, and he tips her head to his, presses a kiss to her forehead and then her temple and when his lips fall to her mouth, she tastes coffee and maple syrup.

She falls deeply into the kiss and there is a pinching in her chest, as if her squeezed-too-hard heart has opened reluctantly. She cannot help but run her fingers from the back of his neck and down to the collar of his T-shirt. It is a layered collage of kisses now, tender-soft and passionately deep, short and lingering. She moves to the crook of his shoulder where the tendons of his neck thicken and lets her mouth fall against the salty hollow of it. There is the oceanic swell of his breath in her ear and she turns again to his mouth.

"Wow," she whispers. It is all she can think of to say.

Her head is cupped in his hands and they nod forehead to forehead.

"Eat," he says. "It's getting cold."

When he rises from the floor to take his seat, sliding his arms away from her as he stands, she feels the rush of cool where he had held her.

He has no idea, she is thinking, watching him cut at his pancakes with the side of his fork, stab, and start to put a double-stack bite of pancakes to his mouth. He has no idea of the way in which a kiss has jumbled up everything inside of her, making her lose her focus, making her forget whatever it is she needs to be focusing on—Tasha, her classes—anything but this man who has made her anxious and suddenly self-conscious and not at all who she knows herself to be. And what is worse than the way she is acting is the way she is *wanting something*, the way she finds herself wanting to feel something and do something she hasn't felt or done in way too long, something which she was—up until now—certain she could live without. She looks at his face now, the broad smooth forehead, the blondish stubble on his otherwise too-smooth cheeks, the lips she has just kissed.

"What?" He stops midbite.

"What?" she echoes. "I didn't say anything."

She thinks she might be blushing, feels a strange heat come up her neck, and drops her gaze to her plate.

His hand falls to hers and she tangles her fingers in his. She feels as if she is standing on the edge of a pool that is winking in the sunlight and doesn't know if she should take the leap—if she is expected to jump or turn away. "Was that . . . *something*?" she finally says.

He looks directly into her eyes and there is just the barest hint of a hopeful smile. "It was to me," he says. "How about you?"

She smiles at him and he breaks into a full grin.

"Okay," she says, carefully untangling her fingers from his. "Next question—just to get my footing here—are you seeing anyone? Is there anything I should know?"

She detects a small crumbling in his face, barely perceptible, but she is sure it is there and now he is about to tell her just what she should have suspected, that it was a mistake.

"Of course not," he says.

She raises her brows just to let him know she isn't convinced.

"I wouldn't have kissed you if I was. I just don't work that way."

"That's refreshing. Good to know."

He puts a forkful of pancakes in his mouth and chews, considers. "What about you?"

She laughs, the idea is so startling to her. "No way, I mean, no, no, I don't."

They smile at one another, and again she feels the rare flush moving up and into her cheeks.

They eat in surprisingly comfortable silence, as if something monumental has been settled between them.

September 5, 1974

I'm laying here in bed and my legs are shaking so bad they're making waves through the coverlet and it's all I can do to keep my stomach from coming up. Uncle Price, Aunt Virgie, and Lacey are all at the church setting the flowers and putting up the long tables in the church hall for my wedding tomorrow. But I am ashamed to even think of putting on my beautiful ecru dress in the morning. I have no business walking down the aisle and into the rest of my life with a fine man like Willy. I am fearful of just what kind of sin it might be for me to marry him.

I can still smell it on me. I smell the smoke and the whiskey and the sourness that clung to him from the long drive here. I can feel him—Lord, I can, the scratch of his face on mine, and his hands pushing up into me.

I don't know how to tell of this, and so I will tell it slow, just as it happened, and in the end of the telling I will read it back to myself and find the very place where I went wrong.

At first I thought it was Little Jim. I saw the red truck—Little Jim's truck—coming into town down a ways when I went across the street to the pharmacy. It spilled off the road a bit and kicked up dirt and grass along the side and then swayed back onto the road again. I thought for sure it was Little Jim and I ducked fast into the pharmacy. From the front door I was at a distance but not too far to see the truck swerve wide and then swing into the

Starting Gate Bar and Grill, spitting gravel and scrunching to a stop with its nose near crashed up against the dumpster.

From the front of the store I watched for a spell, telling Tolly at the counter that I was just window shopping. I watched for a bit and then I could see the truck pull out of the lot and head back out of town the same way it come in, slowing down some as it passed the hardware store then kicking back up again as it moved on. I watched for a spell more and Tolly Martin and me got to talking about my wedding coming up tomorrow and I told her I was thinking of buying a lipstick for my wedding day. My hands weren't shaking so much and I was feeling some relief as the truck did not come by again so I went on deep into the back of the store where all the makeup is.

It's my favorite part of the pharmacy. Everything hangs from little silver rods and is sorted by products—with your lipsticks coming first and moving on to blushes and so on and ending up with nail polish. Everything is then further sorted by color, red being the first color at the top and the pinky-whites being at the bottom.

There is something calming about all those colors spread out in such a way and it soothed me some. I further reminded myself that Little Jim wouldn't have no idea to look for me in here, least of all back by all these makeups. He never seen me in any color but what the good Lord give me so he would never think to look in the back. I spent way too much time looking over lipsticks and trying to find a nice color for tomorrow. I found one called Seashell and figured it was a good color for me.

After I paid at the front counter, I looked careful outside afore I stepped out. Little Jim's truck was surely gone and I felt safe about going straight across the street to the apartment. Just to be sure, though, I came out real slow, looking up and down the road, over at the Esso, down a bit to Farmers National Bank, and just past the stop sign to Kiel's Feed and Grain.

Uncle had closed the store up early on account of getting ready for the wedding, so I went round back to the stairs and went on up. I never locked it. I should have locked the door behind me, but it never did occur to me. Uncle always locks up the store but we never think to lock the apartment door—never have. It just wasn't in my thoughts to throw the bolt we never used or to think anyone could be coming in behind me. I went to the front window and looked up and down the street for Little Jim's truck, just to be sure, and never saw it. Oddly, I remember thinking how pretty the Queen Anne's lace and the tiger lily looked coming up in little dusty patches along the road as it led out of town.

I thought I heard footsteps in the kitchen, but I couldn't be sure of it with the bath water running. I had taken off my dress and slung it over the towel rack and I reached for it real quick. I turned off the water and all I could hear was my heart thumping in my chest, so I turned the water back on and started to put the dress back on the towel bar. That's when the door burst open and Daddy slumped against the doorframe.

My heart jumped straight up from my chest and into my mouth like a leap frog and I could not speak a word. I scrambled behind the door and pulled my dress across the front of me. He yelled for me—as if I was far away—his head rolling on his shoulders, telling me to STEP OUT *and* COME ROUND *and slamming his hand against the doorframe.*

I'm taking you home, girl, he said. You and that little baby of yours. Where's my granbaby? He said he'd borrowed Little Jim's truck, but that didn't make him beholden to Little Jim. He said he whupped Little Jim good for beating me like he did. His words were garbled up some but I heard him say that it was all a long time ago and it was time to let bygones be bygones.

I told him Lacey weren't home and when I backed up from behind the door he grabbed at the dress I held up to cover the front of me. I said, No, Daddy. I said _no_ and I held tight to my dress across my bosoms and he pulled hard at what hung from my arms and he pulled me right at him—I would not give up the dress—like I was on a leash.

I pushed hard at him and he fell backward, but he took me down with him, smashing down to the floor, and I kept trying to wrap the dress around me to cover myself, but he kept wrapping himself in it at the same time, like he was wrapping himself in a blanket. When he had it all pulled from me and his hands were tangled in it, I got up quick from the floor of the hall and ran to my room. I grabbed the spread from the bed and covered myself. He was already in the doorway afore I could pull it all around me. He was coming in slow, none of his body moving now but the shuffle of his feet across the floor, like he was dealing with a spooked rabbit. I told him—though my voice was shaking hard and it came out bumpy—Go home, Daddy, I said. Go on home now.

He began explaining, in that sad sad voice, how he was lonely and needed me and what I had done, running off like I done, was bad. People was talking about him now, he said he couldn't get no work cause everyone lost respect for him. People were saying things, bad things, and he needed me to come home— it was the only way. Me and the baby had to come home, cause that was the only way to show people that he was respectable. I owed him that much, after what I gone and done.

He said things were partly his fault, and that I probably didn't know no better—not having Mama around and all. Mamas have to teach their girls certain things, things not to do and such, and I was all alone that way, so he understood.

I could feel my brain scrambling up in my head when he talked at me. I could feel the back of my jaw lock up, and the stinging in my chest was like a hundred hornets trying to get out. And all I could manage to say was Don't make me come home, Daddy. Don't make me come home. I knew I was crying cause I could taste my own tears, but they weren't the sad kind of tears that come slow and mean something. They wasn't the kind of tears that could wash away the troubles that dredged them up. These were angry shook-up tears. These were the kind of tears that can make your chest hurt cause they seem to take the very air you're breathing right up out of you. These were the kind of tears you can't see through, not clearly, which maybe explains partly why I let him walk toward me with his arms out. My heart needed comfort or it would surely break and for just a second I mistook him for my daddy, the daddy that used to take care of me and say my prayers with me and kiss the top of my head. The daddy who knew my tickle spots and got the fish hook out of my thumb and couldn't give me a spanking—even when I needed one, so Mama always had to do it.

That's who I thought he was—for just a little second. And so maybe I let him put his arms around me, and maybe I even let him rub his hand up my back, but then I remembered. I remembered everything when he started to push against me, pushing me down on the bed. I squeezed my eyes and held my hands tight together across my chest, like a fierce prayer was being said. I heard the clink of his belt and his zipper and I tried to think about breathing. If I could only remember to breathe—but even with my teeth clenched each breath just sucked more of him into me, sucked in the smoke and the whiskey, the marsh and the ocean, the fish guts and the fried meats and seaweed and oyster shells.

When it was done I unclenched my teeth and told him to go. I didn't beg or cry no more. I didn't even have to look at him. Doing what he done had changed him and there was a sorryness about him that hung in the air—even more than usual—and he left quiet-like, sniffling into his sleeve. But daring to ask one more time would I come home and bring the baby.

I have read this over and tried to imagine it different. What I could of done different is nothing. I am nobody special.

All I can see in my head now is the ocean. I can feel it beating against my legs, taking me out, pulling at me, and the salt burns at the raw places in me. I want to be pulled out to the blackest bottom of it. I want to breathe it into me and let it wash out my lungs. I want to clean him out of me and go down into it.

The first time it happened I lay froze through the night and full into the next day. I could not unlock my body to neither run nor hide nor settle my brain to even go about regular business. But the next night something begun to thaw in me and just as the moon come up through the window, I near fell out of the bed and just started walking to the marsh, to where the water trickles against the shore and loses itself in the reeds. I stepped in, barefoot, and felt the muddy bottom suck at my feet. It was dark, but a half moon hung in the sky and cut a ribbon of light straight out to the pool of the black sound. I cut my feet on shells, felt the squish of the muddy bottom coming between my toes, and kept going deeper, trying to find the deepest part of it. I think a snake slipped past my hips and the light of the moon wove and winked across the back of it. I couldn't stop. I couldn't let go of the need to feel the water coming up on me. I was far out when it rose to my shoulders. That's when I knew I had to choose.

And that time I chose to turn around.

CHAPTER 17

The Snake

When Mac arrived that afternoon, Willy was surprised to see that he didn't have Kat with him. "Not my weekend," Mac explained, and Willy found that strange, this shuffling of children between homes. It was one of the reasons he had been so happy to bring May and Lacey home to the farm years ago, to give them a permanent place. He couldn't imagine, thinking on it, what he would have done if May had up and surfaced one day and demanded to split their time with Lacey, or—worse yet—taken her away altogether. He wouldn't have stood for it. He is sure of that now. He hadn't fought for May and he can't be sure why, maybe something to do with never feeling like he deserved her in the first place. No, that isn't right. Maybe thinking he couldn't bear fighting for her if he was just going to lose again anyway. Whatever it was, he knows he could have gone on after her, should have, but didn't, thinking maybe she'd come back of her own accord. But it was different with Lacey. He couldn't say—nor did he want to think about—exactly how, but it was different.

As for Mac, having him around hasn't been such a bad thing so far. Willy is finding his presence amusing, even though right now he is rearranging things in the cupboard as he unloads bags of groceries he brought with him. This is bothering Willy some, Mac shoving Willy's Cheerios to a second cabinet and moving his salt and pepper from the back of the stove to the far side of the sink.

"Spices really shouldn't go on the back of a stove. The heat will make them turn."

Willy isn't too sure what he is talking about. He never considered his salt and pepper to be *spices*. He is a little confounded, in fact, by Mac's constant fiddling around in his kitchen. It just doesn't seem natural. Mac was forever asking for things no self-respecting bachelor had too much business with—like did Willy have any *genuine* vanilla, chai tea—whatever the hell that was—or fresh pine nuts. Does he have a garlic press, a lemon zester? And—dare he ask—does he have a food processor?

"Food processor?" Willy says, knowing he has heard of it, but not quite sure of what it is.

"Yeah, for chopping food."

Willy stares at him for a long second, opens a drawer, and pulls out a cleaver and a butcher knife, both of which have seen better days and bear rusty blemishes near the handles. "Right here," he says, setting them on the counter.

"No, I mean . . ." But Mac stops himself and sighs hopelessly. "Okay, okay," he says, picking up the cleaver, rejecting it, and settling on the second, less damaged knife. "But this is just going to take a little longer. That's all."

"Fine by me," says Willy. And he heads out the door to finish some business at the coop. When he gathered eggs earlier that morning, the chickens were squawking and agitated, more so than usual, and when he flipped the lid to the laying boxes, he was startled by a five-foot black snake stretched out and lazy in the straw and eggs. The perfect shape of an egg bulged from within the snake about five inches back from the head. Normally it would have taken him all of about three seconds to grab a shovel and slice the snake in half with one quick chop. Willy had no argument with snakes—but he wasn't turning his nesting boxes into a feeding trough, either. Best to be rid of the thing. But something stopped him this time. Maybe it was the size. A five-footer was unusually large—you had to appreciate something like that—or maybe he was feeling a little generous about the egg, still perfectly shaped but now encased in shimmering black snake skin. Whatever it was, he didn't want to kill it, a marvel he hadn't quite taken stock of before. The snake, slowed down by the meal, only writhed slightly and pulsed its body to painstakingly urge the egg farther on.

Willy snatched at the snake, picking it up so that its head was between his thumb and forefinger and the heel of his hand touched where the egg was lodged. He dropped it, tail first and twisting, into a feed sack, knotted the top, and tossed it in an old wooden work cart that sat on the shady side of the coop next to a couple of old tires, an ivy-covered woodpile, and some discarded lumber scraps.

Now, coming back to the chicken house, he is thinking again what a damn lame farmer he has become, not even capable of keeping a bunch of hens safe from one old black snake. He picks up the shovel that hangs just inside the coop and comes back out again and around the corner to where the bag lays. The sack isn't moving. He could just slam the shovel down once or twice, toss the whole thing on the compost heap, and be done with it.

He nudges the bag with the end of the shovel. It moves just slightly. He picks the feed sack up and easily undoes the knot. The snake lies twisted in the bottom of the bag, a knotted mass of black scales and muscle. There doesn't appear to be any trace of the egg from this morning. He knots the bag again and brings it around to the back stoop of the house with him where he drops it next to the door.

Tasha is in the sunroom again, on the sofa watching *Bambi* this time and curled against the giant stuffed bear as if it is a pillow. "Hey, sunshine. Want to take a ride on the tractor?"

She shakes her head softly. "Can Carlotta come over again? Bring Thumper? Please?"

"Let me think on that," he says, but there's nothing to think about. That dumb rabbit made her happy and that is what he's aiming for. "I'll give her a call later," he says. "How about that tractor ride? Hmmm?"

She shakes her head again.

"Aw, come on," he says. "It's a real nice day outside."

Just then Mac comes in from the kitchen. He has a dishtowel tucked in his waistband and he is using one end of it to wipe his hands. "What's going on, Willy?" he asks.

"Come on, sugar. Daddy will come, too," says Willy.

"Go where?"

"You will, Daddy?"

"Go where?" he says again.

"For a ride," says Willy.

"On the big tractor," says Tasha.

Willy finds Tasha's tennis shoes under the sofa and hands them to her. She has a hooded sweatshirt on, and she keeps the hood up and the string pulled tight under her chin. It seems too warm to him and he doesn't like to see her with the hood so tight, but she is pretty adamant about it. He wonders what will happen as the weather gets even warmer.

As the three of them head out the door, Willy scoops up the sack by the stoop. He pauses to feel the promise in the afternoon sun. The sky is robin's egg blue and the tree line of birches to the west is the tender green of spring. Tasha and Mac follow him to the aluminum garage, a hundred yards or so from the house, where he slides open the wide doors with a screech and sends up a spray of swallows who take to the sky and swoop like arrowheads. It takes a couple of tries, but the tractor roars to life just as it always has. He backs it out through the wide sliding double doors.

Mac, looking just a little uncertain, lifts Tasha up to Willy and then climbs on himself. He is forced to stand on the sideboard and hold on to the back of the seat. Willy has the sack hanging from the hand he steers with and the other is wrapped around Tasha on his lap.

"Where should we go?" she shouts in his ear over the din of the tractor, and Willy nods to the upper fields.

"Where are we going?" shouts Mac. Willy ignores him.

Willy drives the tractor up an old rutted path, which eventually tapers as they come upon the first field. He then veers right along the low stone wall nearly covered in vines and bramble. A small red fox shoots out of the undergrowth and leaps over the stones once they are nearly upon it.

Tasha bounces on his lap at the sight of it, pointing as it weaves with its tail straight out behind it until it is lost in the timothy. The snake in the bag swings hard against Willy's leg as he takes a sharp left along another slightly graveled trail, bordered on one side by tall pines. The tractor dips down into a damp gully and up again toward a thick wall of pine and mulberry. Willy heads for a narrow opening between the trees that he is constantly clearing in the spring. In the thick of summer, he knows that the ground will be littered with rotting mulberries and the drunken starlings that feast on them. He will have to remember to show that to Tasha, too.

Willy moves through the break in the tree line an

d Mac is forced to suddenly duck down to avoid being swatted by low-hanging branches. Breaking into the upper field is always a pleasure for Willy. It sits atop a small hill, and it isn't until you are actually in the field, having come through the opening, that you even would know it is there.

He turns off the tractor and waits for the hum to clear his ears.

Mac jumps to the ground. "Fabulous," he says, turning in a circle and looking out over the expanse. "This is fabulous."

To Willy, it has always felt just like the top of the world, as if he can touch the sky from here. The boundaries of the field dip down slightly all around so that it seems borderless, as though the timothy tickles the sky in every direction and if you were to run through the fields, there would be no end to it other than the heavens themselves.

Mac takes Tasha from Willy's lap and sets her on the ground. Immediately, she squats on her haunches to watch a grasshopper munching on a stalk of timothy. She squeals and falls back on her bottom when it takes off flying with a startling ripple of its wings.

Willy gets down from the tractor, setting the bag on the seat. He walks over to where Tasha now sits giggling, leans over, and quickly scoops another grasshopper into the cup of his hands.

"Let me see, let me see," she says, pushing herself up off the ground.

"If I open up my hands, he might hop away," Willy warns her. "Here, come look." He peels back his thumbs so that Tasha can see the creature in the cup of his hands. It rolls its eyes and taps the confines of Willy's hands with slender green antennae.

"Oh, Willy, it bit you!" she says, quickly peeling his hands apart. The grasshopper crawls to his wrist like a little jewel on jointed legs. She points to a red-black stain in the palm of his hand about the size of a pencil eraser.

"No, sugar. It threw up on me. They do that sometimes."

"How come?"

"Scare away predators—you know, birds and such that eat them. They just do it 'cause they're afraid of being eaten."

"Or afraid of dying?"

"Could be," he says. "I suppose that's one way of looking at it."

"Me, too. That's probably why I threw up," she says.

"Or maybe you just didn't feel good," says Willy.

"Hey, Willy?"

"Hmmm?"

"You're not even afraid of throw up, are you?"

"Naw, and I'm not afraid of blood, neither."

"Me, neither." She gently touches the grasshopper with the tip of her finger, nudging, and it takes off low across the field, making a sudden sound like a deck of cards being shuffled. Tasha slips her hand into Willy's.

"Wanna take that hood down and get some sunshine on your brain?"

She giggles and uses her free hand to pull the hood down.

Willy feels some small satisfaction in seeing her tufted head bare under a big sky. *It's not so bad*, he thinks to himself.

Mac is wandering through the field in no apparent direction. Tasha calls to him. "Come back, Daddy! Willy has a surprise."

Willy takes the sack down from the seat of the tractor and moves about twenty feet in toward the center of the field. The grass is near knee-high to a man, but the three of them have inadvertently created a small clearing of about four feet in diameter. "Just a little something I wanted to show you," he says, unknotting the bag. Mac stands across from him, brows lifted, curious.

"Stand back, just a bit, sugar," he says to Tasha, waving with his free hand.

He opens the bag, turns it over, and dumps. A tightly coiled bundle of writhing snake falls to the trampled grass. It quickly untwists itself to its full, incredible length, lifts its head a few inches from the ground, and flicks its tongue. It swings in a half circle, flicking over and over at the air around it.

Tasha takes a step toward it, but Willy holds her back. "Now don't crowd him," he says. "He won't bite, but see that tongue of his? Now that's real sensitive. He actually smells with it, and he's smelling us right now."

"Can I pet him, Willy?"

"He won't let you, sugar." Willy looks up at Mac. He is frozen where he stands and staring, horrified, at the snake less than three feet from the tip of his fancy running shoes.

Suddenly the snake swings toward Mac, and with a fierce whip of its tail, shoots like a streak of black ribbon between his legs.

"Jesus Christ!" Mac screams, leaping off the ground as if scrambling to fly. He is nearly knocked to the ground by Tasha as she speeds past him after the snake. "I see him, Willy! I see him!"

Willy watches her run, seeming nothing like the sick little girl who was curled up with a giant stuffed bear earlier. He's pleased, but suddenly struck by a memory he'd rather not have nudge up against the sight of Tasha running through the grass in widening circles, shrieking with abandon. "Help me find him!" she shouts. But Willy is remembering now the last slow days of Beauford. Once he had come to live on the farm after Virgie and Price passed, he had become Willy's constant companion, trudging back and forth to the barn with a sense of purpose Willy never knew the old dog had in him, until, of course, Lacey would be due home from school and then he would wait for her at the end of the drive, curled in the cool grass beside the mailbox, trot beside her up to the house, and spend the rest of the day curled on her bed beside her or spread on the kitchen lino-leum under her feet. In time, however, he became unable to manage the steps to the second floor and took to sleeping downstairs, his back curled to the davenport. As winter crept in, Willy made it a point to stoke up the woodstove before retiring to bed himself, just to make sure the room stayed warm enough for his old bones. By December the dog would still trudge to the barn with Willy, but once there he would settle at the far end on fresh straw and only his eyes followed Willy through his chores. He'd wag his tail eagerly at the sight of Doc Asher, one of his favorite humans, never somehow connecting the man to vaccinations and ear inspections. He'd thump his tail, swishing the straw around his rump until Doc would lean down and scratch him behind the ears. *Hey, old boy, how's it going, hmmm?*

Doc gave him cortisone shots now and again and he'd walk a little more sure of himself for a week or two, his back end not crumbling so much, maybe even taking the steps now and then, but by February even the shots failed to lighten the load he carried.

One morning he wouldn't get up, wouldn't even lift his head to Lacey as she came down the steps. She stooped down and rubbed her hand down his neck, talking soft and low, careful not to touch his hips, so thin now that even through the mats of fur, you could see his hip bone sticking out like an old doorknob.

Willy watched the pair. Watched the old dog's goopy eyes, the way they almost pleaded with Lacey, the way they closed and opened, trying to bear down on her. Willy didn't have to say a thing.

"I guess it's time to call Doc," she said in a papery voice. And they both knew she didn't mean for another shot. "Wait till I get home?"

Willy asked if she was sure.

She was.

When Lacey got home from school, she curled up on the floor beside Beauford, Willy in the stuffed chair, the woodstove cranked to an unbearable warmth. The old dog's uneven breath the only sound, they sat with a heavy silence between them. He'd been a good dog, helluva good dog.

Old Beauford only blinked at the knock at the door. Willy remembers thinking how warm and watery those eyes looked. *Blink, blink.*

Willy went to the door to let the doc in. But then, that dog did the damnedest thing. He lay there looking at Doc and then suddenly, his tail wagged, two, three times, and his hind end got to scrambling till they got a purchase on the carpet, and the dog managed to get to his feet, his front legs wide and his head hanging but rising up as he moved across the room and made his way to the man, tucked his muzzle between the doc's thighs, whimpered, nudged, and stood there in all the dignity he could muster, that tail swishing low. Doc scratched Beauford's head, ran both his hands down his neck, ruffled his fur. *I know, boy, I'm here.*

And then the tears started, first Lacey's, and then, damn it, Willy's own.

Beauford turned his neck to lick the doc's hand and lowered himself down to the floor, sliding his muzzle down Doc's thighs, graceful as a swan settling into her nest, tail still swishing softly.

By the time Doc had his bag unpacked, the old dog was flat out on his side again, eyes closed, raggedy breath filling the room, ready, ready to take his leave of them.

Tasha twirls now in the grass. "I lost him!"

Willy feels the knot growing in his throat, can almost feel the heat of Beauford's breath against his own hand as a breeze shimmies over the field. He turns away, maybe needing a moment, and sees Mac headed for the tractor.

"You alright, boy?" Willy calls to him. But Mac is climbing the tractor with one hand, the other hand spread to his chest, his mouth still open in surprise, and can only nod. Willy is sure he is hyperventilating. "Catch your breath, boy."

Mac nods more fiercely.

"I lost him, Willy. Daddy, help me find him."

"I don't think your daddy feels too good right now," says Willy.

"Jesus, Willy," says Mac. "You could have warned me."

"Don't like snakes?" he says.

"Not a fan," says Mac, stating the obvious.

"Nothing to be embarrassed about." Willy looks out to the field, watches the hood of Tasha's sweatshirt billow behind her as she runs, sees how the western sun casts her shadow long and lean so that her silhouette looks more like a girl of sixteen than that of a small child.

"We're all afraid of something, is all I'm saying." He is waving to Tasha in the field, seeing the way both she and her long shadow wave back to him. The sun makes her scalp shine pink in places where there is no hair left at all. "That's all I'm saying."

CHAPTER 18

A Dinner Party

Seven weeks have passed since Tasha started her treatments. The first round of chemo will end in the next two weeks, and Lacey has no way of telling if her daughter is better or worse. Dr. Oren always says everything is proceeding as expected. To Lacey's way of thinking, nothing about any of this feels expected.

She is packing to head back down to the college tomorrow for two nights and finds herself guilty of looking forward to it, looking forward to the time she will spend with some distance between Tasha's illness and her own life, the life that is taking shape without Tasha in it, the life that is taking shape around Cade. Feeling this way is not something she is proud of and it is a thought she crams back down inside herself only to find that it makes her chest hurt.

She inspects the pile of bras and underpants she has piled on the bed. There's nothing sexy about any of it. What she wouldn't give for an hour spent in Victoria's Secret. She imagines herself in a sexy little thong, maybe black—no, too cliché—maybe aqua, and she laughs at herself. She is too utilitarian for such indulgences. She had owned a thong once and spent the better part of a day trying to remove it from the crack of her bottom.

She tries to ease the cramping that has lodged, rag-like, behind her sternum by reminding herself that as much as she wants to be with Cade, she has not once in the past weeks made the trip unless it was related to her classes. She would never, ever leave Tasha, she assures herself, if she didn't have to. And Tasha has Mac or Willy or both when she is gone. But she and Cade talk on the phone every night after Tasha is in bed and it is something Lacey looks forward to. She takes her phone to her room every evening, opens the window, and climbs out to her smoking porch. It is the best part of her evening. She can relax in the knowledge that Tasha is sleeping and safe and another day of this illness is behind her. She can smoke her cigarette in utter peace, looking out over the pond, watching the bats dip and the fireflies rising while she waits for his call.

Right now, it is a too-warm day, too warm for the last week in May, and it has taken them all by surprise. Heat is something they all prefer to ease into with the longer days of summer. Because of this, the three of them started with a lazy morning, everyone half dressed at the breakfast table, Willy slower to get to the chickens, and Tasha not even thinking to cover her head as she usually does until much later in the morning when she grabbed her pink baseball cap and headed out to the coop with Willy.

Looking out the window, Lacey spies Carlotta's car coming up the drive. It is an older model maroon Cadillac, and she would expect nothing less from her. The woman is a bit of a mystery, a sort of Italian Mary Poppins in their life. She has come to give Tasha her growth factor injection through the port.

Dr. Oren started her on the injections a few weeks ago to stimulate the production of white blood cells. Lacey and Willy were both taught how to do it and how to flush the port with heparin if necessary, but it made them nervous and they kept putting the procedure off until later and later every day. Finally, Willy just called Carlotta and asked for her help with it, and she was all too happy to take care of it daily. She always brings Thumper with her and he sits patiently in Tasha's lap while she strokes his long ears and coos to him.

This evening, Carlotta is also making dinner for the four of them. Willy is nervous about it, Lacey can tell. He's been acting funny ever since Carlotta called at noon to say she wanted to come over and fix them a big Italian supper. Ever since, and in spite of the heat, he has spent the afternoon puttering around the house in a way Lacey isn't used to, cleaning out the refrigerator, moving the salt and pepper shakers from a cupboard to the back of the stove and back again to the cupboard, sharpening the knives. And a few minutes earlier, she had watched him head back into his bedroom again for his second wardrobe change of the day, coming out in a white button-down collared shirt, with long sleeves, of all things.

"Aren't you going to be hot in that?" she asked, peeking into the hallway as he headed into the bathroom.

He just mumbled, turned, and went back into his bedroom, coming out a few minutes later in a short-sleeved collared polo shirt—not a real Polo shirt—this one with a small blue duck emblem the size of a quarter on the breast pocket.

"Better?" he asked, looking down at himself, maybe noticing the flecks of mud splattering the cuffs of his jeans. "Maybe khakis." He turned and went back into his room.

Minutes later she heard his door and stepped out into the hall to meet him.

"Maybe a suit would be better," she said, and he had looked up at her, horrified. "I'm kidding, Willy. You look nice."

He relaxed, starting to tuck his shirt in and then changed his mind.

"Untucked," she said. "Definitely untucked."

"Yeah, well . . ." He headed down the stairs.

"You could be in an L.L. Bean catalogue," she said. He waved her off with his back to her, but she heard him chuckle.

Now Lacey stuffs her practical underwear in her bag and heads downstairs to find Tasha and greet Carlotta.

Willy is helping her in the door with Thumper's cage in one hand and two bags of groceries hefted in his other. Carlotta is carrying a huge empty pot and a canvas bag that looks to be filled with cooking utensils, slotted spoons, a ladle, and an enormous cheese grater.

"Well, hello, hon!" she says to Lacey. "Where's the princess?" Tasha pads into the kitchen, goes straight to Carlotta, and hugs her. This takes Lacey by surprise. She knows Tasha is fond of her, but she's not a child who typically hugs in greeting. The baseball cap is nudged from Tasha's head as she buries herself in Carlotta's ample waist. Carlotta holds Tasha to her with one arm and runs her other hand down the child's head, letting it rest on her neck. Tasha's eyebrows and eyelashes have all but disappeared and so she seems to wear a consistently blank expression, but she is smiling now, and Lacey is reminded of how beautiful she is.

Willy sets Thumper's cage down on the floor and carries the bags to the counter, begins to unload Tupperware containers and a long box of pasta.

"I don't want you to touch a thing, Willy," says Carlotta. "I'm here to make things easier, not more complicated. I'm gonna get Tasha here settled with her meds—and Thumper, of course—and then get right to the cooking. Just leave it all on the counter. Dinner is at six sharp."

"I can help," Lacey offers.

Carlotta waves her hand through the air. "No, hon—I got this, but I'd love your company. Get back to whatever you were doing before I got here and join me later, maybe have a glass of wine with me."

Lacey knows there's no alcohol in the house. It's not a rule, just something that has never shown up. She's not sure why. She's known Willy to have a drink on only a handful of occasions, a single glass of wine at Pisticci after her graduation from Columbia, a beer with the nephews when they celebrated the opening of the new garden center with a barbecue, a shot of Jack courtesy of Doc Asher after he had to put down Beauford on a cold February night many years ago.

"I don't think we have any wine, Carlotta," says Lacey apologetically.

"I was just on my way out to get some," Willy offers.

Lacey doesn't believe him. "Well, sure," she says.

"Red or white?"

"A good, acidic red would be best," Carlotta pipes in on her way into the sunroom with Tasha and Thumper.

Lacey is certain he has no idea what she is talking about. She shrugs her shoulders to him, but he doesn't let on whether or not he knows what he is doing. "Want to tag along?" he asks her.

Of course, she does.

The inside of the liquor store is cold and refreshing, the bottles chilled to a comfortable 65 degrees. Lacey trails behind Willy through the aisles and, knowing he has no clue what he is looking for, she searches the aisle for a red she might know, might assume to be acidic, though she isn't sure herself what that would be.

"A Chianti?" she offers. "A cabernet?"

Willy only shrugs.

"Need some help, folks?" says a voice from behind them.

It is Ronnie Gelpin, an old classmate of Lacey's who had once worked at the pharmacy when Lacey was in high school. She had been forced to endure the embarrassment of buying tampons from him. She hopes he doesn't recognize her.

"Lacey!" he says when she turns around. "I thought that was you. I'd have recognized that hair anywhere."

"Yeah, well." She runs a hand through her tangle of tumbling curls and feels as self-conscious about it as she had at sixteen. "Hi, Ronnie. How've you been?"

"Great, just great. You don't live here anymore, right? Just visiting? And what are you up to these days? You're a doctor—or something like that, am I right?"

Lacey shakes her head, no, but he fires his questions off so quickly without waiting for an answer that it apparently doesn't register with him. "Looking for something special? We got your reds here, your whites next aisle over, bubbly varieties at the end of the next one over. Course, it all depends on what you're looking for." He hops foot to foot, anxious, apparently, to be of help.

"So you work here?" Lacey says, stating the obvious.

"Owner, partial owner. Me and my brothers bought in two years ago when Mr. Jakes passed on. Great guy, but just didn't have a handle on what folks are looking for these days. We had to make a lot of changes, as you can see," sweeping his hand in a wide circle around himself. "But we're doing great, just great. What can I help you with? A gift, or . . ."

"Well, son," Willy interjects, "we're having a little dinner party." Lacey looks at him wide-eyed. *Is that what we're having?* "And what we're looking for here is an *a-cidic* red," pronouncing the *a* in acidic as if he is ready to recite the alphabet. "One of your better varieties."

"Gotcha, gotcha."

"Something Italian," Willy says.

"Right. Now you got your Barolo, here," and he reaches for a deep, dark bottle from the shelf.

"Looks about right," says Willy. Lacey peers over Willy's shoulder to look at the bottle he now holds in his hand.

"Nebbiola," says Ronnie.

Willy looks up at him and blinks.

"The grapes," he says. "They're grown in Northern Italy. Nebbiola grapes."

"That so?" says Willy.

"Can't go wrong with that one."

Lacey peers closer to the bottle. "Oh my God, Willy. It's ninety-six dollars!"

"We'll take it," says Willy.

"Are you serious?" Lacey whispers in his ear, but he ignores her.

"How many bottles?" says Ronny, wrapping his hand around the neck of a second identical bottle. "How many guests you got coming to your dinner party?"

"Four," says Willy. "Better get two bottles; good thinking, son."

"Whoa, Willy . . ." says Lacey trailing behind the two of them to the counter. "Three!" she says. Ronnie stops in his tracks and turns to them.

"You want three bottles?"

"No, no!" she says. "Willy, there will only be three of us having wine. Tasha is *five*!"

"Oh, right." He chuckles, still following Ronny to the counter. "But if this wine is as good and acidic as Ronnie here says it is, we might want an extra."

The two of them stand at the counter as Ronnie rings up their wine. Lacey tries not to shake her head when the total comes to $203.52 and Willy hands him three crisp bills. It doesn't surprise Lacey at all that he carries a few hundred dollars around in his wallet. He never used credit cards. Ronnie has to go to a second drawer to make change for him.

"Been good to see you, Lacey," Ronnie says, handing over Willy's change. He sleeves the bottles in two thin bags and hands them over to Willy. "Hard to believe you're a doctor now."

Lacey is still shaking her head. "Sure is," she says.

Back in the truck Lacey looks to Willy with her mouth open, hardly able to speak.

"Willy," she finally says, "what the hell?"

"Damn," he says. "I don't think we have a corkscrew." And they both burst out laughing.

"Smells amazing!" says Lacey coming into the kitchen with Willy. She leans over the pot and inhales. "My gosh, what is it? It's heavenly." A thick red sauce burps over fist-size pieces of meat, rolled and wrapped in string.

"Braciola," says Carlotta. "Peasant dish. You won't get this in any restaurant around here. Very tender," she whispers, as if imparting a secret.

Tasha tromps into the kitchen with Thumper hanging from her arms, his huge back legs nearly dragging the floor. Lacey goes to take him from her. "Careful, Mommy, rabbits are fragile. Don't squeeze him too hard."

"He's very sweet," Lacey says. The heft of him is like a baby in her arms, his little nose tickling her chin.

Willy takes the never-used wineglasses from the china cabinet. They had been Virgie's and he had simply set them on display in the cabinet years ago in the same way they had been set in hers and never thought another thing about them. Now he brings them to the sink to rinse the dust from them.

"What can I do?" he asks.

"Pour me a glass of wine?" says Carlotta.

Willy goes upstairs to fetch his pocketknife with the corkscrew on it. As he comes back into the kitchen Carlotta is asking, "Did your mother like to cook, Lacey?"

Lacey and Willy stiffen. No one ever talks about May. They look at each other and look away.

"I don't know," Lacey says. "I don't really remember." She can't help but wonder how much Willy has told Carlotta, if anything, about May. But now that she thinks about it—now that she is being forced to think about it—she can remember some of May's cooking. Biscuits. She made biscuits at nearly every meal. And they were served piping hot topped with a slab of cold butter that would melt as it hit the biscuit just a bit but retain enough of the cold when she bit into them that she would lose herself in the mix of the two. And oatmeal, the best kind of warmth on a cold winter morning, topped with thick cream, brown sugar, and, of course, more butter. But, Lacey thinks now, that's all she can really remember. Except—there was a lemon cake, for special occasions, church functions, Easter. Sweet, tart, and so moist it would leave a fine layer of cake in the bottom of the pan that she would drag her little fingers through when the empty sheet cake pan sat in her lap on the way home from church. The memory of it, once forgotten, now makes her mouth pucker.

"How about you?" Carlotta wants to know. "You like to cook?"

"Not so much. I'm capable enough, I guess. Just so busy, and Tasha, well, she's picky."

As if on cue, Tasha is on her toes next to Carlotta as she begins ladling sauce into a gravy bowl. "Are we having a *red* dinner? I hate red dinners."

"How about just some pasta," Carlotta offers. "And maybe a shake?" She points to a cluster of brightly colored plastic cups with snap-on lids on the counter and then begins to put them in the refrigerator. "I made some protein drinks for her," she says to Lacey. "Just one of these a day and she's getting everything she needs."

Carlotta hands the last remaining drink from the counter to Tasha. "Bring this to the table, doll. We're ready to eat!" She puts her arm around Willy's back and ushers him to the dining room.

The meal is heavenly, the antipasto of salty olives, thin slices of pecorino reggiano, artichokes, pickled tomatoes, and freshly torn basil is exquisitely balanced by the wine that Willy can't help but pronounce *perfectly acidic*. By the time they are into the tender braciole and the second bottle of wine, Tasha has, of course, finished three bites of pasta and her protein shake and is settled on the sofa with Thumper.

Lacey isn't sure if it is the effects of the wine or the effects of having a full stomach, or maybe both, but as she watches Willy pat the top of Carlotta's hand and thank her for the meal and she watches Carlotta nearly glow under his gaze, Lacey feels a warmth settle over the table that she hasn't felt in years.

Later that night, while she is tucking Tasha into bed and Carlotta is washing dishes and Willy is drying and putting them away, she can hear the murmur of their voices from downstairs, the sprinkling of laughter, the snap of cabinets opening and shutting. The sounds drift out the open kitchen window and catch in the leaves of the sugar maple outside

Tasha's bedroom where they hang like the promise of a sweet rain.

Tucking Tasha into bed, Lacey asks her to open her mouth and she tips the bedside lamp to get a better look. "Mouth sores still bothering you?"

Tasha closes her lips and nods, yes.

"It will get better, honey. I promise."

"But it doesn't, Mommy."

"I know it doesn't seem like it, but you're getting better." Lacey leans down into Tasha's face, their noses nearly touching.

"You always say that."

Lacey doesn't think she does always say that, but she can't be sure. All she knows for certain is that in that moment, her face pressed to Tasha's and inhaling the very breath the child is exhaling—the breath that has just coursed through her lungs and sent the flush of pink to her face—tasting now, the sweetness of it in the back of her own throat, well, all she knows is that this daughter of hers is rooted to her, tangled in Lacey's core as if they share the same pulse.

"I always tell you the truth," says Lacey.

Tasha blinks, runs her tongue between her lips. They both can hear Carlotta's laughter followed by a gravelly chuckle from Willy and it makes the two of them smile conspiratorially and cock their heads in unison, tracking their footsteps across the kitchen floor below them.

Tasha whispers to Lacey, "I like Carlotta."

"I do, too," and she means it. It is strange, granted, to see Willy breathe a little bigger when Carlotta is in the house, but she likes it, the way they make her feel that what is between the two of them extends to her and Tasha as well.

Tasha settles to her side, and Lacey runs the back of her hand down her smooth cheek. In less than a minute, Tasha drifts off and still Lacey stays, listening to the soft wheeze in her breath, noticing her small pale hand curled next to her neck, the downy bits of hair patching her scalp, the whorl of her ears.

She places a tender kiss on her daughter's forehead, slips her finger into the soft curl of her daughter's fingers that close gently around her own. Outside the windows she can hear the *ting* of silverware going back in the drawer and the running of water. An unexpected breeze sighs at the window and she feels it twine around the two of them, lightly swing the door that creaks softly, and drift down through the heart of the house.

September 6, 1974

I am a married woman and this is my home now. I sleep in a room with two big windows that look out on the fields and the pond, and the branches of the maple tree outside our windows bend down and back with the breeze. Willy is breathing against my shoulder as I write this and his breath is warm when it floats over my neck. I like the smell of him, like good garden dirt and fresh water.

I didn't feel so good this morning, my wedding morning. The ocean was still calling to me from far away and there was something painful in the voice I was hearing. I wondered this morning if I would bear Willy touching me.

I have been wanting him to touch me for so long now, and it don't seem right that Daddy could take away my wanting Willy. Everything about Willy is soft—his lips, the skin under his jawbone where he likes me to put my fingers (and I know this cause when I touched him there he took my hand and kissed it and then held my fingers to him along his cheek and down his jaw to the softness under his face). And his eyes. They are deep gray like a winter ocean, but soft as flannel and I can't help but want to be wrapped up in those eyes of his.

When I saw Willy waiting at the altar for me this afternoon, I could not even manage one foot in front of the other. Lacey stood at the end of the aisle holding on to Willy's hand, and when she saw me, she smiled big as the whole world. Uncle Price had his arm strung through mine and he started on without me, pulling my elbow from my side. But then I seen Lacey waving me down, like she was telling me to hurry on up, we got a wedding to get done here, and I almost jumped to catch step with Uncle Price and went on down the aisle and into my new life.

After the wedding and a fine dinner of fancy chicken stuffed with ham and cheese, green beans, mashed potatoes, and cornbread—all made by the church ladies—and cake and champagne that Uncle Price bought, Lyle and Clint set up a microphone for toasts and such and hooked up a sound system with great big speakers. They played every kind of music you can imagine, from "Delta Dawn" to John Denver. When they played "Could It Be I'm Falling In Love" Willy put his arms around my waist and buried his head next to mine. Later on they played "Monster Mash" and I near died laughing watching Willy dance to it, scooping his bottom and swinging it round, making his arms like monster arms. So I joined right in dancing like I was Frankenstein's bride. I danced with near every man there, starting with Willy and then Uncle Price and moving on down to Moose Braggart who couldn't be more than twelve years old but dances like he was born to it. It was just like I always thought a wedding should be.

Lacey went to bed real easy tonight. She was tuckered out for sure. Aunt Virgie wanted to keep her over tonight but Willy said no, said we were a family now and I squeezed his hand when he said it. I was real proud she was no trouble. Though Willy would've spoiled her and let her stay up all night. Lord, I was nervous, but truth be told I was surprised to find there were many times today I found I was wanting him.

Somehow, just the way he was making me feel, like when we drove home tonight and his hand was on my knee, or the way he wrapped his fingers round the back of my neck and leaned over to kiss me in front of everyone and they all got to cheering and hollering—well somehow those little things were making me feel like I needed him, needed to lie down with him. It was something like how I used to feel with Little Jim, but nicer, not so dangerous.

He carried me in the door with Lacey scrambling behind us. His one arm come under my back and up under my arm and nearly fell on my breast and I would have let him touch me that way. I put my face to his neck and kissed him afore he set me down.

We were quiet for a long time after that.

Willy said he had to go check on the herd and I said I would put Lacey to bed and take a bath. I bathed with my eyes shut. I didn't want to see myself and I wished the water would rise on me and rush down my throat, fill my lungs, fill the parts of me that Daddy had taken and which now were not fit to share with Willy. I scrubbed parts of me raw and came out of the water without looking in the mirror.

When he came in from the barn I heard him drop his boots by the door. He came up to the bedroom in his new suit and stocking feet. I was already in bed, as I thought maybe I should be. He leaned over the bed and kissed me and I felt the cool of the outside on his cheeks.

He told me I was beautiful and it made me laugh to hear it, but I think he believed it because he was really looking at me then, peeling the covers down real slow and looking at me and touching me in a way that was kind of asking if it was okay. Next thing I knew I was touching him back. I never done that before. And we showed each other what was good and even what was not so good.

And while maybe I didn't forget about the water altogether, I couldn't hear it calling to me. But I could hear Willy's breathing and his heartbeat and I could hear the small bursts of breath that tumbled from him when he moved inside me. And I could hear the crack in his voice when he told me that he loved me and fell upon me soft and comfy as a winter quilt.

I must turn out this light and not disturb Willy's sleep. Though he is sleeping like a bear next to me with his leg cross mine and I am drawn to the soft smile on his face and would like to watch it all night long.

Lying here now like I am, feeling this afterward part and knowing he is loving me even in his sleep, I don't want so much to sink in the ocean and go into the black parts of it. Instead I feel more like I want to float. I want to spread my arms in a warm September ocean, look up at the sky, and let the moonlight bounce off of me. I will have to try harder to learn to swim.

September 12, 1974

> *1 dozen lemons*
> *powdered sugar*
> *1 pound butter*
> *find Lacey's church veil*

I will never find that veil and will have to purchase a new one. Willy said he saw her in the cellar catching crickets and wrapping them up in the veil, but he didn't know it was nothing special, he said. I will have to buy a new one for her in town today. This is my first trip into town as a married woman and I am anxious to hear my new name—Mrs. Cherrymill, Mrs. William Cherrymill. I think May Cherrymill may be just about the prettiest name a girl could hope for in a marrying situation.

CHAPTER 19

Together

Lacey is curled in a bed that is just now getting to know the curves of her body. The pillow is soft and deep, and beside her is Cade. He is propped up on pillows and he reaches down to her as she drifts into sleep and runs the backs of his fingers down her cheek. She smiles and turns toward him. He has a clipboard propped in his lap. The team has made it to the semi-finals and it keeps him awake at night. He goes over plays, drawing lines that she doesn't understand the meaning of, X's and O's that she assumes represent the players but she is sleepy and dreamy from sex and when she sees them she thinks of adolescent love notes, as if he is covering a page with her thoughts.

She has slept with him a handful of times and always at his house. She is not ready to have him in her bed, her home that she shares with Tasha. It amuses Lacey now to know that when she is in town, he makes his bed.

They graded final papers most of the afternoon. He had already been through them once, jotting notes in the margins, and she gives them all a second read. He saves the actual assigning of letter grades for her. She understands that some of the students have grumbled that it's unfair to have their work reviewed by two professors, but so far no one has made anything resembling an official complaint. They are getting to the finish line and she is relieved for herself, but also for Cade. His mind, she knows, is shifting away from her class and back to where it belongs, with his players.

She can hear Log's boat putter into the dock, and she imagines the low bow of his cat waiting in the lawn as Lacey stretches her own legs along Cade's and curls up her toes. It's after ten o'clock and he must have been far out in the bay to be coming in this late. She imagines the cat has been worrying over him, maybe not. Log always comes back. It's a Tuesday evening and the bar is quiet, thankfully. The peepers are making their little whistle-bursts and a breeze sifts in from the river and lifts at the curtains.

Tasha is at the farm with Willy, and Carlotta will be stopping by as well. Lacey knows Tasha is in good hands with the both of them.

Mac, too, is wrapping up the semester and will be arriving at the farm in the next few days. He has a conference coming up in Vancouver and so he wants to spend a long week with Tasha before he heads out. Kat is still in school and won't be coming with him, which is a bit of a relief to Lacey, though she would never say so.

Just as she feels herself drifting off again, feels herself taking inventory and knowing that yes, everyone is safe and sound, all hands accounted for, Cade's phone rings. He has the cordless tucked under his thigh and digs for it quickly, tossing her an apologetic look.

"No worries," she whispers.

"I'll take it in the kitchen," he says, starting to toss off the covers.

"No, no," she says, throwing her arm across his chest. "It's fine. Don't go."

"Hey, Mom," he says warmly into the phone, raising his brows to Lacey apologetically.

Lacey smiles and tucks her head to his side.

"No, not busy," he says. "Sure, this is a good time. I'm just going over some plays. Glad you called. How's Dad?"

They talk quietly, friendly. He is clearly happy to hear from her. The class he is teaching has gone well, he's enjoyed it, actually, and he's even learned something as well. But no, he is not inspired to teach literature in the future. What is she reading these days, how's Dad's knee, and yes, of course, he is looking forward to coming up next week.

Lacey can hear his mother's voice but not her words and is struck by how easily their conversation flows, how earnest. She notices his easy laugh and the way he listens, and she looks up to his smiling face that shifts happily in response to his mother's questions, turning more animated again as he asks his own questions of her. Apparently, his father wants to buy a truck and Cade is amused by this. "Well, he always wanted a truck," she hears him say. "It will give him an excuse to wear that camo jacket he likes so much." It is, she can tell, something known between them, between mother and son, *family*.

Thoughts of her own mother trickle in. Her defenses are down, her arms relaxed and draped over Cade, her fingers trailing through the hairs on his chest, her mouth soft against his shoulder. She wonders what her mother looks like now. Still young, she imagines. She would be what—forty-nine? Still young. It has been thirty years since she left. Funny to think of that now. It was so long ago. Does May, too, think of Lacey, she wonders. Maybe she does just as Lacey does and puts her away, locks her away and doesn't speak of her. It hasn't been such a hard thing to do. She has never looked for her—never so much as typed her name into a Google search—and if the urge has ever struck her to do so she has simply whipped her mind away from the urge itself. As long as Lacey has a focus, a goal, a mission, she can put her mother aside, or so she had thought. And always there were goals. College, graduate school, having a baby, raising Tasha. These things kept her mind tight and laser-focused, with no room for thoughts of May. It is when she lets her mind drift, when she is sex sleepy and—dare she think—momentarily happy, that thoughts of her mother dribble into her unlocked mind. At least, that's the way she always thought it was. But now, with Tasha sick and Lacey focused with a kind of angry energy, she unexpectedly finds May slipping in more and more whenever she is distracted from Tasha. Sometimes it is just a kind of wondering. She remembers the silver sliver of scar near the outer corner of her eye and wonders if it is faded into the creases she must surely have by now. She thinks of her voice, the unusual opening wide and then funneling of her vowels, and wonders if she is living north or south, if the Ocracoke accent has melted into a new geography.

She remembers the feeling of her own hand in her mother's, leading Lacey through the aisles of the pharmacy or Carroll's Market, the small tug to hurry her along. And she remembers now, at the mention of

Cade's father buying a truck, *the red truck man*. Well, she remembers the truck, not so much the man. What she remembers of him is that he was big, so big, with a deep gravelly voice and an exaggerated way of saying his consonants so that they bounced hard from his mouth as he leaned from his truck. But mostly, it is that truck, the huge beast of a red truck that flew out of Carroll's Market, spitting gravel and shooting down the long ribbon of road.

She can't help but wonder what would be different now. Would the sheets always be fresh and clean and would May still insist on drying them on a line in the yard or would she have finally surrendered them to the clothes dryer? Would she have eventually installed a dishwashing machine, or would her hands still be water-wrinkled at the end of every meal, her nails always short and clean from the sudsing of dishes? Would there be pictures of Tasha tacked on the refrigerator instead of set in a stack and bound with a rubber band in the dining room buffet drawer?

Mostly though, Lacey wonders now what kind of conversations they would have if May had never left. Would her mother call her on the phone at the end of the day to tell her about the farm, about a new recipe she might try, a new neighbor, a book she's recently finished and thinks Lacey would like, idle chat about the weather and the difference between Harford and St. Mary's County, and would Lacey have someone to complain to about her wild curly hair and how she has moved to the worst patch of humidity in all of Maryland for hair like hers and just what was she thinking? Would they talk of Willy, his arthritis that he never complains about but which she (the both of them?) can see in the way he sometimes descends the steps, the way he bends more slowly to slide into a car.

What would things be like between May and Willy now, thirty years later? Would Willy still rise at the end of a meal and kiss her on the cheek, and would she still smile and tuck her chin shyly at the weight of his hand on her shoulder? Would Willy still bring her the small gifts for no apparent reason that he always picked up whenever he was away from the farm? Writing paper for writing her friend Sugar—Lacey hadn't thought of that name in thirty years and can't believe it has come back to her now—and stamps, funny magnets for the refrigerator, a bouquet of sunflowers, which she thinks now must have been May's favorite flower, hair ribbons and caramels, cinnamon buns from the Amish women, hand creams, and jars of honey. He never left home for the full day without bringing her something small. Would May and Willy sit up in the evenings and think back about the raising of Lacey?

Cade is wrapping up his call, *I love you, love to Dad.*

He leans over and puts the phone on the bedside table and a smile lingers on his face. She is glad for him that there is this easiness with his mother, and she plants a kiss on his shoulder.

She drifts back to sleep, moving in and out of the puffs of a dream, a time in the future when she will wait for Tasha's call on an evening just like this. Tasha, a young woman, away at college, or married perhaps, maybe with a child—or more than one! And Lacey will curl up in a large familiar bed, maybe even leaning into the very same shoulder that cradles her now. In the dream she waits for the call that comes every evening and is reminding herself to tell Tasha about the book she is reading and also that funny thing that one of her students said. Just before they say goodbye Tasha will say, *Can I ask you something, Mommy?*

You can ask me anything.

Are you happy, Mom? I want you to be happy.

She is deep in her dream now. *I am happy.*

September 14, 1974

I have been married a whole week now. I have slept the sweetest nights and walked through the finest days since my marriage to Willy. We went to church this morning and I brought a lemon cake for coffee after. Aunt Virgie reminded me of this as something expected of the married churchwomen. When I brought it down to the social hall afore the service, the other women were dropping off their baked goods and cooing over plates of cookies or blueberry buckle or such. Aunt Virgie took the lemon cake from my hands and, lifting it like an offering, said loud as can be, Oh, May, you made that special lemon cake of yours. This is the best lemon cake in the county, ladies. I was embarrassed by her fussing and the fact that it weren't really my lemon cake at all, but a recipe Aunt Virgie herself give to me and taught me to make.

After church, Mrs. Carter said she did believe it was the best she ever ate and Mrs. Braggart said she never ate a lemon cake quite so moist. Willy had three pieces, smiling with every bite, and Lacey told everyone her momma made the lemon cake. On the way home Lacey kept dragging her little fingers across the empty sheet cake pan in her lap, squeezing up every last crumb onto her fingertips, and licking them clean.

I helped Willy with the herd some when we got home. He said it weren't women's work, but I asked him please, could I help, because I really do like the peacefulness of those animals. They are all the color of butterscotch, but already I am able to tell one from the other among a few of them. They have soft brown eyes and a creamy muzzle. They seem to me to be gigantic animals, but Willy says Jerseys are among the smallest breeds, and they produce the least milk, too, but their milk is real rich, Willy says. Sweet and full of butterfat.

Willy gives them names once they are weaned. But these are not their recorded names which are actually numbers that tell the cow and the bull and the year and so on in a kind of number code. These are just names he calls them in the barn. He explained to me that each year he has a theme—which is kind of like the subject—for calving time and names the calves in that way. One year they was all named after bodies of water. There's Chessie—short for Chesapeake, and Ol' Miss, from the Mississippi River, and sweet Mary for the St. Mary's River. It was Mary who I come to know best as she has a bad teat she stepped on once and tore bad. Willy won't hook her up to the milking machines no more for fear of hurting her, so he showed me how he milks her by hand.

While the machines whirred and chunked at the other heifers, I used my hands and did a squeeze-pull. Streams of milk squirted and tinged and shot into the bucket. Willy, who is all about business in the barn, asked me how was his little milkmaid doing and I felt my heart flutter, but I just kept on working and pulling that milk from her. I was secretly glad I had distracted him.

After the milking, I stood at the paddock door and watched the two men who come to help. They know just what to do, just what is expected of them next, and they do their job without stopping to talk or smoke.

I like to watch the young cows in the paddock. Last year Willy was studying on Native Americans during the winter months and so he named them after Indian tribes. Most were sold off, but the few left are too young to come in for milking, so they run and kick in the paddock. Cheyenne and Cherokee nuzzle each other and make a braying sound to say they are bored waiting for the others. Apache settles herself in to wait by folding her front legs in front of her and then dropping her rump last. She chews her cud as if she has all the time in the world.

CHAPTER 20

Someone to Sleep Beside

On the very rare occasion over the last thirty years, if someone was to mention May, Willy would find himself answering matter-of-factly that he didn't think about her much, had no idea where she was, didn't have no inclination whatsoever to find her. It wasn't exactly the truth, but it is how he would have answered. He did think about her, but what he thought about was the absence of her, the lack of her, the emptiness that had swept in like a thing and replaced the fullness that he had felt with her. He had lived in that void for many years now, and like a buzzing in his ear or black dashes in his vision, it was something he had tricked his brain into ignoring. Now, though, with Carlotta slipping into that void with her loud rolling laugh, her Baltimore endearments—*hon* and *doll* being two of her favorites—and her pale scent that makes him want to lean in closer, and her way of touching his shoulder or hip with just enough pressure to make him want to hold her hand there, a strange thing is happening with the empty place he had in himself that he had ignored for so long. He just can't believe she, Carlotta, this woman so different from May, is managing to squeeze herself into that very same hole May had left in him.

He hasn't told her much about May, just the facts. They were married, she left. That pretty much summed it up in his mind, but when Carlotta asks about her—and, damn, he can't understand what makes her ask—it always makes him feel a little off balance, like he's been tripped on a little snag of memory he didn't even know was there in the first place.

They had been at the grocer, the new one, and Willy hadn't wanted to go, but Carlotta had said that Carroll's didn't carry the brand of Greek yogurt she needed for Tasha's protein drinks and so he had agreed to go to the Safeway even though it was too big and confused him in the way they ordered things with crackers being in a completely separate aisle from cookies and your canned goods split up depending upon if they were considered meat or vegetable, and worst of all some of the things Carlotta wanted—anchovies and salsa—were snuck into aisles Carlotta referred to as *gourmet* and *international*. It always took some meandering and backtracking to find the things he wanted and worst of all it is way too cold in there. But the cold had turned out to not be such a bad thing because it gave Tasha an excuse to wear her hood up. The three of them had been forced to park way too far away and amble across the hot parking lot with Tasha between them. As they jimmied a shopping cart loose from the long trail of carts just inside the store, Willy offered it to a patiently waiting mother of a young girl. She looked to be about four years old and looked up to him with a sweet shy smile and blinking eyes and he was struck by the beauty of her, the long lashes, the tender sweep of little brows, and the hair that was thin but waved gloriously and was pulled up with a mammoth bow at the back of her head. There was so much expression in that tiny face. The little girl looked to Tasha and noticed, perhaps, a strangeness about her, maybe not realizing at first that it was the lack of lashes and brows, the hood pulled tightly and knotted under her chin. Perhaps all she could understand was the blankness in Tasha's face, the eyes just two pools of blue and the cheeks bloated and blotched from the steroids she was now on. She stared at Tasha quizzically, and Willy willed the girl to be silent, to say nothing, for her mother to distract her quickly, for anything to stop what he knew was coming. The girl tilted her face to the side and peered at Tasha and then up to Willy and Carlotta and back to Tasha again, who said nothing.

"How come your mommy and daddy are old?" she finally said. And Willy and Carlotta had both burst out in laughter.

"He's my grandpa," said Tasha. "He came that way."

The little girl nodded, understanding now, and her mother smiled apologetically at the three of them and lifted her into the cart and hurried into the store.

They were still chuckling to one another as they move down the aisles. "It's a shame," Carlotta said, changing the subject as they rolled through the condiments, "that May never got to know this precious granddaughter of hers." Tasha lagged behind the two of them, and Carlotta kept looking over her shoulder to keep an eye on her.

Willy didn't answer, can't imagine what she expected him to say. "We need mayonnaise," is all he said. "You got your Hellmann's and your Safeway brand here."

"Was she a good mother, Willy?"

He turned to look at her with the shopping cart between them, a jar of mayonnaise in each hand. How was he to answer that? Yes, she was a very good mother. Damn it. But he remembers how things were toward the end, the weeks before she left, dragging herself around the house, sometimes in the same clothes for days at a time, once even wearing her blouse inside out, like she had just pulled it from the floor that morning and slipped it on. And then there was the night he was reading to Lacey in the parlor, squished together in the same too-small chair, her legs tossed over his, and he could smell a kind of sourness coming off Lacey. When he looked at her bare feet, he saw the band of dirt embedded in her ankles just above the line where her shoes would have been and he realized that she hadn't had her bath, maybe hadn't had one in a day or two, maybe longer, now that he was looking at the backs of her ears, the slight crust under her nose. May was across from him, in a bathrobe that bore recent coffee stains down the front and she was working her crochet hook, dipping, catching with a finger, pulling, the lines of her jaw hard and thin. She had glanced over at Lacey with a blank look on her face, stared a moment, and then asked, "Lacey, you been playing with my crochet hooks again? I can't find my 7 or my J-10."

"No, Momma." And Lacey had scooched down harder into Willy's lap.

He can't remember now if he said anything or not. Maybe he just stared at her, watching her breath come and go, watching her adjust the floor lamp in an agitated way, huffing, and not looking up at him. Something was in the air and he didn't want to know about it, examine it. He wanted it to go away, like a storm that's expected and suddenly takes a turn.

He turns around now and looks at Carlotta over the shopping cart, waiting for her to explain, wondering where the hell she is going with this, all these questions about May.

"Let's not talk about this now," he says, nodding to Tasha, who trails behind them pulling at her ear under her hood, her face squished in some kind of discomfort.

Carlotta is quiet after that. He knows what that means. He knows she is thinking on it, storing up her questions for later.

Back at the farm, they unload groceries together while Tasha putters at the edges of the pond. Willy had given her a bucket and a ladle from the kitchen so she can catch tadpoles. He let her keep them in the sunroom long enough to watch them sprout the little nodules that indicated legs and then he'd dump them back in the pond. When he brings it outside to her, she is fussing and pulling on her ear again and he suggests she take her hood down when he hands her the bucket. She slides back the hood and he notices an angry rash starting up behind her right ear and trailing the back of her neck.

He pauses her for a moment and looks harder at it.

"Hurts," she says.

"Want Carlotta to take a look?" he says.

She shakes her head, no, rubs it hard with the flat of her hand, which makes her squinch her eyes, and she trudges down to the pond.

"I didn't mean to upset you, Willy," Carlotta says as he comes back into the kitchen. She turns to him from the counter, and he leans over her to shelve the protein powder she had him buy for Tasha.

"Didn't upset me."

"I think about her, you know?"

"Why?" He stops and takes a step back from her. "Why? *I* don't think about her."

Carlotta is quiet, running her tongue between her lips as if she is considering this. She turns back to the counter. "Turkey sandwich?"

But he is bothered now, and as much as he doesn't want to continue this conversation, he can't help but ask again, *Why?*

"Well, let me ask you this then," she says, turning her back more solidly to him so that he can't see her face. "Do you mind me talking about Tony?" And then she turns to him suddenly and there are tears in her eyes that he hadn't been prepared for, hadn't expected at all. "Because sometimes I need to," she rushes to tell him. "Sometimes I'm afraid I'll forget things if I don't talk about him. And what's more, Willy, he's a part of me, and it's like telling you about him is like telling you about me." She tilts her head away from him, embarrassed maybe, he can't be sure. She takes in air and her chest rises up and then falls again. "I loved Tony and I don't ever expect to love anyone in the same way again. I will always have a piece in my heart that hurts—like a rock stuck in here," and she puts a limp fist to her chest. "But maybe loving someone else—starting to care about someone else—has nothing to do with loving him."

He can't help but think that she is wrong—that one thing *does* have to do with the other. He can feel it, the way the emptiness left by May keeps bumping up against the feelings he has for Carlotta, and he is having a hard time reconciling the one with the other, different as they are. But when he looks in her eyes, feels the way they settle over him, the way they are asking something of him that he hadn't realized he had in himself, well, it feels good. It feels right. It feels like a tender and hopeful part of him unfurling.

"I don't mind, Carlotta. I don't mind at all." He steps up to her and puts his hands to her shoulders and she tucks her head against his chest. He doesn't mind at all. He likes her stories. He likes to hear about Tony's summer bocce ball nights, the fact that he always wore a white shirt to church, their fortieth anniversary party in the basement of Saint Alphonsus, the way he liked to get up before dawn and walk to the corner market for a fresh quart of milk every morning. He likes hearing that Tony preferred his sandwiches cut in quarters and the fact that he would only drink her coffee—no one else's, ever. Willy likes to hear about the small things, the way Tony always shouted out the answers to *Jeopardy!*, that he preferred to end his meals with a cup of gelato, and the way he always set the alarm for 6:00 a.m., even though he was up and showered and shaved by the time it went off.

It is as if Carlotta's life with Tony fills in the spaces in Willy's life that he and May never had a chance to live. Carlotta makes him wonder if he, too, would have developed a preference for the way his sandwich was to be cut. How many years would May have come into the kitchen in the morning wearing the pretty white bathrobe he had given her, the sash trailing behind her and the robe falling open to reveal the blue flannel gown she slept in, and would sunflowers have always been her favorite flower?

He wants everything that Carlotta and Tony had. He wants to dance their dance, but, as he strokes Carlotta's back, as he listens to the bubble of tears in her throat, he can't help the sudden and unexpected missing of May that he is feeling. He'd been gypped, somehow. It just doesn't feel right trying to pick up where he left off with a brand-new dance partner, and still, he is amazed by how easily Carlotta has fallen into step beside him.

"Lord knows," she says, laughing between tears and lifting her head from his shoulder, "he wasn't perfect, Willy. He was a picky eater, he blew his nose too much, and he never shut the door when he set on the toilet, but I loved that man and he loved me and I want something like that in my life again, Willy."

He rubs his hand up her spine, feeling the way her back is pinched by her brassiere and rolls over the top of it, so different from May. Everything about Carlotta is different. Here all along he's been waiting for someone just like May to wander into his life—not expecting it, not thinking it would ever happen, but if you were to ask him what he was waiting for, he imagines that would be it, and instead it is Carlotta. That is something to wonder about.

He feels confessional and so he says, "You asked me where May is, and I don't know. No one does. Virgie and me puzzled on it some. Calls were made down to Ocracoke. She was here one day and then she wasn't."

"I don't understand, Willy."

"Look," he says as he rakes his fingers through his hair and then moves to set down at the kitchen table, feeling the sudden distance between them as she stands on the other side of the kitchen. "This ain't the time to talk about it," he says, spying Tasha through the window with a bucket sloshing against her side and making her way to the door.

Carlotta nods and goes to the door to let Tasha in. He is thankful for her arrival. He knows now, he is closer to the edge of telling her what little he knows, what little he understands, and he is going to need to work it through his own mind again first.

"Growing some frogs, are we?" he says brightly to Tasha now.

That evening, after a simple dinner of tomatoes, green beans, and chicken cutlets that Willy devours, Carlotta offers to draw a bath for Tasha before she leaves for the evening. Willy is clearing the table and setting the plates in the sink when he looks over to the table where Tasha still sits. She has begun to whimper quietly, rubbing at her ear again and down to the small pit of her arm. He sets the dishes down in the sink and goes to look at what she is fussing with. He is used to the periodic bouts of whininess due to headaches and, he supposes, a general feeling of illness that she tolerates better—he imagines—than most five-year-olds. But this time when he looks behind her ear and then pulls down the neck of her T-shirt, he is horrified to see a trail of small blisters erupting along a swath of her skin.

"Aw, jeez, sugar. Don't touch. Come on. We're gonna go on upstairs and have Carlotta take a look at this." With this suggestion, she bursts into tears. "Don't worry, sugar. It's just a rash, is all." He scoops her into his arms even as she keeps the one hand tucked under her other arm, and he carries her up the stairs.

Carlotta is bending over the bath, swishing the water with her hand. He sets Tasha down, tears now streaming down her face and head tucked. Carlotta peels back her shirt tenderly.

"Oohh, princess, that hurts, I know!" She looks up to Willy. "Shingles," she says evenly and quietly. "I'm certain of it." And then to Tasha, "Try not to touch, honey."

Carlotta directs Willy to bring her a box of baking soda and asks if there is any Benadryl in the house. He heads to the kitchen and finds the baking soda, but the bottle of Benadryl stashed in the cabinet expired many years ago. *Damn it*, he mutters to himself, tossing the Benadryl and the also expired—he now notices—Pepto-Bismol into the trash. He clambers up the steps again just as Carlotta is lowering a quietly weeping Tasha into the bath. He hands her the box and she dumps the whole of it into the bath and swishes it around Tasha.

The look on Tasha's face, her eyes squinting shut and her little mouth gritting as the water eases up around her, tugs at his chest. "No Benadryl," he says. "I'm gonna run into town and get some."

"Hmmm," she says, dunking a washing cloth and then squeezing it to run water down Tasha's neck and shoulders. "Better go to my house. I have some in the medicine cabinet in my bathroom." Tasha makes a small hooting sound as the water runs down her neck. "Easy, easy," Carlotta said.

Willy looks at Tasha with her eyes clenched shut, the pale pinkness of her, the shine of her scalp, the utter hairlessness like a blind baby mouse—like the nest of them he had once drowned in the utility sink in the basement many years ago, squirming like fat larva, and his stomach feels sick to be seeing it all again, the memory of it rising in his mind at the sight of her helplessness.

"Be right back," he says.

He drives the half mile to her house, a bright little rancher painted yellow with deep-green shutters. He lets himself into the kitchen through a side door and is met by Thumper who apparently has the run of the kitchen itself. It still smells like a new house, like paint and something clean and raw—fresh wood. The kitchen is tidy, just as he would have expected, a huge coffee maker shining in all its chrome, the counter lined with bright-red canisters, two upholstered stools neatly tucked beneath an island countertop. Soft music is playing on the radio, as if he is coming home to a peopled place. Thumper hops to him, stretching the front of himself forward followed by the heft of his large rump, and noses at Willy's shoes. Willy reaches down and draws his finger down between the rabbit's eyes and along the bridge of his nose. Carlotta had told him he liked that and as he does it, the rabbit lifts delicately on his hind legs with his front feet setting lightly on Willy's knee—he is that big—and his ears lay long and flat against his back like two thick locks of human hair. "Can't stay to chat," says Willy, now noticing the litter box in the corner of the room. "I'll be damned," he says to himself.

A baby gate separates the kitchen from the rest of the house and Willy is forced to step over it, as the locking contraption is beyond him at the moment. He feels sure that Thumper could jump it easily if he had a mind to.

Thumper follows him to the gate and sits—curiously, Willy imagines—on the other side of it as Willy makes his way through the living room and into the first bedroom. A bedside lamp is lit, expecting her. The bed is neat and fluffed with thick pillows and a quilt, terribly *red*, a shade he knows he could never get used to. But at the same time, he can't help but imagine Carlotta slipping into that bed, in a long sheer nightgown cinched under her large breasts, maybe with a small bow, tucking the redness of the quilt around herself and that deep dark hair. There is a large photo in a wide gold frame next to the bed, and he stops himself from going to it, knowing it will be a photo of Antonio, maybe the two of them, and he doesn't want to see it, doesn't want it to change what he imagines of them.

He goes directly to the bathroom and slides open the medicine cabinet. It is filled with fancy brushes in cups, tubes and powders, lipsticks, little compacts of color. But he finds the Benadryl amongst these things and some calamine lotion which he isn't sure will be useful but takes with him as well.

He makes it a point not to look at the photo as he leaves the room.

Carlotta is in the bedroom with Tasha, digging through an assortment of nightgowns in an effort to find something that won't irritate the raw blisters. She holds up a long sleeveless tank-top-like sleeping shirt and Tasha nods to it.

Willy holds out both the Benadryl and the calamine to Carlotta and she takes the Benadryl from him.

"Calamine won't do much good right now," she says. "You go on and call Dr. Oren."

Willy kisses Tasha on her forehead and heads down to make the call.

When Carlotta comes down the steps a few minutes later she seems to know instinctively that the only thing she can do is put her big arms around him and hold him there.

"Just how much is she supposed to take?" he says to the top of her head tucked under his chin. "Doc wants her back in the morning. Says they'll probably admit her."

Carlotta runs her hands up his arms.

"Can you stay?" he asks.

She just blinks and looks at him, like she isn't sure what he is asking.

"Tonight," he says. And still she looks at him, cocks her head, but says nothing.

He doesn't want her to misunderstand. He just needs a body next to him. He just wants someone to tell his fears to in the dark, someone who will listen beside him and not say anything he doesn't want to hear, just be warm, maybe hold his hand, curl to his side.

"Sure, Willy. I can do that."

"I would feel better if you would stay."

"You want me to be here for her tonight," she says, as if she is understanding something, confirming it.

"No—yes, no. I want you to stay with me." But he isn't sure she is understanding. "I want you to stay here for me." He takes her chin in his hand. "You make me feel . . ." He stops. How to explain it? "I want you to be here, for her . . . and for me. I want you to talk to me and listen to me." He looks up at the ceiling as if the words he is looking for might be printed up there somewhere. "I want to fall asleep knowing you're next to me and wake up knowing you're still here."

She raises her perfectly arched brows, her forehead furrowing as if she still isn't sure what he is asking, wants him to explain. All he can do by way of explanation is kiss her sweetly on the lips, briefly, carefully, not deeply or passionately, but tenderly, in a way that asks nothing more of her, only that she stay.

"I'll pack a bag for her in the morning," she says. And she kisses him back, a tiny *smack-pop* of a kiss that floods him with relief.

October 12, 1974

> *post office*
> *grocer*
> *black-eyed peas*
> *cornmeal*
> *toilet paper*

Aunt Virgie has set me to worrying. Willy dropped me in town today so I could run my errands. I mailed a letter to Sugar Lee. I wanted to tell her about how my life is here on the farm. Then I went round to Carroll's Market and purchased some of the things we was needing. I stopped by to see Aunt Virgie and she was having chest pains again. She tells me they are nothing to worry about, just a sign that she needs to take it easy.

She sat in the big stuffed chair with the pulled threads on the arm while we talked and it was odd to see her so still, just sitting like that.

But then she says she wants to talk to me about some things that are kind of personal. Did I mind, she asked of me. I said no but already I was thinking that maybe I did. She said she was certain that Willy and me would be hoping to have more babies but seeing as I had some confusion over Lacey and all, was there anything I wanted to know about that kind of thing? I felt all the blood going to my face. I would have paid good cash money to get out of there. She asked me questions about my cycle and I told her I never did think of it that way as it ain't never been regular, so to speak. Well, May, that's what it is, she says to me, like she's a little bit frustrated with my ignorance and so I just nodded my head like I already had an understanding of these things. Then she told me I should keep track of it on a calendar, just a little x to mark when it starts and count the days until it starts back up again and see if I got anything regular so I will know if I am having a baby or not and if it don't come back could be I am with child. I asked her could I fix her a cup of tea? But she said no. I could just sit there and keep her company until Willy got round to picking me up.

So I did, but the whole time my heart was racing round in my chest on account of when I got to thinking about it, my cycle was maybe late, or maybe not, because I hadn't been thinking of it and I didn't rightly know what was regular, neither. I got so I was hardly hearing what she was saying to me for the roaring in my ears.

All I could think was that this couldn't be happening, but then I would think, it <u>has</u> happened and so it could happen again.

I couldn't speak the whole way home. Lacey jabbered between me and Willy and I was ever so grateful. I looked over at her, just once, to see if I could catch any of Daddy in her face, but it just weren't there. She was just a giddy little girl tucked between the two people who loved her best and that is all I could see.

When we got back to the farm Willy carried my groceries in and I walked down to the pond and went in at the edges. He called out to me that it was a little cold for a swim, hmm? And then I noticed I was in up over my knees and didn't even realize it, just knew something felt right about the way it was rising on me. I hadn't even taken my shoes off and so they are drying out at the back stoop right now. Willy wants to know what I was thinking, going on in with my shoes on.

October 13, 1974

I think it started up last on August 31. That would make it about 43 days. Aunt Virgie says a cycle is more like 28 days.

October 15, 1974

   I watched Lacey follow Willy around the barn today. She has to double her steps to keep up with him and it is a sight to see. I have a pain in my back that is at me something awful.

October 17, 1974

   It came today, and I near slid off the toilet to my knees. I feel like I'm cleaning all the bad part out of me and starting new again.

November 16, 1974

   I watched Lacey clambering over bales of straw in the barn today. Without even turning his head to look, Willy put his hand out to her where she stood on top of a bale, and she took hold of it afore she jumped down. He never even had to take his eyes from the machinery he was tending to, but just knew to reach up his hand and hold it there for her to take if the need was to come up.

   She is just like any little girl I see walking in town with her daddy. She asks me where her daddy is. I tell her she doesn't have one. She got Willy instead. This makes her smile like she got the better end of the deal. And she did, too.

CHAPTER 21

Hospital Time

The thing about hospitals, Lacey thinks, is that they suck the living right out of you. Time is warped in a way that makes no sense. It's meaningless and yet she watches the clock on the wall tick the minutes away as if they are all waiting for something and there is nothing to wait for other than its passing. And the air is so sterile—no, not sterile at all, because she knows there are germs hidden everywhere, even as she watches the little round woman with the housekeeping cart swish a wide-headed mop into the corners and along the baseboards but completely miss a twist of plastic, about an inch long, that has lodged under the side table. The air is not sterile, but *neutral*, empty, nothing at all like the air surrounding the silent movie that plays outside the hermetically sealed window where summer has taken hold and ribbons of purposefully planted begonias sway, dogwood petals drift to the greenest grass, pale blue hydrangeas burst forth from mounded bushes, cars roll along, heaving their backsides over speed bumps and sliding into the mouth of the parking garage, and a man-made stream gurgles (but she can only imagine that) along the meandering brick path to nowhere.

Perhaps the hardest part of all is the way Lacey looks forward to visitors and then finds that there is no hope of an earnest conversation in this place. There are awkward silences begging to be filled, self-conscious chuckles that are immediately checked by a side-eyed glance to Tasha, and what is worse is that there is a lack of honesty because it can't be any other way. *How is she,* they ask, and just what is she to say? *Look at her*, she thinks of saying. Just look, with her naked scalp and her wheezing breath and the way she tosses and grimaces in her sleep which is, in fact, an artificial drug-induced sleep that is nothing like the deep sweet sleep she deserves but is something given to her so that she can lose the consciousness of the raw blistered nerves trailing from her ear to her arm to the thread of her spine. She sweats against the sheets that are designed for bed-wetters even though Lacey has told the staff she doesn't need them. (But then there have been accidents. Blame it on the fluids Tasha is getting that surprise her bladder when she is locked in by the pain meds.) *Be forewarned if you plan to place a kiss on her furrowed brow. Her breath is sour.*

But Lacey doesn't say that at all. Instead, she tries to brighten her face. *Good, much better, she's sleeping, she's doing better*, and none of it, none of it rings true in her own ears.

The shingles, she has been told, are not uncommon once the immune system has been compromised. It doesn't happen often, but it can. And it did. It's been five days since Willy and Carlotta brought Tasha in. She was neutropenic, meaning that the drugs killing the cancer had gone into overdrive and were killing the good cells, too—a little friendly fire in the land of leukemia. The ANC count has risen since then and hovers around one thousand. She was still at risk for infection the first few days and so visitors had been forced to wear a mask, but now, thankfully, that has stopped. She hated the way Tasha would wake from her restless sleep and be startled by a masked visitor. The blisters are just now starting to crust and scab over. All of this points to some kind of healing.

Hopefully, she will be able to take Tasha back to the farm in the next few days and so, in fact, Lacey is telling herself, Tasha *is* better, and so it is not a lie. *Good, much better, getting better.* In fact, Lacey has been telling those who call that maybe it would be best to visit once they are home. So Lacey is alone now, flipping through children's magazines and waiting for Mac to arrive. She is anxious to get back to the farm, take a long shower, sleep, if possible, for just one night in a real bed.

Cade's games start tomorrow, and she will miss them. She is sorry to miss them. She had looked forward to bringing Tasha and sitting in the bleachers under a hot sun, hearing the crowds roar and watching Cade pace and slam his clipboard, spit on the ground and pound his fist in the air. When he is running his team from the sidelines, he is nothing like he is with her, and she is fascinated by the opposite side of him. He is staying in a hotel with his team only a few miles from the hospital and when he arrived last night, he stopped by the hospital.

She saw the shock on his face when he saw Tasha for the first time since March. His face fell as he came into the room and he stopped in his own steps. She thought for just a second that he didn't even know who Tasha was, like he'd come into the wrong room and needed to go back out to the hall and check the room number again. Tasha was half-awake and while she didn't lift her head, she did smile up at him. He put his hand on her forehead. "How are you doing, Tash?" When he turned from her to hug Lacey, she was surprised to see the tender twist of his face and the watery flush in his eyes.

"Wow," he said, hugging Lacey. "Wow." He took a deep breath and waited to be introduced to Willy and Carlotta. They were just leaving, Carlotta hefting a big vinyl bag over her shoulder and Willy with one arm around her waist, which he dropped now to shake Cade's hand.

Pleasantries were exchanged, and Lacey saw the obvious way that Willy looked him up and down. She expected nothing less of him. Carlotta, on the other hand, had a hundred questions lined up, after she rambled for a bit about how much she had been looking forward to meeting him (embarrassing Lacey, because she suddenly realized how much she had told Carlotta about him), and please come by the farm after the games, maybe they could have a little cookout once they got Tasha home and *wouldn't that be nice, Willy?*

Willy nodded his head, *sure*, though Lacey knew the idea would never have occurred to him, and then Carlotta started asking about the games, saying she was a big lacrosse fan herself and never missed a Hopkins home game when she lived in the city. She even recalled the names of particular players and coaches from the past. Bob Scott, for instance, wonderful man, did Cade know him?

"He's a legend in his own time," Cade said, smiling, and this pleased Carlotta who nodded enthusiastically in agreement.

"Well, good luck tomorrow, son," said Willy earnestly. "Good luck to you," and he had ushered Carlotta out of the room as she blew kisses to Tasha.

But now Lacey is alone, and Tasha is restless but awake as they wait for

Mac. He is dropping Kat at the farm first and then heading over. She had thought Kat would be in school and didn't expect him to have her and she makes a note to herself to ask him why Kat is here and also to ask it in a way that will feel offhanded so as not to belie the frustration she feels in adding Kat to the already complicated mix of people she is accountable to in some way.

Mac is loud when he comes in, full of ridiculous endearments and silly noises he thinks will amuse Tasha. "Where's my little Russian princess?" he practically shouts when he comes into the room. Then he looks under the bed for her. "Now where could she be?"

"Daddy," she says, a wan smile on her face, "I'm right here," and she puts her small hand on top of his head and spins her fingers in his hair while he peeks under the bed.

He pops up like a prairie dog. "Oh! There she is!"

She sits up a little straighter and her eyes roll over him, looking for tricks up his sleeve. Lacey finds it all a little irritating but she is trying to appreciate the fact that Tasha is engaged in the shenanigans. He is "stealing her nose" and pretending to put it in his pocket. It's absurd and Tasha is way too old for this game, and still, she plays along. "Put it back, Daddy!"

It confuses Lacey, the way Tasha has suddenly woken and become playful. Lacey wonders if maybe she herself has gone too far the other way, hardly able to look at her without feeling the hurt and the fear and then wearing it on her sleeve. Maybe she has, in some way, given her permission to be sick.

Still, she can't help but tell Mac not to wear her out. Of course, he doesn't pay attention to her and is, in fact, making obscene fart sounds against his arm which has Tasha actually giggling and trying it out on her own arm as well.

Lacey feels it now, watching the two of them locked in their games, creeping out of the darkest corner of herself, a nasty little secret. It's a feeling, actually, a perspective she keeps bumping into and can't get out of the way of, and it is this.

She is angry at Tasha for being sick.

She knows this feeling can't be normal. And she knows that all of her other feelings—the fear, the loving her daughter, the instinctual desire to step into her place and take all of her pain from her and into herself—those feelings are stronger than the shard of anger she feels at this moment. But she shouldn't be feeling it at all. A good mother, even a mediocre mother, would never have to come up against such a thought, such a *thing*.

"Is Kat coming, Daddy?"

"Tomorrow, princess. I dropped her at the farm." He turns to Lacey. "I thought she could ride in with you tomorrow."

"I'm not getting back here until pretty late tomorrow," Lacey says. There are piles of errands waiting for her and she has agreed to meet Cade for a quick drink after the games. Just for an hour, she had told Cade, and he had said he would take what he could get. "I have a ton of errands to run tomorrow." It irritates her that she feels obliged to defend her absence from the hospital. And, of course, it is none of Mac's business, she thinks to herself now. She has been here four days running. Just what does everyone expect from her? It is all so confusing, to be so needed, to want to be here for Tasha, to *not* want to be here at all. "Why isn't Kat in school?" she asks suddenly, forgetting her note-to-self in regard to that question.

"Oh, you know," he says, running his hand like a small escaped rodent under the covers and grabbing Tasha's ankle, who laughs and kicks her foot. "She's got a break."

"Where's Diane?" she wants to know.

"Home, of course."

"She has a whole week off school—at the very end of the year?"

"Let's just say she has a little break." He looks hard at her and there is a slight narrowing of his eyes. "Besides," he says, turning now to Tasha. "I'm away all of the following week. I wanted a little time with her, too—with my *girls*," he teases, poking Tasha.

"Where are you going, Daddy?"

Lacey considers and can't help feeling something is amiss. "What'd she do, Mac?"

"Daddy is teaching classes at another college, up in Canada, honey," he says to Tasha, and then more quietly to Lacey, "Let's drop it, Lacey."

"Will you teach them about the Russian princesses?" Tasha asks.

"I'll teach them all kinds of things about Russia, and I'll teach them all about the Russian princesses. "Especially"—and here he puts a finger to her nose—"especially about Princess Anastasia."

"What happened, Mac? What happened this time?"

"Stop it, Mommy," says Tasha, the smile falling off her face to be replaced by a scowl.

Lacey realizes she has gone too far. In an effort to redirect her anger she has swung hard all the way to Kat. It's not fair. "I have to get going, sweetie," Lacey says, rising from her chair. She is anxious to be alone, to be outside, to get away. And she is angry with herself for what she wants. Mac frowns at her as she leans over and kisses the top of Tasha's head.

"Get some sleep tonight," he says.

She is pulling out of the garage and neglects to slow for the speed bump that comes just after she has paid for her parking, just where the sunlight catches the hood of her car and she can't help but rush into it, smashing her bumper behind her. Startled, but not willing to slow down, feeling an urgency she can't explain—or doesn't want to—she accelerates along the empty city street, hoping against hope that she can make all the lights and not once have to touch her brakes before I-83 unfurls for her, for her escape. It is a futile hope, and she finds herself idling at the very first light, trying not to tap at the gas, just a little, just a little nudge through an unnecessary light that stands between her and . . . anywhere, anywhere but here.

She wonders if this is the way her mother felt, when she was ducking down that day. Yes, she remembers that part, her mother ducking down in the red truck as it spun and spit out of the parking lot, taking her away to wherever *away* was. She thinks now, *What a chicken-shit way to leave your kid.*

The moment recalls the numbness that fell from her jaw to her toes as she stood there, watching that truck fly down the road, disappearing into a pinprick of red. She remembers now—as she pulls a cigarette from her purse on her seat beside her, lights it, and immediately feels a heavy sway in her head, it having been at least four days, maybe five, since she has assaulted her lungs this way—she remembers watching the truck and knowing that this was the moment everything had been leading to. Her mother had been leaving her for weeks, had maybe already left her, let go of her, something no mother should ever do—let go of her child. And all that was left was the physical doing of it. The disappearance. Gone, with nothing left to touch of her—or smell of her because the smells are hardest of all to remember. Smell is the kind of thing you cannot draw up raw in your mind but instead you experience the smell and then that experience of it draws up the memory. Right now, she cannot remember the way her mother smelled, but to smell lemon and baby powder and rain is to have her mother, fresh from her own bath, tucking the covers around her and rubbing her nose to Lacey's own. She cannot pull up into her mind the smell of sausage frying, coffee perking, snow in the air, but if she were to walk past a breakfast diner on a wintery morning, she would be caught totally by surprise by the smell of Saturday mornings at the farm many years ago.

Touch, she thinks, touch is another thing altogether, the feel of her mother. Her upper arms, soft and sometimes warm from the sun if she'd been outside doing chores. Lacey liked to snuggle against her arm while May read to her and she liked to touch her face, trace the small scar at her eye, and there was a downy blond fuzz where her hairline met her cheekbones and sometimes Lacey liked to lick her own fingers and smooth it down. "Quit it," May would say, and she'd grab Lacey's hand and kiss it with a little smacking sound.

She is driving by a farm stand now. She considers stopping for corn and tomatoes, but the urge to keep moving won't allow it. She is focused instead on a long shower and fresh laundry. Once well past the farm stand, she regrets not stopping. The season is just starting, and it would have been nice to come back to the farm loaded down with fresh produce. She begins to slow, spying a drive ahead where she can turn around, but is nudged back to the road by a memory of May that she hadn't thought about in years.

May had a sliver of space between her front teeth and she wouldn't eat corn on the cob because of it. She always sliced it off the cob, portioning some to herself and some to Lacey. Lacey can remember this in particular because the summer after May left, Lacey and Willy were at a church picnic and Lacey asked Aunt Virgie to cut her corn off the cob for her. Aunt

Virgie said she wasn't a baby anymore and could eat it right off the cob like the other children. When Lacey fussed that her momma used to eat it that way, too, Aunt Virgie had looked at her kind of funny, thinking about it, and then said, "Her teeth, Lacey, she had a little gap there, remember? She didn't like the way the corn got in there." Lacey can remember that moment as if it was yesterday, the way she had stopped to consider what Virgie was saying, had tried to conjure her mother's face in her mind's eye and couldn't see it, not the whole thing. She could see only the thin space between her teeth, but the rest of her face was suddenly lost to her. It had always been part of the whole of her face and she had never, up until that moment, considered it separately, but in that second, surrounded by the butter-smeared faces of other children, scrambling over their mothers' laps, hanging from their arms, snatching food from their plates, she could not remember the whole of her face. All the pieces of her were coming apart.

She tries now, turning off the radio and sliding up the car window to focus on those pieces, and the pieces themselves are clear and sharp. Like her fingers. May kept her nails short and the thumb of her right hand was missing part of the nail at the tip, owing, her mother had told her, to a fish hook that got in there and festered. Her chest, above the breasts, was very hard and flat, the skin stretching like a drum and her collarbones jutting out like baby bird wings. And her tummy was soft and pillow-like, just a tiny pouf beneath her skirts. Lacey asked her once why she had a pillow for a tummy and was told it was there in case she needed a soft place for a baby to grow. Somehow that made perfectly good sense to her. They were a family, after all. All families had babies, didn't they? She only wondered when theirs was going to arrive.

So, all in all, she has the various pieces that made up her mother with no real hope of ever putting them all together.

November 18, 1974

I am having a hard-earned lesson today. I am learning that I can't never let my guard down, not ever. And I am learning that as much as things change, ain't no way to go back and change what's already done and happened. And what's more, what's done and happened is likely to come slamming back into what's changed and no good will come of it. At least, not for me—and not for Lacey.

What happened was Willy was in town picking up some feed this afternoon and I was sitting on the back stoop watching Lacey down at the pond throwing rocks in. She called me on down to show me some little fish she was seeing. We talked about the difference between fish in the pond and the fish round Ocracoke and I was explaining to her that the big Ocracoke fish can't live in our pond here on account of a number of things including their need to travel the waters and mostly on account of the one is salt water and the other is fresh.

It's been warm these last few days, but when the sun falls behind the clouds you can feel winter hanging right around the corner. I told Lacey to be real careful for just a minute, just one minute, while I went in to get our jackets.

My jacket hung as it ought on the hook just inside the door, but Lacey's was not to be found so easily. She wanders the house in it and then drops it wherever she happens to be when the notion hits her to peel it from herself. I searched the sunporch and then her bedroom where I found it wadded in a ball and half kicked under her bed.

When I came back out I couldn't find her anywhere.

I called out her name. But she don't always answer when her attention is caught up by something else, so I looked high and low, calling her name and telling her she best not be fooling with me right now. I started to head on up to the barn, but as I walked by the pond, just sitting there looking innocent enough, I looked closer and sprinkles of bubbles coming up in the center gave me a lurch in my heart. And just as I was turning to look harder I heard her little voice coming from down near the end of the drive. I couldn't hear what she was saying but she was talking to someone. I figured one of the farmhands had arrived and stopped to chat with her on his way in. Maybe she'd been playing in the ruts the milk tankers make in the drive as she is prone to do and I have told her repeatedly not to do as I am fearful a truck will come in too fast and not see her stooping down in the drive. So I come round from behind the big old evergreen where the drive curves down to the road and looked to the end of it. Lacey was on her tiptoes next to Little Jim's truck, pulling up at the window by her fingertips.

My voice stuck in my throat and when I tried to run my knees locked up and

I almost couldn't go to her. I knew that if I unlocked my knees I would crumble. I could feel everything in me going weak and loose and it was only my knees stuck like cement that kept me upright. When I finally pushed her name out, and it shot up from me, up into the air and glided like a pelican cross the crest of a wave afore it tucked and dove down on her, making her jump back on her toes.

　　Lacey!

　　Afore she could turn around to face me, the truck roared up. I had, by then, shook my knees loose and saw it was not Little Jim at all, but Daddy leaning out of that truck. But when he saw me running to her, he backed up real fast not even looking to see if there was cars coming down the road or even to be careful of Lacey, who had just been on her toes at his window. Then he shot on down the road leaving her standing in dust he kicked. I got to her and scooped her up, holding her so tight she started to cry. She told me to stop it, that I was hurting her.

　　I asked her what he said to her—just what did that man say?

　　She wanted me to put her down, but I wouldn't, so she pushed her hands against my shoulder and wiggled her bottom to work her way down through my arms. I set her to the ground, but took her wrist in my hand and wouldn't let go.

　　I walked hard up the driveway, with long, mean strides, and she had to do little runs and skips to keep up with me. I would have dragged her if she'd slowed behind me. She had to catch her breath as she scampered to keep up.

　　Stay away from that man, Lacey, I told her. You ever see him, you stay away!

　　All along she is talking to me. He said you'd be mad, Momma. He said what did I like so much about Willy's place, and I told him bout the cows and how I swim in the pond and he said we could come and live with him and then me and him could swim in the ocean. I don't want to live with him, Momma. He said you were mean to him and he never done anything to make you be so mean. Can I swim in the ocean, Momma?

　　I was yanking the poor child up the drive and past the pond, looking over my shoulder, listening for that damn truck.

　　He said you were mean to him, Momma, and you don't take good care of him, and he said you promised you would, but you don't.

　　Lacey. Do you hear me? I stopped and spun her hard by the arm so she was facing me. Don't you ever go near that truck again! Never! And that man cannot swim in the ocean!

She looked at me with her lower lip trembling, afraid of me, but there was something more there. I saw something in her eyes I never seen before. I saw her weighing what I had said against what she had just heard from Daddy. I saw her trying to find the truth somewhere in the middle of the two of us. That is just the kind of power he has—to make a child doubt her momma.

What could I have said to her then? Some promises can't be kept? Some promises should never be made at all? But when I got on my knees on that gravelly drive, felt the rocks pinching at my kneecaps, and looked her in the eyes, and I saw how expectant she was, like I could explain everything to her in a way that would make sense, well then, I just couldn't say nothing at all. No matter how far I was reaching into the corners of my mind, I didn't seem able to put my fingers on a kind of truth that would satisfy her. In the end there was nothing at all to say.

He said to tell you he's not mad at you anymore, she said.

I took her hand again, trying to be gentler, and we walked up the drive, not talking any more, but when I got to the pond I held her hand a little tighter as that was the only thing keeping me from walking into the murky middle of it.

December 6, 1974

Willy gave me some money to buy Lacey Christmas presents. He told me I must buy her at least one book and then I can buy for her anything I want. I am going to buy her <u>Blueberries for Sal</u> and maybe another one. Willy brung it home from the library last week and she was fussing not to return it this week. Willy reads to her every night and he says they've read everything the library has to offer. Willy always brings home books for the both of them and he brings me books of poems sometimes. He read a book called <u>The Old Man and the Sea</u> and he read parts of it to me. He wanted to know if it was truthful about some things or if it was just made up. I told him the ocean is so full of surprises you could make up just about anything and it is likely to be true one time or another.

Willy is especially curious about what lives in the sea and he is forever asking me have I ever seen this or that. I seen plenty of sharks, I told him. They tend to hug the shore in the early evening. They swim through the gullies that the waves have washed out and where all the smaller fish are trapped and this is where they hunt. Their fins slice the top of the water and every once in a while there is a thrashing that tells you a shark has taken on something he has had to fight for.

The dolphins seem to like morning better and they will play and splash and dance on a sunny day. Mr. Cooter, who everyone thinks of as a bit of a wampus cat, was right fond of dolphins and used to call them into the shallows. He would wade into the water about hip deep and make snapping and squeaking noises when he saw them playing just over the surf. Certain ones would come up on him and flip water with their tails. He'd get to carrying on with them, whipping his hand through the water in a big half circle, skimming it right back at them. Daddy said it weren't natural and to stay away from him. Mama said Mr. Cooter was just sensitive and sometimes men like that have a way with animals. Daddy said they weren't animals at all, just big dumb fish—and I best stay away from Mr. Cooter. But I knew Mama was right. Dolphins are mammals, which is a kind of animal, and that's cause they breathe air from the top of their head. Willy and me was explaining it one night to Lacey, about how mammals can look just like fish, but if they breathe air they are not really fish at all. They were naming mammals they could think of, like dolphins and whales, and sea lions, and Lacey said mermaids were mammals. Willy said a mermaid was a fine example of what we was talking about as she looks like a fish and lives in the sea, but breathes air. Lacey says now we should try to catch one and it can live in the pond.

CHAPTER 22

Out with the Old

Willy is thinking of whitewashing the coop—thinking of it—but not yet committed to the endeavor. He isn't sure where the idea has risen from and needs to find the source of it before he moves ahead in such a direction.

Earlier that morning, he'd been fussing with the eggs at the sink, wiping them down and packing them in a pile of egg cartons he had set on the counter, planning to run them over to Carroll's Market later in the morning. Lacey was at the hospital with Tasha waiting for Mac to get into town and spell her for the night. Willy knew Lacey was worn thin by it all. He had offered to come in himself, but Lacey had said no, she'd just wait on Mac. Sometimes she was stubborn like that, and he was wishing he had insisted. He didn't like the way Lacey looked to be dropping weight, the dark circles under her eyes, the quiet of her lately. He was thinking of calling her again, insisting this time that they switch off until Mac arrived, when he heard Carlotta's car come up the drive. They had moved past the place where they called one another first to announce a visit and he was glad of it. Now, when she just showed up, he felt a pleasant kind of hitch in his heart. Seeing her unexpectedly was like taking a sip of cool water, not knowing he'd been thirsty until he got it to his mouth and then he couldn't stop himself from drinking it all down. That's the way he felt watching her come out of her car, followed by bags and boxes and sometimes, but not today, that rabbit of hers.

She moved across the lawn, past the hydrangeas blooming as blue as the sky, bags hanging from her arms and a big box set on her hip and he met her at the door with her hands full and a smile on her face that was bright and busy. He held the door wide open to her as he took a bag from her hand and another from her shoulder.

"Morning, hon," she said. "How'd you sleep?" She always asked him that and it was funny to him as sleep wasn't something he thought much about until she started asking. She kissed him quick on the lips, making a little *hmmmm* sound as she did it, and then proceeded to announce what she had brought with her—tomatoes from her little garden, fresh basil, some puzzle books for Tasha, birdseed for the feeder she had brought him the week before, and—surprise—a brand-new coffee maker just like the one he had seen in her kitchen. "They had red, black, and cobalt. I figured you for a cobalt man," she said, hefting the box off her hip and onto the counter. "Your coffee is just awful."

"I've been told."

"A percolator, Lord." She laughed and shook her head at the same time. She proceeded to remove the coffee maker from the box and set it up on the counter, looking around for a place to put it. The counter was cluttered with eggs and cartons and a stack of casserole dishes to be returned to neighbors and, of course, the reasonable place for it would be right where the percolator set nudged against the refrigerator and the toaster. She unplugged the percolator and stuffed it in the trashcan, its dull chrome cap and the filmy glass top-knob of it sticking out above the trashcan so the lid couldn't be closed.

"I'll take it down the cellar," he said, moving to lift it from the trashcan.

"Don't be silly," she said. "What are you going to save that old thing for?" She rubbed his back solicitously and laughed. "Trust me, you'll never go back to that thing once you have coffee from this coffee maker. One thing I know is coffee."

"Just seems a waste to throw it out," he said. He'd had that percolator more than thirty-five years and it was a marvel to him the way he could still rely on it to spit and bubble every morning. Sure, sometimes he had to jiggle the cord to get it started, and maybe the coffee wasn't the best, but he'd gotten used to the bitterness of it and he didn't mind the grounds at the bottom of his cup every morning. Furthermore, it was one thing to be bringing in something new, like the birdfeeder he was now accountable to every morning, but it was another thing altogether to be throwing out the old things that he was used to.

He let the percolator sit and went back to his eggs, side-eyeing it poking out of the trash. It nagged at him and he considered removing it from the trashcan later and stowing it in the cellar.

"Don't go digging that thing out of the trash," she said, reading his mind.

"I've had it for more years than I can count," he said with a chuckle.

She nudged him out of her way at the sink to run water in the pot and then stopped to look out the window to where the barn had once been, the foundation rising up in ruins. Willy saw her look, stopping what she was doing to lean in on her elbow. He came up behind her and looked as well.

"Must have been something," she said.

"Sure," he said. "Things was different then, with the cows and all the business around here, milk tankers rolling in, and Lacey underfoot."

"And May, of course," she added.

"For a time." Beyond where the barn had once stood, he could see the gentle rise of the land. The timothy was a rippling blanket of new green reaching up to a blue sky and a scattering of curdled clouds. It was a view he couldn't have seen had the barn still been there.

She turned and kissed him on the lips, patted his shoulders, and turned back to the sink, sliding the egg cartons out of her way so they wouldn't get wet from the splash at the sink. "Well," she said tenderly but matter-of-factly. "Now you have chickens. You had cows. Cows are gone, and now you have chickens."

He moved beside her, gathering up the packed eggs in his arms.

"Cows was better," he said, trying to make a joke of it but not really feeling it.

"Nope," she said brightly. "Just different. That's all. One's not really no better than the other." She turned her head to him and said earnestly, "It's a shame about the cows, Willy, really. I imagine it was real hard on you. But now you have chickens, all these delicious eggs, best in the county, from what I hear."

He gave a small *harrumph*, thought on it a second and said, "Reckon things just change is all." The knowledge of it settled heavily in him again, barns falling down, wives running off. He watched Carlotta, the largeness of her in a bright-green blouse and a big gold medallion-like necklace hanging down between her breasts, her dark brown eyes with the swipe of blue color on the lids, the full lips painted a deep red—always, even after he woke to her that first morning with her next to him (and the first thing she had said to him was *how'd you sleep?*). He was surprised by the redness of her lips, like they'd just been stained that way from years of lipstick, and he looked at her now and couldn't imagine what it would be like to not have so much color in his kitchen. And just how could that be when he had loved the quiet pastel of May, of May with her caramel-colored hair, her pale shoulders, the shy smile, the slender wisp of her when she walked around the house in her white robe, and no makeup, not ever, and he had loved that about her, too.

Carlotta put a cup of coffee down in front of him and stood back to watch him. He rolled his eyes at her with a smirk on his face and took a sip.

"Hmmm?" she said, her brows rising up.

"Good," he said. "Good." And it was.

"Well, there you go," she said.

"Yup, here I am."

She went back to the counter and poured herself a cup. "What's the plan for the day?"

"Mac's dropping Kat here at the farm and then heading over to the hospital to relieve Lacey. I'm gonna drop off these eggs and maybe," and he heard himself say it just as the idea was occurring to him, "and maybe I'm thinking of whitewashing the coop."

He is still thinking on it, set at his kitchen table. Eggs have been delivered and his lunch has been eaten, and there is a whole afternoon in front of him. Now that he's thought of whitewashing the coop, he can't understand what is stopping him from getting to it. He is not a man who deliberates over chores. Something needs to be done and he just adds it to his list and does it.

Just as he is thinking of rising to it, Mac arrives with Kat in tow. He goes out the door to meet them and, truly, it is like Mac is dragging her from the car with an invisible rope. She is sulkier than usual, refusing to look at her father and moving slow enough that even Willy wants to tell her to get a move on. She has to be reminded to get her bag from the back seat and when she does, she swings it onto her shoulder so fast it knocks her off balance and she steps quick to right herself. There is huffing and grumbling, and she doesn't even acknowledge Willy but walks straight past him into the house, letting the door slam behind her.

"I don't think she'll be much company for you," says Mac.

"Never needed much company," Willy says. "Come on in. Carlotta packed some supper for you and Tasha. Remind me to give it to you."

Once in the kitchen, Willy looks at Mac and can read the strain on his face. He's tired, they all are, but it's more than that. They can hear Kat upstairs in the bedroom, and there is some *thunk*ing and the sound of a window opening.

"Here," says Willy, nodding to the cooler on the counter. "Carlotta don't like the fact that Tasha's eating hospital food."

"Awful stuff," Mac agrees.

"You better get going, boy. Lacey's been there four nights now and she won't leave until you get there." He sees Mac eyeing the new coffee maker. "Gift from Carlotta," he says.

"Nice," says Mac, stepping up to the counter, leaning in, and running his hand down the cobalt casing of it all like a man might caress a shiny new sports car. "Nice," he says again.

There's the sound overhead of a window stuttering open followed by a *thunk* that is likely Kat flopping on the bed.

"She won't be any trouble," Mac says, lifting his eyes to the ceiling to indicate the room where Kat is now banging around.

"I know that," says Willy, waving him off.

Willy thinks Mac will go up and say something to Kat before he leaves, and he looks to be thinking of it, but then drops his shoulders in a defeated way, sighs, stares up at the ceiling hopelessly, and heads out the door with the small cooler hanging from his shoulder like a pocketbook.

Willy has hauled cans of paint and brushes from the aluminum barn to the side of the chicken coop and is setting out his tools on top of the wood-pile. He has found a bucket of asphalt shingles and plans to make some repairs to the roof and maybe change out some bad hinges before he gets started. Lacey pulls in and he waves to her, watches her sit in the car, her head tilted back, her fingers drawing her hair up over her forehead. She opens the car door, sets her leg out, and still doesn't rise from the interior.

He knows she is tired. The hospital time is hard on her for too many reasons to count. Suddenly, she is slamming her car door and making her way to him. He stands up straighter, recognizing that stride of hers. She has something to say and she is going to spit it out and chances are good he's not going to like it much.

"Willy," she says, standing in front of him now with her arms crossed. "We have to talk."

He looks up at her, wide-eyed, but says nothing.

"We have to talk about May."

December 21, 1974

Little Jim's truck was seen in town again today. I only know cause Uncle Price sent Willy straight home from the hardware store after Doc come in the store and said he just passed that red truck on the road. Willy came in the door calling my name out loud even afore he had the door full open. I came up from the cellar with an apron full of potatoes and saw him looking kind of shook up and pale, kind of like he had a whole lot to say but didn't know how to get started.

I asked him what was the matter, but first he had to know where was Lacey and had anyone come to the house. I can't be sure what he was thinking or what exactly Uncle Price told him. I suppose Uncle Price told him about the time Little Jim came to the store and scared Lacey so bad.

He called Little Jim my old beau and he weren't mean about it, just want-ing to know was there anything unsettled between the two of us and where did Lacey fit into all of this?

I stood on one side of the kitchen and he stood on the other and it felt like there was a whole country between us. I told him Lacey didn't fit in anywhere except here with him and me. He asked me was I sure about that. I told him there weren't nothing in the whole world I was more sure of. I rolled the potatoes out of my apron and onto the counter where they thunked around, and I brushed the dirt off me. I asked him real casual like, was he sure it was Little Jim who was seen in town? Because maybe it was just a stranger with a similar truck. I was thinking, of course, that it could have been Daddy again, and truthfully I would have rather it be Little Jim than Daddy hunting me down again. And why, oh why, does Little Jim keep letting Daddy take his truck? I can only think Daddy must have whupped him good for beating me a long time ago.

Willy told me Little Jim must still be carrying a torch for me, and I had to smile at his old-fashioned way of putting things, like what Little Jim and I had was some kind of tender romance.

That's when I stepped across the kitchen floor and wrapped my arms around him. I didn't say a word for a long while, and neither did he. Then I told him Lacey was napping and I asked him to come upstairs with me. Then I kissed him with the kind of kiss I never thought to give a man in the daylight hours.

I surprised him some, I think, but he drew his hands harder around me and then moved one hand under my blouse and across my breast and I felt his fingers dance across my skin. He had a sad but ever-so-grateful look in his eyes as he moved me toward the stairway. I had to stop him a second to go lock the back kitchen door.

December 22, 1974

> *cranberries*
> *ginger ale*
> *cotton balls*
> *witch hazel*
> *cinnamon*
> *popping corn*

Lacey and I are going to string popcorn tomorrow night. Mama used to do that with me, too. Daddy loved the look of it and he always said so. It was darn near his favorite thing about Christmas, he once said. Only our dog, Swamp, once ate it all off the tree, string and all. Mama caught him in the middle of his shenanigans with string hanging out of his mouth and when she pulled it out, yards and yards of string and popcorn come up out of him. Mama just cracked up laughing and Swamp made funny yacking sounds. Better this end than the other, she told him.

Daddy came home later that night and saw that all the popcorn was gone. He was three sheets to the wind by then and all his racket woke me and Mama up from a sound sleep. Mama told him what happened and he said what was wrong with her, and why didn't she just make some more or was it so damn hard. Mama tried to hush him some and said me and her was going to make more in the morning. It damn near is morning, he told her, and then he said if she weren't going to make popcorn then he would. Then he asked her again, tell him how it happened and when Mama didn't say nothing I started to tell him about Swamp and how Mama pulled the string up out of him.

He looked over at Swamp curled up tight in the corner with his face to the wall, but looking at us with the whites of his eyes showing and his tailing thumping soft and anxious-like on the floor. Daddy staggered across the room and Swamp curled up smaller and tucked his tail in tighter. Sonofabitching dog was what he said. Swamp loved that man, but he knew trouble when he saw it brewing.

Daddy went at him like a shark, kicking him once and then stumbling back, circling round, and coming back at him again. If he could of bit a piece of meat out of that poor dog I think he would of. Swamp just yelped each time and pressed hisself harder into the corner.

Truth is, I think now Swamp could have taken him down, but some creatures don't know when to stop loving somebody, even when they don't deserve it no more. It was a surprise to me, him going after poor Swamp that way. That man never put a hand to me when I was a child, nor Mama, either. But thinking back now I think Mama must have been sick by then and maybe they both knew it and one thing I know is that Daddy is different when he is afraid of something being taken from him.

But Mama stopped him. She could always stop him from his worst self. She was yelling, Let's make popcorn. I'm making the popcorn, Duane. She slammed the kettle on the stove so hard that I jumped. Du, she says, I need some help with this popcorn over here.

Daddy turned his back on Swamp and told Mama that she was finally talking a little sense and was that so hard after all. Swamp shivered in the corner and I wanted to go to him, but I was afraid of making Daddy notice him again. Daddy shoved Mama away from the stove with the weight of his shoulder, turned the flame up real high and poured half a jar of corn into the kettle.

In less than a minute corn was flying out of the kettle like something wild. Daddy had forgot to put a lid on it. Corn shot everywhere. Swamp slunk real quiet into my bedroom and Mama ran around like a crazy lady looking for the lid to the kettle. Daddy took up a dustpan and began swatting flying popcorn out of the air. He laughed so hard and looked so silly that pretty soon Mama got to laughing, too, and it was all she could do to get to the stove and turn off the flame. Kernels still shot from the kettle for another minute or so, and Daddy swung at them with all his heart and soul, only to finally send himself tumbling into the wall where he slid to the floor and slept till dawn.

December 23, 1974

He is still in town and I don't understand how he is doing it. I don't know where he stays as it is too cold now to sleep in the truck and the roads are getting full up with snow. I told Virgie I didn't think it was Little Jim but likely Daddy instead, but she is certain it is not Daddy as he don't even have a driver's license. But I know that don't matter. I wanted to tell her that I <u>know</u> it is Daddy and not Little Jim and has anybody actually seen Little Jim? I started to say all this to her but then I couldn't say no more. There is something so shameful deep inside of me that makes me not want to say in words that it is my own daddy hunting me down like this and for what reason that would be I cannot even say out loud. It is easier to let them all think it is Little Jim for if they knew what I know about Daddy the shame on me would be too much. I couldn't stand up in this county under that kind of shame. I couldn't pretend to be the good momma I am trying to be to Lacey, the good wife I want to be to Willy. Even though Aunt Virgie knows about Lacey, she has never since that day spoken on it and I am grateful to her.

What happened was I sold some smocking work to some of the church ladies at the Fall Bazaar and so I had a little extra pin money for Willy's Christmas present. I was hoping to get him an electric razor like the ones they sell in town at the pharmacy. Aunt Virgie thought it would make a fine gift and then she asked Uncle Price and he said, why, he would like to have one of them hisself for a Christmas present.

Willy dropped me off at the store and Aunt Virgie and I went across the street to pick out our gifts together. We got the last two razors left in the store as they have been real popular this year. We was standing at the counter paying for our purchases, laughing and smiling between ourselves as to how clever we were to get the last two razors, when I looked out the store window behind the cashier and saw the red truck shoot through the stop sign in the center of town.

I couldn't be sure at first that it was Little Jim's, and so I didn't say anything, but Aunt Virgie saw it, too, and real quick we went back across the street to the apartment and up the back steps.

Snow was starting to fall again and it had settled a half inch deep on the porch railings. Aunt Virgie slammed the door so hard that the snow clumped down off the ledge. Once we got in we didn't say a word about what we saw, but it hung in the air like a bad odor you don't make mention of. She put on a pot of tea water and said she had to speak with Uncle Price and would be right back up. She took the inside steps that went down into the store. This time I locked the back door.

I still needed a few things from the grocer only a little way down past Farmers National Bank, but I weren't going to leave Aunt Virgie's until Willy come to pick me up. I figured he and Lacey could just come to the market with me for a minute.

By the time Willy and Lacey got there he could tell something was wrong. Lacey kept asking me did I see the snow, and while I heard her question over and over again, I couldn't quite remember if I had answered it. I felt like I was on the other side of a screen door from the two of them. I told Willy I needed a few things from the grocer and Aunt Virgie suggested he drive me over.

We come down through the store and Uncle Price was standing by the front door watching the road. He was locking up a little early, he said. Business was quiet. He unlocked the door for us and watched us go to Willy's truck. The bed was loaded with hay he'd just picked up from Mac Dougarty's place and it was all covered with a dusting of snow that blew off in an instant when we pulled out on the road.

Lacey didn't want to go in the market. She wanted to stay in the truck and watch the snow fall. Willy said he'd sit with her. I leaned over Lacey's head and kissed him on the cheek. I'm not sure why I did that. I think it confused him some.

Marybeth was behind the cash register when I checked out with my items. She asked about Lacey as she always does as she has a little girl, Franny, about the same age. Difference is Marybeth and Jed are very old to be the parents of such a young child. She is forever telling everyone how Franny is a miracle and they never did think they would have a child so late in their marriage. I have to bite my tongue to keep from telling her that I think Lacey is a miracle and I never thought I would have a child before my marriage.

In any case, Marybeth kept chattering away at me and I had a hard time breaking off from her. I kept looking over her head and out the window, checking on Willy and Lacey in the lot, but she would just get to chattering and clear forget to ring my purchases. The store was empty except for me and so I guess she felt a bit lonely. I finally told her to have a merry Christmas and I would surely see her in church on Christmas morning, and then I took up my shopping bag and went out the door.

When I got to the parking lot Willy was gone. I could see the tire tracks from his truck in the fresh snow and they led around to the back of the store where the deliveries come in. Just as I started to walk around the side of the store toward the back of the building, Little Jim's truck come flying up the road and spun real wide into the lot. I backed up against the building and it was Daddy pulled up beside me leaving only two feet between me and the clapboard siding. He leaned from the driver's side and rolled down the passenger side window. Smoke near tumbled from the truck and rolled down its side. He told me to get on in and don't sass him none. He reached across again and opened the door, but when he did, the door fell open against me and hung between me and the open doorway to the truck.

I told him to go home. He wanted to know where the baby was. A bottle of Wild Turkey rolled out of the truck and fell to the gravel lot, but the snow cushioned its fall and it only rolled and clunked against the wall of the building. I told him again to go on home. I'm a married woman now, I reminded him.

Then he tried being real nice and said it would only be for a little while. Just come on home for a visit. I said maybe I would do that sometime and he looked at me with those damn sad eyes, like he was the loneliest creature on earth. He said he sure did miss me, and it weren't natural, him being alone and all. He ordered me to climb on in and we would go to get the baby and have a nice Christmas together.

Don't sass me, May, he said. Get on in this truck now.

I was inching my way along the wall and back up to the front of the store, but he had sense enough to inch the truck along with me, though he seemed hell-bent to crush me between the truck and the wall of the building. He told me he'd been driving around all afternoon looking for me. He'd been to the farm, but I weren't there. I wondered if he'd gone inside the house, then figured for sure he had.

I told him, Go on home now, Daddy. I'll see you real soon. We'll come for a visit, me and Willy and the baby. I didn't want to say Lacey's name out loud to him. She could just go on being the baby.

I could tell he was getting angry with me and he would of reached for me and pulled me in if the car door hadn't been between us, but just then Willy and Lacey come driving round from the back of the store. I looked up at Willy, grateful to see him and shamed at the same time. Instead of coming faster, Willy slowed his truck down and then stopped altogether. He was close enough that I could see he was watching us, but too far for me to read his face.

I have to go now, Daddy, I said. I told him go on home now. And I pushed the door shut and squeezed between the truck and the store until I was free of him. He shot out of the parking lot with the horn screaming a big goodbye in my ear. Willy started to pull up real slow.

I got in the truck and set the bag at my feet, and Lacey rambled on and on about the snow and how Willy showed her how it fell in the little stream behind the store and disappeared into nothing. My hands were shaking and there was a sick feeling in my stomach that started to come up with every bump and turn. Willy never said a word, never even looked at me. When we got home and Lacey run through the kitchen and up to her bedroom, he just asked real quiet if he'd been coming round.

I told him nobody been coming round. He asked me did I suppose he'd be headed back down tonight. I told him it seemed likely. I took the popcorn out of the bag and dropped it straightaway in the trashcan. I told him we oughta get some of that fancy tinsel for the tree tomorrow. I said that would be real nice for a change.

December 24, 1974

When I watch Lacey skip around the parlor in her slippers and then stop to peer up at the ceiling because she thinks she heard reindeer, well I never think for a minute that I would change anything that brought me to this place, to Willy and Lacey and this farm. I belong here. Everything feels like it's right where it should be and the ocean is so far away, only a whisper in my head that hushes up when I see Willy coming in from the barn, walking through his own icy breath, or Lacey dipping her toe into her bath water. Seeing these things, it is like coming up from the bottom of the ocean and they are the air I gulp.

Christmas 1974

Willy is real pleased with his electric razor. Lacey liked near about every-thing she got, but she says best of all is the paint-by-numbers project Willy picked up for her last time we went to Towson. We go into town there every so often to pick up several things at the Hutzler's department store—socks and underdraw-ers, a new church tie. This last time he also got a new white shirt and some dress socks. I got a new church dress and stockings. At Christmas they set up a special toy section with giant candy canes and cottony snow all around. There are plastic elves with heads that turn this way and that, and reindeer that swish their tails by way of a motor, and ladies in red hats to wrap your purchases in shiny red foil paper. That's where Willy saw the paint-by-numbers. It said <u>ages eight to twelve</u> on the box, but Willy says he knows she's smarter than most eight-year-olds and she can certainly paint according to number. When she is finished she will have a painting of horses running through a field of sunflowers. Although already she is saying the numbers are wrong and she will paint it as she likes.

Willy gave me a new white bathrobe and some toilet water that smells like lemons. Lacey found that real darn funny that I would want to put water from the toilet on me.

At church we had a live baby Jesus on the altar. Moose Braggart and his sister Taffy-Lynn were dressed as Joseph and Mary. They were kneeling next to a little cradle with a plastic baby doll in it. Pretty soon we all knew that the doll belonged to their sister, Elly, who is four and who sat most unhappily in the second pew back from the altar. She was surely not pleased to see her baby doll being used in such a fashion. Twice she wiggled and squirmed up out of her daddy's arms and tried to make her way to the altar to snatch that doll from the cradle. After much fussing and a little bit of name calling between brother and sisters, Pastor Ray finally took the doll from the cradle and handed it back to her in her pew. Her mama turned a hundred shades of red when he did that, but Elly just hugged that dolly like she was never gonna let it go. Well, of course, then it seemed Taffy-Lynn did not feel right worshipping at an empty cradle. She looked near about tears and finally made like she was leaving the altar, too. Now Beau and Lana McDowell have a fat little baby boy who just happened to be sleeping away in Lana's arms at the time. That's when Lana went to the altar and lay down her little baby boy. Pastor Ray thanked her for _giving her only begotten son_, and the service went on just regular as could be—though the baby did pass gas after a time and Pastor Ray said that should only serve to remind us that Jesus was a real human being who once walked among us.

We will have supper at Aunt Virgie's place tonight. She said I'm not experienced enough to cook this kind of meal, but she will teach me. I made a sweet potato pie, her recipe, that I will bring along.

Christmas Night

The back door was swung wide open when we got home. I was the last one out because I had to run back in and get Clint and Lyle's present that I forgot *under the tree. I know for certain that I closed that door. Fact is, when I look at my hand, I can even recall the feel of the door when it jimmied over the frame and clicked into place. I had their chess set wrapped and tucked under my right arm and it was my left arm that pulled the door shut. I haven't got a shred of doubt about my closing that door.*

I told Willy I must have been careless. He was angry with me, I could feel it even though he don't say much. While he unloaded presents from the car, I bolted the basement door at the top of the steps. I threw on all the lights, too, and checked the closet and behind the sofa.

Willy said to check for critters when he came in the kitchen door. He told me I couldn't imagine the damage a squirrel or a coon could do to this place.

The house is icy cold now and the wind has howled through the kitchen and blown the papers around. It doesn't feel like what we should of come home to on Christmas night.

Willy said, Jesus, what was I thinking? I just told him I was sorry, but he shook his head at me like I was near hopeless. Lacey was asleep in the truck on the way home, but the cold woke her and now she is fussing with Willy about leaving the hall light on. I hope he will leave it on for her. Even though it's so cold I can see my breath, the light makes me think it is warmer than it is.

CHAPTER 23

The Search Begins

Willy is digging through a drawer in the bedside dresser on May's side, though he has begun of late to think of it as Carlotta's side, as she has twice slept over in the very same place where May once slept. He hasn't opened the drawer in years and inside he finds crochet needles, strands of fine white yarn, a tube of ChapStick, tweezers, a dried-up pot of night cream—which he cannot help but open to find the contents cracked and yellowed and now scentless, plus an emery board, Q-tips with fuzz-bloomed ends, cotton balls, two white flat shiny button-like discs that he remembers to be the earrings she wore on Christmas Day and—what he is looking for—a stationery box with a smogged plastic lid.

He settles himself on the edge of the bed and brings the box to his lap to open it. The stationery, he knows, was one of his small gifts to May. He had given it to her the first time he had left the farm for the day after they were married. He was only headed up to York for the afternoon to pick up a used bucket loader for the smaller of his two tractors and then to an Amish farm where he planned to check on one of the bulls he was considering for breeding. He made it a point always to see the bull in person before he purchased the sperm. Temperament was important to him in breeding. He didn't need calves that would eventually give him trouble in the barn, especially not now with a young child running around. May was sleeping when he left, curled into a question mark with her hair splayed across the pillow. He had looked at her and thought he was the luckiest man on earth.

The day before, she had asked him for writing paper to write to her friend Sugar and he had torn paper from a notebook. He made up his mind then to stop at one of those Hallmark stores in York and get her some proper stationery.

Opening the box now he finds a ballpoint pen—chewed on the ends—and a book of old eight-cent Harry Truman stamps, paper clips, the few remaining pages of yellowed stationery with a border of strawberry vines, and the slip of paper he has come in search of. It is Sugar Lane's address in Ocracoke Island. He knew there wouldn't be a phone number.

He takes the steps slowly and goes into the parlor where Lacey waits for him. She has her computer on her lap and has set a little device with a blinking green light on it beside her on the side table. Willy doesn't understand the internet but he has been listening to her complain about it, or the lack of it, since March. He has promised to look into it but has no idea how to go about doing so.

"My hotspot's not working," she says when he comes back into the room.

He doesn't know what she is talking about.

"Oh, wait, here we go." She scowls at the screen and Willy takes a seat across from her on the davenport, fingering the slip of paper in his hand.

"No *May Cherrymill*. But let's try *May DuBerry*." Willy watches her type and leans forward to see if he can see what she is looking at. "Nothing," she says. She looks up at him and asks, for maybe the third or fourth time, exasperated with him, "You have no idea what this Jim guy's last name was?"

Willy shakes his head, no. She is frustrated with him, he can tell. But he doesn't think he ever knew the man's last name. "They just called him Little Jim." By *they*, he is referring to Uncle Price and Aunt Virgie, Lyle and Clint as well.

"Can you call the nephews and see if they remember?"

"Really? You serious? Right now?"

"Yes, Willy, please! You said you'd help."

"Not sure what it is I'm helping with."

He has, in recent days, begun to feel like he is closing some doors and in doing so, he's begun to realize just how nasty a draft had been blowing over his heart the past thirty years. "I know you say you been thinking on it awhile, but I can't quite see the point here. I told you everything I know. I'm not hiding anything from you, honey."

"Oh, Willy. I told you. I'm being haunted." She stops her typing and looks to him. "No, really, I mean it. I can't shake her. She won't get out of my head. I spent thirty years not thinking about her and now, other than Tasha, it's all I think about. I'm curious, that's all."

"Here," he says, rising and handing her the slip of paper with the address on it. "No phone number, like I said, but here's her address. Probably has a phone by now. You could call information down there and see if she's listed." He watches her type again.

"*Duane DuBerry,*" she says slowly as she types.

"Course, she probably got married and likely has a different last name . . ."

"Got him," says Lacey. She pulls the computer up farther onto her lap and reads to Willy. "Body Washed Up on Shores of Kill Devil Hills Believed to be that of Duane 'Du' DuBerry, Medical Examiner Says."

June 6, 1975

The badly decomposed body found on the shore of Kill Devil Hills on May 29 is believed to be that of missing Ocracoke resident, fifty-two-year-old Duane DuBerry. DuBerry has been missing since April 30, when he was last reported seen by Ferry Master Robert Kreen who ferried DuBerry to Ocracoke Island. The lapse in identifying the body is partly attributable to the fact that DuBerry was not report-ed missing, as he was often known to leave the island for periods of time to whereabouts unknown and had indicated, according to two residents, that he planned to relocate to Key West, Florida. Medical Examiner Dr. Marshall Emerson reports no foul play is indicated and the drowning appears to be accidental.

Lacey and Willy lock eyes. "Yeah, well," Willy says.

"I wish there was a photo. I'd like to know what he looked like. Did you ever meet him?"

"Nah. The coast guard called here after they found him. She'd been gone about a month by then. I just said she wasn't here and I'd give her the message," he admits now. "You know," he says quietly, "I just kept thinking she'd be back, hoping."

"Aunt Virgie didn't think much of him. I remember that." Lacey shakes her head and asks, kindly this time, "Will you call them?"

"Sure, sure," Willy says, and he shuffles from the room to make the call.

Lyle answers the phone and Willy can tell he is surprised by his question. Lyle's not sure about it, hasn't thought about that rascal in years but he will think on it.

"What brings this up, Willy?"

"Ain't me. It's Lacey," says Willy, twisting the cord around his arm.

"Bingo!" yells Lacey from the parlor. "I found her!"

For a second he thinks she's found May and is certain his own heart will stop, but then he hears Lacey say, "Sugar Lee Lane, owner of Sugar's Cottages."

"Think on it some," he says to Lyle. "Ask Clint if he can recall anything. You know Lacey. Once she gets a bee in her bonnet over something, she don't give it up."

Lyle says he will talk to Clint. He asks after Tasha and says they will both stop by to see her once she's home. Willy heads back into the parlor to look over Lacey's shoulder.

On her computer screen, she has pulled up a picture of three small cottages in a grove and there is a clear blue sky and a wide expanse of water in the background. Suddenly she is flashing through photos and lands on one titled: Your Host, Miss Sugar Lee Lane.

"Is that her, Willy? I think it's her."

"I reckon it's her. I told you, I never met her." He is looking closer at the picture and is reconciling it with what May had said of her. *She has the most sparkly blue eyes, Willy, and she ain't but four-foot-nothin'.* In the photo her hair is pure white and long, frozen in the lift of a breeze and her eyes are surely the sparkling blue May had said they were. She is chubby, he thinks, in that way that short women are and it can't be helped. There are deep lines in her face that take him by surprise as he has pictured her in his mind and she was always young, with the dark hair May had described and so to him she was always just a girl. "That's her, that's her friend," he says. He puts a hand on Lacey's shoulder and is grateful when she gives his resting hand a pat. "Weren't no sense in going on after her," he says. "And like I said, Virgie made calls down to the coast guard station. She asked after her, but they didn't know nothing. Said this Jim character had left the island for Georgia or Virginia or someplace I don't recall, and I figured the two of them didn't want to be tracked like animals." He takes a seat across from her on the sofa.

Lacey looks over at him earnestly, and he knows she is going to be very careful with what she has to say. "I wanted you to bring her back, but at the same time, something inside me told me she *would* be back. I guess I was used to her leaving." She looks at him for a long moment, takes a deep breath, and starts again. "I watched her get in that truck. I watched her duck down in the seat as it drove off and I knew she made a choice that didn't include us . . ." Her voice trails off, but she doesn't stop. She only says the next cautiously, stepping, he knows, around his feelings. "I have a hard time understanding you not going after her . . ."

"I thought she'd come back," he interrupts her. "I did, Lacey. And damn, I just couldn't find the sense in forcing her to come back." He runs the massively knuckled paw of his hand down his chin. "He'd been coming around, you know. And he weren't no good. I knew that. But she was young and maybe foolish, and I just hoped she'd come to her senses."

Willy isn't sure what else he can say. It seemed at the time the right thing to do, to wait, to let her figure it out. But now that he is being forced to look it square in the face, he is thinking he was wrong. But one day just led to another, and another, and before long he had resigned himself to having been left—didn't like it—but resigned to it, claiming the emptiness of it that felt so familiar, the kind of thing a man could get real comfortable with, like the way a man don't mind the smell of his own gas he passes, even though he knows it's a foul thing.

But there is something else he is recognizing now, and he can't tell her this. Is sure he will never say it aloud. There was always a niggling fear after she left that she *would* come back. But it wouldn't be for him. It would be for Lacey. And he was certain that if she came back it would only be to take Lacey away. And the more the days went on, the letting loose of May, the more he found he couldn't bear to lose Lacey, couldn't possibly bear to lose her, too.

"Well, now what?" he says. Lacey just stares at him, blankly, lassos her hair from her face and pulls it into a massive mop on top of her head. When she doesn't say anything, he says. "Suppose you're gonna do whatever you're gonna do."

"I don't know what I'm going to do," she says firmly.

A toilet flushes overhead and they both look to the ceiling, having forgotten that Kat is upstairs. She's been holed up in her room since she arrived, and Willy is reminded that there will be three of them for supper. "Figuring on heating up one of them casseroles for supper," he says and rises on what feels at the moment like the ricketiest of knees.

Kat joins them at the table and picks at her food, separating peas from noodles from chicken out of a cheese-laden casserole.

"How's school?" says Lacey, and Willy knows it is a loaded question in so many ways. Lacey has already shared with him that she is suspicious of the fact that Kat is here this week, so close to the end of school. "Almost finished, hmmm? That must be nice."

Willy can see the girl squirm, her face twisting into a knot, and he wishes Lacey would let it drop. Kat nods to Lacey and then drops her fork to her plate, pushes back from the table so that her chair squeaks across the linoleum, but doesn't say anything.

"How 'bout some ice cream?" he offers, rising from the table and shooting Lacey a look with narrowed eyes. Lacey mouths *what*, shrugs her shoulders, and goes back to eating.

Kat declines the ice cream with just a shake of her head but takes her plate to the sink and asks Willy if she can watch some television. He tells her of course, no need to ask, and reminds her that there is a jumble of VCR tapes in the box beside the sofa.

"They're all little kid tapes," she says.

"Yeah, well. That's true."

"*American Idol* is on tonight," she says, and he asks her what that's about.

"It's a reality show." He looks at her for an explanation, having no idea what she means. "Like a major talent contest for singers," she says, "and they're sometimes really good but the judges—Simon Cowell—he's the main judge and he's like ruthless, man—the worst. I mean—*really*. But if you're good enough you can win a major recording contract. And you know it's really hard to be a star and you have to take a lot of criticism, which is what Cowell always says— that you have to be able to *take it* if you're gonna *make it* in the business, so it's, like, for their own good, you know?" She is animated and he is surprised. It's the most he's heard her say since she arrived earlier that day. He agrees, or nods his head as if he does, but really doesn't have an opinion on the matter. "I think I'll eat my ice cream in there. The show starts in a minute," she says.

Willy pulls two ice cream cartons from the freezer and tells her to help herself. He watches her, suddenly enthusiastic as she digs into the deeply frozen ice cream, watches the thin muscles of her arm strain. "Need some help?" She steps aside and he piles the bowl with more than he intended, happy to add the calories to her thin frame, and she heads to the sunroom, reaching behind herself to shut the door.

Willy and Lacey sit at the table in silence, each with their own dish of ice cream and there is the clinking of spoons and the casting of eyes toward the sunroom before he finally says, "You oughta let it rest."

"What?"

"This thing with her," he says, nodding to the sunroom. "She ain't your kid, Lacey."

She looks at him wide-eyed, huffs, and drops her spoon in her bowl. "She hates me."

"And you don't even like her," he says.

"That's not true, Willy!"

He purses his lips and raises his brows at her, inviting her to rethink it. "It's not true!"

"You catch more flies with honey than vinegar, all's I'm saying."

"You're ridiculous."

They sit in silence for a while until Lacey turns to him and says maybe she'll send Sugar Lane an email.

With that, Willy sits up a little straighter at the table and looks around the room, his eyes casting about as if May has just materialized in a million different places but all at the periphery of his vision—in the corners of the room, at the kitchen sink, at the window. He can see the hem of her lemon paisley skirt swish by, but when he looks down to his side there is only the bare old yellowed linoleum. He sees the flick of her fingers across the table-top, but as quick as his eyes fall upon them, he finds only the porcelain curve of the salt and pepper shakers. And when he is certain he is seeing the curl of her hair behind her ear and the tilt of her forehead when her brow is wrinkled with concern, he realizes to his astonishment that it is only Lacey, pressing her hands to her brow and smoothing a lock of curls behind her ear. She rests her elbows on the table and runs her fingers back and forth over her brow.

"Maybe," she says, "when things calm down, you know, when Tasha's better, I might go down there."

Willy is alarmed. He hadn't prepared for an all-out search. "Aww, you don't wanna do that."

"You could go with me, Willy."

"Oh, oh, no. I don't think so. I don't think so, Lacey."

"Well, I can't do it without you." She picks up her bowl and spoon and takes them to the sink. "I don't want to do it alone. So I guess I'm not going to do it." She turns to him and leans against the sink. "I'm getting way ahead of myself, Willy . . ."

"Damn right, you are."

"I don't really want to find her, Willy," she admits.

"Then you need to explain to me, Lacey, just what the hell you do want."

She shrugs. "I just want her to get out of my head," she says sadly. "And I don't know how to do that." She crosses her arms and looks around the kitchen. "Maybe it's just time to sort this out."

"This don't make no sense. Not now."

"When then, Willy?" and he can see that she is starting to get angry with him. "When would it have made sense? Maybe thirty years ago? Maybe when she first left us."

"Us? She didn't leave us, Lacey. She left me."

"You can't be serious," she says, a look of incredulity on her face. He looks at her and runs his palms down his lap. He works his jaw as if to say something, but nothing comes out. "You're kidding me, right? I mean, you couldn't possibly think this is all about you—do you? You're not that selfish, Willy. You couldn't think this had nothing to do with me. I mean, God, Willy. I was just a little girl. My mother left me!"

"That's not what I meant. What I meant was— Aww, you don't understand." He waves his hand at her as if to dismiss her.

"You're damn right I don't—"

"What I'm saying here is that she didn't mean to leave you. She *meant* to leave me. That's all."

"And what was I? Collateral damage?"

He doesn't understand her question. "I don't know," he said. "I just don't know—what she was thinking or—"

"Then maybe it's time to find out." She turns and begins to wipe down the counter and then sticks the soggy carton of ice cream back in the freezer.

"I don't think so," he says to the back of her. "You know, I got no business going after her now. There's Carlotta. What would she think? And it's been a long time, Lacey. I've kind of settled things in my mind, you know?" He rises from the table and can hear his own knees crackle. *Now what would May think of that?* he thinks suddenly. Just what would she think of him now with his creaking knees and his stiff back and the browning spots on the backs of his hands. He looks out the window. And his fallen down barn, and his chicken coop and the fact that he has had his heart swiped by Carlotta. "She's still your momma," he says. "But she ain't my wife."

December 28, 1974

> *eggs*
> *Tang*
> *cheese*
> *brown sugar*
> *nail clippers*

Kotex
Jell-O 1-2-3

It's quieter around here now. The cows are dried off for the next couple of months and Willy has less and less to do. He likes to read stories to Lacey in the evenings. Three days ago he started reading her <u>The Long Winter</u> by Laura Ingalls Wilder, who writes all kind of books about a family living on the prairie a long time ago and Lacey has been waiting for snow ever since. Willy says it's coming. He can smell it. We will just have to see.

December 29, 1974

Snow, snow, snow. I never felt such quiet in my life. And I never knew quiet could be so heavy on your ears.

December 30, 1974

Willy is plowing out the drive so we can get back and forth from here. I have never seen so much snow in my life. We never had snow like this on the island. The phone lines are down, too, so I can't call Aunt Virgie and check on her. Lacey went out to play in it but could get no farther than the clearing Willy made between here and the barn. She was chilled to the bone in no time. Willy says as soon as the phone lines are up again he will phone over to the Owens' place as they have seven children from nine years of age on up and are sure to have spare boots and mittens and things for Lacey.

She has outgrown what she has from last year and I didn't think of these things for her afore this cold weather set in. I never expected so much snow.

December 31, 1974

If I ever get to town again I will need these things:

eggs
Tang
cheese, Swiss and American
brown sugar
nail clippers
Kotex
Jell-O 1-2-3
peanut butter
Ovaltine
iodine
Q-tips
tapioca
canned tomatoes
sturdy thread for smocking (white and blue)

Latch hook for the bathroom door—Willy says he never had no need of a lock, but he never had a five-year-old round, neither. When he needs his privacy he has taken to shoving the small chest of drawers that's in there right up against the door. Lacey hears that thing squeaking against the floor and suddenly she is right on the other side of the door telling him she needs to come in and what is taking so long. He is surely a patient man.

January 1, 1975
   The moon is full and the stars are hanging like crystals in the sky and sparkling down to the pond. I been looking through my window and I never seen anything like it. There is a stillness all round us. Back home there was never a quiet like this. There was always the ocean. The heartbeat under everything. And there was always a sway and a swish in the scrubby trees and the reeds along the shore. But here there is a quiet that falls down over everything. It is like when a ringing you didn't know you were hearing stops ringing in your ear and what is left is a quiet that you are newly grateful for. The snow glows almost blue under the moon and where the earth rolls the snow bounces the light back up at the sky.

I opened the window and stuck my head outside and the difference between out there and in here is not the cold at all. It feels like the air outside is bigger and emptier than the empty insides of any one place could ever be.

January 5, 1975

I wrote to Sugar Lee this morning, though I won't be able to post it for a couple days. Her last letter says Daddy disappears for days at a time and no one knows where he is. He takes Little Jim's truck, she says, and Bob Kreen who runs the ferry says he's been running Daddy to Hatteras and sometimes across the sound. Then he don't see him for days afore he'll just show up and want to be ferried back, no money in his pockets to pay, of course. Sugar says she don't know why Little Jim tolerates the taking of his truck like that. I figure Little Jim ain't got much use for it anyway. Not much in the way of paved roads and nowhere to go to anyways. He just bought it to show off. Daddy probably made him feel real bad about beating on me and tells everyone that's why I left. So now Little Jim is feeling beholden.

I would like Sugar Lee to visit me here this summer when she is done with school. Willy said it would be fine with him and so I am looking forward to it. I wish she could come now for she would be amazed to see this snow, as the only snow we have ever known back home is equal parts wet and slush and the flakes of it fairly come dripping from the sky afore they hit the ocean.

I miss my friend something terrible and sometimes there is a longing to speak with someone who knew my mama and remembers a time afore things changed so. I would like to sit with Sugar and picture our mamas talking to each other on the porch, her mama shucking corn and mine repairing the men's fishing nets. I wonder if she still recalls the sound of my mama's laugh when they would get to talking about another damn fool thing the men gone and done. It is nice to be known by someone who can fill in the holes in your remembering.

January 15, 1975

Willy has but one cow to milk, just enough for the three of us here. Calves are knotted up in their bellies, waiting for the end of March when Willy says we'll be having calves all over the place. When the weather is mild some days, he'll put some of them in the paddock and they bay and paw at the frozen ground and shake their heads and the snot flings from their noses and freezes in the air. Willy tends to repairs around the place and looks over papers from the DHIA—that is the Dairy Herd Improvement Association—which offers him information about bulls he is considering breeding with this June. Willy says at one time he and his pa used to put the bull they liked out in the pasture with the cows and by the end of the month they all got bred. That don't seem right to me.

Now Willy says he just looks through the booklet and papers he gets and then he matches up the things he likes about the bulls with the cows, checking butterfat mostly, and then he buys the raw material, which is sperm, and I only know that because I felt real dumb and I asked Aunt Virgie and she told me. He puts it right on in them hisself, which is not a pretty picture to my mind.

I suggested to him that maybe we could purchase a couple of bulls and see who was getting along with who afore we set them out to do their business somewhere. He looked at me like I likely had six heads afore he slapped his knee and cracked hisself up laughing. I was angry at first and I wouldn't look at him, but just stood at the counter peeling the parsnips with my back to him. But then he come up behind me and put his arm around me and says that is what he likes best about me. He likes best about me that I have all kinds of ideas about how everybody can just get along nice.

Don't make me feel stupid, I told him. Just don't do that to me, is what I said. He said I weren't stupid, not by a long shot and he was sorry if he upset me but I was awful damn touchy. Then he kissed the top of my head and said he meant it. I was real smart.

I told him there was a whole lot I didn't know how to do and he said, like what? I thought mostly of things like cooking, which I was learning but none too fast, or driving a car, or how to tend to the marigolds Aunt Virgie had me plant along the stoop, but mostly it was the swimming. I still don't know how to swim, I said to him. I can't do it. It's like something just won't let me be on top of the water. Something pulls me down. He promised to teach me to swim when the pond is warm enough this spring. I made him promise that even if I was hopeless, he had to be real darn sure Lacey learned to swim all by herself. I made him promise.

February 25, 1975

Willy is worried the alfalfa done heaved. The ground has been frozen deep for a long time and Willy says frozen ground is bigger than not frozen ground and so it just bursts open throwing up the seed. I don't like the look of him with lines of worry cutting across his face. The cows are being got ready for calving and Doc Asher was here yesterday. Seems a couple of heifers never settled last June and Willy will probably have to butcher them soon. He said he knew one of them wouldn't take and he should of butchered her for veal last spring. He was talking of Iroquois. She was a freemartin, he told me, twin to a bull, and that usually means she's sterile and can't have no calves. Now she's gone and cost him a whole year's feed and care. I told him don't tell Lacey, but what with his worries and all, he got short with me and said she was gonna have to learn the ways if we was gonna live here as a proper farm family. He was thinking about this from the easy chair in the parlor and when I got up from the sofa to walk past him, he reached up and grabbed my hand. Don't worry none about this, May, he said to me. He said he tended to get a little restless this time of the year.

We put on our coats and went up to the barn to check on things, just to make sure everything was as it should be. The cows were all in their stanchions, munching from the troughs and letting shit go in the gutters. I don't even mind the smell. Willy keeps them all so clean and he hoses down the gutter twice a day. They just chew their cud and clip-clop their feet on the concrete. They turn to watch us with big blinking eyes and steamy puffs of their breath make clouds around their heads. Iroquois is smaller than them other yearlings, and her udder is small, too, and odd shaped, with short teats poking out from it and to the sides. She was rolling her head side to side and the shank jingles. Then she took to tossing her head up in the air, snapping at the shank and looking with her big warm eyes at me. I believe she knows she is locked into dying.

March 28, 1975

Willy put a big old bolt on the bathroom door and he put it too high for Lacey to reach. Somehow or other she managed to get it locked when she was in there, but she couldn't manage to stay up on her toes long enough get it unlocked. She was in there howling and fussing so that I couldn't talk her calm enough to unlock it proper. Then she starts to pull out the drawers of that little dresser in there so she can stand on them and work the bolt. I could just see that whole bureau toppling over on top of her—and me stuck on the other side of the door. I just screamed at her to move on back and I put my shoulder into that door so hard the whole thing bust wide open. Now we not only got no lock, but we don't got much of a door, neither.

March 29, 1975

Willy weren't too mad about the door. He seemed mostly worried about us being okay. He says he can fix the door but the three of us need to have a little talk about privacy. Lacey piped in that she would like to have that talk cause she never gets any privacy. Willy says she is a loony bird.

March 31, 1975

Calving time. The barn smells like baked blood and dirt and sweet with fresh straw, but it's a warm smell. Calving pens are separated from the stanchions where they stand and eat and get milked most of their lives. So even though the birthing must be truly terrible, I'm sure they feel like they have deluxe accommodations right now in them big wide stalls. I wonder if they know they won't have long with their new babies? Course, some of them have been through all this before. Maybe they learn after the first time not to get too attached—or maybe they learn to give all the loving they have right fast because time is too short.

I would like another baby, but it just ain't happened yet. I would like to know what it feels like loving it growing inside of me though I surely can't think how I could love another child the way I do Lacey.

CHAPTER 24

The Date

The next morning Lacey finds herself rising later than usual, the last hour of sleep having been a collage of odd dreams breaking apart and fusing together again as she tossed from sleep to foggy waking and back into sleep again, picking up the last threads of a dream and then weaving it into something else altogether. She dreamed of her mother, young and fairylike, talking to her with the simplest of words that Lacey, try as she might, could not decipher but knew to be endearing. May, wrapping the two of them in the folds of her skirt. Lacey batting the skirt from her own face, pulling at the folds to free herself and reveal her mother's face that she has been longing to remember, but then she finds that she is in reality dragging the bedsheets from her own face and she is alone with the only sound that of the predawn waking and chirping of the birds outside her window. She freed her arms and rolled to her side and felt her mother's hand in her own, warm and tight, walking her into the pond, the muddy bottom oozing between her small toes, the pull of her mother's hand, the water rising around her, oddly warm and thick, the air cool above her knees and then as she wades deeper, the warmth of the water rising to her waist and then her chest, and she is anxious to sink down into it, roll to her back and float. She thinks she could even breathe beneath it, such a notion being the thing of dreams. Her mother is beside her, holding tight to her hand, the water only at May's own mid-thigh, and one hand holds the hem of her paisley skirt in a balloon of fabric to her side. May stops abruptly, as if she has come up against something beneath the surface of the pond that blocks her way and she uses the hand locked in Lacey's to direct Lacey forward, beyond where May now stands, toward the center of the pond—sending her on into the deeper water. Lacey doesn't want to let go of her hand, but her mother twists her own hand free of Lacey's and tells her to *go, go*. She can *do this*. She doesn't want to make her mother angry, make her sad. Lacey turns to face May, though still, she cannot see her face as a bright sun orbs precisely above May's head and the brightness is too much to open her eyes to, and so she leans back to float, her eyes closed. The water is so deliciously warm. When she opens them again a breeze has caught the fabric of May's gathered skirt and May is rising with it, out of the pond, her toes dripping pearls to the surface of the water. *Don't be silly,* her mother is saying, *of course you can breathe underwater.* May is rising toward the horizon and calls back to Lacey. *If you can't swim, you can surely walk across the bottom to the other side. You can.* With that, gravity pulls Lacey to the murky bottom and though she struggles at first, she finds it is true, she can breathe underwater. She knows it is a gift from her mother, this magic, and that the saying of it was the giving of it. *You can be anything you want to be, Lacey.* But the mud is thick and hard to pull her small feet from and she knows her mother is going away, floating like a hot air balloon across a blue sky. Lacey is not sure she herself will make it to the other side, the mud is so greedy, and the water is too thick to rise up through.

She wakes sloppily, relieved, to a room filling with light—but not her mother. She burrows back to the pillow, hoping to find her, and hears the sound of cabinets opening and closing, Willy chuckling, footsteps in the kitchen. There is the smell of coffee. She is dreaming again, surely, and May is in the kitchen, making Willy's breakfast and he is talking to her in that hushed conspiratorial way of her childhood where she can hear the low soft rumble of his voice though not the words. But then she hears a bold laugh, melodious, not at all like May's, and realizes it is Carlotta.

It is late morning now and she has so much to do on this one day she is free from the hospital. There is laundry, and she planned to return the assortment of casserole dishes, Tupperware containers, and cake pans to various neighbors who have been dropping off more food than they can possibly consume and so have overstuffed the freezer so that it sometimes requires a great deal of rearranging to shut the door. And damn, it is too late to reach Cade and wish him good luck before his noon game, as they are already at the stadium warming up and she wouldn't think of calling him while he is working with his team. Lastly, she wanted just a little time to get on her computer, maybe write a letter to Sugar Lane, maybe not. She considered calling her but ruled that out as well. What she wanted, she thinks now, pulling on her bathrobe and knotting her hair on top of her head with a wide clip comb, was just to *think* about it, about what she will do, if she will do anything at all.

"Morning, doll," says Carlotta when Lacey comes into the kitchen. "How'd you sleep? I hope we didn't wake you up?"

"Gosh, no," says Lacey, "I meant to be up two hours ago."

The phone rings and Willy goes to answer it, patting Carlotta's shoulder as he moves past her and smiling in Lacey's direction.

"Well that's great news," he is saying, giving a thumbs-up to both Lacey and Carlotta and mouthing *Mac* to Lacey. "Lacey's right here if you want to talk to her." He sets his mug down on the counter and raises his brows to Lacey, asking if she wants to take over the call, pointing to the phone at his chin. "Sure, sure, I'll tell her. See you in time for lunch. Good news. Thanks for calling."

Lacey sips at her coffee and waits. Willy tells them both that Tasha is being released from the hospital. Dr. Oren believes she is better off recovering at home now that her counts have risen again. Lacey is relieved, not just for Tasha, but privately she is relieved to not have to head back to the hospital herself. Her mood lifts as she sips her coffee and thanks Carlotta profusely for the new coffee maker.

"That's great news, hon," says Carlotta to Willy, and Lacey is charmed by her endearments, but further surprised by the quick kiss she plants on his cheek and the way he can't help but smile and pat her back as she moves past him to stow the milk in the refrigerator. She has a Post-it note pack on the counter and she goes back to writing on slips and attaching them to the casserole dishes and a small box stuffed with plastic containers. "I've got everything labeled for you, Lacey," she says. "You got the nephews, the Owens, the Ashers, the Braggarts, your friend Franny." She points to each piece as she rattles off the names. "I always like to return a gift of food with a little something," she says with a sigh, "but I just haven't had a moment to make anything."

"Now, Carlotta," says Willy. "That's just ridiculous. Tell her, Lacey."

Lacey looks at them both, not sure what they're talking about, and shrugs to let him know she has no idea what this is about.

"She seems to think you gotta return a gift with a gift," he explains, pointing at Carlotta. "She says you can't just say thank you for your kindness and return the dish without giving them something in return."

"It's just something I've always done," says Carlotta matter-of-factly.

Willy looks to Lacey and rolls his eyes.

"Well," says Lacey, "it does seem a little redundant."

"Oooh, I just feel so bad about it," says Carlotta. "It's not the way I like to do things."

"A gift is a gift. Shouldn't come with no strings attached."

"It will just make people feel guilty, anyway," Lacey offers.

"Doesn't seem right," says Carlotta.

Lacey shakes her head and smiles. "I need to get dressed and get going," she says. "You two can debate this yourselves. I'm not weighing in any more. What are you two doing today?"

"Willy has chores today so I'm going to head back home. Get my morning housekeeping done."

"She likes my coffee better than hers," he teases.

Lacey waves them both off and heads upstairs to dress. The day is looking better. Until she gets to the bathroom and finds it occupied. She had completely forgotten about Kat. She starts to knock, raises her hand to the door, thinks better of it, and goes to her room to wait her out. First come, first served in a one-bathroom house. She used to shout just that from the bathroom when Willy would stew on the other side waiting for her. Still, fifteen long minutes later she can't imagine what the hell Kat is doing in there. And Willy used to wonder the same thing, she remembers now. *For crying out loud, Lacey, how long does it take to pee and brush your teeth?* She makes a mental note to herself to have two bathrooms before Tasha is a teenager, which would, of course, require a move—something she has never seriously entertained, but the idea of it, of gathering up her shallow roots from her rental cottage and settling deeply into fresh soil, is appealing in a surprising way. It is as if in the last few days some (some, not all) of her armor has been stubbornly peeled from her and the tenderness it has revealed, the rawness, is not so awful. It is like the Mercurochrome her mother used to put on her skinned knees, stinging at first, but meant to start the healing.

When the door to the bathroom finally swings open, Lacey rises from her bed and meets Kat in the narrow hallway where they are forced to sidestep one another. Kat emerges wearing only a long T-shirt that falls to mid-thigh. Her hair feathers to her chin, which is tucked, eyes averted as she swings her own shoulder to the side to let Lacey pass. Lacey's mind is still nestled in the future she has imagined for herself and Tasha, a future where she and a teenage Tasha reside in a two-bathroom household. Kat, for the mere flash of a moment, as the sunlight streams behind her, looks to Lacey so much like an elongated version of Tasha that Lacey audibly gasps and takes in the scent of minty toothpaste and soap. The scent is delicate, reminding her of babies damp from a bath and wrapped in a freshly laundered towel. Reflexively, there is an immediate bittersweet swell in Lacey's chest, as if something tender has been ripped from her arms.

"Kat . . ."

Kat startles and blinks, lifts her eyes to Lacey and looks away. There is just the barest pursing of her lips and the hint of a scowl forming on her pale face, but it never fully forms. She clutches a large ziplock baggie to her chest that is filled with jumbled toiletries, the neck of a shampoo bottle poking out from it and a bar of soap slimed in the bottom corner.

Lacey doesn't know what it is she wants to say, has no idea why she has said anything at all. "Am I rushing you out?" She hopes she sounds kind, considerate, but she can't be sure.

Kat shakes her head, no. She's finished. The bathroom is free. She's sorry she took so long.

Lacey looks at the way her hair falls over her eyes, the blue blush of a vein at her temple, the blinking of her blond lashes as she looks down to her toiletries and then at her feet, the toes long and pale, bearing the last chips of black polish. Kat rocks back on her heels, stretching her toes upward in a way that makes the tendons in her feet rise in taut bands. She has her father's long torso and boney knees. Tasha once had the same stick-straight blond hair.

Stepdaughter, Lacey thinks now. The word implies that so much more should lie between the two of them. But Lacey doesn't know her, knows nothing, really, of this girl's life. She only knows something of how it fits into Tasha's life. They are all, she and Mac and Tasha and Kat, the linked sets of a Venn diagram. She remembers now the language of statistics, a course she nearly failed in undergrad—*universal set, complement, disjoint sets, proper subset, unions, and intersections*—all of which suddenly resonate with her when she thinks of the four of them, the bumping and blending of spheres. She reaches for the bathroom door, releasing them both, and Kat slides into her own bedroom.

Lacey is underdressed, wearing only a short cotton navy wrap skirt that sashes and ties at the side and a simple white T-shirt, and of course, her standard flip-flops. Sure, there are some women in jeans and tank tops, but they are the kind of jeans that fit like a second skin and bear designer labels and their tops are sheer and silky and meant to perfectly drape their breasts. And the shoes—the heels on them—are a symphony of *clicking* and *clacking* when they walk in groups of two or three, leading with their pelvis and sashaying their hips. She looks down at her own feet. She could have at least gotten a pedicure. She's only had maybe three or four in her life, and each time she was disturbed by a total stranger touching her feet, struck by the trust it required to let someone wield sharp implements against her soles. Instead, she had shaved her legs and wrangled her hair into a pile on top of her head and powdered her cheeks with blush, swooped her eyes with mascara, and considered it all an improvement of sorts.

She is waiting for Cade and he is late. She is sitting alone at a bar halfway between the farm and downtown Baltimore, though she was more than willing to drive the distance, but Cade had insisted they meet halfway.

She had canceled their late afternoon date once she learned that Tasha was coming home, and then Cade had offered to come to the farm instead. But she was sure she detected some reluctance in his voice, and it would have been a bit awkward anyway with Mac and Kat there as well. His team had lost its first game, making it their last game, and was knocked out of the semifinals, and he wasn't hiding his disappointment. He didn't want to talk about it, he had said on the phone, but in the same breath he rambled about *fucked up plays*, ground balls that should have been theirs, a lousy call that left him steaming, and an injury that should have resulted in a penalty. It was a shitshow, he said, but he didn't want to talk about it. So she is expecting him to arrive sullen and cranky and it is a side of him she has never seen and so she is not sure how to work with it, how it will make her feel, if she will be expected to work him out of it.

When he does arrive, she spots him first and there is a hangdog look on his face that she doesn't recognize and it makes her feel responsible, almost immediately, for his mood. She swivels on her stool to catch his eye and as he spots her his eyes light up and his steps quicken, weaving between a gaggle of young women without taking his eyes off her.

"You," he says, hugging her and not letting go until he has breathed her in, "are the best part of this day." With that, all her trepidation drips away. He smells of clean soap and water and while she is hungry, hasn't eaten a thing all day and was looking forward to a leisurely dinner on what would be their first real date, she wishes instead that they were curled next to one another in his bed.

"How's Tasha?" he asks, and she tells him that she is tired and cranky, a little sassy. She had been especially angry when she was told she couldn't go near the chicken coop—not until her counts are a bit higher—and no Thumper visits, either. It's hard to see her so cranky but they are all relieved to have her home.

He asks if Lacey is troubled about having left Tasha at home in order to meet with him but she says no, that Tasha has Mac and Willy at the house, Kat as well, and of course Carlotta hovers as if she is her flesh-and-blood grandmother, so Tasha is well taken care of, though she can't really make it a late night and she's sorry about that. He nods, understanding.

By the time they get to a table the bar is swarming with patrons. Everyone is so young and happy and thousand-watt smiles are flashing, eyes are darting over one another, inventory is being taken, sights are being set. It is not a scene she is familiar with, and she is grateful for the intimacy of the two of them.

He is utterly disappointed, he tells her, about the game, but by the time they are seated he is telling her about Marcus's sweet goal off the pipe and the fact that when he had to replace an injured player—goddammit— with a third string middie, it was beautiful. The kid has a lion's heart and he's only a freshman. Didn't know he had it in him and that's something to bank on for next season.

"You know," he says. "We were a long shot." She nods, though she didn't really know. "No one expected us to get this far." He rests his chin in his hand with his elbow on the table. "Would have been sweet to win," he says wistfully. "I really wanted it." She thinks of his pages and pages of diagrams, all those *X*'s and *O*'s, the lines running here and there, a language she doesn't know, and she wonders what will become of those pages. Will he crumple and toss them for having been failures, or will he rethink and fine-tune them? How does all of this work?

She tells him a bit about May, about having found Sugar Lane, but when she tries to stay detached from what she is saying—*not sure if I'll reach out to her or not*—as if it is just a little something that she has stumbled over, she finds she is invested more than she wants to be and is not ready to share the jumbling of half-baked ideas she has had concerning it all. She changes the subject before he has a chance to weigh in and tells him about Carlotta and the silly idea of having to bake something to return the neighbor's dishes. He agrees that it's a strange idea—like writing a thank-you note for a thank-you note. "It's pretty serious between the two of them," she says, smiling, and she leans into him, giggling a bit. "She spends the night!" She knows this because yesterday afternoon when she got home from the hospital she noticed how neatly his bed was made, the corners tucked precisely, and when she went farther into the room to look, she could have sworn she could smell Carlotta, the scent of lavender and honey.

"Think he wants to marry her?"

"Wow," she says. "I hadn't thought about that." Suddenly it occurs to her that he probably *can't* marry her.

"Why not?"

"I think," she says, and there it is again, the strangling hold of the past pulling her back, like going underwater. "I think he's still married to my mother."

CHAPTER 25

Sisters

Tasha had been asleep for an hour or more when it started, having been tucked in by Carlotta before she had left for the evening. Kat was in the sunroom by herself, and Mac, having been anxious and unsettled ever since Lacey left earlier that evening, had wandered into the sunroom, paced to the window, dug in the box of VCR tapes, forcing Kat to lean to her side and around him in order to see the television, and finally settled down on the sofa beside Kat, releasing a long and heavy sigh as he did so. Kat ignored him. Mac stared blankly at the screen. "What are we watching?" he finally asked.

"*Miami Ink*," she mumbled. "It's about a tattoo parlor in Miami."

From where Willy stood in the doorway, he could see the frown start to take shape on Mac's face. Kat leaned forward, her elbow to her knee, resting her chin in her hand, and focused hard on the screen.

Willy watched Mac side-eye her as he leaned back deeply, reaching his arm out to drape the end of the sofa. By the time he had stretched his long legs out in front of him, locked his feet by crossing his ankles, Kat had risen to her feet, turned on her heels, and stormed from the room. Willy had watched it all from the doorway, all the huffing and puffing, as he pretended to be occupied by the frozen pie he was thawing on the kitchen counter. Willy had turned away as Kat brushed past him and stomped up the stairs.

"Do *not* wake her up, Kat!" Mac shouted to her as she banged on each step with purpose.

And with that warning, the door slammed over their heads. The slam was louder than any Willy had heard in years, and he thought he heard plaster falling between the walls. That was all it took for Mac to jump from the sofa, taking the steps two at a time. (The last time Willy had heard a slam like that, he had found a freshly laundered marijuana pipe in the clothes dryer and had taken off after Lacey in the very same way.) "What did I tell you?" Mac was shouting and Willy followed on gravelly knees, certain that if the slam hadn't woken Tasha, which was unlikely, whatever was about to ensue was sure to do it.

Willy figured the fact that Lacey was out on a date with her new fella might be what had been twisting Mac up into a knot all evening. Even though it had been at Mac's urging that she had agreed to meet Cade for dinner. At first she had said no, she was just going to cancel altogether as they had planned to meet close to the hospital before Lacey was to come in and relieve Mac for the night, but Tasha's coming back to the farm had changed everything and she was saying she was just going to catch up with him another time. Mac had insisted. *Go have a good time. You deserve a break*, he had said, but Willy had seen a flash of something close to sorrowful on his face at the mention of Cade. He wondered how much Lacey had told Mac about him—how much there was to tell.

"Leave me alone!" Kat shouted from the other side of the door. But Mac threw open the door to the room Kat and Tasha shared. Willy was just glad they had no locks on the doors as there was no doubt Mac would have put his shoulder to it.

Mac flicked on the overhead light and a frightened Tasha sat bolt upright in bed, pale and startled, her eyes like wet saucers, the tears a result of both confusion and—Willy couldn't blame her—genuine fear.

Seeing her that way wrangled something in Willy, and he pushed past Mac who stood, his chest rising, working the muscles of his jaw. Willy swooped down onto Tasha's bed, putting his arms around her and not knowing what to say to her but finding it in him to mumble, "Everything's fine, sugar, just fine." And then turning to Mac, who loomed at the doorway, he said, "You ain't yourself, son. Settle this in the morning."

Kat, for all her bravado, was scrambling to the other side of her room, crawling across her own bed and backing against the wall and the whole time screaming at Mac to get out, *Get out, I hate you!*

Mac looked from Tasha to Kat and back to Tasha, gathering himself, and his eyes finally landing on where Willy sat, arms around Tasha, but shaking his head firmly, staring hard at Mac—a warning, *Do not carry this no further.*

"Go on. I'll settle this down," said Willy, and it was not a request. To Willy's surprise, Mac let out a pained growl of a sound and turned on his heels, headed down the stairs.

When Willy came down minutes later, Mac was sitting at the kitchen table with his head in his hands. He didn't lift his head when Willy walked in, just mumbled an apology into his own hands. "Jesus, I'm sorry. I'm sorry about that."

"I ain't the one to apologize to, but I'd appreciate you not pulling some damn fool stunt like that again." He slid the chocolate cream pie from the counter and put it on the table between the two of them, took two plates and forks and a serrated knife from the drawer, and set down across from him.

Now, jabbing at it with the knife, trying to find a less frozen place to start carving out a piece, Mac confesses to him that Kat has been suspended from school for a week and that is why he had to bring her to Baltimore.

"Diane is at her wit's end with her," he says to Willy. "She has to work, and she can't watch her every minute." Willy slides a piece of pie to him. "I shouldn't have brought her here. It's not good for Tasha."

"Nope, you're wrong there. She's your family."

"Diane blames me, you know. She says it's because of the divorce she acts like this." He looks up from the pie to read Willy's face.

"Well, she's probably partly right there."

"What? I don't see how she can blame everything on the divorce. Lots of kids have divorced parents." He shoves his fork hard into the pie so that it clinks against the plate. "They don't turn into juvenile delinquents."

"No," Willy says, considering for a moment, "but the way they behave probably has everything to do with how their family's put together."

"You don't really think that, do you?"

"Sure. Good or bad, growing up is just a reaction to the world around you. Don't mean bad parents make for bad kids. That's not what I'm saying.

Just means that if you weren't divorced from her mother, she would probably behave in a different way, maybe not any better, just different."

Mac slides his plate away from himself. "She graffitied the entrance to the school, of all the damn things."

"That right?"

"Destruction of property. Lucky they're not pressing charges. And then . . ." he says, pushing back from the table. "And then she went and tagged it."

Willy has no idea what he is talking about.

"She tagged it," he says again. "It's like a signature—not her name— but a signature, sort of, so the kids all knew who did it, and of course, she got caught. I just don't get it. You would think she wanted to get caught, destroying property and then signing it."

"Don't be stupid, boy. Course she wanted to get caught."

"Huh?" Mac is looking at him in disbelief.

"It's like you said, she *tagged* it, like she wanted to get caught, so it follows—she wanted to get caught."

"Why?"

"How the heck should I know? You're her father," he said, pointing his fork at him. "Figure it out. I've done most of the thinking for you already." He shrugs his shoulders and goes back to eating his pie.

They are quiet for a moment, Mac watching Willy and Willy pretending not to notice, not looking at him, still angry about the outburst.

"You know, she was a really happy little kid, Willy. Just like Tasha. But she is one miserable teenager."

"Lacey was miserable as a teenager, too."

"You telling me it's a 'girl thing' and Tasha will be miserable, too?"

"Lacey near drove me crazy. I was forever trying to figure out what I done wrong to make her act so damn feral."

"What'd you figure out?"

"Nothing. Just stopped blaming myself is all. About the time she went off to college she started coming 'round again."

Mac gets up from the table and takes his plate with him. With his back to Willy, he rinses his plate at the sink. "Hey, Willy, just between the two of us, did she talk about me much? I mean before you met me, before Tasha and all. Did she tell you about me?"

"Nope."

"I was just wondering."

"Not a word." Willy finishes off his pie without looking up. "Never said a word." It wouldn't have been like her, Willy knows. Dating, boyfriends. There'd been a brief boyfriend in college, and Willy only learned of him when Lacey called to say he was driving her home for winter break and *please, Willy, don't make a big deal out of it.* The boy stayed over one night before heading home to Nashville. Willy can't even recall his name. He was never mentioned again.

"Well," says Mac, turning from the sink. "I'm gonna turn in." He stands, expecting something, but Willy doesn't say a thing. "Night, Willy," says Mac, but then he only stands still at the sink, leaning against it, as if he has something to say and it is twisting around in his gut. "I'm sorry about tonight."

"Yeah, well."

But still he stands there, just casting about with his eyes. "Willy, there's something I have to tell you about me and Lacey." He runs his hand down his chin and looks into the corner of the room. "I mean, I feel like you deserve to know, that maybe I owe you an explanation of sorts."

Willy sits stock-still, blinking at him. He isn't keen on confessions. He doesn't fancy being put in a position where he is expected to absolve someone.

"I loved Lacey, Willy. I really did. I wanted to marry her, but she didn't really want it, you know? She's so—so damn—she's so stubborn, and independent, and . . ." He stammers, and Willy senses he would like to have his sentence finished for him.

Lacey is all those things, but Willy has always known that about her, and it has always made him all the more certain that he'd need to be there for her if ever she was to stumble over herself and not know how to ask for a hand back up. So now he can only sit there and watch the boy nearly hang himself over his own words. He doesn't know how to help him or even what is expected of him.

Mac suddenly looks deflated. He heaves a sigh. "But it was my fault. I bailed on her. She just didn't seem to need me—or want me, for that matter.

Don't you think it's sometimes better to slip out quietly when you're not wanted around, rather than hang around and make a bigger mess of it?"

"I don't know, son. I wouldn't know about that." But he did, and he had the feeling that, while he and Mac had walked similar paths, he wasn't anxious to get back on the trail right now. "She has her ways, you know?"

Mac nods. "Just the fact that she never even mentioned me to you. That says something about her, or us, I think."

"Lacey never did talk much about anyone, even her girlfriends. She was kind of private that way," he offers.

He gets up from the table with his plate and walks it over to the sink, patting Mac on the shoulder as he walks past him. "Night, son."

The next morning, Willy comes around the corner of the coop to find Kat sitting on her heels against the outside of it, her back curled into a C, her arms resting on her knees, and a cigarette to her lips. He watches her pull it from her mouth dramatically, narrow her eyes to the sky, and blow a long, thin banner of smoke. It is early, much earlier than he would have expected to find Kat up and about.

She quickly snuffs out the cigarette in the dirt and stands, grinding her heel to it.

"Pick that up," says Willy. "Chickens is worse than goats. They eat that and you owe me some chickens." He thinks for a second she will deny it, and maybe she is thinking of it, but then she looks down, digs in the dirt with the toe of her sandals, looks back up to Willy, and stoops to pick the butt up, finally sticking it in the front pocket of her denim shorts. "You're up early," he says.

She doesn't answer him, barely makes eye contact, but she doesn't walk away either, so he hands her one of the two baskets lined in rags for gathering the eggs and waves her ahead of him toward the door of the coop. As soon as the door opens the clucking begins, softly at first and then building as it always does.

"It smells like shit in here," she says.

"That would be about right." He nudges a small red banty off her roost to get at her single egg. They aren't big layers, his chickens, but the eggs are of a good grade with thick plump yolks that have a rich orange color and sit high in their whites.

"What do you do with all these?" she asks, as her basket begins to fill.

"Eat 'em and sell 'em."

"Who comes all the way out here for eggs?"

"I deliver," he says. "Mostly to Carroll's."

Between the two of them, they have just slightly less than five dozen eggs.

Back in the kitchen he pulls cardboard egg cartons from the pantry. After wiping the eggs down to a dull polish with a damp cloth, he sets them in the cartons, creating an even four dozen, and stows the rest in the icebox. He hands the cartons to Kat and tells her she is welcome to come with him to Carroll's to drop them off.

When they pull up in front of the market, Kat offers to take the eggs into the store for him. Willy suspects she wants to buy cigarettes. He takes her up on her offer only because he knows Carroll's doesn't sell cigarettes anymore—ever since Franny's father died of emphysema. In the year it took for the last of his lungs to disintegrate like rotted lace, Franny had managed to alienate the tobacco sales rep so badly that he wouldn't have sold them to her again even if she begged him.

Kat comes out of the store five minutes later looking disappointed and hands him his bills through the window before going around to her side.

"Pretty lucrative business you're in, huh?"

He doesn't say anything, just pulls the shift down on the steering column and clunks into gear.

"I mean, I guess three dollars a dozen is a lot for eggs. My mom never pays that much. It's like, a dollar or something at the Piggly Wiggly back home. But, still, you can't live off of that, can you? How do you live off of chickens?"

"First of all," he says, pulling out into the traffic, "I don't live off of it. I'm a—I had a dairy farm. My herd had to be destroyed—TB. Happens sometimes."

"Cows get TB, like you mean tuberculosis?"

"Uh-huh."

"What do you do when they get sick like that?"

"You sit back and watch the government load 'em all up, every last one of 'em, even the calves born the night before, and then they take 'em off and butcher 'em, cut 'em up, and try and figure out how it happened in the first place."

"They can do that? Do they pay you for them or anything?"

"Pennies on the head."

"Oh." She is quiet for a spell. "Then what, you take up chicken farming?"

"Something like that," he says.

They are going over a small bridge now that stretches over a trickling finger of the reservoir and he watches her strain her neck to peer down over the sides. The water is calm and slick with no breeze to speak of.

"We used to live on the water," she says. "When I was little. We lived on the St. Mary's River. When my parents split up, I moved to Virginia with my mom." She is fidgeting with the rubber seal around the window and it flakes with age, crumbling under the picking of her nails. "He came back after a while." She looks over at Willy and he feels her looking at him, though he doesn't look back. "Did you know that? That my dad came back to live with us?" She says it as if she already knows full well that he had no idea. He has no idea about anything that has to do with Mac and Lacey.

He doesn't answer.

"Well, he did. After Tasha was born. But then he left again. He's a jerk."

She picks again at the window. Her nails are short and ragged, the cuticles paint-stained black. "I think he has commitment issues," she says. That seems to satisfy her for the moment and she changes the subject. "But seriously, is everyone around here stupid? Why would they pay you more than three dollars a dozen for eggs when you can buy eggs for eighty-nine cents?"

"My eggs are better," he says. "Good cooks like my eggs and they pay more for them. Carroll's sells them for four, maybe five dollars a dozen."

"Cripes, that's a lot for eggs."

He has to agree, but he knows the eggs are in demand. There are three different caterers in the area that will only cook with Willy's eggs, and there is an omelet chef at the Classic Catering Team who insists on them for his private events.

"Can you, like, taste the difference or something?"

"You can taste the difference, a little bit. But it's more a matter of chemistry. My eggs are better to cook with. They have more protein and they make baked goods rise better."

"Oh," she says. "Cool."

"Yeah," he says. "Cool." He can't help smiling to himself at that. "Plans for today?"

"Yeah, right. Like what is there to do around here?"

"I got a chicken coop to whitewash."

"I'm in."

April 2, 1975

Daddy phoned the house here today. It's funny because my heart sank into my bowels when I heard his voice, but at the same time I felt a need to know how he was doing. That's just what I don't understand—how it is I keep caring, wanting him to settle down and find some piece of contentment that don't have nothing to do with me—but at the same time I don't never want to see him again. I asked him was he eating good and did he have work lately. He goes to Sunday supper at Miss LaBleu's place sometimes, and of course there ain't much work but the mullet been running some.

I think he was sober. He didn't start crying and he didn't tell me to come home. He said he wanted to see the baby, though. That's when the real sick feeling come down my throat, dripping like something bitter, and I told him I had to go. I had chores to do. He said maybe he would come on up and visit sometime, but there was a whining in my ears and I didn't hear anything else if he said it. I just real gentle put the phone back in the cradle as if it never rung in the first place.

April 15, 1975

The weather is funny around here. Cold and wet one day and warm enough for just a sweater the next. I never can tell if Lacey is dressed right. Keeping a jacket on her is darn near impossible. She gets herself all heated up and just wiggles herself right out of it wherever she happens to be. Willy is forever bringing her jacket down from the barn. She can't stay away from them calves.

I think Willy's naming plan is out the window this year. Lacey has taken to christening them all herself and the names are catching on in a way that makes Willy shrug his shoulders and join in. Some of them she gives simple names, like Midnight for the one born at midnight, and Bonnie named after her favorite baby doll. But one of them, a little guy who nurses at the teat like a sloppy little monster and gets milk to spraying all over his muzzle, is named Cap'n Crunch cause he's <u>so sweet and stays crunchy even in milk</u>. And one is Weebles because she wobbled all over the place the first time she stood up and <u>Weebles wobble but they don't fall down.</u>

Willy has a rule about naming the calves that they don't get named until they're taken from the cows and a decision is made as to which ones the farm is keeping, but Lacey changes a lot of the rules.

April 17, 1975

I sure do miss some spring things round here. Yesterday I got up thinking I would go in search of some poke. I had a great and terrible urge to have some of them tender young shoots on buttered toast with a sprinkling of salt and pepper and a glob of sweet butter melting on top. I looked in all the places I would expect to find the rosy-green shoots coming up—under the trees by the edge of the pond, at the edges of the fields where they slope toward the woods, even along the shady parts of the roadside. There was none to be found and so I asked Willy, does it grow round here? When I explained it to him he said he thinks I'm talking about inkberry or pigeon berry and while he's seen it some he says there ain't much of it until the weather warms a bit more and there ain't no need to go scavenging for supper like a bunch of buzzards.

It hurt my feelings some to have him say that. I never thought of it as scavenging. Though I suppose I been eating that way all my life. I been eating what's taken from the sea, and I been eating what's left behind. Example is, most winters there'd be at least one good run of scallops. I remember one time down at

Green Island it looked like thirty truckloads had been dumped on the beach and all Ocracoke was down there skimming out the fattest ones. For the next week we ate supper knowing just what everyone else on the island was having, too.

Come to think of it, the biggest difference between me and Willy might just be the fishing and the farming. I spent all my life waiting to take what the earth give up, and he spent all his life putting into the earth what he wants to get back.

April 18, 1975

I saw a snapping turtle in the pond today. They ain't pretty like a sea turtle. They're all rough edges and thorny looking with a sharp little beak of a nose and beady little eyes that got no color to speak of in them. I told Willy about it, cause I know they're mean and could bite clean through a toe, specially little ones like Lacey's. He says keep Lacey away from the pond till we can catch him.

Course, I tell Lacey to stay away from the pond and what does she do? She marches her little fanny right down to the edge of the pond, puts her little hands on her hips, and starts scouting the muddy edges for the snapping turtle. Lord, I wonder if all children do the exact opposite of what you tell them to do.

April 20, 1975

I cannot write today's happenings because it makes my body jump and my fingers shake so the pen gets to bumping round on paper.

I have been running after my own happiness ever since I first come up to Maryland, and it done always outrun me. Sometime I get close enough to wrap my fingers round it, and I feel like I surely will not let it slip away. Then—maybe I squeeze too hard—but it goes right through my fingers like sand, and I got nothing left but grit-covered hands and an urge to step into deep water. There is a damp kind of darkness coming over me of late. I know there is no getting out from under it.

April 21, 1975

Daddy was here yesterday, in my kitchen. He set hisself in my pretty chairs and he drank from Willy's mug. He traipsed round my kitchen with his muddy boots and, worst of all, he run his hands down my daughter's arm and poked her belly with his fat dirty finger and made her cry.

Willy left for Harrisburg early yesterday morning to look at some equipment. I don't think to worry about being here without him as the hired men are here much of the time. It was early, about seven this morning when I heard the truck in the drive, but I was busy in the kitchen running string around a slab of pot roast for our supper and I thought surely it was one of the men. Next thing I know, my kitchen door is opening and Daddy is letting hisself into my house. Hello, May, he says, like I should be happy to see him.

He helps hisself to the coffee, which has been perking since five and likely tastes like dirt, pouring it into Willy's favorite coffee mug that was sitting on the counter and which is not yet washed, and drops his back end into one of my chairs that has the new quilted seat covers I made.

He wanted to know where the baby was, but I couldn't answer him even if I wanted to as my tongue felt like glue in my mouth. Lacey was still in bed and I crossed my fingers and prayed that she'd stay there. I no sooner work that prayer through my heart and mind than I hear the toilet flush. Next she starts bumping her bottom down the steps the way she does, sitting down and sliding with a thump to the next step till her feet reach the last step and she stands and leaps to the floor with her arms in the air.

She sees him right off when she comes in the kitchen, and so she comes right on over to me and wraps herself round my leg, twirls up in my skirt, and slides a thumb in her mouth.

Daddy starts jabbering away at her about how she don't remember him and his feelings is hurt and ain't she pretty and all—looks just like her grandmother, God rest her soul. Even though she don't, not at all. His voice is a painful thing in my ear that has settled in the corners of my mind like broke glass. I cannot bear the feel of his words. I cannot even imagine what this sight would do to my mother and for the first time ever I am grateful for her passing on.

I used to think none of this would have happened if she was still living. But I'm grown up now and I know that what is in him has nothing to do with Mama being gone. Oh, maybe some things would of been different. Maybe she would of protected me a little longer. And I want to believe she would of taken me away, but it likely still would of happened. It's his nature. Nature does as it pleases.

I told him, Daddy, go home. Then Lacey whispers, is he my daddy? Daddy wants to know where my husband is and I don't answer him. He says he come to take me and the baby home. That's when my knees start to buckle and I had to push Lacey hard against my thigh with one hand and hold the counter with the other. The baby needs a real daddy, he says, nodding his head to Lacey.

I told him to go. <u>Go now</u>. But when he got up out of the chair and come across the kitchen at me, the crying come upon me and I could not read his face for the blurriness of my tears. I scooped Lacey up and held her tight in my arms and she wrapped her legs around my waist and dug her face under my hair.

I whispered, <u>please, please, please</u>, and he kept coming at us so close that I could smell the goaty smell of him mixed up with the coffee he just drunk. He tells me I gotta come home cause of what a awful shame I brung him. He says people been talking trash about him and me, and the baby can show them all how everything turned out just fine. Then he reached his hand out and dragged it down Lacey's arm.

That's when I stomped my foot real hard, so hard I felt the floor travel up the bone of my leg and I could feel my hip tremble from it. NO! I shouted at him. And to my surprise he stepped back from me, right away starting to put that look of hurt feelings on his face. Lacey got to whimpering under my hair and I held her tighter and tried to shush her.

He told me I gone and upset the baby and what was I thinking. He steps toward us again, like he will try all this again, and pokes a finger at Lacey's belly. He tells her there ain't nothing to cry about. Lacey presses her whole self harder against me.

Leave her alone, I tell him, and right then I'm thinking I'm going to have to kill my own daddy. I don't see no way round it and I'm thinking on how I can grab the kitchen shears that I know are right behind me on the counter from where I was cutting the string for the roast.

He looks at me with that sorry-sad face of his. He tells me again I brung shame to him and I owe it to him for to come on home with the baby.

I hear trucks coming up the driveway now. More than one—maybe three or four of them. And Lacey whispers that loud kind of whisper that children got, Toby and Sam are here, Momma. Toby and Sam are Lacey's favorite farmhands. Right away Daddy starts to look a little nervous, backing up and saying he didn't come to hurt nobody, just wanted to visit with his grandbaby some. And when am I coming to visit. Be sure to bring the baby.

When he left, I locked the door, and for the rest of the day I made Lacey move from room to room with me as I tended to chores. I also slipped the kitchen shears in my apron.

April 22, 1975

I can't breathe so good today. I feel like the air is made of dirty water and I am drowning in my own breath. When I changed the sheets this morning, there was a stain from the loving we had a few nights back. I run my hand over it and felt the sheets go crisp in the place under my fingers and my tears just got to falling like rain. I don't hardly know why.

Lacey followed me around all day and when I said maybe she should go on up to the barn and visit with Willy and Toby and Sam, she says she's just going to stay with me today and be my sunshine, like in the song I sing to her, "You Are My Sunshine." I told her I sure could use a little sunshine today. She just smiled and put her hand in mine. It felt warm, but fragile as a baby bird and all I could think was how was I going to keep her safe.

April 23, 1975

Ivory soap
sugar
molasses
bleach
cornflakes

Quick Oats
lard
cotton balls
Jell-O 1-2-3
coffee
kidney beans
rice
condensed milk

Seems I'm darn near out of everything. Willy was none too happy this morning with no coffee to start his morning off. He says he will carry me to town later today to get the things we need, but I don't think I can go and I told him so. He asked me why and all I could say was I'm feeling quamished. I got no way to make him understand what I'm feeling—the blackness of it, the way it come into my lungs and feels like one long sooty breath I can only wash out by breathing underwater. Now just how do I explain that to him?

I saw the snapping turtle again this morning. It come up out of the water, beaky little nose first, and hauled itself up on the mud. He looks to be a million years old and I would bet he's always been living in the pond right here, under our very noses, but nobody thought to look for him. I think maybe he has always been waiting here, mean and nasty as he is, for someone to start looking for him—someone who knew he done had to be down there somewhere. Now he hauls hisself up here and by way of introduction he drops his sharp little jaw and shows me a wormy tongue and his pale pink insides.

What I cannot believe is the difference between him and the sea turtles back home. He is sharp, chiseled like a rock, and colored like mud and clay. A sea turtle is green and gold and smooth, almost looking like velvet on the edges. And the eyes have a gleamy look, sad maybe, but wet and huge, like eyes on children. It is hard to understand how the world carries two creatures what can be so much alike and so much different.

April 24, 1975

The sadness what has got a hold on me lately will not ease up. Seems it clings to my very skin and I heave it with me this way and that as I go about business.

April 25, 1975

Lacey come at me today waving a big old fan she made out of newspaper. I asked her what the heck she was doing? She is filled with spit and vinegar today. Then she tells me she's just blowing away my black cloud. She's gonna need a nor'easter for that.

April 26, 1975

Willy is getting frustrated with me. Last night I made biscuits and gravy with chipped beef. He left the table hardly saying a word. I asked if maybe he could carry me to the grocer tomorrow, but he knew I was only asking cause it seemed I should go, not cause I had intentions of any kind. My stomach feels poorly.

April 28, 1975

> *milk of magnesia*
> *Ivory soap*
> *sugar*
> *molasses*
> *bleach*
> *cornflakes*
> *Cheerios*
> *eggs*
> *bacon*

Quick Oats
lard
roasting chicken
lemon pepper
condensed milk
margarine
cotton balls
elbow macaroni
rice
kidney beans
Jell-O 1-2-3
cornmeal
Vaseline
ketchup
mayonnaise
peanut butter
Palmolive
bananas
tinned peaches
tomato paste
coffee
wieners
baloney
canned mushrooms
creamed corn
Velveeta
tinfoil
wax paper
Epsom salts
cream of mushroom soup

We hardly got spit left around here to eat. I asked Willy if he could go to town __for__ me, but he said he can only take me in and come back and get me at Virgie's. He says I should understand and not be pouty about it knowing how busy he is with the cows this time of year. I don't see why he can't take an hour, maybe less, to run some errands. Now just what exactly did that man do afore I come along. Surely he got hisself to the grocer? It is darn near all I can do to get out of bed in the morning. I don't see how I can manage a trip into town and a visit with Aunt Virgie—specially with Lacey along. I can hardly put one foot in front of the other.

CHAPTER 26

A Party

This summer that thus far has sat so heavily around all of them is now thick with August heat, the sky itself scalded a bright white. The hydrangeas have parched crisp on the bushes and from the kitchen window Lacey can see that the potted impatiens Carlotta has set along the walk are hanging forlornly, the blooms dropped and smattering the pavement like bright melting candy.

There is talk of a late afternoon storm and the three of them, Lacey, Tasha, and Willy, debate the prediction in light of the barbecue they had planned for the evening.

"We'll just move indoors if we have to," Lacey says. She moves back and forth at the counter, chopping celery and shredding carrots for a pasta salad she will prepare, making neat piles and scooping them in handfuls from the counter to a large bowl she has set out. It is a celebration of sorts, though no one has really said so aloud. Tasha has completed another round of chemo treatments. Her counts are better, hopes are high. Restrictions have been lifted to some degree, and while they must stay close to the hospital, there are no longer the thrice weekly trips to contend with. Lacey wipes strands of hair from her face and takes in a damp breath, exhaling through pursed lips to blow the trails that cling to her forehead.

"Don't put much stock in weather reports," calls Willy. He is speaking to her through the screen door where he is settled with his pipe on the stoop.

"It's happening," says Lacey over her shoulder. "It's just a matter of when and if it's going to ruin our party."

"I like storms," says Tasha, who is stretched out on the kitchen floor on her back, her limbs spread and a cup of yogurt balanced on her chest. She opens her mouth and drips the yogurt into her mouth with a spoon. Lacey turns to watch as the yogurt lands with a plop on Tasha's cheek, missing her mouth altogether. Tasha wipes it to her lips with her finger, giggling. "You're a silly goose," says Lacey. "Wouldn't it be easier to eat that at the table?" But she is just glad to see her eating again and doesn't really care where or how she does it. "Want a carrot?" she says hopefully. But Tasha just shakes her head, no, and continues to drip yogurt.

"Tell me again who will be at our party?" Tasha asks.

Lacey recites the guest list. The nephews, Franny and Duffy, their boys, Carlotta—of course—and Cade.

"Not Daddy and Kat?"

"Nope. Sorry. But they'll be here next weekend."

"How long until our party starts?"

"About one *Bambi* movie and a *Rugrats* show." A spinal tap is the length of a commercial. A visit with Dr. Oren is how long it takes to rewind the *Pollyanna* tape.

Tasha sets the spoon in the near-empty cup on her chest and the weight of it sends it toppling, splattering yogurt to the floor.

"That's why we eat at the table," says Lacey. She hands Tasha a sponge and Tasha rises to a sitting position and wipes the yogurt from the floor beside her, hands the sponge back to her mother, followed by the spoon and yogurt cup. She smiles sheepishly and Lacey notices that perhaps her lashes have begun to come back. She leans down closer to her. Yes, there is the palest feathering of lashes and perhaps even a dusting of eyebrows tracing the crest of her forehead. She puts her hand to Tasha's head and feels the faint tickle of new growth in the palm of her own hand. This, she had noticed days ago. It is the color of toast, not the white blond of before. Some things, Lacey knows now, will never be the same. Things will be different. There will always be a before and an after.

"Don't mind a good storm," Willy says over his shoulder. "Cool things off around here."

Lacey comes to the door and peers through the screen. The air is expectant, waiting for change. "Barbecued chicken, pasta salad, and corn," she recites, "and remind me what Carlotta is bringing?"

"She's doing her baked beans and tomato-something-or-other."

"Perfect." She looks to the whitewashed coop. It is refreshed in a way she didn't know was possible. Framing was added to the plywood door and the door itself had been painted a bright, happy blue at Kat's suggestion. Along the foundation Willy had allowed Kat to paint clusters of red tulips on lime-green foliage that now rise pert and perfect in contrast to everything else that droops from the heat. By the time she and Mac had left that week, Kat was splattered in periwinkle and her mood had shifted in a small but perceptible way that had everyone breathing a little easier around her. The chickens high-step in the yard and along the edges of the fencing, their heads bobbing. Lacey can't help but think they seem happier.

Before Kat and Mac had left the last time, Lacey had gifted Kat with a set of cosmetic bags. She had been picking up a prescription for Tasha and spied the set, two black canvas bags trimmed in silver metallic with a tiny parade of silhouetted white chickens trailing across the bottom, and immediately thought of Kat, a thought instantly followed by the realization that she had never bought her a gift before, not for birthdays or holidays—not even a card. Sometimes her own selfishness surprises her. But something has shifted in recent weeks, as if her heart has been pried open and she can no longer control what trickles into it. Lacey had left the cosmetic bags on Kat's bed with a simple note. *Thought you might like these*, and while Kat hadn't gushed enthusiasm, she had tapped on Lacey's bedroom door and mumbled *thank you*. Lacey had only said *glad you like them*, even though Kat hadn't actually said she did. After they left Lacey found the soap-slimed ziplock baggie stuffed in the bathroom trashcan.

Willy blows a puff of smoke from his pipe and the cloud of it falls beneath the thicker air, drifting across the lawn. He holds the bowl of the pipe in the cup of his hand and fingers. "Nope," he says, "don't believe this storm is happening anytime soon."

They hear the crunch of a car and both turn to watch as Cade pulls in the drive. Lacey steps out the door and around Willy to greet him at his parked car. When he opens his door to her, cool air rolls out along her bare shins. He has been coming up at least once a week and sleeping in the sunroom until the house quiets down and she tiptoes down to retrieve him back to her room, giggling like teenagers as they slip up the stairs and collapse in her bed. In a house with a no-locked-doors policy she has, in any case, taken the precaution of installing latch hooks on the doors in her bedroom, one to the door that opens into the hall and another on the door that opens from her room to Tasha's. She didn't even tell Willy, just took the liberty of doing so because it was the right thing to do.

Willy had made mention of it a few evenings earlier. He had called down to Lacey in the parlor—where was Tasha's heparin for flushing her port, as Carlotta was expected soon—and Lacey had hollered back that it was in her own room on the bureau, but when he tried to enter through Tasha's bedroom into Lacey's he had found the door latched from the other side. When he came back downstairs, he had nudged her shoulder and said since when did they have locks on their doors? Lacey had only shrugged but just this morning she discovered also that there is now a latch on Willy's door. She has known that Carlotta occasionally stays over, but no mention has ever been made of it and Tasha seems not to have noticed. By early morning Carlotta is dressed and in the kitchen making breakfast and no one is the wiser as to whether she has spent the night or just popped in that morning. They are discreet, just as Lacey has tried to be. But this is something she is thinking now that the two of them should discuss in light of the fact that Lacey will not be returning to school in the fall and has in fact taken a leave of absence through the fall semester. There is the burden now, of explaining these *sleepovers*—of both Cade and Carlotta—to Tasha.

How much explaining is necessary, she wonders now as she wraps her arms over Cade's shoulders and kisses him quickly. Once again, motherhood confounds her and she will have to think on this, but for now she is only happy to see him, and she smiles uncontrollably at her own good fortune.

By late afternoon and just as the other guests are arriving, a stiff hot breeze has picked up and the sky has gone from white to a pale dove gray. Carlotta has filled the bird feeder and watered the impatiens and they have perked back up in their pots, waving a cheery hello to Franny and Duffy as they come down the walk.

"Hey, babe," says Franny, handing over to Lacey a bag filled with corn on the cob. "I even shucked them for you." She hugs Lacey and Lacey notices over Franny's shoulders her two young boys. They are ten and nine, or somewhere thereabout, and Lacey feels a nudge of guilt at not knowing their exact ages. Michael, the older of the two, shuffles shyly down the walk but lights up at the sight of the chicken coop where the chickens are dusting themselves and raising dirt clouds. The boys head straight for the coop, as children tend to do when visiting the farm, and Tasha, who is trailing after Carlotta as she sets condiments at the picnic table, meanders after them, first being sure to snug her baseball cap firmly on her head. Lacey is sure she is set on explaining to them the finer points of chicken farming. Duffy is shaking Willy's hand and then Cade's and everyone is set to the offering and passing of drinks while Willy tends the old black Weber grill he painstakingly cleaned that morning. Cade has met Lyle and Clint already and greets them with enthusiasm as he fills a cooler with beer and bottled waters and Carlotta sets a hefty pitcher of iced tea on the table.

"They okay?" asks Franny, nodding to the boys standing with their fingers twined to the fencing and staring in at the chickens.

"Oh, sure," says Lacey. She calls down to Tasha to let the boys in the chicken yard but not to chase the chickens or forget to close the gate. She puts an arm around Franny and begins to usher her into the house but Franny stops her.

"Oh, no, not until you introduce me to Cade." Lacey smiles, hefts the bag of corn to her hip, and leads the way to where the men have gathered around the cooler. Franny hugs Lyle and Clint, referring to each of them as *Lynt*, an old joke from many years ago when she once had trouble telling one from the other. It's a joke they never tire of and they break into wide matching grins at the reference. Cade shakes Franny's hand warmly and Lacey steps back and feels a sort of pride she isn't used to in showing him off to her dearest friend in the world.

Quite suddenly Lacey thinks of her mother, the thought taking her completely by surprise as she imagines what it would be like to present Cade to May, going so far as to wonder if she would like him, would feel Lacey had chosen well to let this man into her life. Would May take him aside and admonish him in a kind-natured way to be good to her daughter? Would she pepper him with questions about his aspirations? His intentions? Would she take Willy's hand and whisper in his ear, *I like him*? Curiously, Lacey never thought these thoughts of Mac, never yearned in her imagination to see the two of them, her mother and Mac, seated beside one another laughing over childhood photos of Lacey, but with Cade—with this man—she is thinking just that, that her mother could tell him stories about Lacey swimming in the pond, the time she fell in face-first at the edge while chasing a bullfrog through the reeds and came up sputtering, with nothing but muck in her hands. May could tell him how Lacey loved to ride on the paddock gates, how she wrinkled her nose at green beans, how she once sassed a farmhand for smacking her favorite heifer, Mary, way too hard on the rump when she refused to get in her stanchion. (And Lacey would cut in by way of explanation that Mary was the one with the damaged teat that she had told him about and that she, Lacey, had a particular soft spot for her, and he never should have done that.) She imagines Cade grumbling about how Lacey is forever misplacing her keys and May would be reminded of the way as a child Lacey was always losing her socks, her hair bands, a favorite trinket, and what was worse, she had a fidgety habit of picking up things that weren't hers, fiddling with them, and setting them god-knows-where, so that May was always having to look all over the house for her crochet hooks and knitting needles, pantyhose, a missing earring, her church veils, the red leather notebook that was always set beside the bed until Lacey got to fooling with it, trying to decipher the pretty script, at which point May would take it from her and slip it in her bedside drawer if Lacey hadn't already wandered away with it.

It occurs to her now, watching Franny take Cade's hand and then, with a what-the-hell flip of her hair, drop his hand and lean into him with a hug as if she can't help herself, so happy is she to meet him, that those days, the days of May, are a part of Lacey that she has worked hard to pack away. And now, she is reconciled to the fact that these days are at the core of herself, and that May's leaving stole them away. She was a happy child, a loved child, and the missing of that, the great effort she has made since that time to put that part of herself on a high shelf, stow it away like old china that never gets used anyway, well, perhaps the efforts have not served her well. Maybe it is time to reconcile the past with the present.

By the time they sit down to dinner, the breeze is lifting the edges of the paper tablecloth. The pollen-topped surface of the pond is rippling as if a skin is being pulled from it and the birds are urgently flying in clusters across the sky.

There is much laughter and too many questions asked of Cade, at least in Lacey's opinion. Does he like coaching, where did he go to school, where did he grow up?

He is skilled at deflecting the attention, Lacey notices, turning the tables with similar inquiries of his own. Of the nephews, he asks about their hardware store, shares his frustration with having tried to buy a simple roll of duct tape at Home Depot and coming out thirty-six dollars poorer with a caulk gun and three kinds of caulk that he never really needed in the first place.

"That's the whole idea," says Clint, lifting his fork and pointing it at Cade. "Did'ja know that no two of them stores are set up alike? Hmm?" But he doesn't wait for an answer. "And I'll tell you why that is. Why that is," he says, "is so you don't get too familiar. You go to a different Home Depot thinking you know just where the duct tape is and it's someplace altogether different than in the other store you're used to."

Lyle adds his two cents' worth. "They *want* you to walk around and not be able to go directly to what you're looking for, so you'll pick up other things along the way."

Cade says he never thought of it that way, but it makes sense now that he thinks about it.

Willy says he feels the same way about the Safeway. Franny and Duffy share a look, nod in agreement. They have decided not to sell the store, Duffy announces. He says that instead they have decided to make some changes, offer things you can't get at the bigger Safeway, like Willy's eggs, for instance, and locally grown produce. He's actually in talks with several farms, including Hurline's, regarding organically raised beef and pork.

"Times change," says Willy. "Calls for innovation. If you can't be big, be better."

Afterward, the carnage of chicken bones rests on paper plates and the mouths of Franny's boys are splattered and smeared with barbecue sauce. Franny takes a napkin to her youngest boy's face and he squirms away from her, asking instead for permission to eat the brownies they had spied earlier on the kitchen counter, courtesy of Carlotta. Lacey is once again grateful to Carlotta, as she herself hadn't thought about dessert at all. She looks to Tasha, brows raised, and asks if she would like to go and get them from the kitchen. The boys will help her. She breaks into a smile and scrambles from the table to fetch them. The boys follow her and moments later they return, Tasha carrying the huge platter across the lawn. The boys grab their brownies from it as she walks, nearly tripping her, and Lacey takes in a breath as Tasha stumbles, pitching forward, but steadies herself, her eyes never leaving the tray she holds in front of her. The cumulative effects of the chemo include a loss of balance, which may or may not get better with time. Time—something Lacey waits for the passing of and then regrets the loss of. A conundrum rooted in point of view, she thinks now.

Tasha sets the brownies on the table and then follows the boys down to the pond. Out of earshot now, the adults begin to pepper Lacey with questions as to how Tasha is doing.

Lacey tells them they are still visiting the hospital once a week for blood counts, and there is the occasional bone marrow aspiration and such, but as they know, the treatments are on hold for a time. She watches Tasha now, squatting on her heels at the edge of the pond, likely pointing out the tadpoles. The boys hover at her shoulders, peering into the pond, but soon they are scampering around the edges, tossing stones and running through the cattails.

"She looks good," says Lyle. "Hair growing back, I noticed."

Lacey and Willy, even Carlotta, all nod in unison.

"Hell of a thing," says Clint. "Hell of a thing."

"So the chemo is done?" says Franny.

Lacey explains that she will need maintenance chemo off and on over the next three years. They start a milder form of it in late October. She doesn't want to talk about it and stops herself, nearly ignoring the squeeze of Franny's hand on her knee. She looks away, but hears Willy say, "But she's doing good now, real good."

Over the pond Lacey can see a darkness invading the sky and the wind is picking up, knocking over Willy's empty cup that rolls across the table and lodges under the rim of the pasta salad bowl. "Might get that storm after all, Willy?" she teases. The leaves of the maple tree above their heads are swishing and the sound builds and tapers. Still, there is no rain, though there is talk of moving inside. The darkness to the west moves closer and a sudden gust of wind sends wadded napkins rolling like small tumble-weeds across the lawn. Carlotta suggests clearing the table before they are all caught in a downpour and Duffy rises from the table to chase down the errant napkins that have lodged in the shrubbery. Willy says he needs to tend to the chickens who are squawking and scolding one another at an especially fervent pitch. He wants to lock them up ahead of the storm he says isn't coming. Cade offers to help.

Franny starts to clear the table but at the same time mentions that they should be on their way ahead of the weather. "Go, go," says Lacey. "We've got this, really."

It takes Franny many minutes and finally the stern demands of Duffy to wrangle the boys and by that time the table has been cleared and Lyle and Clint are settled in the sunroom because Carlotta has shooed them away from kitchen duty. Tasha trails behind Carlotta in the kitchen, pulling out Tupper-ware and tinfoil and finally climbing on a chair at the counter to help with the packing away of leftovers. Franny pokes her head in to say a final good-bye, the door slamming on her heels with the wind behind it and causing her to wince. Lacey hugs her, thanks her for coming, for the corn, and waves her away. "It'll be nice to have you around this fall," says Franny. "I'm sorry about the circumstances, you know, but glad to have you around just the same."

"Love you, girlfriend," says Franny.

"Same," says Lacey.

Carlotta sends Lacey into the sunroom with iced tea for Lyle and Clint.

Lyle is pacing, his hand pressed to his lower back and Clint is settled on the sofa nursing the last inch of beer in his cup. Lacey watches him swig down the last of it as she hands him the glass of tea in exchange for his empty cup. "Cuttin' me off?" he says with a gruff smile.

"Wanted to talk," she says. Lyle turns to her from the window—beyond which the sky is now a deep gray-black, the branches of the mulberry at the far side of the pond dipping and swaying in unison, the leaves flipping to reveal the silvery undersides—and settles into a chair.

"About your mother, hmm?" says Lyle. She nods. "We been thinking on it, Lace." He tips his head to his twin. "Neither one of us can recall his last name."

"All I can recall is *Jim*," says Lyle. "And you know, Lacey, we don't think he was your father anyway." They share a look between the two of them, Lyle to Clint, both nodding and drawing back their shoulders as if they have agreed to something in advance. Lyle pulls his shoulders back, waits for Clint, and when Clint says nothing at all, he leans forward toward her from the chair where he is sitting. "I'm sure of it, Lacey," and proceeds to tell her what he recalls of the one time he remembers Jim coming to the store, threatening May, wanting to know who Lacey's father was.

The news is distorting to Lacey, shifting her recollection of the past, especially when Clint goes on to describe Little Jim jumping around at the counter *like a jack rabbit*. "Little guy," he says, "and spittin' mean. You were there, but you was just a bitty thing, maybe three years old. You don't remember?"

She shakes her head, no.

"Nuisance, he was. Kept coming back into town. Never stopped in anywhere that we heard of. But Uncle Price had us watching out for that damn truck. If he was said to be in town, we sometimes locked up early. Uncle Price didn't want no trouble from him."

This is not at all what she recalls of the red truck man. In her memory he is big, so big, and somehow the word *Daddy* is attached to him. She can remember that. She is nearly certain of it. Her memory banks are jumbled and she blames herself, blames herself for having shelved everything for far too long and now, pulling out the dusted-over memories requires a great deal of wiping down, reexamining the once-discarded contents, paying special attention to the cracks in it all where the smudge of time has settled.

She is flipping it over through her mind, seeing that truck, knowing it was the centerpiece.

She watches Carlotta now through the doorway, moving about the kitchen, chattering to Tasha, gliding purposefully along the edges of the counter, her hand coming to rest now and then on the small of Tasha's back where she stands on the chair, steadying her. She can see the man now, in the haziest of ways, the tracking of mud across the kitchen floor, the loud slurp from a coffee mug gripped in his fists, sounding like a large animal at the water trough. Her mother's grip at her, Lacey's own legs wrapped and locked at her thin waist. The pressure of her mother's arms around her.

"May was a good mother, damn good mother," says Lyle, as if that settles everything.

"Young as she was," says Clint.

Branches are whipping against the house now and the first smatterings of rain are pelting the windows. Lacey stands and begins to shut windows. Carlotta calls out that she and Tasha will get the ones upstairs. Lacey jiggles down the old windows and hears the door slam. Cade and Willy are laughing between themselves, having run in from the now raging rain. The wind is whipping through the trees, raising a hum with the swishing of leaves, and an empty trashcan rolls across the yard and along the coop. As Lacey comes into the kitchen, Cade is starting to head back outside to get it when a flash of lightning throws the room into instant bright stark light and is followed in the new dark seconds later by a crack of thunder so loud that she feels it in her feet and they all startle, Willy visibly flinching through his shoulders and then all of them breaking into foolish grins at the surprise of it all.

The nephews decide to take their leave, even though Willy encourages them to wait it out. But they want to check on the garden center, make sure everything is closed up tight and they brave the rain and wind, ducking their heads and making a run for their truck with everyone laughing and waving goodbyes. *Drive safe, go slow!* Lacey watches from the kitchen window as they make their way down the drive, its gullies running with muddy water already.

"This is something!" says Carlotta coming into the kitchen. The thunder rolls and the lights flicker. They collectively moan and eye the ceiling, then break into smiles again when the lights flick back on.

Willy goes to the cellar steps and reaches along the narrow shelf that lines the stairway, taking two flashlights down and closing the door just as the lights dim again and the refrigerator drones down.

"Uh-oh," says Tasha. "Mommy?"

Lacey takes her hand in the dark. There is a rolling of thunder and a tremendous *bang* that makes them both jump and then Lacey gives a nervous laugh. "I'm right here, sweetheart."

Willy tests the batteries and hands a flashlight to Tasha. She shines it around the room, resting an orb of light over each face, her mother, Willy, Carlotta, and Cade—everyone accounted for—everyone breaking into a smile and squinting their eyes when the light falls on them.

Willy brings two candlesticks from the dining room and sets them on the kitchen table, digs his fingers down his shirt pocket to retrieve a pack of matches, and lights them, creating an intimate glow at the kitchen table that invites them all to settle around it, Tasha climbing on to Lacey's lap and shining the flashlight under Lacey's chin.

"Still hot as dickens," says Willy. He gets up from the table and opens the kitchen door to the screen, weights the door against the wind with his work boots set beside it. The stoop is covered, but a wet mist still makes its way into the kitchen on the wings of a whipping wind. A pad of note-paper flutters on the counter.

"I used to love thunderstorms as a kid," says Carlotta, patting Tasha's shoulder. "Especially at night, the way everything would light up and go dark again. Oh, it was fun!"

As if on cue, the world lights up in a bright searing flash and goes dim again.

In that moment, Lacey sees the look on Tasha's face, knows she is not convinced that this is fun, but she is trying to find the adventure in it, looking anxiously among the adults to gage the truth of what Carlotta has said.

Lacey never did love thunderstorms. They don't scare her. They just make her uneasy, afraid that she will find the world rearranged with every flash of lightning, that one flash might reveal the boughs lifting on the tree outside her bedroom window and the next reveal them crashing and clawing at the glass, weighted by a downdraft. She can remember an evening so many years ago, waking to a storm and her childhood bedroom suddenly illuminated, set just as it should be, her books scattered across the floor, her blankets knotted at the end of her bed, the hallway empty, she is certain, and then with the next flash her mother stood at the doorway, her fair skin made bloodless by the searing flash of brightness and the *bang* of thunder so loud she thought the world was cracking open. The light so brief and bright that she could not read the look on her mother's face. It is such a pale memory and she cannot now recall if it was real or not, if it was before or after May left. It would have to be before, of course, but then again, she can't be sure. The storm might have folded into her dreams that night and she will never know for certain.

She is so entwined in these thoughts, so mesmerized by the glow of candles, as if they are seated at a séance, that she doesn't feel the snuggle of Tasha under her chin, the weight of Cade's arm on her shoulders, the *tap-tap* of Carlotta's hand on her arm, doesn't even recognize the soothing purr of Willy's voice as he asks, "Lacey, you okay?" And then Cade chimes in. "Earth to Lacey?"

If she can't be certain as to whether or not it was a dream, whether or not it was before or after May left, then just where is the line between the two?

"Mommy?"

She folds herself back into these people, the people she loves, looks to them with a small shake of her head, and realizes that May is among them, always has been.

PART 2

Autumn 2005

CHAPTER 27

From: SugarsCottages.com
To: <u>LCherrymill@SMdC.edu</u>
September 15, 2005, 9:59 p.m.

Dear, Dear Lacey,

    I have read your email letter near 10 times now and alls I can think is, LITTLE LACEY CHERRYMILL. You cannot have any notion of how thrilled I been to hear from you. I think of you and your mother more than just time to time. I thank you so much for writing me your letter. Imagining you a college professor, of all things! Whiles I can tell you many things about your mother and my friend, I am most sad for what I cannot tell you. The last time I saw my friend May was many years ago when she was sixteen. As you know, she lived in one of the cottages here. We have three now but at the time there was only the one she lived in and the one I was growing up in here. I have built a third since that time as I now rent the other two of them to guests in the summer, which I will tell you is a lucrative business for me as we are swarming like flies with the tourists in the summer months. Winter is quiet and more like the old times round here and that is when I think of her most, because that is when things are lonelier and it would be good to have my dear friend about. And I think of you, too. For I do think of you often and have taken to wondering many times about you and Mr. Willy but do not think to write as the last time he wrote me when she first left many years ago there was such sadness in his words, him telling me to be sure and tell her she could come home whenever she wanted and he would take good care of you until then, but after so much time passing since that letter, it seemed best to let things be.

Now you ask me who was your mother's boyfriend named Jim and who might have been your daddy but that is an oddly put question. Your mother did have a boyfriend for a bit of time named Jim Skole who we called Little Jim as he was no more than five foot tall and a bundle of fighting mean, but that is a funny thing about him and I will tell you more. You should know he was most definitely not your daddy as I was there when you were born and he weren't even a bit of an idea in her head at the time. My own mama delivered you in my bedroom the night you were born and Lord, I was scared when it was happening. Your mama was scared too and the whole time she was thinking she was dying as she had no idea she was having a baby. Now you may be wondering how a thing like that is even possible, but stranger things have happened. I have since read articles in the newspaper and on my computer about young girls and even full-grown married women not having any idea they was having a baby. When you were born your mama was only thirteen years old and her own mama, Miss Ruth, had gone on and passed from a terrible cancer that I assume now was OVARIAN CANCER. May was certain as the day is long that the same thing was happening to her, too. It was my mama who said to her, NO, MAY, YOU ARE NOT DYING BUT YOU ARE ABOUT TO HAVE A BABY. My mama sent me out of the room but I stood at the doorway and I heard her ask who the daddy was and May did not know, did not even believe she was having a baby. She said the cancer had been growing all summer long in her, was biting at her even, and she would surely die as her mama had. But lo and behold, you were born pink and squalling and my mama sent me up the lane to tell her daddy who would be your grandfather. And that is another story I will tell you. Then my daddy went on up to the coast guard station to call your aunt Virgie in Maryland (God rest her soul as I am so sorry to know she is no longer on earth as she was a kind woman) and she come down and get the both of you and took you up to where she lived. We all agreed it would be best not to make mention of this to anyone and all these years we kept our promise but it was your grandpa who likely told of you and rumors and speculation was all over the place.

When May come back you was probably near a year old and she just went on back to school like nothing happened. But she was sad most days and missing you terribly and I was the only friend she had to listen at her sadness and hear of the kind of child you was growing into. She took a bus up to see you sometimes and once spent near the whole summer with you as I recall, and we weren't none too surprised when she just up and disappeared to Maryland and never came back. And that is just the point I am getting at. She never did come back. There was some rumors that there had been a beating that made her leave for good and as by that time she was riding round town with Jim Skole most afternoons, it seemed likely if there had been a beating it had come from him. But then she moved permanent to Maryland and married Willy and her letters to me were happy things about her life on the farm and about you.

When we all started hearing that she had up and disappeared from you and Willy, some did think at first that maybe she had taken off with Little Jim, but that was proved wrong. See, round about that same time (and it is hard to know the order in which these things all happened), the coast guard got a phone call as I understand it and came to check your grandpa's house and talk with him about where she might be and if he had heard from her. But he weren't there and was always disappearing anyways. Near a month or more went by before we learned of his drowning and no one was in the least worried about him missing before knowing the sad truth (least not any more than usual as he was known to drink and disappear and had often said he was moving to Florida anyways). Little Jim's truck was there the night they come by, I remember that, but that was not unusual as Little Jim did not seem to fuss much with your grandpa borrowing his truck. But then about a week or so after, Little Jim come and pick up his truck and he come by our cottage and told me and my folks he was headed up to merchant marine school in Norfolk and that is just what he did.

Now the thing about Little Jim is I never liked him much and didn't trust him neither but what I wanted to tell you about him is that five summers ago, he just come on back to the island for a visit with his little family of three boys and a pretty little wife. Seems he stopped his drinking and bad ways and settled into a nice life up in Virginia. He was coming back to MAKE AMENDS, he said. And one of the ones he wanted to see was your mother. Now don't that beat all? He was sorrowful clear through about not being able to find her and I will say I believe it crushed something in him that had been hopeful to make things right with her. He said his meemaw had wrote him when he was in training years back and said rumor was May was coming back to the island but she had not yet. She had left Willy and some thought she had left with Little Jim, but that was not the case, of course. But still, he had been hoping she had come back eventually so he could speak with her.

I did think to reach out to Mr. Willy and let him know what I knew of Little Jim but so much time had passed and I thought it might be best to let things go. It has bothered me some these last years and bothers me more now that I have heard from you. I am glad to have heard from you and know that you are doing good, being a college professor and all. I hope someday you will think of coming to Ocracoke and I can show you where your mama grew up. It has changed a lot over the years and then maybe not at all. I modernized some things but tourists seem to like the old things too so there are things that haven't changed at all and the guests say they like the VINTAGE FEEL of it all. Course I had to put in air conditioning and a dishwasher and remodel the old bathrooms mostly, but they always remark on the old pine floors what have to be refinished every year from all the sand and grit that scratches them good. I prefer a good linoleum floor any day! You are welcome to be my guest at no charge as it would be my pleasure to host May DuBerry Cherrymill's daughter.

Thank you for writing to me and for your questions which I am sorry I cannot answer but I would be pleasured to talk more with you about your dear sweet mother.

Sincerely,
Sugar Lane

P.S. I forgot to tell you some things about your grandfather but if you come here there will be stories from the old-timers so you should know that he was mostly a decent man until your grandmother Ruth passed on. He didn't get over her passing too good and had a habit of going over to the graveyard and hollering his woes to the dead and anyone within earshot. That is how I think most folks learned of May having a baby. He would hang about crying that May took the baby away and shamed him. I hope it don't bother your feelings by knowing this. He was not always right in his head and could be a bit of a wampus cat. You are best knowing that his drinking got the better of him though he weren't always that way. The other story I was going to tell you of him is that when I went up the lane to tell him you had been born he behaved strangely to me, saying he knew it was coming and acting afraid that what he knew was coming had come after all. I have not since squared in my head how it was he seemed to know when I believe surely that May herself did not know. It is true, thinking back, that she put on a pouf of weight around her belly that summer but not nothing like what would make one think she was with a child. So I can only tell you that if anyone knew who your daddy was it would have been only your grandpa and your daddy hisself and sadly your grandpa is not here to tell.

Lacey reads to the bottom of the email and then starts at the top again. *Dear, Dear Lacey …*

None of it makes any sense to her now. She knows with absolute certainty that her mother climbed into that truck and ducked down in the seat as it ripped out of the parking lot. And now, after so many years of knowing something with such precise detail, it is not possible to reconstruct the memory in any other way. She wonders now, where is the crack in her memory? Where is the gully of pertinent detail that she is missing and what has washed into it?

She hits the response key and begins typing.

CHAPTER 28

Planning a Trip

Willy is hosing down the insides of the coop, aiming the stiff spray of water at the rafters and then down the walls, washing the grime and soggy down feathers away as best he can. The chickens are fussing at being locked out while he does this, and he knows they will not appreciate his efforts and will instead come back in clucking at the changes, eyeing the fresh pine shavings and the dripping laying boxes, hefting themselves to perches where they will scan the floors and walls and one another before finally settling in with a fat satisfied fluff as if they had done the work themselves and are plumb worn out from it all.

He aims the spray at the abandoned cartilage of a mud wasp comb glued in the corner, though he knows it won't come loose. *Darnedest things*, he thinks to himself, the way they build a home of spit-up paper that doesn't even flake as he attacks it. He has a sudden urge to take the time to chisel it away but then doesn't see the point in it. Just let it be, he thinks to himself. Ain't hurting nobody to be there and he knows that once abandoned, they won't take up residence again.

Carlotta is in the kitchen with Lacey and Tasha, planning their trip, the one that he doesn't want to go on, that he has told them time and time again he doesn't want to go on, but seems no one is listening. Instead they're in there planning menus, Carlotta already making a list of what she needs to bring along, looking at maps and scheduling the sights they might want to stop at on the way. The plan, thus far, is to leave in two days at the butt crack of dawn in order to make the last ferry that evening from the mainland to Ocracoke.

He should've put a stop to it before everyone got so carried away, that is what he is thinking now.

The whole coop is raining inside from his efforts, the water dripping from the rafters and he has backed himself into a corner and finds himself having to wait for it to stop its dripping so that he can make his way to the doors.

At first he had just said that Lacey should check with Dr. Oren, that maybe it wasn't a good idea to be so far from the hospital, but Lacey said she'd already done that. Lacey was sitting at the kitchen table with her computer in front of her explaining that it would be a ten-hour drive but that they could stop at a hotel on the way if they got tired, or just switch off drivers between all of them. That had been two days ago, and he had hoped she would just drop the whole cockamamie idea.

He was thinking to himself at the time that there was no way he was going to ask Carlotta to go with them on a trip to the town that his runaway wife grew up in but, dang it, Lacey jumped him on that one, too.

"I've already talked to Carlotta and she thinks it sounds wonderful."

He didn't believe her, looked at her across the table as he felt his jaw drop. "You asked her already?"

Lacey just nodded. He continued to stare at her and she looked up at him. "What?" she said. "What?"

He threw his hands up in the air, just couldn't believe she wanted to do this, wanted *him* to do this with her. But she knew what he was thinking. "Look, she's not there, Willy. Never was there after she married you, I don't think. I don't know where she is and probably never will. But I want to see where she grew up. That makes sense, right? I never got to see where she grew up." She looked around the room and back at her computer. "And besides, it's supposed to be beautiful there this time of year."

"What are you looking for, Lacey? Hmmm?"

She didn't answer at first, appeared to be completely immersed in her computer screen, but then, quietly, she said, "I just want to get to know her somehow, Willy." She looked at him quickly and then away, put her elbow on the table and her hand to her chin and then said, so softly that he wasn't sure she wanted to be heard, "I've spent so long trying not to feel anything at all. But I've come to realize she's a part of me. I'm a part of her, and I just want to feel her again, get some idea of who she is—was."

What he wanted to say was that he *didn't*—didn't want to feel any of it again, the pain or the wondering, the distance between them the last weeks before she left, the confusion, the anger, or the love of her. Didn't want to feel any of it and how could it make any sense to drag Carlotta through it as well?

Lacey took a breath and pulled back her shoulders. "I know that on some level it's unfair of me to ask you to come along."

"Damn right it is."

"But I promise you this is not some mystery I'm looking to solve. I don't have an agenda here other than I just want to see where she grew up, get to know what she was like—maybe talk to Sugar about her." He raised his brows, letting her know he didn't believe her. "And I want you there, selfish as that is." The look on her face softened painfully. "It's hard to explain, Willy, but this happened to both of us and I can't separate myself out of it anymore. It was the three of us—you, me, and May—and then suddenly, it wasn't. It was just you and me and this big damn hole. I feel like I have to go there and reconcile how she once fit into our life—both our lives—and then she didn't." She looked up at him and waited, but he was at a loss for words. "*That's* the hard part right now, trying to figure how this ghost of her fits into our lives now."

"It don't make no sense," he said, "going down there. There's miles of beaches down the coast we can go to. Don't have to be there." He stared at her, but she didn't answer. "You're not selfish," he says finally, thinking it's important to let her know he knows that about her.

Lacey ignored him. "Tasha has an appointment Monday morning so we can leave on Tuesday. Cade is going to meet us there on Thursday night—best he can do with his schedule—but we don't have to get back until Sunday."

He caught himself wondering what kind of things he might see in the ocean, maybe dolphins or a shark. And he had always wanted to see a horseshoe crab. May had said they were big old prehistoric-looking things and moved like molasses on the shores of the sound, stinking of rot if they got flipped while mating and couldn't get back to the water before the sun done them in. He recalled the way she carried on about the scuttling sand crabs, the way they buried themselves in the sand in between the washes of waves. He couldn't even imagine that back when she had told him about it—it seemed so impossible, to burrow so fast between waves as if they'd never been there in the first place.

"I'm not at all comfortable with the idea of staying on at Sugar's places. That don't seem right," he had said.

Lacey only said the cottages looked nice in the pictures and it would be interesting to see the cottage her mother grew up in. "You don't have to stay in that one," she said. "There are two, right next to each other, I think." She flipped the computer around to show him the pictures but he only glanced and looked away, not even sure what he was supposed to look at. "It *would* be weird for you and Carlotta to stay in her actual house."

"You think?" he said. "You think that's the only thing weird about this?"

She smiled at him and said she knew he would feel differently once they got there.

"What about the chickens?"

"Franny's going to take care of them."

He had promised to think on it. That's all. And with that the whole damn thing had snowballed without him. He begins now to make his way across the coop, coiling the length of hose as he goes. He cannot believe that Carlotta is on board for this. It makes no sense to him, but when he had tried to ask her about it the night before, she had said it sounded lovely, *lovely*, as if they were headed to a tropical island where they would drink fancy drinks with umbrellas and lounge in hammocks. It would be good for Tasha to get away from the farm for a while, she had said, and good for him too, for all of them. And if they didn't go now, they would have to wait until spring, in which case it would be all the more difficult if Lacey was back to teaching. This was the perfect time for such a trip. And Sugar was being so generous, letting them stay in the cottages for free. It would be foolish *not* to go! She was curled in his bed beside him and she leaned in and kissed him on the mouth and May wasn't even a flicker in his mind when he kissed her back.

April 29, 1975

Me and Willy had some row yesterday. He was wanting to know what the hell was wrong with me. We got no coffee, no sugar, hardly no clean dishes. He says I'm not even taking care of Lacey so good and she's been wearing the same dirty pants and shirt going on four days now. I didn't think it was true at first, but then I took her on upstairs to get her clothes off the floor and get them ready for laundering and I see maybe he's right and she's wearing the same thing for a number of days now. I could smell a sour smell that clung to her shirt and around her neck.

I bathed her right away, washing rings of dirt from her neck and between her toes. I sudsed her hair and piled it high on her head like one of the fancy ladies down to the Hutzler's department store, and then I held the hand mirror up for her to see herself. The sight of herself made her get to giggling and I couldn't help it none, either. I got to laughing with her and it felt good, like it was shaking something loose.

When the water begun to cool, I got her from the tub to wrap a towel around her. I was pulling it from behind to bring it round the front of her and I couldn't help but look at her good, looking like a little pearl, her skin all smooth and new. Her shoulders are delicate and flutter when she gets to laughing, as if they oughta been wings, and her belly is a ball of a thing. Between her legs is only the tiniest fold, like the fold you might find in a peach, and everything inside the fold is tucked away, like a secret she doesn't know she carries.

I ran the towel all over her and then wrapped it tight round her and pulled her to me. On my knees we were nose to nose and she smooshed her face up at mine. I'm glad we're not going with that man, she said to me. I like it better here with Willy. Don't you? I could only nod and her face moved up and down with mine. Then she broke free, happy and certain that everything was right as rain, and bounced foot to foot. Her wet curls broke from the towel and then it slid down her head and over her shoulders. She asked me if tomorrow could be a happy day and I told her it could be any kind of day she wanted.

milk of magnesia
Ivory soap
sugar

molasses
bleach
cornflakes
Quick Oats
lard
cotton balls
orange juice
Jell-O 1-2-3
cornmeal
Vaseline
ketchup
peanut butter
razors
flour
brown sugar
bacon
vinegar
eggs (or get from Olsen's if not good)
toilet paper
4 pounds ground beef in 2 packages
wheat germ
6 pound roaster
1 pound round steak (cut to 4 pieces)
applesauce
bananas if good
aluminum foil
Jergens hand cream
Kotex
vanilla
spaghetti
egg noodles
cottage cheese
3 loaves bread
tunafish 4 cans

tomato soup
Dippity-Do
baloney
Ritz crackers
tapioca
rice
1 pound scrapple

Ask Marybeth when strawberries come in

CHAPTER 29

The Road

The departure is not going smoothly. Seems Lacey had told Tasha she could bring *Biggy*—the giant stuffed bear Carlotta had given to her last spring, but of course, there was no way Biggy was going to fit in that car once they had packed everything. Tasha had come down the steps dragging that big bear like he was a passed-out drunk, bouncing him down the steps and through the kitchen, and Lacey had said no, there was no way he was going to fit in the car and Tasha had thrown herself across him, wrapping her arms over the girth of him, like she couldn't stand to leave him behind and it was the cruelest thing to ask of her. Lacey had said don't be ridiculous and that had just made matters worse. Carlotta intervened, suggesting they pick some of her smaller stuffed animals and had taken a sniveling Tasha back up the steps to gather a near dozen of her favorites. When Willy finally locked the kitchen door behind them that big damn bear lay out on the floor like an abandoned body.

The car is now packed to the hilt and Willy finds himself having Lacey stop midway down the drive so he can open the hatchback and re-arrange the bags that sit too high and, he is certain, block a clear view out the rear window. Frustrated, he has pulled the cooler from the back to make more room in settling the bags and then has to have Carlotta step from the car so he can put the cooler between Carlotta and Tasha in the back seat. Inadvertently, he sets the cooler on top of a pink unicorn and a much-prized gopher-like thing, all of which sets Tasha to whining again. He digs them both out from under the cooler and hands them to Tasha whose lap now overflows with the menagerie of creatures.

An October sun is just breaking through the sky to the east as they hit the main highway, and by midmorning Willy has cracked the window on his side, asking Carlotta if it is too much wind on her, and then settling back as best he can. He is familiar with the roads as far as Norfolk (the farthest south he's ever traveled on farm business), but after that it is all new to him and the patchwork of fields and farms seem odd—crops he hadn't thought about, cotton bursting from their clam-shaped husks, pumpkins poking their color through tangled vines, ruffled rows of blue-green collards and deep purple kale. The fields of sunflowers are something to see and he points them out to Tasha, the way their heads all turn to the sun like choreographed dancers.

Tasha wants to know how long until they get there.

"Two *Shrek* tapes and one *Power Rangers* show," says Lacey.

Willy isn't sure that's exactly right and he worries they may not make the ferry.

"Where's my books?" asks Tasha. "Did you pack the one Willy is reading me?"

"Which one is that?" says Lacey.

"*The Lion, the Witch and the Wardrobe*," says Willy. "Don't worry, sugar. I packed it in my bag." He had spied it in the parlor that morning, open to the page he had been reading to her from last and he had thought to stuff it in his duffel bag. He's a little pleased with himself right now for thinking to bring it. It had been Lacey's copy and Tasha had found it on the shelf in Lacey's room. The psychedelic cover illustration had caught her interest—two children and a handsome lion crashing through a lush world swirling with mythical creatures, a centaur, unicorns—what child wouldn't be intrigued? He had started reading it to her a few nights ago and at first, he wasn't sure she was following, or even interested, for that matter, picking at her toes and interrupting him to ask questions that had nothing to do with the story. But as soon as little Lucy had gone through that dang wardrobe (and he'd had to explain just exactly what a wardrobe was, too), she was hooked.

Lacey looks over to him, surprised maybe, that he remembered the book, and then lifts a hand from the steering wheel to high-five him. He chuckles. "Willy for a win!" she says. He settles back in his seat. Maybe he's not so bad at this vacation thing.

But he doesn't like it, just the same, doesn't like the idea of this trip, though he has tried the last two days to resign himself to it. *She ain't there*, he tells himself. She ain't there and this is just something Lacey has got to do, and he owes it to her to go with her and face whatever it is he's been keeping his back to the last thirty years. Still, he knows he's been lassoed into this and would never have chosen to make a trip like this if he hadn't felt the sting of guilt, like a snag of barbed wire caught in his heart. Like this is the wound he bears for having not done what he should have done thirty years ago.

And just *what* should he have done? Made no sense to him at the time to go chasing her down. You can lead a horse to water . . . and all that kind of thing. But he wasn't going to go try and change May's mind when she already made it up to do such a thing, leaving him like that. Virgie had said he oughta shuck off his pride and get on down there—here—where they're headed now, but it wasn't his pride holding him back, he thinks now. Just what it was he can't be sure but when he looks over at Lacey driving, her curls tickling her cheeks, the blink of her eyes on the road, hears the sound of her voice pointing out the herds of cows in the fields, the way she looks to the mirror and adjusts it to better keep an eye on Tasha as well as the road, well, he thinks now, he was just cutting his losses is all.

There is a quick stop for a picnic lunch before they continue on through the late afternoon, passing through Avon and a stream of brightly colored buildings with big signs boasting the best of this and the best of that. Crossing another long bridge, Lacey points out the fishermen and their trucks and SUVs dotting the shores below. Carlotta says it all looks like a painting, like it just couldn't be real, the green grasses and the blue of the sky. Willy studies the series of canals that weave through the grasses and can't help but imagine what it would be like to travel them in a canoe or one of them tippy-looking kayaks he has seen pictures of. Coming back down to land level on the other side of the bridge, Lacey points out the swans that float in stiller waters. Egrets and herons pick their way through the shallows and something is weaving a silky rippling trail through the water.

It looks like they will make it—the last ferry out of Hatteras—and Willy isn't sure if he is relieved or just resigned to it.

Waiting to board the ferry, they all unsnap their seat belts and wiggle and stretch as best they can in their seats. "Isn't this exciting?" Carlotta asks Tasha, and she bobs her head, yes, craning to look out the window. The ramp is set down and the wide gates swung open. Willy holds his breath and looks over the sides as Lacey bumps the car forward to the belly of the ferry. Lacey makes Tasha wait until all the cars are parked before letting her out. They clang up the metal stairway to the bow and Willy feels the wind tunneling down the stairs, carrying the smell of salty surf and the caw of gulls.

On the bow the wind whips into their faces and Willy's eyes tear. "Are you cold?" he asks Carlotta and he begins to shrug off his jacket, but she stops him, wrapping a flapping shawl around her shoulders. "I'm just fine," she says into the wind, her face pleating at the corners of her mouth with the wideness of her smile.

Willy and Carlotta sit down on a stiff plastic bench sheltered a bit from the wind and he holds her hand, their fingers tangled, while Lacey explores the boat with Tasha. The ride is smoother than he expected, and he finds himself mesmerized by the wake rushing along the sides of the boat and the way the gulls effortlessly drift along beside them.

When they dock, Tasha runs to the two of them. "We're here!" Lacey, taking Tasha's hand, leads them all down into the belly of the ferry and back into the car where they ease out of the ferry by way of the rickety planking again and onto a small lot that ends at the beginning of a ribbon of road. There are no houses or stores, just swaying seagrass and the road cutting into it for the several miles that lead to the village.

Willy feels a lump lodge in his chest. It is dark and hard, as if it has settled too comfortably, and it makes it hard for him to swallow. He turns in his seat and asks Carlotta if he can trouble her for a bottle of water from the cooler. The low-set sun winks hard at him from the surrounding water, making it difficult to look beyond the surf without squinting.

As they near the village, small homes spring up at the sides of the roads. Crepe myrtle, heavy with dark pink blossoms, and twisted oaks dot the tiny lawns that are framed by white-washed and weathered pickets. Roses clamber over tipping arbors and here and there a cat or dog slips out from under a porch, circling in the cooling grass and settling back down.

In the heart of the village, Lacey drives the too-narrow streets looking for the turnoff to the cottages. She holds a sheet of paper in her hand and keeps looking to it as she turns down streets that come to abrupt ends or turn suddenly to dirt. The directions, she mumbles to Willy, make no sense to her now that she is here. She hands the sheet of paper to Willy, but he can make no sense of it, either. It frustrates him that he can't help. "Just stay on this here road a bit," he says. "It should come up soon," but he isn't sure himself. Eventually they find themselves heading out of the village on a road too narrow to turn around on. Finally, she travels down a graveled lane that narrows the farther they travel.

"Are we lost?" says Tasha.

Lacey ignores her and Willy can see she has more weighing on her mind than just getting there. There is a tightness in her jaw and she stares straight ahead at the narrowing road as if she is daring it to end somewhere. The road closes in around them to where small gullies run on either side of it. Willy hopes like hell no one is coming the other way. He also wishes he was the one doing the driving. He never did like being a passenger. A sharp turn in the road is followed by a four-foot-wide washout that Lacey doesn't slow down for and which sends her rear bumper smashing and dragging in the dirt as she crosses it.

"Mommy, I have to pee," Tasha whines.

"I know you do. We're almost there."

"You said that already."

Farther down the dirt lane, Willy can see a couple of rooftops peeking out over the brush.

As she drives nearer, he sees two almost identical clapboard houses rising up out of the scrub and a third smaller, more modern ranch-style house that looks to have been plunked down to the left of them both. All three are set on three or more feet of pilings, the gaping space beneath them partially hidden by dusky pink sedums.

Lacey slows down and pulls up against a low picket fence that rises like bleached bones out of the dirt. Beyond the fence is a mottled green yard dappled with dandelions. Tasha scrambles from the car and Lacey opens her own door, warning Tasha to wait for her before she goes shooting through the open gate into the yard.

Willy opens the back door and offers Carlotta his hand and the four of them walk under an arbor dripping with orange trumpet flowers and through a small gateway. The path they are on splits to three paths and veers off toward the houses. Bougainvillea cascades from baskets that hang from the porch eaves. Geese are landing just beyond on a still marsh that sparkles in the dusk from a setting sun.

Willy tries to feel the peacefulness of it, tries to settle his mind down, but it is hopeless. It isn't at all like where he had imagined May growing up, but then, he can't figure just what he had expected. Long shadows weave and shift across the houses and yard. He had never imagined the color of it, the mix of pale and deep greens, the water sparkling as if it has been glittered by a child, the sun melting in molten colors into the western sky. He realizes now that he had thought of May as stepping out from a black-and-white world and into his. He is certain that he never really knew her, only knew who she had been during the short time she had been with him. He *is* self-ish, he thinks now. He is selfish, and this is what he deserves, this sudden crashing and burning of his memory colliding into this very real place.

"Hello?" Lacey calls out as they come into the yard.

"Helloooo?" says Tasha, when no one answers her mother's call.

Within a few seconds, the front door of the ranch house to their left opens and a small woman with white hair plaited into a braid falling over her shoulder comes out on the porch. She wears long denim shorts that land at a pair of pudgy knees and a man's undershirt that is snug against her wide hips. She wipes her hands on a dishtowel as she comes down her front steps into the yard.

"Well, well, well, little Lacey Cherrymill," she says, her smile as wide as the still waters that spread behind her.

CHAPTER 30

May's Place

The thing about Sugar Lane that startles Lacey, the thing she hadn't expected, is the sound of her. It is not Lacey's mother's voice, but her way of speaking, the way the words arrange themselves, the way she remarks on the high tide and it comes out more like *hoi toid*, the very same way her own mother would have said it. Something like a cross between a brogue and an Appalachian accent, Lacey thinks now.

Sugar is showing Lacey around the cottage, pointing out the two small bedrooms, the remodeled bath (that Tasha scurries to immediately upon entering the cottage and is in there now, with the door ajar and shouting back to Lacey—*Mommy, it has a squishy toilet seat!*) telling her what is original, what has been remodeled. It's the original woodstove, explains Sugar, but the ceiling has been *put up* and raftered, ceiling fans have been installed. And though the porcelain kitchen sink, now yellowed with age, has always been here, *the spigot works is new.* Likewise, the floors are the original pine, but she has had them pickled to a dusky white, had seen it in a magazine, and Lord, what a trouble it was. The *Frigidaire,* (which is not a Frigidaire at all but a GE brand, as Lacey notes by the small round blue logo on the freezer door), is brand spanking new, as the last one had puttered out a few weeks ago. It was what May would have said as well. *Lacey, fetch me the strawberries I done cut up earlier in the Frigidaire.*

Tasha comes from the bathroom, still pulling up her pants in a way that has the seam twisted over her hip.

"She sure is a pretty little thing," says Sugar.

"My real name is Anastasia," says Tasha, trying to twist her pants into place.

"My, that's a mouthful. I for sure never heard a pretty name like that afore."

Lacey leans down and helps Tasha straighten her pants, reties a loose shoelace, and stands to brush the top of her head with the palm of her hand.

"Course, all the furniture is brand new 'cept a few things." She walks toward one of the bedrooms. "Not much in a way of closet space but you got your wardrobe there. I could not of fetched that big ol' wardrobe out. Paid a feller good cash money and he couldn't do nothin' 'bout it. Too dang heavy and too dang wide for the doorway. I says just leave it." She waves her hand at it. "Now yous can store your things in there, but the drawers is wonky, it bein' the humidity and all, so the drawers ain't no good to you on the bottom, but there's a good length of hanging rod in there."

Tasha's mouth perks into a perfect O and her eyes widen. "A real wardrobe, Mommy! Just like in my book!" She runs to the wardrobe and swings open the doors, sticks her head deep inside.

Lacey wanders back to the main room and Sugar follows her. They can see Willy outside. He has wandered down to the water's edge with Carlotta. Lacey suspects he doesn't want to come in, isn't ready, and is waiting for Sugar to return and show him and Carlotta to their own cottage. He has retrieved the bags from the car and set Lacey's and Tasha's on the steps of the porch as well as the cooler that holds Tasha's meds. But he didn't dare come in, didn't even look up when he set them down. Lacey is tempted to call out to him, to tell him that there are no ghosts, in fact, there is not a whiff of her mother anywhere. Not anywhere in the mix of old and new. She tries to imagine her mother in these rooms, standing at the sink, digging in the wardrobe, stepping out to the porch to look at the geese peppering the surface. But May will not come to her. This is not a place Lacey knows of in any way and she cannot tie it to a vision of her mother. But Sugar, the way she speaks, digs into Lacey's memory banks.

"So this here's everything," says Sugar, sweeping her hand around the room. "Must be something," she says, "seeing all this for the first time. Feels a bit odd, a bit much, maybe?" Lacey only nods. The truth is she had wanted to feel something, something more, but she simply cannot reconcile this place—with its pickled floors and rattan ceiling fans, its huge deep-blue sofa and raftered ceiling—with what she had expected. She thought she would feel something of her mother here, but once again, May eludes her. The disappointment blooms in her, making her chest hurt, and she is suddenly exhausted from the long drive.

"I'm pleased to tell you anything more I know but I done told you most in my email letter."

"You sound like her," Lacey says, turning to her. "Not her voice, but the accent, the way you put your words together." She leans her backside to the kitchen table and then slides down into a chair. "I like hearing you talk," she admits.

Sugar looks suddenly uncomfortable, as if her mind is taking a step back from Lacey. "We been said to talk funny," she says.

"I don't think it's funny," says Lacey. "It's nice."

Sugar opens a kitchen cabinet and points out dishes and serving bowls, then opens a drawer. "You got your flatware, your serving pieces, dish towels." She opens another. "Couple of postcards, pad of paper, pens," though she pronounces *pens* as "pins."

Lacey nods. "Thank you, Miss Lane. Thank you for everything." She says it sincerely, trying to heal over the earlier moment when she might have offended her.

"Oh—call me Sugar," she says. "I gotta say it, Lacey Cherrymill, I could be looking at your mother right now. It's something, imagining what she would look like now. You are a DuBerry, for sure. Your girl, though, she don't look so much like you?"

"I look like my daddy," shouts Tasha from the bedroom.

Lacey tips her head to the room. "She does," she agrees. "But she's got my spit 'n' vinegar." She has no idea where that has come from, it surprises her as it comes out of her mouth, like she has channeled her own mother in saying it. *Lacey Cherrymill, don't you sass me. Why, you is filled with spit 'n' vinegar today.*

Lacey swings Tasha's bag to a bed that is covered in an aqua comforter. She finds Tasha inside the wardrobe, her stuffed animals arranged around her like an audience.

"That looks cozy," she says.

"Can I sleep in this room? Can I sleep in the wardrobe?"

Lacey tells her she can have the room, even though it's the larger of the two, but no, she cannot sleep in a closet, silly girl. She unpacks a stack of books and sets them beside the bed, sets Tasha's pajamas on the bed itself. The walls are paneled in pine that has been painted too bright a yellow. A long white wicker full-length mirror runs from the low ceiling to the floor, and inexpensive prints of sea life—shells and tropical fish—cover the remaining walls. She leaves everything else packed in Tasha's bag and sets it on the floor.

"I'm going to pull together some supper for the four of us," she says, but she is wondering if Willy and Carlotta will even come eat with them or if she should bring it over to their cottage. As she heads back to the kitchen, Carlotta is coming up the steps.

"Our cottage is just darling," she says, looking around. "Almost exactly like this one, but we don't have a woodstove like you have here. But we have a nice, big island in the center so there's plenty of counter space. Isn't this wonderful?"

Lacey asks after Willy, and she only says he is settling in and they were thinking of getting a bite out, how does she feel about that? Lacey is tired after so much driving and hands her the keys to her car. "Have a good time," Lacey tells her. "I'm beat. I think we'll just dig something out of the cooler and get to bed early."

The next morning, Lacey wakes to watch the mist burn off the marsh. She steps out on the small covered porch wearing just a long T-shirt of Cade's and pulls down on the hem of it, making sure it covers her underpants. When she had slipped it over her head last night, it still carried the smell of him and with it, the pang of missing him.

Dragonflies dip and dash all around the porch rail and at the slippery edges of the water, only a stone's throw from where she stands. Sugar is in the yard, wearing exactly what she had worn the day before, hanging pure white sheets to dry on the line.

She waves to Lacey and then takes the laundry pin from her mouth to pinch a corner of a towel to the line. "My cousin Beanie runs the grill in town. Says breakfast for all yous is on the house this morning."

"Oh, that's nice," says Lacey. "Thanks." Though she's a little disappointed to be suddenly locked into an obligation. She goes inside to put on pants so she can extend the invitation to Willy and Carlotta.

Tasha has wandered from her room, rubs her eyes, and looks around. "This is where your mommy lived?"

"When she was a girl," says Lacey. "It didn't really look like this back then." She doesn't know why she feels the need to tell her this but something about the coffee table books with titles like *The History of Ocracoke* and *Life on Ocracoke*, the *Coastal Living* magazines, as well as the framed island map on the wall, the shiny appliances on the kitchen counter, the small plaque over the door that says *DuBerry Cottage* makes her think that it is important that Tasha know that May didn't grow up in a vacation cottage. Lacey heads to her room where she pulls on a pair of shorts and calls to Tasha to put on her bathing suit and a pair of shorts as they are headed out to breakfast. "We have a big day ahead of us!" she shouts to Tasha.

CHAPTER 31

Breakfast with the Locals

Willy is sitting on the front porch with his pipe in hand watching Lacey and Tasha make their way toward him. Tasha is wearing a bright lemon-yellow bathing suit and pink shorts and sporting red heart-shaped sunglasses and her baseball cap. They are holding hands, but Tasha breaks away to chase two geese at the water's edge. They honk and flap, swooping up and then gliding long to skim the surface. Willy's happy to see Tasha sprint to the water's edge. It's swampy and sloppy and she loses a flip-flop in the muck, stoops to pick it up, and stays squatting on her heels, poking at something in the mud. "Snails, Mommy! Come see."

Lacey waves to him and detours to Tasha's side. She stoops down beside her and Willy watches the two of them, their backs to him, and cannot help but think of watching Lacey and May at the edge of the farm's pond, peering into the water's edge, scooping frogs and poking at the banks with sticks, as if, maybe, they were both enchanted children rather than mother and daughter.

He slept well last night, if only because he travels so rarely that once asleep, he never chanced to wake and find himself in a strange bed until morning, and then, comforted by the sight of Carlotta beside him, the sun making wide stripes across her hips beneath the blankets, he turned to her, put an arm across her, and fell back into another twenty minutes of sleep. He is glad for her company, for her business in the kitchen behind him now, for her morning smile, her question upon waking—*how'd you sleep, hon?* Grateful for the way she swung her robe around her shoulders and had padded out into the kitchen to begin brewing coffee, and thankful, mostly, that she is a buffer between him and the conjuring of May.

The air is still and damp, and he had watched the mist cast off across the sound before Lacey and Tasha arrived. It was an ethereal thing and had spooked him some, tugging at some part of himself and then it vanished as if it had never been there and now he can see clear across the dazzling water.

Lacey tells him of the breakfast offer, says she feels she can't really turn it down. Willy isn't thrilled but does his best to seem cheerful. Sounds like a fine idea, he tells her. Carlotta steps out on the porch and they discuss the logistics. They will go into town for breakfast by car and then Lacey will rent a bicycle with a seat for Tasha and ride to the public beach. Carlotta wants to poke in some of the shops.

The four of them slide into a booth with Willy settling in last. His knees still ache from yesterday's long drive and he stretches them out under the table, careful not to kick at Lacey, who sits across from him. The place looks to be filled mostly with locals, older men in T-shirts and caps that they set on the table as they take their seats. There doesn't seem to be many tourists, far as he can tell, other than a chatty bunch of middle-aged women at the table behind them, discussing the shops they want to pop into, the best place for drinks in the evening. Their voices are loud with an occasional burst of shrill laughter breaking out as they talk over one another, and Willy considers moving to another table but doing so will require the folding of and subsequent rising on his sore legs again. Tasha is on her knees in the booth spinning a carousel of syrups in small glass pitchers and asking Lacey, which one is *regular*.

In less than a minute, a middle-aged woman with yellow hair knotted in a pastry-like swirl at the back of her head is standing at their table, leaning back on her hips, thumping a small notepad against her chest. "You're a DuBerry, alright," she says. "Sugar said I'd know you the minute I set eyes on you. I'm Beanie, and breakfast is on the house, folks. You sure do got your grandaddy's cheekbones—like an Injun—and your sweet mama's eyes."

Introductions are made all around, and Willy can only nod and shake the hand Beanie first wipes on her apron and then offers to him and around the table, even taking Tasha's hand in hers and saying what a pretty little thing she is.

How much would they know about him, about him and May, his complicity, as he has come to think of it recently, in her disappearance and with that thought fresh in his mind he is startled when Beanie turns to him and says, "You're May's husband. I heard that. Hard to believe she was a married woman. Of course, she was so young when she left here."

It stumps Willy to some degree because he isn't her husband—not anymore—but then again, he is, and all of it was so long ago, so far away.

Beanie taps the shoulder of the man sitting behind Lacey. "Uriah, you ain't gonna believe this, but this here is May DuBerry's girl." She is beaming like she has just conjured Lacey out of thin air.

"Well, I'll be," he says, turning to look at her. "I'll be damned." Willy watches the man's jowls shake as he speaks, notices the deep creases in his forehead and the strip of paler skin where his cap had been on his head. Lacey turns in her seat and puts her hand in his gnarled one and he shakes it heartily. "May's baby. I'll be damned."

"And this here is Willy who May married up to Maryland!"

"I want pancakes," says Tasha to Willy. "What are you getting?"

"Ain't seen your mama in more 'n thirty-some years, but I could be looking at her right now," he says. Willy feels oddly relieved to have it confirmed once more that May is not here, that he doesn't have to worry about looking out the big front window and seeing her walk down the street or turn a corner and run smack into her.

"Let me get your order here," says Beanie. "You first, little one."

"Pancakes!" says Tasha. "With regular syrup."

Everyone places orders and Beanie hurries away from their table. Carlotta pats Willy's knee and he places his own hand on top of hers. A moment later Uriah is rising from his table and standing at the end of theirs. His voice is deep and gravelly, but he keeps it low. "It's been a pleasure to meet you all," he says. He stands blinking, working his heavy jowls as if he has caught food behind his teeth. Lacey looks up at him expectantly, waiting. He clears his throat. "Real sorry about your grandfather," he says. "It was a long time ago, but we knowed each other, back in the day."

"I never met him," says Lacey. The old man hesitates, shifts side to side on his widely planted feet. Lacey tells him she knows about the accident, but lets her voice trail, inviting him to fill in the details for her.

Uriah puts his hand to his chin, appears to think on it. "He was a friendly kind of man," says Uriah, and then his voice softens even more. "But alcohol didn't agree with him. Everybody knew it. Nobody held it against him. Had a hard time of things when his wife gone on, I can tell you. Near broke him when she died, that's for sure." He clears his throat. "Not much else to tell, I reckon. He just took a turn with his drinking and then, the accident and all." He lifts his hands as he says this, palms up, and drops them to his pockets. "May was a nice girl," he says. He smiles now and a faraway look sweeps down his face. "I remember her dancing with her daddy over to Jake's. We'd all come in after a big run and stink the place up with the sweat of a long day fishin' and the jukebox would get to goin', soda pop for the kids, liquor for the men, oh, we had ourselves a fine time them days." He shuffles a foot back and forth. "Du would have his girl, May, out there, twirling and swinging her around. Reckon that was about the last time I saw the two of them together. She was just a young thing, maybe twelve, thirteen years old? Oh, sure, we had some good times."

Willy finds himself nodding along as if he knew these things as well, though he didn't, had never thought to ask May about her father, about her mother, about who Lacey's daddy was, about her life here on this island. Always he had just let May talk when she felt like talking about the things she felt like talking about. And he can't help but wonder now if that was selfish of him, if there were things she wanted to tell him but he just never asked and so she never did. Looking back, it didn't seem right that he never asked, especially given how much he asks of Carlotta, always wanting to know about her life in Little Italy with Antonio. Why, just *why* had he never asked these things of May?

He looks over to Carlotta, her eyes wide, her hand reaching across the table to pat Lacey's, her chin dipping and her head cocked, as if she can feel what Lacey must be feeling and can help her absorb the past. And that is just the thing. He never felt he could take on whatever it was May was leaving out, had left behind, and which she was—if he were to be honest—likely hiding from him. There had always been a feeling in his gut that she was spooked somehow, that she had run from something and found herself running smack into him, into Willy, and he couldn't afford to spook her more, or she might turn and run from him, too.

Turns out, she ran anyways.

The breakfast crowd is thinning, and Beanie starts collecting salt and pepper shakers and the ketchup bottles off the table and adding them to her tray.

Willy takes a twenty out of his wallet and slides it under his plate. He is stuffed with pancakes and the sweet residue of maple syrup stays with him. Beanie wouldn't let them pay for the meal. But he wants to make sure the tip is enough to say a proper thanks.

"How long you here for?" Beanie calls from a table in the back corner as he watches Tasha hop down out of the booth and reach for her mother's hand.

"Until Sunday," says Lacey.

"Stop in again," she says. "Best breakfast in town."

Lacey thanks her, Carlotta echoing her gratitude. "Delicious," Carlotta says. "Perfect way to start the day."

The four of them walk down to the corner where they are told there is a shop that rents bicycles. Tasha asks for her own bike, and there are some with training wheels on them, but Lacey says no, this will be safer, but she will teach her to ride a bike when they get back to the farm. For now, she rents a bike with a child carrier seat on the back.

Willy helps her load their towels and sunscreen and a small bucket of sand toys in the bike's basket. He lifts Tasha to the seat, checks her helmet, and waves them off down Howard Street under a canopy of old oaks.

Carlotta takes his arm and they continue down the street. The air is sweet with a scent he doesn't recognize. There are only a few cars on the street and most of them are older models, scabs of rust on the fenders and over the wheel wells. They walk past galleries, ice cream shops, and antiques stores. Carlotta laughs to point out an old percolator coffee pot set in the window of one of the shops. It is flanked by wooden shoe forms and Willy mentions that he has a few of those around, too. At Carlotta's urging, they climb the wooden steps to have a look. The inside of the shop is cool and dark with the only light coming from oddly placed lamps covered in silk shades, the shelves crammed with familiar things, a pile of doilies set on the ledge of an open cupboard next to a stack of dusty books, old blue canning jars—of which he has a full box in his cellar back home—wooden handled tools for punching leather, meat grinders, white porcelain pitchers, an old shaving mug with a ragged soft-bristled brush, and a velvet tufted chair not so different from the one at home in his own parlor. He can't help but wonder briefly if the whole farm was robbed while he has been away and trucked down here to this antiques store. Something bittersweet blooms in his throat when he picks up an old hand drill, turns the smooth handled crank and watches the mechanisms lock together to spin the large bit. All of these artifacts from the past, familiar in a way that draws both memories and a disturbing realization that their time has passed and they are now only objects of curiosity, relics of the way things once were in a time that he can't say for sure was better or worse than where he is now.

Different, just different, is what Carlotta would say, if he were to ask her. He watches her now, opening a child's jewelry box and nearly purring to herself when the tiny ballerina pops up and begins a tinkling pirouette. "I had one just like this as a child," she says to Willy. She opens and closes it two more times before she spies a set of displayed teacups on a coffee table and stoops to pick one up by its thin handle, turns it over in her hand. "I just love this old pattern," she says. It is covered in gold and red roses and tiny blue birds, their wings spread in flight. "But you know, I don't really miss drinking out of them. Too delicate. You ever notice how the porcelain got too hot and by the time it cooled enough to drink from it was cooled too much?" Willy shakes his head, no, he never did. "And they're so thin and shallow, always sloshing over the edges. Beautiful to look at but I prefer something a little heavier these days. Give me a good mug anytime." She sets the cup down gently in its saucer with a wispy sigh. They leave the shop hand in hand, Willy tucking scraps of woken memories away, and head into the sunny day.

CHAPTER 32

A Confession

The water is warmer than Lacey expects. They play at the surf, digging their toes in the sand and making deep footprints and then watching the waves wipe them away as if they'd never been there.

They walk the beach and Tasha stops to squat on her heels like a little samurai facing into the surf, daring the ocean to come at her. A swell of water rolls over her feet and slaps up to her face. She coughs and sputters as Lacey swings her up to her hip and out of harm's way, the water curling and swirling at Lacey's legs.

With Tasha's arms locked around Lacey's neck Lacey swims into the surf with Tasha. Lacey is a strong swimmer, though the ocean is less known to her. She feels its pull taking her out and rolls to her back so that Tasha rests on Lacey's upper body. They swim lazily just outside the breaking waves.

"Can you touch the bottom?" Tasha asks her.

"Nope, but I'm a good swimmer," she says. "I've got you."

"Did your mommy teach you?"

"No, honey. She couldn't swim very well." And it is an odd thought to her. Her mother, having grown up on the water and yet never learning to swim. "She tried. She just never could do it." It is strange to her to think of it now, the way her mother was constantly wading into the pond, sometimes even in colder weather, wading hip deep, chest deep. Lacey can remember watching her, the straight set of her back when she walked into the pond, and once, as she recalls now, even with her shoes on. But then she would always stop, sometimes not even turning around but just backing her way back up to the bank.

"Can you teach me to swim?"

"Not here," says Lacey. "But Willy taught me how to swim back at the farm. This water is too rough to learn to swim in," she explains. "But you can learn in the pond just like I did. Maybe we'll have him teach you, too."

They build a sandcastle with an elaborate moat and Tasha pronounces it a grand success when a foamy wave slips up to its edge and pours down the well that circles their creation, runs through it, and rushes back out to sea without damaging the castle.

Just as Lacey is applying a second coat of sunscreen, her hands working gently over the port under Tasha's skin, the tips of her fingers carefully running the edges of it, imagining that it will one day be nothing more than a scar that Tasha can boast of to her friends—*oh, that. I had cancer as a child, but I'm fine now*—just as she flips the top with a snap back on the tube, Lacey points to the surf.

A pod of dolphins is threading their way just beyond the breaking of the waves. They leap and arc, slip-stitching along the surface and falling with splashless grace back into the water. Lacey takes Tasha's hand and walks to the surf where they squint to track their journey along the shore's edge.

For a late lunch, they eat fried shrimp on a picnic bench outside one of the small restaurants in town and follow it up with ice cream. Lacey notices the freckles now sprinkling Tasha's nose, and while she knows the sun to be an insidious thing, she is happy to see the bloom of freckles, this evidence of a day played out under sunshine.

Once back at the cottage, they are welcomed by a platter of peanut butter cookies. The beds have been made and fresh white towels are folded and set on an old steamer trunk outside the bathroom door. Tasha heads straight for the cookies.

"Only one now, and you can have more after your bath."

"I don't have to take baths on vacation."

"Says who?"

When Willy comes to the door, Tasha rambles on and on about their day, telling him about the dolphins and the sandcastle and swimming in the ocean. She takes his hand and pulls him across the porch to bring him into the cottage and show him the platter of cookies. "Can Willy have one?"

"Of course."

"Sugar brung us some, too," he says. He lets his eyes scan the room, and Lacey watches him carefully. "Place looks just like ours," he says.

Lacey relaxes, slides down into a chair and offers him a seat across from her.

"Carlotta and me picked up some scallops in town. She's making a fuss over supper right now." He sits across from her and she slides the plate of cookies to him, but he shakes his head, no. He's saving room for dinner. Never had scallops before and Carlotta promises him he will like them, though he's not so sure.

Tasha asks if she can go over and visit with Carlotta. The door to the porch slams at her back. Lacey rises and watches from the doorway, making sure she doesn't dawdle at the water or wander off course in that way she tends to. She comes back to the table and sits down across from Willy, flips her hand to the room. "No ghosts," she says.

"Nah," he says. "It's nice here."

"Are you glad you came?"

"Wouldn't say that," he says. "But not sorry, neither." He smiles. "How about you? Is it what you wanted?"

"Yes and no." She takes another cookie and considers. "God, get these away from me," she says, sliding the plate toward him.

He looks to her expectantly, waiting for an answer.

"Not sure what I wanted." She brushes her hair from her face. "No, that's not true. I guess I wanted to get to know her through this place. But it was so long ago and there isn't much of her here. And I get the sense that everything's changed so much over the years."

He lifts his hands from his lap, threads the fingers together, and brings them down with a small *thunk* on the table. "Some things I been thinking on," he says. He clears his throat, brings his hands back to his lap where he runs them up and down his thighs as if he is working the kinks out. "I should've gone after her, Lacey. I should've done that, and I been thinking on just why I didn't."

"I know, you said you thought she'd come back. I did, too."

"That's true," he says, "but maybe not the whole truth. See, I got to taking care of you, trying to figure on how to take care of you, and . . ." He stops, swallows so hard Lacey can hear it, see the rise and fall in his throat. "Things had been a little rough, you know, before she left." He blinks hard, once, twice, lets his eyes fall and stay that way for the length of a heavy breath, opens them directly to her. "She was acting strangely, wandering around the house in dirty clothes, not wanting to leave the house, sometimes dragging you around like she couldn't let you out of her sight and other times clear forgetting you were around at all, and I'd ask after you and she'd act like it was none of her concern, where you was or what you was up to."

Lacey considers this and a trickle of memory drips in. Yes, she remembers this, the way she would find May, knee deep in the pond and she would call to her and still she wouldn't answer, wouldn't turn around and look at her. Other times she'd make Lacey follow her from room to room, upstairs to make the beds, back down to check the locks on the door, back up to finish pulling up the bedcovers, down to the cellar with her to do the washing, out to the barn to check on Willy, her hand gripping at Lacey, pulling her along, clawed to her.

"The worst of it was her quiet," he says now. "Quiet like I never seen in her. She had nothing to say to me. Couple days before she took off, we had a hell of a row, and then after, she didn't have nothing to say to me." He drops his head and then lifts it again. "I got after her some about not taking good care of you," he confesses. "You was running around dirty, wearing the same clothes for days, once still in your pajamas when I come down in the afternoon. No food in the house, no supper on the table, no coffee in the morning. Even gettin' rude with Virgie, telling her maybe she ought not to be coming over without calling first and she ought to know that was just common courtesy." He shakes his head side to side. "After all that woman done for her."

Lacey thinks on this. There is a haze to it all, but she can see Aunt Virgie standing in the kitchen with a look of hurt on her face, her chest rising and falling, the way Virgie ran her hands down over Lacey's shoulders, held her to her, and her mother, her mother so angry, pulling Lacey from Virgie. Then, Willy coming down from the barn and walking into the middle of it, looking from May to Virgie, and his eyes settling on Lacey, maybe seeing the confusion that was digging into her. "What's going on here?" he had said. Virgie had looked to him as if she wanted to ask something of him, opened her mouth to say something but nothing came out and then May pointing at her, saying she was *meddlin' in what wasn't none of her business.*

After Virgie left, May and Willy had gotten into an argument, the only one Lacey ever remembers between the two of them. The whole time, May held tight to her hand, gripping it so hard Lacey's fingers tingled with numbness, and finally May had stormed from the room, Lacey locked to her by a fierce grip, dragging Lacey up the stairs and running a bath, stripping off her clothes so hard that Lacey felt the hard drag of them at her skin, her shirt pulled over her head and her ears peeling under the tug of her shirt.

"Thing is," he says now, "after she took off and I started taking care of you, well, I almost got afraid she *would* come back—but not for me, Lacey. Not for both of us. Just for *you.*" He looks directly at her, as if he is owning up to a terrible crime. "I was afraid she'd take you away," he admits, and with this confession he slumps in his chair, swipes his hand across the tabletop. "She didn't seem fit, you know, to take care of you."

Lacey doesn't know what to say to this. Doesn't know how she is supposed to feel. The late afternoon sun is slipping in the sky and bears hard at her through the window, causing her to shift in her chair. But something has turned on its head and the light has caught her memories in a way that illuminates the corners, the crevices, the cracks she has been trying to fill.

"Maybe she wasn't," she says. She remembers now, looking from her bedroom window to an early spring day filled with promise, sunshine, the rise and fall of the men's voices turning out the cattle after milking, the earthy rich smell of the barn drifting back to her, and turning from the brightness to see her mother at the doorway, her face blank and shadowy, her fingers kneading into knots, her mother on the edge of something lifeless and raw. "Maybe she wasn't fit to take care of me. Maybe, Willy, you did the right thing," and in offering this up, this absolution, she feels a rush of gratitude that she hadn't seen coming, knows now the unsteady feeling she had around May the last weeks, as if May wobbled between two worlds and either dragged Lacey along or forgot her altogether.

She reaches across the table and takes his hand in hers. It's so big, has always been so big around hers. She squeezes and he lifts his other hand from his lap, places it over hers. She knows now that she had been miraculously caught in the depths of a fall, cushioned by this man with the deepest of hearts.

Willy says the jury is out on scallops, even though he ate everything on his plate and helped himself to the last few remaining in the pan. Tasha refused to even try them, but Carlotta had prepared a pasta dish with an agreeable aioli sauce and Tasha devoured it.

They sit on the porch at a weather-beaten picnic table that jiggles when Tasha leans on it. Lacey and Carlotta sip their wine.

"Okay," says Lacey, smiling and draining the last of her wine. "Better get this one back for a bath."

"No bath," says Tasha.

"You go on and get that bath and I'll come over and read more to you from our book," Willy offers.

Walking back to their cottage, they spy Sugar on her front porch and wave to her, Lacey shouting out a thank you for the cookies.

She draws a tepid bath, mindful of the pink blush of sunburn Tasha now has on her back and shoulders. At one point, Tasha tries to re-create the ocean's waves and sloshes water over the side of the tub. "Easy," says Lacey, but she really doesn't mind. It's reflexive, like telling her to be careful at the pond's edge.

By the time Willy arrives Tasha is in her pajamas and has dragged a pillow and blanket inside the wardrobe where she plans to hunker down and listen to Willy's reading. Her animals are set around her, a small audience of blank, beady-eyed stares. In trying to climb into the massive wardrobe, Tasha had tried to pull out the bottom drawer to make a sort of step, but the drawer was truly sealed by the humidity, swollen shut just as Sugar said it was. She clambered up in with a little boost from Willy and settled in the corner.

Lacey takes a shower while Willy reads and then slips into her sleeping shirt and her robe. The reading goes on for a long time and she can hear the rise and fall of his voice. She digs in her bag for a pair of warm socks and can hear him, stopping the reading to answer one of Tasha's questions that may or may not have anything to do with the story itself. She can hear bits and pieces and can tell he is at the part where the young sisters find the body of Aslan bound and muzzled. She worries that it will frighten Tasha the way she herself had been frightened by it as a young girl. *If you've been up all night and cried till you have no more tears left in you . . .* She goes to the refrigerator and takes out a bottle of white wine, her mind pulled by a thread back to the conversation she had earlier with Willy . . . *you will know that there comes in the end a sort of quietness.* Her mother's leaving had always been the thing never spoken of. *You feel as if nothing was ever going to happen again.* Her mother's disappearance had tamped down a mysterious hush over all the years that followed. And then, this other thing—Tasha getting sick—had shifted the weight of her leaving, had changed the way it draped her, and Lacey believes now that she has outgrown the way she wore her grief. Or perhaps it never fit her properly in the first place.

She pours her wine and takes it to the table. Willy is still reading, and she can't believe Tasha is still awake. When he comes from the room a few minutes later there is a sheepish look on his face. "She's asleep in that dang wardrobe," he says. "Not sure how long she's been out like that. I just kept reading and plumb missed her nodding off."

Lacey smiles. "She's exhausted. I'm not surprised."

"I can move her to the bed," he offers. But she waves him off, noticing the stiff way he is carrying himself, the way he has been rubbing his knees all evening. "She's wanted to sleep in that thing since we got here. I'll just move her when I go to bed. Glass of wine?"

"Nah, thanks. I better head back."

"Dinner was great," she says. "Tell Carlotta I said so." He pats her back as he moves past her, his hand *scritch*ing at the fabric of her robe, and tucks the book under his arm. She watches him steady himself on the railing as he descends the steps.

A moment later there is a loud creak from Tasha's bedroom, like that of a heavy tree limb preparing to fall, and then just as quickly she hears a deep *thunk* as if a heavy window has slammed. Lacey jumps from her chair, tipping it over and runs into Tasha's room. At first nothing looks amiss but when she looks to the wardrobe, she can see that the bottom of the wardrobe has collapsed under Tasha's weight. Shockingly, Tasha barely wakes, tired as she is, though she has been dumped to the farthest corner of it. Lacey scoops her out and lays her in her bed. After removing the blanket and pillows from the wardrobe and covering Tasha, she assesses the damage.

The whole back left side of the bottom of the wardrobe has collapsed into the drawer below it and is now wedged in there. There is no way Lacey can slip even a finger in there to try and pull it up, and the drawer below it is now firmly locked in place by the bottom corner piece that has wedged itself into it.

In the kitchen she looks for a tool of sorts that she might use to pry the floor of the wardrobe up. She rejects a couple of sharp knives and picks up a long metal spatula. If she can slide it down the back of the wardrobe, she might be able to flip up the floor piece.

Just as she is making her way back to the bedroom, her phone rings. It is Cade and she settles on the sofa, spatula in hand, to tell him just what she is dealing with. He tells her to leave it, he will fix it when he gets there, but she can only imagine Sugar spying the destruction tomorrow while they are out, and the guilt is too much. She drops her voice to a whisper and carries the phone and spatula back into the room to further assess the destruction.

"I think I can do this," she says, but it is nearly impossible with the phone wedged between ear and shoulder. "I'll call you back in five," she says, and sets the phone down on the floor beside her as she works the spatula down the interior of the cabinet and under the wedged wood. There isn't much room to maneuver and it is difficult to get any leverage, but eventually she manages to pry the corner up and with a small twist of her wrist, the whole piece shoots up out of the corner. She jiggles the drawer below, and to her surprise there is a small pop, and she is able, with some effort, to pull it out with a screech that makes Tasha roll over in her sleep.

The drawer holds a small musty blanket that releases its sharp odor immediately. It looks to be a baby blanket and has large, loopy crochet stitches. Next to it is a pair of women's black patent leather pumps, scuffed at the heels, the vinyl peeling back in strips. She pulls the drawer completely free of the wardrobe and tries to set it back in again, but every time she slides it to close, it jams on something. Pulling the drawer out again, she uses her phone as a flashlight and, on all fours now, leans in to look for the obstruction.

Wedged far in the back is what looks to be a bound book. She reaches deeply into the depths of the wardrobe and pulls it out. The book is about five by eight inches, with a stamped red leather cover in a sort of paisley design. It is nearly an inch thick, and a pale green mold clings to the corners of it and along the spine.

She recognizes it immediately. But it is wholly impossible that this artifact should be here, this place that she knows May never returned to. She lifts the book from its mildewed grave, turns it in her hand, flips the pages with her thumb, and the sharp odor assaults her. It is not possible. Everything she knows, everything she has carefully dusted off in her memory these last months and tucked away with a kind of reverence is spinning into chaos. Her life without May had been like the scrap of black paper trailing from the cutting of a silhouette, the subject inadvertently discarded and only the negative space left in its place. But this discovery, this dropping down of May's shadow, shifts that space like a trick of the light.

She opens the book and begins to read.

CHAPTER 33

Everything Is as It Should Be

Willy reaches his cottage and climbs the steps to Carlotta. She is waiting for him, a glass of cool water and two aspirin in her hand. Willy reaches out and takes them without questioning her, swallows and thanks her. She takes the glass from his hand and sets it beside the sink. He goes to the sofa and lowers himself slowly. "Come sit beside me," he says.

She sits, nods a head to his shoulder. "This has been fun," she says. "Thank you for inviting me."

Willy gives a small laugh. "Seems more like you invited me," he says, placing a kiss on her head. "And I'm glad you did." He is being truthful. Being here isn't at all what he expected. There's been an odd reconciliation in his mind, part of it having to do with the fact that May isn't here, isn't a specter waiting to pop out at him, and part of it having to do with having settled some sort of truth between him and Lacey earlier. He doesn't feel absolved, isn't even sure if that's what he wants. No, there is a layer of guilt that still weighs on him, but he has begun to feel that he can stretch his hands out from under the crush of it all, working his fingers toward whatever lies beyond the rubble.

Carlotta leans forward and pulls the coffee table closer to him. "Put your legs up, darlin'. Give that aspirin a chance to work."

"Aw, it ain't too bad," he says, but lifts his legs anyway.

"What should we do tomorrow?" she asks. "Visit that old British cemetery we walked by today? Might be interesting. And there's a light-house we could drive to. Maybe we could eat dinner out?"

"Anything you want," he says. He reminds her that Cade is expected tomorrow. He is suddenly struck by how that will feel, what they will look like walking through town, people mistaking their little party for three generations—grandparents, parents and child—a lineage, all on vacation together. "Anything you want," he says again, and his chest expands with the possibilities.

CHAPTER 34

In the Pages

December 18, 1972
My heart feels like it's all stretched out, working out the kinks it got from being tied up in a knot for so long . . .

Lacey begins reading cross-legged on the floor, leaning back against the old wardrobe, the musty smell still rising around her, but the light is dim and the writing is so small, in some places nearly indecipherable. After a few pages, after flipping back and forth through the pages, noticing the different colors of the inks, the way the script goes from small to smaller, Lacey gets up off the floor of Tasha's room, grabbing her phone from the floor beside her, flicks out the light, and heads for the sofa. Some of the pages are mildewed and hard to read, and sometimes May has written in a script so small that Lacey wishes she had a magnifying glass to read it.

She has to keep going back and rereading sections because it isn't making any sense to her at first.

Who'd you whore around with, May? I done ask every last man on the island and no one's got a clue who the little bastard's daddy is . . .

The words have a surprising sting in them, even on paper, and Lacey flinches as if she is actually still perched on her mother's hip and the words are smattering into her.

> *It was kind of a funny situation I was finding myself in, I explained to Aunt Virgie. I couldn't let Daddy know Little Jim beat me, cause Daddy would surely kill him. And I couldn't let Little Jim know the truth about Lacey, cause he'd kill Daddy.*

Lacey has to read it again.

> *And I couldn't let Little Jim know the truth about Lacey, cause he'd kill Daddy. And in all that mess—of one wanting to kill the other—no one would really be doing it for the reasons they would claim. No one was watching out for my honor. They was just men watching out for their property and willing to kill each other on account of who owned the parts of me.*

An unexpected wind is kicking up over the sound and through the screen door, bringing with it the salty musky scent of low tide. A queasiness brews in her stomach as she continues.

> *Aunt Virgie says that I am never ever to go back to the island. Furthermore, neither Daddy nor Little Jim are ever coming to carry me back, not ever, she says. He is no longer her brother, she says to me. He is dead to her.*

Startled by the ring of her phone in her robe pocket, Lacey jumps up, the vibration of it synced to the swoosh of the wind, and fishes it out of her pocket, holds it to her ear and waits, unable to answer, her mind still back on the pages.

"Lacey?"

"Hmm?"

"You didn't call back. Everything okay?"

She doesn't hear him, isn't paying attention.

"What's wrong?" he asks.

"Nothing. I'm fine." But as she says it, even as she tries to believe it, the full weight of what she is reading is bearing down on her, prickling through her flesh and wriggling under her skin.

"I found something," she says. "Something weird, Cade. I found my mother's diary. The one she kept when I was a kid."

"What diary, where?"

"Here!"

"What?"

"Yeah." She drops her head into her hand, presses the phone harder to her ear. "It doesn't make any sense. Doesn't make any sense at all. She never came back here. I don't know why it's here."

Cade thinks maybe someone else left it there, maybe it's not May's diary at all—is she sure it is? How does she know, has she read any of it? Is she *sure* it is her mother's? Is she *sure* she never came back?

Yes, yes, it's hers and she is reading it now, but it's confusing. She looks at it now, the pages open, the script so pretty, so small, looping the pages, her writing extending far into the margins, the lines of writing squished up against one another so that the letters from one line to the next are almost touching.

The next entry is written in pencil, smudged and faded. She can't concentrate on it while on the phone to Cade.

September 2, 1974

It's been a long time since I last wrote. After that time last year when Little Jim come to the store and I had to tell Aunt Virgie about him and about Daddy, too, well, I just lost the heart for writing anything down anymore. Seems I couldn't avoid looking at the truth once it came from my lips—but I sure didn't want to write about it.

Cade tells Lacey to enjoy reading it. It will be fun to get to know her mother this way, through a journal. Who cares how it got there? That's not the point, is it? She was lucky to find it, he tells her.

Lacey knows he doesn't understand, doesn't know what is rising off the pages. She asks him when he thinks he will get here tomorrow but she is distracted and asks him again before they hang up. She reminds him that the last ferry is at six o'clock, and he says that won't be a problem. He's leaving at 5:00 a.m.

Lately I have begun to feel good inside, like a quamishness is being cut out of me. I still have some worries now and then, like the fact that Little Jim has been seen in town at least two times that I know of yet.

Quamishness—Lacey has never seen the word in print, never even heard it again after May disappeared from her life, but she remembers it now. Especially toward the end (what she thinks of now as the end). May would say she was feeling quamish, sick to her stomach. There were other words, too, funny ways of saying things, odd words that were never uttered again in the house after she left. Lacey can't think of any of them now, but they are there, hanging in the air, wavering just outside of reach of her tongue.

The more she reads, the more the pieces of her mother begin to flicker. She begins to see May again for the first time in a very long time. Lacey can see her rolling out pie crust on the counter, flour swiping her cheeks, her forehead. She can see her in the white bathrobe, sashed like a princess at the waist. And Lacey can see May run her hand along the back of Willy's neck while he sits in the parlor chair, Lacey in his lap, and reading *Blueberries for Sal* for the fifteenth time.

She also begins to remember the look in her mother's eyes shortly before she left, a hunted rabbit. May was exhausted. Lacey can remember that now. The way May's hair was flying around her face all the time and the way she would drag herself through the bedrooms in the morning half-heartedly pulling up the bedcovers.

Hours later, and still Lacey is only halfway through it, so difficult it is to decipher, and she keeps flipping back through the pages to reread an earlier entry, let it settle with her in a different way, with her stomach churning and her bladder squeezed into a knot. She hears Tasha call out for her.

She rises off the sofa, the muscles of her legs aching as if they haven't moved in hours, and quite possibly they haven't, but have remained curled beneath her, and she goes into Tasha's room. The sight of Tasha in her bed, awake, but still flirting with the remnants of a dream, stops her for a second at the doorway. Tasha is too vulnerable, too ripe, half-asleep and floating between two worlds and trusting Lacey to keep her safe in both of them.

"Mommy?"

"I'm right here."

"I'm thirsty."

"I'll get you some water."

"Can I have a cookie?"

"No cookies at night, sweetie," she says, and Lacey is amazed at the way her own voice sounds so calm coming from her, so certain, so much like a mother's voice cloaked in reason. She goes to the kitchen and takes a bottled water off the counter, squeezing off the top as she heads back into the bedroom and hands it to her. Lacey sits down on the edge of the bed and watches her drink, her lips puckering over the mouth of the bottle, her head tipping back, her throat pale and tender as she swallows. The bottle still to her mouth, her eyes tracking to Lacey.

"What's the matter?" Tasha asks her, handing the half-finished bottle back to her and tilting her face to the side.

"Nothing. What do you mean—what's the matter?"

"You look funny."

"I'm tired, sweetie."

Tasha reaches up with both her hands and holds them to the sides of Lacey's face. "Me, too," she sighs. "We're almost like twins, aren't we, Mommy? We think the same things." Tasha drops her head back to the pillow and Lacey kisses her on the forehead, pressing her lips hard as she does so, and then rises from her side.

"Mommy?" she calls as Lacey is reaching the doorway. "Don't be sad, okay? It will make me sad, too, if you get sad."

"I'm not sad, Tasha. Go to sleep now," she says softly. And truthfully, she isn't really sad. Though there is a kind of numbness descending. She takes the book from the sofa and carries it with her to the bathroom where she brushes her teeth, scrubbing at the gumminess in her mouth, and climbs into bed, begins to read again.

April 30, 1975

There is a wretched smell come over me from the road and my heart is cracking in places for want of Lacey and Willy. How I come to be here is a long story. I don't know where the beginning is but I know I have had some time now to think of it and it begun long afore I even started writing down in this book. So I will start with yesterday.

Yesterday Willy dropped me to the market. I had my marketing list right here in my book, and it was a big one, giving as I been neglecting my chores and such and we had days ago run out of most everything. Well, of course I had Lacey with me and I was figuring on her amusing herself with little Franny for a while so I could concentrate on my marketing. Franny is only five, but already Marybeth and Jed got her set to chores in the store and her and Lacey will do things like stamp price stickers on the canned goods—though the stamping gun has to be held with two hands while the other child holds the can steady—or they will take all the empty crates out back behind the store, though they can barely carry one at a time and Lacey has got splinters in her fingers afore for carrying them. Jed always gives them a soda pop and a box of JuJuBes when they're done and they like to sit on the back stoop or play at the stream out back.

Took me near an hour to do my marketing, as I figured it would, and I had said to Willy to pick me up near four as that would give him time for us to get back to the farm for evening chores and I could still get a good meal on. I told him I would fix chicken-fried steak, mashed potatoes, stewed tomatoes that Aunt Virgie put up last summer, and some of them bread and butter pickles he likes so much. He asked me do I got any dill pickles put up, but no, I only got the sweet ones and the bread and butter ones, which he likes fine anyway. I probably sounded irritable when I told him that, but I was trying to make things up to him and it didn't seem like he was going to make anything easy for me. I said I would make some biscuits, too, and did he want buttermilk or baking powder? He said he didn't know the difference so make what I like. That kind of stuck in my craw, as I have worked terrible hard at learning to make the two kinds. But I didn't say anything.

Well, Lacey and Franny got to playing out back of the store down by the stream, which ain't at all deep so it is fine by me. Willy always gets fussing be-cause she comes home with her feet and shoes all wet and he says she is going to get sick but I got my feet wet near every day of my life and I don't think I ever had a cold, just bellyaches I'm sure got nothing to do with wet feet.

So I finished my marketing and I wheeled my shopping cart out the front of the store and around to the lot on the side of the building. Jed sent a boy to help me, but I said no. I was going to have to wait a spell for Willy right here in the lot. The boy offered to go get Lacey from round back, but I said no to this also as I was only waiting and I could get her from round back once Willy come by.

I knowed better. Or I should of. But at the time I can only say I was feel-ing better, feeling like maybe the darkness come over me lately was lifting. My mind was off thinking of the supper I would fix, and the turn in the weather of late that was keeping Willy in the fields longer into the evening, the way the days was stretching out some and maybe I could shuck off the nastiness what done got to me this winter.

It was just like I blinked and Daddy was there. His truck pulled up so the bumper was against my knees and my back was to the clapboard siding of the store. He told me to get on in and where was the baby? He took my bags from the cart and started putting them in the truck behind his seat. He smashed them in there hard so I felt sure he done broke my eggs and smashed up all my bread and bananas.

Lana McDowell pulled up at the front of the lot and nodded to me as she went to get her baby from the basket she got strapped in her car. I felt shame wash down me like scalding water and I could not look at her.

I scooted from the front of the truck, feeling the bumper skimming my legs, and went round on the passenger side thinking I could scoot by, but Daddy got hisself out of the truck, went behind the back of it, and came round fast so he was right up on me afore I knew it.

He tells me get on in, May. He says I ain't no damn fool and I know he ain't going to hurt me. Then he looks round the lot like he's looking for something lost and asks me again where's the baby? I told him I didn't know where she was, and he asks me what kinda lame-ass mother I'm trying to be not knowing where the hell is my baby and this is exactly why it's time for me to quit acting like a jackass pretending to be all growed up when I can't even take good care of my own baby.

I told him she was with Willy, not back at the farm, but in Harrisburg, long way from here, running errands and such.

He laid his hand to my shoulder real firm and clamped there like a clamshell got hold of me and tells me he ain't never hurt me and he ain't going to hurt me now, but I should do as I am told as he is my father and that is what Mama would want of me. There was a buzzing in my brain, but even through it I could hear Lacey's and Franny's shouts behind the store.

He says, well, makes no difference. Important thing is to get me home and drive some sense back into me. We can take care of the baby later.

The door of the truck is open now and all around me I see the people I have come to know here. Mrs. Carter from church is being dropped at the door by her husband. Moose Braggart is loading up his momma's car. Doc Asher is walking into the bank across the street. Mrs. Olsen is scooting three of her children into the store while another hangs from her neck and wipes his nose on the collar of her shirt.

None of these people is looking right at me, but I know they see me. They see Daddy. They see his hand on my shoulder and they know what it means. They know what I done. It is of no matter to them if I step into this truck and disappear forever out of their lives. They know I don't belong here with decent people who make lemon cake and pickle beets and plant marigolds and whitewash fences and scrub linoleum and fiddle at weddings and read stories to their children. I can do all those things back to Ocracoke—they ain't saying I ain't capable. They're just saying I don't belong here doing those things with them. I can see it mostly in the way they <u>don't</u> look at me. They just flip their hand hello and look strangely to me. But they don't really see me.

The shame was a fire on my face. I felt like I been playing a make-believe game and forgot it weren't real. Even through the hornets in my head, I could hear Lacey's voice around the corner. Everything else was just noise, but her voice was sweet and clear as church bells on Sunday morning. I heard her shout to Franny, who must of been downstream from her, if she can come back and play at the farm and she will ask her momma if it's okay and Franny can see the new calves.

Warm air was coming from the cab of the truck. It was thick and sour. The floor was covered in sand and corn chips and an empty quart bottle of

Pabst. Daddy says be a good girl and get on in. Do as I am told. We will come back for the baby later, he says.

Right then I heard Lacey shout—I'll go ask my momma! Daddy's hand was still clamped on my shoulder and I could smell salt and mullet blood and the sticky-sweet liquor he chased with the beer, but most of all I could hear the gravel beneath Lacey's feet and I knew she would turn the corner, fly right on in at me and pound her body against mine. Her arms would wrap round my legs and she would breathe all raggedy in and out and ask me if please, please, please can Franny come back to the farm with us? She would bounce on her toes and tilt her head up to mine and plead with me—say yes, say yes!

And that's when I knew for sure, if Daddy don't get me and her now, he will just keep on trying. He will always come back. He will always be at the edges of my life trying to haul me back into his, no matter where I am.

That was when I got on in, the sound of Lacey's feet busting out through that parking lot. I didn't want her to see me, didn't want Daddy to see her. I shut the door myself and slunk on down deep in the seat. Daddy stumbled round to the driver's side looking mighty proud of hisself, but surprised, too. He told me I was a good girl and don't worry none about the baby. We will get her later.

I never opened my eyes to see if Lacey come flying around the corner. I just squeezed them shut and prayed she wouldn't see me.

Just go, Daddy. Just go. And the truck shot out on the street so hard my head flew back against the seat. And just like that my life is gone behind me.

I cried the first hours down, but then I was all cried out. I am dry as dirt now. No tears. I done did this to myself. Daddy near run us off the road three, four times and every time that truck started to go I would just grit my teeth and wish it to keep on going, right on off into the lines of trees or over the rails of one of them long bridges where I could just sink on down to the bottom of the water that run under it.

Now it is nearly morning. We are stopped by the ferry waiting for it to take us over. Daddy is speaking with Bob Kreen. I know he ain't got no money to pay our way and I am not telling him I got twelve dollars in my pocketbook. I am slumped against the door trying to gather up the early morning light for to write by. Mr. Kreen don't know I'm here, else he would come to say hello. I told Daddy not to tell no one yet. I said we'd make a surprise of it. I cannot bear to look no one in the eye. He parked far back in the empty lot, thinking a surprise is a good idea.

The seagulls are cawing and screeching, swooping down into the gravel lot and flipping back into the sky. One large dirty gull with a twisted wing, trailing a three-foot line of fishing wire, struts beside the truck, looking at me with a cold round eye like he is welcoming me back to hell.

It's morning now, sun full up. I fell asleep in the truck whiles we rode the ferry. I guess my mind just give up and shut down. Daddy rode the wash the whole way back home rather than take the new highway. I heard the tires slurp at the ocean and the whole truck was leaning into the sea driving that whole long way. All manner of shorebirds got throwed up along the way. Mr. Lane used to drive me and Sugar along the beach when we was girls just for the pure adventure of it.

The house here is oddly cold and the wind is whipping up, making the yaupon bushes bend down all around, but I am careful to stay away from the window. I don't want the Lanes to know I'm here. At first, when we came down the drive past Sugar's house, I wanted to leap from the truck and run to her and Miss Bunny, but the shame of what is happening here makes me more likely to crawl under the house instead.

When I was a little girl I used to crawl under the house whenever I need- ed the dark and quiet of it. Most times it was just cause it was so damn hot everywhere else. But sometimes it was cause Daddy was acting odd again, being mixed up and not knowing what he done the night before. Sometimes he'd have blood on his face or hands and Mama'd be worried. She'd be fussing and trying to get him to think it over—like was he at the ice house—was he packing last night. The ice house was open near all night and Daddy worked it when he couldn't get out on a boat. But not getting out on the water sometimes got him to drinking earlier, too. Then he'd get confused and Mama would worry he'd gone and done something.

Swamp didn't like Daddy in a mood, neither. He would crawl under the house on his belly and he would let me put my head on him and I could lay there looking at the floor joists which was more like little rafters in my underneath world. Me and Swamp would be under the house watching spiders in the rafters with the pine needles spread out like a blanket of cool under our backs. I would imagine I would get no bigger and could live under the house forever. I dearly wish for another living body aside of Daddy in this house right now and I am sad that Swamp is long gone.

Daddy was telling me the whole way down the beach about how when we get the baby back everything will be just like it used to be. He calls me Ruthie sometimes, but I don't say nothing about it.

He has been sleeping in his chair near four or five hours now. I have reconsidered off and on going on over to Sugar's but I know Daddy will not give up coming for me and it feels like it would require some explaining I can't explain—to tell them why I am here and why I don't want to be and why I got in that damn truck and why, why, why. I am mostly fearful that he will get Lacey here. Also, truth be told, I am tarred in a layer of something disgraceful I can not peel off of me without ripping the very skin I'm in. I know now in what ways I brung this on myself.

It is not as if I don't remember crawling into Mama's bed. I know I got in that first time to find the smell of her, to feel the warm of where she used to lay, but the only warm was coming off of Daddy and I kept inching into it until I had curled into him. He smelled like Mama's soap from his bath that morning. I should have knowed better. Daddy put his arm over me and I tried to find comfort in that. When he rolled over on top of me and kicked my legs apart, it was as if a beast had come to life atop me. I did not know what was happening, only that I could not breathe and I could not move him from me. I felt his hands working down there, fumbling round, and I thought if I could just say something, work some words up out of me. When the pain came it was like nothing I ever felt before. I truly did not know what part of him could be tearing me in two like that. I thought surely this is how I would die, with my body split in two and my insides shredded.

When he moved off me I dared hardly remember to breathe again. I took tiny little breaths, barely enough to keep me conscious, for fear of waking the monster again. I did not move. I lay there the rest of the night, so still I could almost believe I had turned to stone. A sticky wetness came from me all through the night and puddled up cold under my bottom.

When Les Tate banged on the door that morning and Daddy rose up he said nothing to me in the bed next to him. He pulled on his long johns and then his oilskins, cinched them hard and left the house, leaving just a trail of heavy sighs and grunts from the bed to the door. I was froze there a long time after, feeling the ache where he had been and afraid to see what he had done to me.

Daddy didn't come home that night, or the next, and I knew I had done something terrible to send him away from me.

Daddy is squirming some in his chair now. I must put this book away now, for I wouldn't want him poking in here.

It is after one o'clock in the morning, Lacey notices when she looks at her phone. She has arrived at the last entry. The next page is blank, and the next, and the next. She closes the book, pounds her head back on the pillow, opens the book again at the beginning, flipping through the pages, stopping now and again to puzzle something out.

I asked him real casual like, was he sure it was Little Jim who was seen in town? Because maybe it was just a stranger with a similar truck. I was thinking, of course, that it could have been Daddy again, and truthfully I would have rather it be Little Jim than Daddy hunting me down again.

It's not that Lacey doesn't understand what she has read. It's that she doesn't want to, is searching for another way in and out of it all, a way that points in any direction but the one she is pointed toward. And farther down.

I wanted to tell her that I <u>know</u> it is Daddy and not Little Jim and has anybody actually seen Little Jim? I started to say all this to her but then I couldn't say no more. There is something so shameful deep inside of me that makes me not want to say out loud that it is my own daddy hunting me down like this and for what reason that would be I cannot even say out loud.

There is a sickness rising in Lacey's stomach that she has kept at bay by sheer force of will and her head is aching perhaps as much from the late hour and the thirst that she has only now noticed as from the contents of the book in her hands. Still there are so many questions that gnaw at the possibility of sleep. And the question remains, just what happened to her mother? It is cruel of her, the specter of her that rises in her mind's eye, to have left just this much of her and so much unanswered. But May was here, in this house, and now this is the last that Lacey knows of her and it is, Lacey clearly understands, more than she knew of May before, maybe more than she wanted to know, and it has turned everything on its head, making what was known before wobble against what she is coming to understand. The nausea is rolling through her stomach but she refuses to give in to it, breathes deeply between her teeth and stills it so that she can rise carefully from the bed to relieve her twisted bladder and gingerly sip some water at the bathroom sink, right from the faucet.

Once back in bed, she puts her head down and finds herself sinking into a restless sleep, waking every hour or so to flip her pillow, throw the covers off, pull them up. There are dreams but they are rooted in the here and now, this house, these waters, this room, and so when she wakes a last time just before dawn, she is certain she has not slept at all.

The first morning cup of coffee hits her stomach hard and sets her hands to shaking. She has no desire to eat but takes a cookie to the front porch just to get something in her stomach and absorb all that is grumbling below her waist. It is early and Tasha is still asleep, the sun barely rising without any fanfare at all. There is nothing promising about the light that seeps pale and gray through a thick mist and over the lawn. She goes back to her room and picks up the book, the mustiness rising out of it again. She could smell it on her hands when she slept—or didn't—all through the night.

She takes it to the porch with her coffee and her phone, knowing it is too early to call anyone, knowing there is no one to call, but it makes her feel less alone somehow, to touch her phone, like she carries a small lifeline should she need it. She swings her legs over the bench of the picnic table, feeling the bare wood rough against the backs of her thighs and thumbs through the book from back to front, watching the flip of different colored pens and pencil lines, once, twice, and then her thumb snags on a small gap at the very end of the book where pages have been folded in half lengthwise against the spine. She opens the book and absentmindedly unfolds the pages. There is another entry—a hidden one, undated, but written in the same ink as the last entry she had read the night before—at the back of the book.

The moon is sitting way up high in the sky like a pearl. The sky is clear and bright and it calms my head so I think maybe I am thinking clearly and with sense for the first time in a long time.

When Daddy woke up out of his chair he was hungry. There was a big bowl of oysters in the Frigidaire and they still had that salty-sweet smell so I figured he got them only a day or so ago, afore he come up to Maryland. I made some potato cakes just like Virgie taught me, fried them in fatback, which was luckily not rancid as I expected. Daddy ate everything up telling me the whole time what a good thing it was, me coming home, and how now we got to get the baby. Then he said don't be a damn fool again—Ruthie—and run off on him cause he done told me more than once that he come after me even if he have to follow me into the ocean. He will bring me back.

I just let him blabber on, picking up his potato cakes with his fingers, slicing open the oysters and slurping them down, tossing the shells in the bowl so that they clinked against the stoneware. He goes on to me about how everything is going to be just fine—just like before, he says—once we get the baby back. I got no idea now who he thinks the baby is. His mind is near gone, is all I know. He don't seem to know who I am or who he wants me to be. He tells me to put on the coffee. He ain't had a good cup of coffee since I been gone. Mama's percolator is not electric like Willy's—so it takes me a minute to remember how to do it. I got the stove lit and ground some stale old beans in the box. He goes out the door to fetch a bottle from the truck and comes back with a pint of something that makes him wrinkle his eyes when he drinks from it.

After I put the coffee down in front of him he poured a little drink into it. For near an hour afterward he set at the table and rambled on to me while I tried to keep busy. He told me I had plenty of chores to catch up on. There was laundering to do and the sheets was in need of changing. I needed to get to the market, he said, as there was damn near nothing to eat. I thought about all my groceries gone bad in the truck right then and maybe I should bring a few things in what hadn't gone spoiled yet. I told him I still got groceries in the truck from yesterday. And he says well, what was I standing around waiting for them to just walk theyselves in. Go on out and get the groceries, Ruthie, he says to me. And what the hell is the matter with me lately.

I whisper that it's me—May—more to remind myself than to inform him of something he don't care to know about anyway.

I nearly slunk to that truck, so afraid I was that Sugar or Miss Bunny would be looking out their window over the yaupons and see me here, and at the same time I kept hoping they would. After I brung in the first bag he is sitting at the table staring at his empty bottle with big old watery eyes. He watched me for a spell, going through the bag, taking things out and separating what is spoilt from what is still good. He says this is exactly what he's talking about. How am I going to take proper care of the baby if I can't even get my groceries put away proper.

Well I guess I had just about enough by then cause the tears started coming like a tide come in. I take good care of her, I told him. I do. And then I had to lean on the counter some on account of my heart was being squeezed tight and a weakness was coming into my knees. He says, Quit your crying, Ruthie. I ain't saying you're terrible at it. I'm just saying little May's going to need a mother with her wits about her, is all. He got on up like he was trying to comfort me but I know better. I know him now.

I said for him to stop it, just stop it, Daddy. But my tears was coming so hard I was drowning in them and they was taking all my air up out of me and truth be told I couldn't be sure I was saying anything at all. His arms keep moving on me, wrapping around me like old mangrove roots, a root prison that's holding me with barely enough room to breathe air at the water's surface. He says he forgives me for running off, his voice all whiskery and digging into my neck— and don't worry, we will get the baby back and everything will be just like it used to be.

I backed up to the sink and felt the cold porcelain bowl against my backside, but the more I squirmed and wriggled about, the more tangled up I got in him. He was pulling down the sleeve of my dress, dragging it down my shoulder, pinning my arm to my side and I was caught, like in a net, like one of them sea turtles, and I was surely going to drown and the more I fought it, the faster my dying was going to be.

I remembered right then, of all the times, about the sea turtle I watched Little Jim dress on the docks one day. It came in near drowned, but not quite, tangled in Cooper Ryley's net and Cooper got to cussing about having to cut and mend his net. Little Jim said he'd take care of it if he could take the turtle, too.

Strange to think my mind carried off this way.

He got to pressing parts of hisself against me and a noise came from the back of his throat that was weighted and thick. In all my squirming from him I managed to get my back to him so that his breath heaved ragged on the back of my neck and fell so thick it near stuck to me and run down my spine. But even with my back to him, I knew he had no concern for how he would take what he was set on getting.

He was working my dress up, clawing the clean cotton in his dirty hands and I could hear the tiny snap of the threads along the seam, pop, pop. I could feel the drag of the fabric and the pull and the twist of a length of it that he was dragging over my hip and then, with the fabric clenched in his hands, he anchored me to the edge of the sink basin.

I could think now only of that turtle, and I rolled my backside, made a shell of it, meant to drag myself down into it. I said to him, he couldn't for the love of God know what it was he was doing.

His other hand wedged between my legs and pulled at my panties as if they was a nuisance. I thought I heard myself say no, no—near about a hundred times, but there was no breath behind my words so they fell out of me like I was choking up sand. He kicked my legs apart and let go his belt.

But I was thinking of that turtle and how it was near dead when Little Jim worked into him, cutting off his tail and fins, hacking off his head with those big eyes dripping death at me. The blood run on the dock and down the slats of the boards back to the water and I remember stepping back cause I got nothing on my feet and the blood was coming at me. He peeled back that shell with a mighty sucking sound and started digging into the insides. The heart was still pumping, blood gushing in little tidal waves all around. And he reached in and grabbed the heart and slapped it down on the dock.

It lay there, just pumping, real slow and quiet-like, but pumping, like it had a job to do, come hell or high water, and damn if it weren't going to do exactly what it was made up for doing. It was near an hour to sundown and I watched Little Jim dress that turtle, all the while going on about the soup his meemaw would make and the little steaks he would grill after soaking them in rye for a day or more.

Still, all that time, the little heart kept pumping, hopeful as it was. And then the sun slipped down by the mouth of the sound, hushing the whole wide world. And I swear to God hisself, that heart pumped its very last just as the sun fell like a glob of hot caramel into the cold water. Little Jim had a cooler full of meat and he shoved off the scraps, including that heart, to the gulls and over the sides of the dock for the bottom feeding scavengers like crabs and such. It didn't mean nothing much to nobody, least of all a sea turtle gone and butchered already.

Hard to believe I was thinking all this while Daddy was working hisself over me. I was thinking about how my heart just keeps beating, too, even when I feel near dead inside. I got to thinking how sooner or later the sun was going to come down on me, too.

Strange, how my mind settled on such a thing.

When he was done he kept me pinned that way, trapped against the sink. He told me he ain't never going to let me go again. I would follow you anywhere, he said.

I could only let my vomit fall and splash down in the basin.

He is washing now. He told me to run the tub for him and so I did and he got on in. I am standing at the counter here and feeling him running out of me and it's burning, but I won't sit down. I just let it keep on coming from me, his poison running down my legs.

I heard the ocean like a song with a rhythm that matched my heartbeat. It called on me and I told it to hush now, be quiet. But the sound of it was pounding through me.

That's when I knew. That is _how_ I knew, by the way the ocean beat to my own heart.

It doesn't want Daddy, but it will take him if that's what it takes to get me. So this is how it will be . . .

I will tell him I am leaving here. I am going far away, Daddy, where you cannot touch me. He will follow me. He would follow me anywhere, he says.

I'll stand at the doorway and tell him again, I'm leaving, Daddy, and he'll move to the door to catch me, but I will run and the door will slam behind me. I'll hunker down in the yaupon waiting for him to follow. And just as I see him come round the corner of the house, I will shoot out of the scrub like a jackrabbit. He'll see me because I'll let him see me. I'll let him think he can reach out and snatch me. Then I'll go down the drive, my bare feet slapping at it so that he can hear me, too, and know that I am running away from him. The moon will light the way across the lane to where the dunes start to roll into the ocean.

If he slows down, if he stumbles, I'll slow down, too, and wait for him. If he falls, I wonder if he will hear the ocean begging for me in the palms of his hands. I can feel it even now, in this house, right through the soles of my feet. He'll pick himself up and maybe yell out for me to come on home.

I will go over the dunes, going up, pulling the sand down with my feet and hands, but still moving, all the time moving, up the dunes and over and up and over. The moon will hang in the sky like a promise and when I am up on the last rise and looking down to the ocean, I know what I will see. The moon will be a path of white light, cut deep and sparkly across the ocean and down into the very heart of it.

I will surely hear him at my backside, crying for me, heaving hisself over the last dune and swearing to bring me back on home. Might be I have to wait a spell for him now, but I will be careful to stay out of his reach. It is hard not to go on ahead without him, for the aching in me makes me thirsty to be drunk on ocean water until I spin down to the bottom of it.

When he gets to the top of the last dune I will already be coming down to the surf. If I look back I will likely see him sliding down the sand on his knees. I will have to run across the sand to the surf and the fiddler crabs are going to be dancing this way and that, the moon flashing on their shells when they scuttle at the pounding of my feet. The sand is going to be soft and deep and hard to push up and out of from the balls of my feet, but when I start to breathe the spray into my chest the sand will get harder under me and the waves will be reaching for me, tangling at my ankles and pulling this earth out from under me. I can turn my back from the ocean long enough to see if Daddy is behind me. He'll be crying now, wailing like a baby for me to come on back. He will follow me anywhere, he says, for to carry me home.

I will head for the path of moonlight and push hard. A wave will come up to take me and pull me from the shore and out. But I will not let it take me easily, not yet. It must take him too and I will wait for him.

I will hear the splash of his body falling into the water and turn to see him rise up out of the surf before another wave breaks over him.

I am pushing through the water, feeling the gritty floor of the ocean on my feet and the sting of it between my legs.

Catch me, Daddy.

I am afraid the ocean will spit him back, but I call out to him and he shoves hisself harder into the black water, aiming for me in the moonlight.

Suddenly the ocean floor falls away under me and it is just me and the water. The cold presses against my chest and makes me suck in the last air I will ever breathe. I want to float for just a second, just to be sure he is behind me, but I can't—not without Willy.

I will hear Daddy crying, begging for me to stop and there will be fear in his voice of a different nature. I believe he will be thinking for just a second that he's less afraid of losing me than he is of dying. But he won't have no choice no more. He will be claimed by the ocean as surely as I been all this time.

My face stays over the swell long enough to hear him suck in water and I know it is burning its way into his insides, going where he don't want it to go.

It won't hurt none for me. I will take the ocean like a lover I have waited for and ached for with every part of me. I can take the ocean deep down into me, knowing that I have been drowning for a long time anyways.

If I open my eyes under the water and look up, I can see the moon like I am looking through rippled glass. I can hear the surf pound, and I can feel myself being lifted and dropped, going deeper every time the water lifts me and lets go.

If, at the last moment, I think I see the rippling figure of Lacey on the faraway shore, if I think I hear her voice calling out to me and calling me back to her, maybe I can remember the feel of Willy's hands under me and I can rise up out of the water one last time to tell her she is safe now. She is safe. I will tell her that, for me, drowning is too easy and life is too hard. And I will tell her—and this is important—I will tell her to hold Willy's hand in deep water.

Lacey looks up to see Willy and Carlotta walking along the water's edge. He waves to her and all she can do is try to bring air into her chest, try not to choke on it, remember to draw it in. And let it go and draw it in again.

CHAPTER 35

What to Do with What We Know

It is not a beach day, slightly cooler, a pale sun, a breeze whipping up now and again that borders on chilly. Tasha is spending the morning and into the afternoon with Willy and Carlotta. They took her to Beanie's again for breakfast and Lacey begged off, saying she had a lousy night's sleep for some reason, would they mind if she passed and Carlotta had said of course, go back to bed, that's what vacations are for. The three of them had trudged off happily, and Lacey had watched them go, waving a long good-bye as the car went slowly down the lane with Willy at the wheel. There were pancakes to look forward to. Maybe, Willy had said, they would buy a kite and head out to the lighthouse. Perfect day for it.

Lacey spends the morning carrying May's diary around with her, afraid to leave it unattended so that it can spill its contents to another unwitting victim. Occasionally she picks it up, flips through, rereads a passage, the afterburn no less vicious on a second or third read. She sets it beside her bed as she makes up the bedcovers and fluffs the pillows, keeps it tucked under her arm when she picks Tasha's nightgown and sandals up off the floor. When she goes to the porch to retrieve her coffee cup and sees Sugar making her way down the path toward her, she quickly carries it inside and slides it into a kitchen drawer before heading back out to the porch.

"I didn't see your car and figured you were gone for the day. I was just headin' over for to make up the beds and bring you all some fresh towels. I can come back."

"Oh, don't worry about that," says Lacey. "I was up early. Beds are made. Have a cup of coffee with me?"

"Why sure, if it's no bother."

Sugar set the towels on the trunk outside the bathroom and grabs the damp ones flung over the ends of doors and bedposts.

Lacey takes a mug from the cabinet. "Cream or sugar?"

"Nope—just black." Sugar comes back into the main room and drops the towels to the floor beside her.

Settling at the table, she unzips her jacket, a long-sleeve gold velour thing with the word PINK in huge letters and now split in the middle by the zipper descending between her breasts. Her white hair is in the same braid, curving to the left over her shoulder and tied off with a rubber band at the end and she tosses it back off her shoulder. Lacey is still amazed by the sparkling blue of her eyes, the lids heavily hooded, the lashes still dark, but the brows threaded with white and unruly. Sugar doesn't lean back in the chair, but leans forward instead, like a woman not accustomed to making herself comfortable. Lacey notices her hands, the nails short, the cuticles rough and embedded with dirt as if she's been digging in a garden.

"New Frigidaire running okay?"

"No problems at all," says Lacey, as brightly as she can. She looks to the refrigerator and back to Sugar. "I was wondering something." Sugar raises her eyes over her coffee cup, eager to help without even knowing the question. "When my mother's father was found drowned." She has worded it so carefully, *my mother's father.* "No idea what happened?" Sugar shakes her head, no, and Lacey goes on. "Any other drownings around that time?" Sugar continues to move her head side to side. "I mean, do you think he was alone when he drowned? Did he fall off a boat or something?"

"Oh, I doubt it, honey." She smacks her lips twice, puts a hand out on the table, caresses the wood. "No, honey, I think—and I hate to tell you this—but I think he just got damn drunk, as usual, and was wandering around like a wampus cat like he done all the time, wailin' and carryin' on and who the heck knows, hmm? Maybe a big old wave just come knock him down. Maybe he fell off a dock somewheres. You know, we got wicked tides and he was missing a good time before he washed up. And he washed up a good ways away." She looks at Lacey and looks away, takes a breath and starts again. "I don't wanna go speak ill of the dead, and I sure don't want to cause you any trouble in your heart, Lacey, but he was a drinker and your mama worried about it. In her letters to me she would always ask about him, about his drinking, where he went, if he was still on the island, cause he like to go off island time and again without word to nobody."

Lacey tells her she was just wondering, that's all. Just wondered if he was alone or with someone, just thinking about it lately. Sugar drinks her coffee in gulps, as if she is finishing off a cool glass of water, and sets her empty mug back down on the table. Lacey tilts her head to the pot, offering her more, but she declines. There are chores to get to. She rises and zips up her jacket, tells her it should warm up again by this afternoon. "It's right airish this morning." But she says the wind is supposed to shift. Lacey wonders how she knows this and then thinks that living here must mean that you *have* to know these things. Suddenly, the fragility of the whole of the island becomes apparent. She thinks of tsunamis and hurricanes and finds it a marvel that the island is still here at all.

Sugar gathers the towels from the floor beside her and Lacey rises, looking around the room to the plastic philodendron that sits in an old spittoon atop the woodstove, the stack of board games—*Life* and *Monopoly* and *Operation*—set on an open shelf along the far wall next to frayed paperbacks, the large framed print of the Ocracoke map on the wall. She imagines what the room looked like thirty years ago, on the night May came back. What would have hung on the walls? Would she have fired up the woodstove to take the chill out of the air that she felt when she came into the house after having been away nearly three years.

I dearly wish for another warm living body aside of Daddy in this house right now and I am sad that Swamp is long gone.

Lacey goes to the sink with both coffee cups in her hand, leans forward to the back of the sink to reach the sponge and dish soap and is suddenly startled by the pressure of the hard porcelain across her own hips. *I backed up to the sink and felt the cold porcelain bowl against my backside, but the more I squirmed and wriggled about, the more tangled up I got in him.*

A startling wave of nausea moves through her, causing her to drop the mugs where they clink and roll in the bowl. She recovers them quickly, holding them up to inspect for cracks, shows them to Sugar—no harm done!

Sugar smiles where she stands at the threshold. She is not concerned, only wishes Lacey a good day. She is making her way down the steps to the lawn and Lacey follows her to the porch. She is cold, colder than the air warrants, feeling a chill that requires the chasing of a deep warmth.

"Sugar?" she calls as the woman makes her way through the yard. "Mind if I start up the woodstove?"

"Sure. There's some lighter wood 'round the side there." She points to the side of the house where the hammock of trees spreads. "Stove matches in one of the drawers in the kitchen, I believe."

Lighter wood. That's what her mother would have said. Willy would bring in the kindling and she would say, "I got a basket here for the lighter wood, Willy."

She takes the diary from the drawer, tucks it under her arm, and heads outside, around the house where it is even cooler under the trees and the breeze sends the leaves to swishing, and gathers the wood in her arms all the while keeping the book pinched between her arm and ribs. She leans over, arms filled with kindling and a few larger logs, to peer under the house into the dark.

When I was a little girl I used to crawl under the house whenever I needed the dark and quiet of it.

Lacey can't imagine needing the dark so badly. She can't imagine there was any comfort to be found under this house.

Back inside she dumps the wood to the floor, quickly steps on a centipede that swims out of the pile and shivers to know it was in her arms just seconds ago. She moves the plastic plant to the coffee table and, kneeling down in front of the stove, arranges the wood the way Willy had taught her, crisscross with the ability to suck wind between the layers. When the match fails to catch the wood, she looks around for paper and, spying none, shrugs and rips a few empty pages from the book. It is oddly satisfying to tear at it, and she makes no apology for doing so. Wadding the paper and tucking the crumpled pieces under the stacking of wood, she strikes another match and they catch instantly, three small balls of paper flaming individually, licking the wood and finally setting the smaller twigs to crackling. She closes the door partway to create a draft, watches everything erupt, the flames leaping, and then closes the heavy door and twists the handle to lock.

In minutes the stove is warm to the touch and half an hour later the heat is swirling around like a warm blanket being tossed over her, and still the chill in the deepest part of her bones persists.

She will make some tea, something to warm herself from the inside. She finds a box of teabags in the cupboard and sets a pot to boiling. She hears her phone ring back in her bedroom but is compelled to go back to the pile of kindling and grab the book from the floor before going to her phone. By the time she reaches her room, the call has dropped. She calls Cade back. The sound of his voice is deep and so sweet it makes her teeth hurt. He misses her, can't wait to see her. He is thinking he will make the two-thirty ferry. She realizes he must have left before sunrise but doesn't bother to do the math. There is a physical ache rising in her chest and she is certain some of it, not all of it, but some of it, would be purged by the telling of everything. There is also the unwillingness to heave everything back up again. It is something she is compelled to sit with, let roil in her gut, and she wonders if it is even fair to share, to try to pass part of the burden to Cade, to make him accountable to her pain in some way.

Besides, she thinks now, she is fine. Just fine. There have been no tears so far, just a deeply painful rearranging of her heart in her chest, as if it is crawling away from a cramped place.

Now, lifting the diary to her lap as she sits cross-legged at the stove, she acknowledges that she is, in fact, in danger of suffocating under the collective weight of all she knows, feels the many bits of it creeping under her skin, worming its way to her heart, snacking on her memories and making holes in the whole of them so that she is left with only a mealy residue of what it is she once thought to be true. The resentments she has used to buoy her the last thirty years are being gnawed away.

The thing about secrets, Lacey thinks now, is that the longer they smolder, the bigger the inferno once they meet the air.

Her first instinct last night as she read had been to bring the diary to Willy, to sit him down and say look—*look, you were wrong, we were wrong. She didn't mean to leave us. She loved us!* It seemed, at the time and in the moment of discovery, like the right thing to do, like he deserved to know. But this morning—the literal unfolding of the hidden pages—has changed all that. Perhaps it is still something he deserves to know because it is always best to know the truth. (She isn't sure why she thinks that is so, recognizes it as a flimsy platitude though it feels grounded in something, and isn't that the nature of platitudes? Because to say otherwise, to say a secret should remain a secret, well, that feels indefensible as well.) Just look at what has happened in not knowing over all these years! Look at the shape it has taken, look at the haunting it has conjured. Look at the blame we have wordlessly passed between one another like a forkful of bitterness—here, taste this, it's awful, right?—but the truth itself is not something he deserves to sit with in his belly, not something she wants to see churning at his insides.

She looks back over the years with Willy and cannot get out from under the love. And what did she do with all that love? She grew and flourished with it and then turned her back on the source of it, not visiting enough, not calling enough, not ever thanking him, until she needed it again, until Tasha got sick and Lacey needed the buoying of Willy to hold her up and walk her through it.

I will tell her to hold Willy's hand in deep water.

She marvels now at just how easy it was to take what she saw before—her mother, allowing a man to hurriedly gather her groceries in his truck, place a hand on her shoulder, and usher her into his truck and drive out of her life—to take that single and precise moment and let it become a known thing, to let it shape itself into a memory of something that was true to her, how the lines of it led without a wiggle directly through a place she would inhabit for thirty years. *The man in the red truck came by and helped Momma put her groceries (their groceries—the groceries that belonged to the three of them) in his car and then she got in and ducked down and left them.* That was what she had seen, what she knew to be true, and in telling Willy she had not shed a tear. Inside she had trembled, had felt the flopping of small fish in her belly, but she knew it to be true. And why? Because the starting point to it all had begun even before, with May's leaving and coming back, with her moods and her sadness. The line of it all had no beginning and no end, until now. The book in her hands is the serial comma that has changed the meaning of everything. She, Lacey, can live with the redrawing of that trajectory but she will not—has no right—to take the sorrow that Willy has traveled, that he has reeled into himself and rearranged and shifted in his heart to make a welcome place for Lacey, for Tasha, and even Carlotta, and turn it into another kind of jagged-edged sorrow that would cut into the scar tissue of his known world and from which an entirely different kind of convalescence would be required of him.

It takes many minutes to feed each page, one by one, to the flames. Starting from the back of the book and working forward, even the blank pages, no longer reading them, not even scanning the words, just watching the pretty script curl into itself, the pages flutter and shrivel to black, gone in a wisp of smoke. Once the fire is fully fed, she holds the shell of the book in her hand, presses her lips to it, and, grateful now for the chance to do so, kisses her mother goodbye, and tosses the leather to the kiln.

The stench of the burning leather seeps from the stove and Lacey has no choice but to breathe it in, recognizing that her mother's secrets are now her own, that she has filled her lungs with the bitterness of it and the blood that courses her veins has oxygenated on a story that she alone bears the burden of, her heart pumping a tragedy through arteries, invading the threads of capillaries so that May's story is both deep within Lacey and rising to flush her cheeks.

Cade arrives right behind Willy, Carlotta, and Tasha, everyone laughing and recalling their day, the long ferry ride, the kite that tangled in the dunes, the many steps of the lighthouse and the view—so breathtaking and worth the climb. And oh my gosh, it's so hot in here! And what is that smell?

Lacey apologizes. She was chilled and the woodstove got away from her. No, in answer to Carlotta's concern, she doesn't think she's coming down with something. In fact, she hardly ever gets sick, and Willy nods his head in agreement. She opens the window and exchanges the strange stink of scorched leather for that of a swampy low tide that will rise again by evening and fill the house with the scent of all it carries; the salt, the damp, the unfurling tendrils of seaweed reaching for the surface, the hatching and growing of fish and snails and crabs, and the decomposing and falling away of all that has gone before.

CHAPTER 36

A Day at the Beach

Willy had risen later than he was accustomed to. He had woken at dawn, as he usually did, trickles of light fingering the blankets through the scrubby pines, listening to the gentle clatter of Carlotta in the kitchen, but had lain back into the bed instead. In the quiet of the bedroom, he could hear the slow, lonely honk of a goose, could feel the rise and descent of it, and then another, so unlike the squawk of chickens. He lay with his fingers laced across his chest and stared up at the low ceiling, examining the unfamiliar patterns of water stains, the way they bled and faded, lapping at one another.

He recalled what he had told Lacey two evenings ago, played it again in his mind, the look on her face, like something dawning and blooming but yet to take shape. What would come of it all, if anything? Yesterday, she had begged off joining them for breakfast and sightseeing, claiming she hadn't slept well. He had worried at the time that she was avoiding him. But last night she had seemed strangely content, leaning against Cade's shoulder after dinner, sliding her hand across the picnic table to pat the top of Willy's own while he recalled the climb up the lighthouse steps and the more painful descent. Maybe it was time to see a doctor, she had said. She would ask Dr. Oren for a recommendation, and he had waved her off at first and then said, on second thought, maybe he should consider it.

He heard water running in the kitchen, the rattle of cups being taken from the cupboard, the scratch of a chair being pulled out. Morning sounds that should have pulled him from the bed, but instead he had found himself taking inventory, trying to sort his crimes and placing them in categories—the forgivable, the heinous, the accidental—and he kept moving them from column to column in his mind, never really able to see things tally in the way he had hoped. Falling in love with a woman half his age: accidental. Not going after her when she took off: heinous. But then he thought of how May was the last weeks and wondered briefly if it was, in fact, forgivable. Not saying anything in the last weeks before she left—that fell into a new category of gross negligence. It all sat heavily with him, each fact like a cold, smooth stone that he could feel the heft of. He could stack them in piles only to watch the weight of one tumble and spill the others, or he could line them up along the edges of his mind until he had built a low wall of regrets that he was forever tripping over. When he finally rose from the bed and placed his feet firmly on the sun warmed wooden planks of the floor, he imagined his transgressions toppling from his lap, one over the other and scattering around him. He stepped carefully, feeling the bones and tendons in his knees, the way they connected to one another, each part relying on the other and counting on the moments ahead, the moving forward of another day, to ease the ache. There was the drifting scent of coffee calling to him.

They ate fried donuts at the market for breakfast and then had to stop at a clothing store to buy Willy new swim trunks. When he had put his old ones on that morning—and Lord, they must have been twenty years old—the waistband was so dry-rotted that they shimmied down to his hips as soon as he took a step. Carlotta was already in her suit, bright red, of course, with a wide swath of black shiny fabric running diagonally across her breasts. She had her arms threaded through the sleeves of a tent-like black dress covered in sequins and when she popped her head through and smoothed it down the front of herself she had looked to him and giggled, shook her head, no, he couldn't possibly wear those things. He amused her for a bit, prancing around with his pants falling nearly to his knees, walking with his legs wide to keep from exposing himself further. She had laughed herself to the point of tears and then held out her hand to take them from him. He'd finally stepped out of them and handed them over, watching her wipe the tears from her eyes as she crumbled them into the bathroom trashcan.

His new swim trunks are bright pink, at Tasha's insistence, and he surprised everyone when he agreed to buy them, asking the clerk to cut the tags from them as he stood wearing them at the counter. In the same shop they purchased five beach chairs, stowing them in the back of the car and headed out to the public beach.

Now, on the short drive to the beach, Willy mentions he hopes to see them dolphins Tasha had carried on about. Tasha tells him about how they shot water from a hole in their heads like a fountain. He explains to her now that they are sea mammals, that they breathe air but can hold their breath for a very long time. The windows are rolled down and he feels the warmth of the sun on his elbow set to the edge of it. Tasha wants to know just how long they can hold their breath and he turns to see her suck in air and puff her cheeks against sealed lips. He begins to count for her, one . . . two . . . three . . . He reaches seventeen and the air explodes from her lungs.

"A dolphin can hold his breath ten minutes or more," he says.

Lacey looks back to him from the rearview mirror, brows raised, surprised he knows this. She has been quiet most of the morning, not unhappy, he thinks, but as if she, too, has been settling things in her mind, tallying up the past, maybe seeing things a little differently. He tells himself that they must talk—again—that he must make it clear that all accountability falls to him.

He has surprised himself in knowing how long a dolphin can hold its breath but remembers teaching Lacey about sea mammals long ago. He can't help but chuckle now and goes on to tell Cade that Lacey had declared mermaids a perfect example of a mammal that lived in the ocean and she would, in fact, like to have one in the pond. He sees Cade look to Lacey, reach across the seat and pat her leg. "Aww," says Willy, still laughing and shaking his head, "I could tell you some stories about her and her ideas." He makes a note to himself to tell Cade more, tell him about the way she named the cows, the swim medals she won in high school, the way she wanted those dumb chickens for her sixth birthday that had started the whole dang thing, the way Beauford always waited for her at the end of the drive, how she could pitch a hairbrush out a bedroom window in a perfect arc. There was so much to tell him about this daughter of his.

He watches Lacey come down to her knees in the sand to slather sunscreen on Tasha and snug her cap down on her head. The locals are right, of course. Lacey looks so much like May. But he realizes now, when she lifts her sunglasses to her forehead and with the sun shining hard on her face, that there is now the faint feathering of fine lines from the corners of her eyes. She is, he understands, older than he ever knew May to be, but he never got to see May get older, never had a chance to watch the changing of her through the years. In some way, he is watching May now. So much alike are they that it could be May rubbing a second glob of sunscreen on Lacey's small shoulders, cupping them in the palms of her hand and swirling, dragging the milkiness of it down her arms, dabbing it on Lacey's upturned face. But it isn't May. He is watching their daughter, their granddaughter.

Cade has brought an umbrella and Willy helps him dig it into the sand. "You ever been to the beach, Willy?" asks Tasha.

"Nope," says Willy. "But your grandma spent a lot of time here. Fact is, she grew up here at the ocean."

"Do I got a grandma?" Tasha turns to look over her shoulder at Lacey.

"Uh-huh," says Lacey, "Daddy's mommy and my mommy are your grandmas. But they're not alive anymore."

Willy finds that strange, to think aloud of May as *not alive*, but he knows it is the easiest way to explain her absence to Tasha. He watches the pelicans skim across the surf, tuck, and drop to the water like a rock. There is a clumsiness to it that surprises him, the way they fall away without warning. He points them out to Carlotta, and they watch together, a small gasp coming from her as another beast of a bird *thunk*s to the water.

"What's a grandma like?"

"Like a grandpa in a dress," says Cade from where he has settled in a beach chair just outside of the umbrella's shade, a paperback book spread on his lap and the pages flipping in the light wind when he takes his hand from them.

"A grandma is just a woman who is a little older than your mom and loves you a lot like your mother does," says Willy.

"Oh," she says, filling up her bucket with sand. "Like Carlotta."

"That's right," he says, winking at Carlotta who tilts her face to him and smiles. He closes his eyes and leans back in his chair. "That's right." He knows that Carlotta is not May, is not replacing May, but he is reeling his mind back to the here and now. Carlotta is *here*.

"I'm going for a swim," Lacey says, popping up from where she is kneeling behind Tasha in the sand. "Will you guys keep an eye on her?" She nods to Tasha.

Sure, they say. No problem.

Willy watches her walk down to the water's edge. When the surf swirls around her ankles, he sits up a little straighter. When a cold wave crashes up her thighs and makes her stretch up on her toes for a second, he nudges Cade. "You go with her, son," he says. "I don't like her out there alone."

Cade sits up and looks at her. They both watch as she dives into the surf and then bobs to the surface again. She turns back to them and waves her hand in the air, lets herself sink, and then pushes up again, breaking the surface with a splash.

"Be careful!" Willy calls out to her, not knowing if she has heard him, worried that the water is too rough, wondering what she knows of currents and undertows.

"Don't worry," says Tasha calmly. She gets up from where she sits in the sand and walks over to Willy. She pats his arm with a small sandy hand and then breaks into a wide smile. "Don't you remember, Willy? You taught Mommy how to be a really good swimmer."

Acknowledgments

A writer spends a good deal of time alone, just her and her keyboard, but a fully fleshed novel, particularly a first novel, rises out of the work of many. Likewise, an author's craft, too, is honed in equal parts by the writer herself and those with whom she surrounds herself. In that regard I have many people to thank. I've been fortunate to have the best of the best at my back—from professors, critique groups, writers, editors, publishing professionals, friends, and family.

In no particular order I want to thank poet Michael Glaser for encouraging a younger undergrad version of myself who had big dreams and was just beginning to find her voice. Heidi Vornbrock Roosa, thank you for your encouraging critique of a very early draft of this book and your detailed attention to choreographing scene. William Black, thank you for tuning my ear to works I would have never discovered on my own and for your late-night writerly conversations that made me want to join the club. Jill Morrow, thank you for your early reads and helping me to put the meat on the bones. Author and professor extraordinaire Elise Levine, you have been pivotal in my growth as a writer and I haven't the words or space to thank you for your in-depth critiques and the wealth of knowledge you share so graciously. You are synonymous with craft.

Cheryl Pientka, my wonderful agent, just how do you thank a person who stood by you for over a decade simply because she read your words and believed in you? You're tenacious and amazing. I am one of the lucky ones who got an agent and a friend in the same deal.

Tanya Farrell, thank you for jumping in with both feet and an abundance of enthusiasm. Charting the unknown has been so much more fun with you at my side.

Blackstone Publishing has made this entire ride a pleasure. Your collective professionalism and your willingness to hold my hand along the way is much appreciated. Haila Williams, thank you for taking a chance on a fledgling writer. I know I speak for all the writers to whom you have given an opportunity—you rock. Madeline Hopkins, thank you for your patience with typos and for your attention to all the developmental details that made this a better book. I can't believe my luck to have been paired with you.

Lynn Chambers, Kelly Gill, and Denise Andrews . . . dear friends, your early reads of this novel, your willingness to be gut honest as to what was working and what was not, your enthusiastic responses to the scenes you loved, and yes, your honesty regarding what you didn't love, all means more to me than you will ever know. You never told me what I wanted to hear but what I needed to hear. And this is a better book because of you.

Debbie Curro Collins, Susan Perkins, and Renee Bland, thank you for believing in me through the years and then acting as if you weren't the least bit surprised when this book came to fruition.

Dr. Graham Redgrave, I can only say you made me brave.

My beautiful sister Jennifer Sapp, you are my best friend and my favorite cheerleader. You always thought more of me than I deserved, but you make me aspire to be the person you think I am.

My daughter Kelly, thank you for continuously letting me borrow from your childhood. They were the best of times. I hope I make you proud, if only to make up for all the times I've embarrassed you.

My son Jamie, your unwavering belief in me is overwhelming and trips my heart. And yes, nothing says *Celebrate!* like a mariachi band.

Lastly, my husband John, so much to thank you for. Thank you for your most careful reads, for demanding honesty on the pages, for asking the questions that shifted the course of this book. Thank you for the morning coffee, picking up the slack in dog walks, and your willingness to invest yourself in my dreams. I'm not certain I could have done this without you, but I'm glad I didn't have to. Joy is best when shared and I am so blessed to share my joys with you. You are my heart.

SHAWN NOCHER'S compelling short stories have appeared in numerous literary magazines, including *SmokeLong Quarterly*, *Pithead Chapel*, *Eunoia Review*, and *MoonPark Review*, and she has been longlisted or won honorable mentions from both *SmokeLong Quarterly* and *Glimmer Train*.

She earned her master of arts in writing at Johns Hopkins University, has given wings to two children, and lives with her husband and an assortment of sassy rescue animals in Baltimore, Maryland, where she writes in a room of her own. This is her first novel.